All The Things We Didn't Say

Sara Shepard

W F HOWES LTD

This large print edition published in 2010 by
W F Howes Ltd
Unit 4, Rearsby Business Park, Gaddesby Lane,
Rearsby, Leicester LE7 4YH

1 3 5 7 9 10 8 6 4 2

First published in the United Kingdom in 2009
by HarperCollins*Publishers*

A CIP catalogue record for this book is available
from the British Library

ISBN 978-1-40745-663-8

Typeset by Palimpsest Book Production Limited,
Falkirk, Stirlingshire
Printed and bound in Great Britain
by MPG Books Ltd, Bodmin, Cornwall

FSC

Mixed Sources
Product group from well-managed
forests, controlled sources and
recycled wood or fiber
SA-COC-1565
www.fsc.org
© 1996 Forest Stewardship Council

For my mother, Mindy Shepard

Behind you was a poster for the DQ Butterscotch Sundae, and next to you were the gleaming, shuddering machines that dispensed the ice cream. Mark catapulted over the counter and gave you a big hug. 'Here she is,' he said, clapping his hands on your shoulders. You looked familiar. It was probably that I'd seen you around – at a picnic, in the halls at school, in the bleachers, in the aisles of Charles Kupka's Drugs, *The Finest Apothecary in Western Pennsylvania*. You smiled at me and extended your hand, so formal. 'Hello,' you said. You smiled with all your teeth. 'Hello,' you said again.

You lived down the street from Mark. When you were little, you stole tomatoes from his garden. He used to chase you with a garden hoe with his eyes closed, chopping and chopping. But then, a month or so ago, Mark was up on a ladder, touching up the eaves of his house with white paint, and a bee came and scared him and he fell off. When he opened his eyes, flat on his back on the grass with the wind knocked out of him, the ladder still tilted against the roof, you were

1

standing there with your wavy blonde hair and your milkmaid face and your wide, vine-ripened mouth. 'I realized I loved her right then,' Mark told me. He had been dying to introduce you to me for a while, but I'd been working so much that summer and had hardly been around.

I don't know what made me go into Dairy Queen alone the next time, knowing what I knew. Mark had been my best friend since third grade, when we were both punished for sticking chewing gum to the underside of our desks. Perhaps it was because you said hello twice. Perhaps it was because Mark joked, that first time, 'Now, don't go stealing her away, Rich. She's mine.' I don't know why he said that – I'd never stolen anything from Mark in my life. But maybe it got into my head, started whirring around. Maybe it was your dove-gray eyes, the way your hands were chapped and red from the Dairy Queen freezers, the way you swayed a little, winsome and uncertain, when you dispensed the ice cream into the pale yellow cone. The first time I went in alone, you pretended to forget my name. All you said was, 'You're Mark's friend, right?' The second time I came in, you said, 'It's freezing. All this snow, in October. You seriously want ice cream?' The fifth you told me bits and pieces about your life.

You told me that you and Mark were secretly engaged. He wanted to get married as soon as you graduated – you were a grade behind us, so it was still a whole year away. You sat on the steel sink in

Dairy Queen's back room, surrounded by ice cream mix, boxes of rainbow sprinkles and glamour shots of the Buster Bar and the whorish, frothy DQ Float – *Go ahead and splurge! Get it with Tab®!* You told me how afraid you were, that you weren't sure if Mark was the guy you were supposed to marry, how you thought love was supposed to hit you like a spark and you weren't sure that had happened. 'But I'm a good person,' you always said when we pressed against the shelves of the walk-in, your lips tasting like caramel syrup. 'I still do chores and everything.' 'It's me, I'm the terrible one,' was what I always said next. I wanted you to be blameless, pure. 'He's my best friend. I'm the bad person here.' I touched the six freckles clustered together by your right eye, a constellation. I even gave the freckle-cluster a name, though I can't remember it now. That's probably a side-effect of what I've been through – so many precious memories have been yanked away forever.

The eighth time I told you everything about me. That winter, I took you to the old, abandoned drift mine, one of my favorite spots in all of Cobalt. We looked into the black, gaping mouth in the side of the hill to avoid staring at each other. You shivered and said coal mining had to be the scariest job in the world, trekking into those dark, uncertain caves. 'I'm sure miners get used to it,' I replied, but you shook your head and said you couldn't see how. I told you that my father looked perfect on the outside, but he hardly ever ate dinner with us anymore. I couldn't remember the last time we'd had a conversation. It was always sports on TV, or long hours at work, or time spent at the new golf club closer to Pittsburgh. He wanted me to play golf, too – he got me a membership to the country club a few Christmases before. 'Golf is a good skill for your future,' he said gruffly, ignoring my lack of enthusiasm. 'I'm grooming you for better things.' The only thing I'd wanted that year was a set of encyclopedias, but my father said I could just use the encyclopedias at school. When new encyclopedias showed up on our doorstep a few weeks later, my father frowned, thinking it was a mistake. 'It's not,' my mother said quickly. She'd gotten last year's set at a discount from a door-to-door salesman, practically for free. When my father turned his back, she winked at me. I read those encyclopedias cover to cover, starting with A and ending with Z. I loved M; it was so thick. There were so many fascinating things in M. *Myelin. Mummification. Melanoma.*

I told you about the scholarship to Penn State – first that I'd applied, next that I'd been interviewed, and that I was waiting to hear if I got it. 'You will,' you assured me. 'But that means you'll leave me.' I told you I'd never leave you. I told you I'd take you to college with me. 'I'll pack you in my suitcase.' I took your small, tan hand and said, 'I'll marry you right now.' I said I'd go get my minister's

4

license so I could marry us myself. You took a whack at me – you liked to slap the air when things were funny – and said we would need witnesses. I said, 'How about this mine? It could be our witness.' The coal was as silent and solemn as God. You looked away then. 'You know we can't,' you said. We were quiet for a while after that.

Then there was the party at Jeff's house. I had gotten there late, so we met in the hall, me holding an empty cup, on my way to the keg, you holding a sleeve of Ritz crackers. I couldn't wait to show you the letter I'd received that very day, the one I hadn't shown my family or anyone else yet. It had Pennsylvania State University's prowling lion logo on the top. I unfolded it, thinking you'd be proud of me, but your expression clouded. And then you told me – you just blurted it out, two words. I said, 'Are you sure?' And you said, 'Yes.' And then I was talking and not thinking, or perhaps thinking too much and talking to avoid saying what I was thinking. Just as your eyes started to fill, Mark approached. We straightened up fast. 'What are you two talking about?' Mark asked, swaying, his breath acrid and hot, so wasted and not even an hour into the party. He touched your boob right there in front of everyone, his beer sloshing over the lip of the cup.

Mark took your arm and you turned away. Jimi Hendrix came on the stereo. I walked over to the plate of crudités on Jeff's parents' kitchen table, but they tasted like sawdust. When the song ended, you found me again. 'Mark wants to go, you said. But he's . . .'

You looked at Mark, swaying in the doorway. It was obvious what you were asking – you'd just gotten your permit but didn't feel comfortable driving Mark's car yet. This was usually a treat for us – Mark would drink too much at a party, and I'd drive you both home, dropping him off first, making sure he got into his house, sometimes even guiding him to his bedroom. Then you and I would drive for hours, rolling slowly across the bridge, along the winding roads to the woods, past the junkyard and lot of abandoned tires. Talking about everything and nothing, simply being together.

But we both knew there would be no after-hours drive that night. Looking back, if only I'd have ushered Mark into the back bedroom so he could lie down for a while. If only I'd have breathed, put things in perspective. I should have taken your hands and said, 'I'm sorry. This is great.' Instead, I rolled my eyes and said, 'Give me the keys.' On the way to the car, you said loudly to Mark that you didn't want to run away and get married anymore, that you wanted to do it right here. You wanted to invite all of Cobalt. Mark threw himself into the backseat, groaning, and you got in the front, next to me. When you stared at me, imploring, I should have stared back, but I gunned the engine hard, gritting my teeth as Mark made a gagging sound. What you'd said in the house

6

throbbed inside of me. The words paraded in front of my eyes, obscuring my vision.

I started down the slick, twisting road. One minute, it was peaceful, dark. The next, there he was, paused right in front of us, blinking in the moonlight. I saw his antlers first, then his broad, brown chest. You screamed. My foot fumbled for the brake. I met the animal's wet, shiny eyes, and then there was that groan of metal. Things were white and chrome and loud and then quiet. Leaves fluttered to the ground. I came to with my head on the steering wheel. I saw your rose-petal hand first, folded neatly in your lap. The glass from the shattered windshield, shimmering on the dashboard and Naugahyde seats, looked like thousands of diamonds. I thought that I could mount a shard in a gold band and give it to you.

'Hello?' I cried out. No one answered.

I saw you once after that. The hospital walls were a sterile green. You were in a gown with faded blue flowers all over it, something you never would've worn in real life. I was afraid to touch you. Plenty of other people were there to do it for me. They did all kinds of things to you, tubes in places, bags in others, needles in veins, tape covering up half of you, a metal cage around your head. Did they find tiny Ritz cracker crumbs in your mouth when they tried to breathe for you? Did they remark on the strawberry smell of your hair? What did they do with your charm bracelet?

7

Where did they put your diaphanous, paisley-printed blouse, the one that hid so much?

They say I should write letters to everyone, even those that are difficult to write, even to those to whom letters cannot be sent. But my hands feel like they're being pulled toward the center of the earth, like they have extra gravitational properties. My thoughts plod like dinosaurs. I've had so much done to me in the past few years, so much prodding, so much electricity jolted into my head; and so much of it, I fear, hasn't really helped. But through it all, I have never forgotten you, nor have I forgotten the secret you and I share forever. I hope you know that I am desperate to always remember. I hope you know I'll cling to everything about you as hard as I can. Although, I guess you don't know anything, now. I guess you don't.

PART I

BROOKLYN, NEW YORK, DECEMBER 1992

fun saver

CHAPTER 1

She'd been away for just a few days when a biology substitute told my class the most important and wonderful piece of information I'd ever heard.

And then he was pulled out of the classroom forever.

Before this, Mr Rice had been invisible. The blazers he wore to Peninsula Upper School – one of the finest schools in the Brooklyn Heights-to-Park Slope radius, to quote the promotional materials – were never wrinkled, and he always combed his thin, wheat-colored hair into wet-looking lines. There was nothing extra-curricular in any of his previous lessons, and with his droning monotone, he made the processes of cell division and photosynthesis and the intricate innards of a paramecium seem far less fascinating than they truly were. But on this particular day, Mr Rice drew a double helix on the board, tapped it with his piece of chalk and said, 'Everyone, this is what your whole life is all about. It's all you need to know about anything.'

The class fell silent. 'DNA makes up everything

inside of you,' he boomed. 'It determines what you look like and how you think, if you're going to get sick and whether you're smart or stupid. All you need to know about yourself is right here in this little molecule. Everything about your future, everything about your past. Nothing else matters, and you can't change it. It's passed down, directly, from your parents. You can't escape your parents and your parents can't escape you, as hard as either of you might try. You're tethered to them for life.'

Everyone murmured. Jennifer Lake raised her hand, then put it back down quickly. 'Even the DNA that may not code for anything,' Mr Rice went on, his voice swooping up and down, the way a hawk climbs and dives. 'The stuff that's called junk DNA. It *does* code for something – something *huge*. It codes for the secrets, stuff we never admit to anyone. Once we crack its code, we'll have the answers to everything, but right now, I think the only beings that understand junk DNA's secrets are the aliens.'

Mr Rice turned and drew a dish-shaped space-ship on the board. An eggplant-headed alien peeked out the top, and Mr Rice etched a dotted line beaming right to the helix of DNA. The sweat on his forehead reminded me of the beads of water that gathered on the outside of a plastic bottle on a hot day. A couple of boys at the back coughed insults into their fists. But Mr Rice's words echoed in my mind. *This is what your whole life is about.*

12

You can't escape your parents and your parents can't escape you.

Before this, our school's principal had missed every other instance of unorthodox teaching, so it was something of a surprise when his face appeared outside the classroom door. Then there was a knock. 'Everything okay, Mr Rice?' He stuck his head in. His eyes glided to the slapdash spaceship on the chalkboard.

I stared at the spaceship, too. There were so many things I worried about. I'd always been a worrier – my father said worrying was in our blood. Just one week before, one of my most pressing worries had been that I would drop my set of keys to the apartment onto the subway tracks. I was so obsessed with the precarious danger of it, I flirted with the idea of pitching the keys down there willingly, just to know what would happen. But if I did, I would have to sit on the stoop in front of our apartment building, keyless, until my mother returned home from work. I didn't want to imagine what she would say, the pinched, disappointed shape her face would take.

I used to worry about the lone gray hairs I often saw sprouting from my mother's head, terrified that she was showing signs of advanced and debilitating age. When she started to shut herself in the bathroom for hours at a time, talking quietly on the phone, I worried that she was hiding a horrible sickness from the rest of us. I pictured a devastating disease ripping her apart, her skin peeling off in curls, her heart blackening. When we received a catalogue from the Vitamin Shoppe in the mail, I put it by her plate at breakfast, convinced its glossy pages contained a miracle pill. But she pushed the catalogue aside. My father absently flipped through it instead, commenting on the high price of spirulina tablets and chromium picolinate diet pills. In all my what-if scenarios, I never envisioned my father physically ill. The dark hours he spent under the covers were due to something different, not sickness.

What had happened to my family a few days before this was something else entirely – something far bigger than anything I'd even dared to consider. But Mr Rice's words made me think that maybe I didn't have to worry about it after all.

The substitute's shoulders slumped as he walked into the hall with the principal. As soon as the door shut, one of the fist-coughing boys snorted, 'What a *loser.*' Someone threw a balled-up piece of notebook paper at the alien spaceship. One by one, like dominoes falling over, everyone began to talk, to forget. I was the only one who didn't laugh.

The following day, when my father told me that Claire Ryan and her mother were coming over to visit in a few minutes, I was struck dumb. Just because I was friends with someone a couple years ago didn't mean we liked each other now. I thought my father understood this.

'Claire?' I shrieked. 'Are you sure? Why?'

'Her mother wants to talk to me, that's why,' my father explained. 'And she's bringing Claire because she thought it would be nice for you two to see each other again.'

The doorbell rang. I looked at my father. He was wearing plaid slippers and had the same Pfizer t-shirt he'd been wearing for days. Our house had magazines piled by the fireplace, empty soda bottles on the coffee table, and a crooked, un-decorated Christmas tree in the corner, needles all over the floor. It was amazing how messy things could get in just two weeks.

When my father opened the door, Mrs Ryan looked right – perhaps a bit thinner, a little ragged, her blonde hair not as smoothly blow-dried as it used to be – but Claire was different entirely. Her eyes were the same, those blue-green eyes everyone used to be so jealous of. As was her thick blonde hair, the hair she used to toss over her shoulder so effortlessly, and her pretty, bow-shaped mouth, the mouth every boy wanted to kiss. But her cheeks were puffy. The rest of her body was, too.

I couldn't stop staring. Look at the way her t-shirt clung to her arms! Look at the pink flesh around her neck! I actually gasped, although I tried to pass it off as a hiccup, hitting my chest for effect like I was working something down my esoph-agus. Everyone knew Claire was back from Paris and her parents were divorcing, but no one knew *this*.

15

Mrs Ryan looked at me. 'Hi, Summer. It's so nice to see you again.'

She pushed Claire forward. 'Say hi, Claire.'

'Hi,' Claire mumbled.

'How was France?' my father cried. 'You two look great. Very European.'

He didn't even notice how different Claire looked. My mother wouldn't miss something like this.

My father asked me to take Claire to the roof to show her the view of the city, as if Claire hadn't seen it thousands of times before. Although her view wasn't from this side of the river anymore – what everyone also knew was that Mr Ryan was retaining his apartment on Pineapple Street in Brooklyn Heights, near us, and Mrs Ryan and Claire were renting a place in a mysterious Manhattan neighborhood called Alphabet City.

'Go on,' my father said, making a shooing motion with his hands.

When we reached the roof, Claire looked at the buildings across the East River. Back when we hung out a lot, we had names for each of the buildings we could see from my apartment – the tall pointy one was Lester, the squat one on the harbor was Fred, and the twin towers were Scooby-Doo and Shaggy, the only two characters on the show worth caring about. I glanced at Scooby-Doo – One World Trade – and counted twenty-two flights from the top and three windows over. My mother's office. I'd never been inside it, but I was certain there was an official-looking name plaque on her desk, *Meredith Heller-Davis*. The room was still dark. I squinted hard, willing the light to come on.

Claire ran her finger along the edge of the charcoal grill. There was rust on it, but we used to cook out on the roof a lot. All four of us, my mother, father, my brother Steven and me, we would come up here and point at the boats and buildings and eat hamburgers. My father used to bring up a boom box and put on a bunch of old jazz tapes, even though my mother preferred music that, as she put it, 'actually made sense.' When it was time to eat, my dad turned his back and whipped up a condiment that he said was his Aunt Stella's Famous Special Sauce. Once, I remarked that it tasted like nothing but mayo and ketchup mixed, and my mother snorted. 'Stella probably got the idea from Burger King,' she said with a laugh. My father chewed his burger. 'Stella's a good woman,' he said stiffly, not that it was in question.

Later, my mother and I would watch the boats on the East River through binoculars, making up stories about some of the yachters. The man in the sailboat named *Miss Isabelle* still lived on his parents' estate. The man in the yacht with a naked woman figurehead had made his fortune by patenting the long plastic wand used to separate one person's groceries from another on the belt – how else could a man with such a tacky combover own a boat that big? When it was Steven's turn with the binoculars, he always aimed them at the buildings across the water, watching the people still in their offices, working. 'What do you think they're doing in there?' he asked out loud on more than one occasion. 'I bet they're doing math,' my mother or I always suggested, struggling to remain straight-faced. Steven's love of math was an ongoing joke between my mother and me; we were convinced that he slept with his graphing calculator under his pillow.

Claire's belt was fastened on the very last notch. 'So my new neighborhood is weird,' she informed me, as if we'd been talking every day. As if I knew everything about her – which I kind of did. 'Last night, I saw a man dressed as a woman.'

'How did you know?'

'I looked at his arms.'

I'd never been to her new neighborhood before, this mythical *Alphabet City*. When kids at our school traveled into Manhattan, they went to SoHo to shop, or to the Upper East or West Sides to visit grandparents. No one ventured into the East Village, and definitely not to the avenues with the letters.

The Staten Island ferry chugged away from the west side of the island, spewing a contrast of black oil and crisp white waves behind it. 'So.' Claire tapped the top of the grille. 'What's new with you?'

'Not much.' I kept my eyes on the ferry. 'Same old, same old.'

18

Claire curled her hand around a rusted spatula. 'I heard about your mom.'

A hot fist knotted in my throat. What did everyone know about *my* family?

Before I could reply, a noise interrupted us. Claire's mother clomped up to the roof. My father followed. 'Time to go,' Mrs Ryan announced.

Claire crossed her arms over her chest. 'We just got here.'

Mrs Ryan gave her a tight smile. 'We have a lot of things to do today.'

'*You* have a lot of things to do. I don't.'

'Well, you have to come with me.' Mrs Ryan's expression didn't falter.

'I can ride the train by myself.'

'Seriously. Time to go.'

Claire put her head down. 'Fuck off.'

My father's eyes widened. Mine did, too. I'd never heard Claire swear.

Mrs Ryan swallowed, then stood up straighter. 'Fine.' She turned around stiffly and started back down the stairs. My dad and I stood there, waiting to see if Claire would move. She didn't. My father looked blank. He wasn't good at dealing with things like this.

Claire sighed. 'Unbelievable,' she eventually said, and stood up. The doorway down from the roof to our apartment suddenly looked too narrow for her to fit through.

My father and I walked them to the door. We watched them out the window as they marched

19

toward the subway, not talking, not touching. The wind blew, shaking the plastic bags caught in the trees.

'Did Claire ask you anything about it?' my father murmured out of the corner of his mouth.

I shrugged. 'It's none of her business.' *Or yours,* I wanted to add.

'Claire's your best friend.'

'*Was*. Two years ago. For like a second.'

He jingled loose change in his pockets. 'It's okay to talk about it, you know.'

'I don't need to talk about it. There's nothing *to* talk about.'

He looked at me desperately. The jingling stopped.

'There *isn't*,' I repeated.

He pressed his thumbs into his eye sockets, breathed out through his mouth, and made a funny *choooo* noise, like a train pulling into the last station stop and easing on its brakes. Then, he patted my arm, sighed, and went into the kitchen to turn on the TV.

Claire was born one year, one month, and one day before I was. When we were friends for like a second two summers ago, she liked to remind me of this when she held me down and tickled me: 'I am one year, one month, and one day older than you,' she would say, 'so I have full tickling privileges.'

She was going into ninth grade and I was going

into eighth. We were forced to be around each other a lot that summer because our mothers, who both worked in the events department of Mandrake & Hester, a high-end private bank, had become best friends and rented a share on Long Beach Island. When my mother told me about it, I panicked. Spend eight weeks at the beach with a girl I didn't know? I didn't even like the ocean. And I wasn't very comfortable with strangers.

My mother wanted me to like Claire – and even more, for Claire to like me – and at the beach, it didn't seem that hard. Claire's long, ash-blonde hair became knotted and caked with sand, and her full, pretty lips were constantly coated with Zinc. She wore ratty t-shirts and cut-offs, and she roughhoused, tackling me into the surf. She indulged my need to spy on our mothers, who liked to sunbathe on the beach and read magazines. We had a foolproof system: the lifeguard stand was on a mound by the dunes, and all we had to do was duck behind where the lifeguards hung their towels and our mothers had no idea we were there. They talked about chauvinistic men at the office, places they wished they could visit, the new male teacher at their ballet studio in Tribeca. I waited to see if my mother would talk about me – maybe in a bragging way, hopefully not in an irritated way – but she never did.

In July, our mothers signed us up to be junior counselors at the town's day camp. Claire was the only person I spoke to and who spoke to me.

Everyone loved Claire, though. She could play the guitar, beat anyone in a race across the sand, and she petitioned the camp to let us build a twenty-person ice cream sundae, exhausting the kitchen's supplies. Three different junior counselor boys had a crush on her, and kids followed her around as if she was made of cake icing.

That fall, I switched from St Martha's, a private Catholic school in Brooklyn Heights, to Peninsula Upper School, where Claire went. Seventh through ninth graders were in one building, and high-school sophomores through seniors were in another. Claire was the only person I knew who went there, but I certainly didn't know who Claire *was*. If I had, I wouldn't have acted like such a juvenile around her, stealing stacks of orange-yellow 500s from the bank when we played Monopoly, constantly playing the beach house's Nintendo even though I barely touched our console at home. And I *certainly* wouldn't have done that dance when I won the Mega Man Six tournament, the finale of which involved flashing Claire my pink bubble-printed underwear.

On September 3, I barely noticed a tall, beautiful blonde girl climb aboard the school bus. 'Get your butt over here!' a guy at the back of the bus screamed at her. Other guys made *whoo*ing noises. 'Where've you been all summer, Claire?' a girl cried.

Claire? I started up, alarmed. The blonde girl in the pink shirt and form-fitted jeans took off her

22

pale sunglasses. There were those familiar blue-green eyes, that lush, pink mouth, but her hair was so smooth, her clothes so brand-new. She whipped her head around, as if looking for someone. I slumped down in the seat and pretended to be fascinated by my lunch, a cold can of Coke that had sweated through the brown paper lunch bag, a smushed PB&J, crammed into a Ziploc. Finally, Claire walked to the back and fell into a seat with one of the girls.

'Anyone sitting here?' asked an Indian boy who I would later learn was named Vishal. My hand was still saving the empty seat next to the aisle for Claire. I curled it away into my lap and squeezed myself as close to the window as I could.

When the bus pulled up to our school on Lincoln Street, I stood up, but Vishal grabbed my sleeve. 'I think we're supposed to let them off first,' he said, in his loopy I-didn't-grow-up-here accent. And there they came, Claire among them, shoving each other and laughing, all of them with clear skin and hiking backpacks even though there was nowhere around to hike.

Claire noticed me cowering behind Vishal. 'Summer!' She stopped short, holding up the line in back of her. 'When did you get on?'

'I was here,' I said quietly. 'I got on before you.'

'Claire, c'mon!' A girl behind her shoved her playfully.

But Claire didn't move. 'I didn't see you.' She seemed honestly sad.

'I was here.' My voice sounded pathetic. Claire noticed, too; her lip stuck out in a pout.

The next day, she made a big point to sit with me on the bus. The day after that, too. The whole time, she was up on her knees facing the back of the bus, laughing with them. 'Just go back there,' I said on the third day, pressing my body against the cold, drafty window, my knees curled up to my stomach because I'd stupidly chosen the bus seat above the wheel.

'No, it's okay.' Claire moved her knees to the front. 'So what's been going on with you? Are you liking school? Wasn't I right – isn't it easy to find your way around?'

'I'm busy reading this,' I snapped, staring at the oral report schedule for my American History class. I was to give a report about the Gettysburg Address on November 14, more than two months away.

'Summer.' Claire wore shiny lip gloss. Her earrings were dangling silver pears.

'Just go.'

Claire shrugged, then monkey-barred from seat to seat, listing sideways when the bus went over bumps. Maybe I should've told her to stay and sit with me. Maybe I should've asked why she hadn't suggested that we *both* go back and sit with them. But I was afraid what the answer might be – what fatal flaw of mine prevented her from introducing me around. I told myself I was being charitable, a real friend, letting her go off there alone. I'd given her a gift.

By the time the end of the year rolled around, if Claire and I passed each other in an empty hall, all she might say was, 'Steal any Monopoly money lately?' I hated her by then. I'd begun to blame Claire for everything that was going wrong – that, two weeks before, I had woken up and realized I'd peed in the bed. That a window in our front room had been broken, and my father asked my mother to call to have it replaced but she argued that *he* had fingers, *he* could call to have it replaced, and it *still* wasn't replaced because they were at some sort of standoff, and there was still a huge crack in the window, sloppily sealed up with duct tape. That I would probably die an old maid without ever kissing a boy. That my father had begun to spend whole Saturdays in bed, and that my mother didn't take me shopping anymore.

One late May afternoon, I was in keyboarding class, typing line after line of *the quick brown fox jumps over the lazy dog*. Two girls in the front row leaned close together. 'Claire Ryan is moving to France,' one whispered to the other. 'They're taking the Concorde.'

I typed a whole line of nonsense so it seemed like I wasn't listening. *France?*

I found out later – not from Claire – that her father had taken a position at his company's Paris office. They had rented a three-bedroom apartment in someplace called Montmartre. I wanted to ask Claire about it, or wish her well, or tell her good riddance, but so many people always surrounded her, all the way up to the very end, that I never had the chance.

The excited chatter that Claire was returning from France had started a few weeks ago. Claire hadn't told anyone the news herself, but someone's father worked with Mr Ryan and had found out the details. Claire would be attending Peninsula again, but she would be in tenth grade with me, not eleventh. People nudged Devon Reyes, Claire's old boyfriend, saying that Claire had probably learned a few tricks, living in a country that was so obsessed and open about sex. And me? I didn't have any reaction to the news, and no one asked me for comment. The time we were friends felt as far away as my birth.

But it surprised me that Mr and Mrs Ryan were getting a divorce – Claire had never seemed worried about her parents' marriage. After Mrs Ryan and Claire left our apartment, I followed my father into the kitchen. 'Perhaps Mrs Ryan just needs a private vacation,' I called out to him, as if we'd been dissecting the Ryans' divorce for hours. 'You know, some time to herself. And then, after a while, she'll move back into the Pineapple Street apartment, and everything will be fine. It's probably what all couples need, I bet.'

My father looked at me for a long time. His eyes were watery. 'Maybe,' he said, eating from a bag of pretzels, letting loose salt fall to the floor. He tried to laugh, but it came out as more of a sniffle.

CHAPTER 2

The night after Claire came over, my father declared we had nothing to eat in the house, which wasn't an exaggeration. We hadn't gotten the hang of shopping for ourselves yet. But now that we were on our own, we could go out to dinner wherever we wanted, which usually meant Grimaldi's.

Grimaldi's was this pizza place down under the Brooklyn Bridge. The pizza was so good that people lined up on the streets for a table. My mother hated eating there because the tablecloths were checkerboard, there were too many children, and they only served pizza for dinner. She hated that all the tables had wobbly legs, and that the wine specials were on a little card-stand next to a pot of fake flowers. As my father, brother, and I piled into the little dining room, I tried to see Grimaldi's imperfections through her eyes; I scoffed at the place's paltry selection of sodas, offering Pepsi instead of Coke. I sneered at the paper napkins. That awkward autumn when Claire was pretending she was still my friend, she came here with my family. Just as we were sitting down in a booth, Claire spotted some of the girls from the bus across the room, *sans* parents, sharing a basket of mozzarella sticks. Claire waved at them enthusiastically, but I shrank down in my seat. 'Why aren't you waving?' my mother hissed. I shrugged; Claire pretended not to hear. Later, I heard my parents talking in the kitchen. 'Summer should have more girlfriends,' my mother said in a low voice. 'Does it matter?' my father answered. My mother murmured something I couldn't hear.

I caught a glimpse of Claire this morning in the courtyard at school, just as I was dashing outside to the breakfast cart to get coffees for the popular girls in my first-period French class. Claire was talking to Melissa Green, one of her old friends. Melissa had a frozen, terrified smile on her face, trying to focus only on Claire's eyes and not the rest of her body. When Claire said goodbye and turned away, Melissa's expression twisted. She ran back to a gaggle of waiting girls and they started whispering.

'So what do you think Mom's doing right now?' I asked my father as our Grimaldi's waitress took our order and trudged away.

'I don't know, honey,' my father said wearily.

'You should try and call her,' I suggested.

'She'll call when she's ready.'

'Mom probably wants *you* to call,' I said. 'She could be surrounded by younger guys, wherever she is. She could get tempted, just like Mrs Ryan was tempted by that younger French man.'

28

My father set down his fork. Even Steven, who had been poring over advanced calculus problem sets – he was a freshman at New York University, but lived in our apartment instead of the dorms – looked up with mild interest. 'Excuse me?' my father sputtered.

I repeated what I'd heard from the girls in French class. 'She had an affair with a younger Frenchman from their local *boulangerie*. Claire caught them. And that's why she's so fat: she ate to console herself. It makes perfect sense.'

'That's ridiculous.' My father looked aghast. 'And Claire's not *fat*. She looks fine.'

'Fine?' I echoed. '*Fine?*'

He sighed wearily and excused himself to the bathroom, squeezing down the narrow hall next to the brick oven, which was covered almost entirely with black-and-white snapshots of scowling old women in aprons. My mother once remarked that it was disgusting how many people in New York City – in the whole of America, really – were getting so fat. My father retorted that obesity sometimes wasn't someone's fault. What about genetics? What about depression? And my mother sighed and said, 'Honestly, Richard, what would you do without me? You can't go telling Summer being fat is okay!'

I wanted to call my mother right now and tell her that I would never, ever believe being fat was okay. And if only she'd seen me doling out coffees to the French class girls in the courtyard this morning – there were such grateful smiles on their faces, and we'd all walked to French class together in a happy, laughing clump. She could've dropped by the school; other parents did it all the time. *That's my daughter,* she would've thought, if she'd have seen me. And maybe her mind would've changed about us – about everything – just like that.

When I came home from school the next day, my brother was sitting at the kitchen table. He was always parked at the table doing math, even though he could've used NYU's facilities instead. His glasses made his eyes look enormous.

'Did anyone call?' I asked.

'Nope.' He didn't raise his head.

My smile drooped a little. I continued to stare at Steven until he finally looked up. '*What?*'

'Nothing.'

'Then go somewhere else!' Steven had my mother's angular face, but we both shared my dad's oversized nose. When we were little – when Steven and I were sort of friends – we started a secret club called The Schnoz. Our father mystified us both back then, with his brilliant white lab coat and all his tics – the specific pastries for breakfast, the long runs often at night, the dark, dreary moods that would come over him like a thick wool blanket. We decided that he was secretly a superhero, a mix between a mad scientist and a stealthy GI Joe – Steven was obsessed with the military. Our club mostly consisted of spying on my father while he watched television in the den, looking for superhero clues. But then, Steven turned ten and announced that if he didn't win a Nobel Prize by the age of 20, he was going to enlist in the Special Forces. My father laughed and reminded Steven how clumsy he was – he'd probably shoot himself in the hand while trying to clean his gun. The Schnoz disbanded pretty much after that.

When he got older, Steven went to Stuyvesant High, the smart math and science school in the city. My mother didn't ask if I wanted to take the test to go to Stuyvesant. My parents had a huge argument about it – my father said Stuyvesant was the best place for me, but my mother insisted that Peninsula was better because it encouraged the liberal arts. 'But she's not interested in liberal arts!' my father bellowed. 'She likes science! She won three elementary and middle school science fairs at St Martha's!' My mother rolled her eyes. 'We should let Summer choose for herself,' my father bargained. 'She's going to Peninsula,' my mother said. 'End of story.'

Even though my father was right – I wasn't that into art or history or English – I liked Peninsula fine. And anyway, girls who went to Stuyvesant were nerds who never got boyfriends. Everyone knew that.

'Do you want a soda?' I asked Steven, turning for the fridge.

'No.'

'We still have the orange stuff Mom bought for you.'

'Mmm.' His pencil made soft scratching sounds against the paper.

'It looks like you're running out, though. But Mom will probably be back in time to buy a new case.'

He kept writing. Steven had hardly said a word about her since she'd left, so I didn't know what I thought I was going to achieve, fishing. Steven had hardly spoken to her anyway, except to ask if she could wash a load of his whites. He probably didn't even care that she was gone. Although, was that possible? Yes, she and Steven were very different – she was so *glamorous* – but Steven had to have some thoughts about it. Just one teensy feeling, somewhere.

'Summer, there you are.' My father appeared in the doorway. 'I have a favor to ask you.'

He led me to the living room, and we sat down on the couch. 'Mrs Ryan just called. She wanted to know if I could tutor Claire in biology.'

I stiffened, surprised. I'd looked for Claire at school today but hadn't seen her anywhere. 'You said no, right?'

'I said I was too busy.'

I tried not to laugh. Lately, my father's version of busy was piling magazines for recycling and watching the home shopping channels – he liked the old people that called in. He probably hadn't even gone to the lab all week.

My father picked up one of the little plastic figurines from the toy ski slope he'd bought on a trip to Switzerland. It came with four little Swiss skiers, each with a blanked-out, stoic Swiss expression. Steven had been obsessed with the ski slope when my parents brought it home, but it had become more of a Christmas decoration. Last night, on the walk home from dinner, there were suddenly fairy lights on our neighbors' banisters and Christmas trees in their front windows. It made our naked, untended-to tree in the living room seem so obviously neglected, so I went down to our basement storage space, found the Christmas box, and brought everything up myself – the ornaments, the Santa knick-knacks, the ski slope, even old holiday photos of all of us unwrapping Christmas gifts, my father inevitably wearing a gift-wrap bow on the top of his head. The stuff wasn't that heavy. And it was sort of fun to decorate on my own.

'Perhaps you'd like to tutor Claire instead,' my father suggested.

I shook my head. 'I'm kind of busy, too.'

He rubbed his hand over his smooth chin. 'Busy with what?'

I didn't answer.

'Well, I've already set it up,' he breezed on. 'She's coming over in ten minutes.'

'*Dad.*'

He placed the plastic skier at the top of the hill and let go. The skier zipped down. My father caught him at the bottom, tweezed his little plastic head between his thumb and pointer finger, and

33

guided him back up the side of the slope, simulating a chairlift. He made a *brrr* sound with his lips, impersonating a motor.

When I was down in the basement getting all the ornaments and stuff, an invitation fluttered out from a box. It was for a Christmas party at Claire's house from that first year I'd attended Peninsula. The night of the party, my mother asked why I wasn't getting ready. When I said I'd rather watch the Christmas marathon on TV – they were playing *Rudolph, Frosty,* and *The Year Without a Santa Claus* back-to-back, a stellar lineup – my mother blew her bangs off her face. 'It's not a crime Claire has other friends,' she chided. 'It wouldn't kill you to be friends with them, too.'

As if it had been my decision. As if I'd orchestrated things that way.

The doorbell rang. Mrs Ryan stood in the hall. 'Claire's down at the deli,' she said, walking right in. 'Thank you so much for doing this, sweetie. It's a huge help.'

I grumbled tonelessly.

'Is your dad home?' She looked around. 'He invited me over for coffee, but I wasn't sure if he was mixed up, since it's so early. I didn't think he'd be back from work yet.'

I felt a flush of embarrassment. 'He had a half-day.'

Mrs Ryan walked into the foyer, smiling at our family pictures on the wall, many of them over ten years old. She reached into her pocket and pulled out a disposable camera. It was covered in green paper, and there was a picture of a woman and a little kid, probably meant to be her daughter, sitting on the edge of a motorboat, smiling so blissfully that their teeth gleamed blue-white. 'Fun Saver', the camera was called.

I pointed at it. 'My mother uses those, too. But she also has a Nikon. That's probably what she's using for her trip.'

Mrs Ryan advanced the camera slowly. 'How are you holding up, Summer?'

'I'm great. Really excited for Christmas.'

'Your mother . . .' Mrs Ryan shook her head. 'It's so unexpected. I mean, I just talked to her a month or so ago. She gave no indication . . .'

I stared her down. 'She's on a trip. No big deal.'

Mrs Ryan blinked hard, as if she'd just run smack into a wall without noticing it was there.

'I mean, it's not even worth talking about,' I went on. 'Like, not to Claire or anything. She probably has enough on her mind anyway, right?'

Mrs Ryan shifted her weight. Then, she peered into the hall. 'Oh. Here we are, honey.' She gestured Claire inside.

Claire wore a heavy blue polo shirt and a long black crinkle skirt. The elastic band stretched hard against her waist. There was a blossom of acne around her mouth. Before she left, Claire's skin was clear and glowing. Maybe France poisoned her.

'How about I get a picture of you two?' Mrs Ryan

suggested, holding the Fun Saver to her face. 'The friends reunited.'

Claire rolled her eyes. 'God, Mom. No.'

'Come on. Just one. Stand together.'

There was a frozen beat. Finally, I took a step to Claire. We used to pose for pictures with our arms thrown around each other, our tongues stuck out. Now, it felt like the corners of my mouth were being held down by lead weights. Claire gave off a heated radiance, as if shame had a temperature. There was a fluttering sound. When the flash went off, bright, burnt spots appeared in front of my eyes.

'Beautiful.' Mrs Ryan advanced the film and placed the camera on the little table in the hall. Claire and I shot apart fast.

My father emerged, saying, 'Hi Liz', and that he'd put a pot of coffee on. The adults migrated toward the kitchen. Suddenly, I didn't want my father hanging around Mrs Ryan. Sometimes he gave up too much of himself. And Mrs Ryan was tainted with marital strife. Some of it might somehow rub off on him, like a grass stain.

Claire disappeared down the hall to the bathroom, but I stayed where I was, glowering at the Fun Saver on the hall table. I wanted to tear off the wrapping and rip it into thousands of pieces. I slid the camera into my pocket. If Mrs Ryan asked, I would tell her I had no idea where it went.

I found Claire standing in my bedroom doorway.

Her eyes swept over the piles of clothes in the corner and the holiday trees and singing Santa Clauses on my dresser – I had Christmasized my room as well. 'I forgot how big your room was,' she said after a pause. 'My room on Avenue A is so small. And my room in Paris was even smaller.'

There was a flowered bra on the floor, the kind that hooked in the front. I noticed a gray flannel nightgown, too, the one with the kitten silk-screened across the chest. A speech bubble above the kitten said, 'I love to sleep'. I stood on top of it.

'So,' I muttered. 'Biology?'

Claire shrugged. 'Sure, if you want.'

'So what's the deal? Didn't you take it last year?'

'Yeah. But I totally sucked at it.'

But you used to be so good at everything, I wanted to say.

I looked around my room and realized there was nowhere for us both to sit. This probably would've made more sense at the kitchen table. Finally, I pulled my chair over to the bed, and Claire sat down. I plopped on the bed, pulled my biology book out of my bag, and opened it. 'How far behind are you?'

'I got lost around cells and genetics.' Claire sat very upright in the chair, her hands folded in her lap.

'Because it was in French?' I asked.

'No.'

Because you're fat? I pictured fat clogging up her brain, impairing her memory.

I flipped to the start of the genetics chapter.

Claire leaned over and tapped a drawing of a tightly wound coil of DNA. 'I heard a Peninsula sub freaked out about genetics on Monday.'

I raised an eyebrow. 'Kind of. I was in the class.'

'What happened?'

'It was this guy, Mr Rice. He was subbing for Mrs Hewes – she's on maternity leave. He told us that DNA is magnetic. We're stuck with our parents, and they're stuck with us, whether we like it or not. DNA can explain everything we do, except we're too stupid to understand that yet. Only the aliens can understand it.'

'Aliens?' Claire giggled. 'Even my teachers in France weren't that messed up.'

'He didn't seem messed up, really.' I clutched a pillow close to my chest, curling away from Claire. 'Maybe our school is just being narrow-minded.'

Claire stared at me. 'You *believe* him?'

'I just think it's an interesting theory. I don't believe the part about the aliens.'

She shifted positions, moving closer. 'So why do you think it's interesting?' Her tone of voice was curious but delicate. It was the same voice she'd used when we were friends, as if I were the most fascinating person in the world.

After a thoughtful moment, Claire added, 'Is it because you like the idea of everything happening for a reason? Or that, if you looked hard enough, you'd be able to understand why people do the stuff that they do? Like why they go away without telling you where they're going?'

38

If she said one more thing, I would punch her puffy face. I would point out that she wasn't one to talk – she'd found her mother fooling around with that young Frenchman, after all. I pictured Claire throwing open the double doors to her parents' bedroom, seeing Mrs Ryan and the *boulangerie* baker tangled in bed together, the sheets on the floor. The baker was wearing a black beret and nothing else. The soles of his bare feet were dirty, and so were his hands.

Claire pressed her lips together coyly. Even in her current state, she could be her old self with me – the one who always said, *It's okay. You can tell me. I'll still like you.* But she didn't like me in the end, did she? She didn't let me into her world; there was something horribly wrong with me. Maybe it was an obvious thing, something a lot of people saw.

Still, I thought about the thing bumping around inside of me. The thing I was afraid to admit, even to myself. Part of me wanted to tell her. Part of me needed someone to tell.

'Do you remember when we used to roll down the hill in the park?' Claire asked quietly.

I bit my lip hard, startled. 'We used to have races.'

'Rolling races.' Claire made a small smile. 'That was fun.'

'And we used to play a lot of Monopoly,' I said, as if just recalling.

'You were always the guy on the horse.'

'And you were always the shoe.'

'And I used to tickle you.' Claire giggled.

'I hated that.'

'C'mon. It was so much fun.' Claire looked thoughtful, then wily, almost like she was considering tickling me right then. She moved toward me. In anticipation, I moved back on the bed and jerked my foot away quickly, sideswiping the softness of her stomach. It felt substantial and . . . *mushy*.

Claire jumped back and crossed her arms over the spot on her stomach that I'd kicked. I tucked my foot underneath the bed skirt. 'Sorry.'

'I was just getting my highlighter,' Claire mumbled. It had fallen on the floor; she reached down for it. At that moment, the holiday tree came on. It was on a timer, playing a different Christmas song every fifteen minutes. This time, it was Perry Como singing 'Mistletoe and Holly'. Claire and I both jumped.

The mood changed fast, from light to awkward. Claire sat back down and we went through the rest of the biology chapter on genetics and then I took her through cells. She got it right away, which made me wonder if she'd really failed biology at all. I duly explained mitochondria, the nucleus and vacuoles, evolution and natural selection, the chemical composition of proteins and carbohydrates. I left out fats on purpose. Claire pretended not to notice.

★ ★ ★

When my father was young, he was in a car accident. He and his friends were driving home from a party, and they were going down a twisty road and hit a deer. This was when my father lived in western Pennsylvania.

It felt like a story I'd learned in history class, repeated again and again each year. My father's friend's name was Mark, and Mark's girlfriend's name was Kay. Kay was sitting in the front passenger seat. The car crashed in such a way that her side was crumpled, but Mark and my father were unharmed. My father got out of the car and saw the deer, dead and bloody on the ground. Then he ran over to Kay's side and took one look at her and passed out. He woke up later in the hospital. Kay was in a coma. Later, she died.

My father brought it up at the oddest of times. The last time he talked about it, we were walking into the Village Vanguard jazz club – I was the only one in the family who would go there with him. 'I basically saw the girlfriend of my best friend die,' he whispered, just as an older black man hobbled onstage to the piano. 'Sometimes I think about how different my life would have been if that accident hadn't happened.'

Different how? He wouldn't have gone to Penn State or met my mother? He had been a senior, and my mother had been a freshman. They'd met in line at one of the university's dining halls. But my mother paid my father no attention. Even though he was handsome, he had a strange accent.

41

He was from a part of Pennsylvania that people from the Philadelphia area shunned.

My father won my mother over with persistence. There were gaps in the story; next, it jumped to the part about my mom getting pregnant with Steven. My father was in med school by then. He'd gotten an offer to intern at the NYU Downtown Hospital. My mother, who was fascinated with New York, dropped out of her sophomore year of college, moved to New York with my father, and had Steven.

I once asked my mom if she and dad would've been friends in high school. 'Probably,' my dad said right away. 'I was well liked back then.'

Behind her hand, my mother shook her head. When my father left the room, she said, 'We grew up in very different places.'

My father was a collector. He collected fossils, bugs preserved in blobs of amber, ships in bottles, and snow globes. 'I like things that are trapped,' he explained. 'Too many things leave us forever.' He even had a way of trapping memories – every time we got a ticket from a parking garage, he wrote a few details about where we'd parked and where we'd been and what we'd seen on the back of the stub. He did this with dry-cleaning slips, movie-ticket stubs, restaurant receipts, throwing it all in a big leather box at the foot of the bed. 'All of these things are important,' he said. 'We'll want to be reminded of it later.' He'd been doing it the whole time I'd been alive.

Sometimes, when my father spent whole weekends in bed, I crawled in with him, and we watched cartoons. My father laughed at them as much as I did. When I got out of bed, he stayed, but I still thought I'd accomplished something. 'Mom thinks you're being lazy,' I said to him once, not that long ago. 'I'm not lazy,' he answered, 'I'm just sad.'

He got sad a lot. Once, my father started crying in a line at the movie theater, putting his face in his hands and shaking. My mother made him go around the corner to an alley because everyone was staring at us, wondering what was wrong. I thought I should go after him, but my mother grabbed my arm. 'Don't,' she said. 'He'll be fine.'

'What's he crying about?' I asked.

My mother just shrugged and rolled her eyes. 'It's so embarrassing,' she hissed. 'I don't know why he can't just pull himself together. But it's like he can't help it.'

I wanted her to explain. What was so embarrassing? Crying? Feeling? Should I be angry at him, too? The movie posters blurred in front of my eyes. When it was our turn to buy tickets, we bought three, one for me, one for my mother, and one for my father. We waited for him to return from the alley, and then we went in the theater together.

Last Friday, when I came home from school, I found my father sitting at the kitchen table, looking at an envelope. His name was written on the front in my mother's handwriting. She'd made the *R* in *Richard* very big, but the letters got smaller and smaller, descending into almost nothing. The *d* at the end wasn't much bigger than a pencil point.

'What's that?' I asked.

'Nothing.' He covered it up with his hand.

We went to the ice cream parlor on the Promenade despite it being early December and cold. My father, well over six feet tall, towered over everyone else in the little shop. He was wearing the black wool overcoat my mother had bought for him. His face was clean-shaven, his thick, light brown hair combed off his forehead. He bought me an espresso milkshake, which I loved, even though they made me twitch. We sat in a little booth in the back, and he ate a whole scoop of butter pecan before he told me that Mom had gone on a work trip. She'd probably be back in a week or so; in the meantime, could I help him keep the house clean?

I said sure, no problem. I'd been helping keep the house clean for the past few months anyway, ever since my mother's job had become more demanding. But I could tell there was something more. It was so easy to tell when my father was lying – his cheeks got very pink, and it looked like he was literally holding something in, like a sneeze. 'Okay, okay, Mom isn't on a trip,' he blurted out, as if I'd harshly interrogated him. 'She's gone.'

His facial features seemed scrambled, like those tile puzzles where you have to move the pieces

44

around to make a coherent picture. 'What do you mean, gone?' I asked.

He blotted his eyes with his sticky ice cream cone napkin. 'She wrote a letter. But it wasn't very clear.'

I felt an uneasy stab and let out a whimper. 'No, Summer, please don't cry,' he said desperately. 'I don't know what to do.'

He bent over until his head touched the top of the table. His shoulders shook up and down. A few minutes went by, and he didn't stop. 'Dad?' I touched his shoulder. 'Come on.'

'I just don't know why this happened,' he blubbered.

By this time, a horrible feeling was sloshing through me. I thought of the things I'd done wrong, all my shortcomings. This could be because of me. Because of something I wasn't.

But I couldn't have my father sitting in the ice cream shop, bawling. 'Dad.' I took him underneath the arm and pulled him up. 'She's probably just . . . overworked. I saw it on *Oprah*. People in this country get only ten days of vacation, but people in Europe get thirty. She probably went somewhere where there aren't any ringing phones.' It poured from inside me. When I finished, I reviewed what I'd just said, not sure if it made any sense.

He raised his chin. Some old ladies in the next booth over were staring. 'Do you think?' my father asked, his face red and wet.

'Yes.' I said it so confidently, I almost convinced myself.

My father ran his hand over his hair. 'Jesus, Summer.' He bumped into me, hugging my head to his. 'I'm sorry I just did that. That's the last thing you want to see, huh? Your crazy old dad, losing it in the ice cream parlor?'

'It's fine,' I said.

He looked at me, nodding. 'You're right. She's on a trip.'

'She's on a trip,' I whispered back.

It wasn't much to hold onto, but I held onto it anyway.

CHAPTER 3

Another weekend passed. Another Monday, another Tuesday. Her mail, a week and a half's worth by now, teetered unopened on the hall table. None of us dared to move it. Moving it might mean one of us had come to a conclusion, a decision. So the pile continued to grow unabated, her name on every credit card offer, every magazine, every catalogue for shoes or clothes or home decor.

Tuesday night, I woke up to the moon gawking at me through the window. It was so large and round and perfectly centered in my windowpane, for a moment it felt like the moon was all mine.

When I went downstairs to get a glass of juice, the boxes of Christmas cards my mother had bought right after Halloween were on the table, as was my mother's Kelly-green address book. The cards were on heavy card stock, and the envelopes were foil lined.

Earlier today, Claire had come over for biology tutoring. A week had passed since Claire had returned from France, but I hadn't seen her at school except for that first day. I wanted to ask her about it, but it didn't seem like something I should bring up in front of my dad, who sat at the kitchen table with us, staring at this very same box of Christmas cards.

'How does one write a Christmas card?' he muttered. 'And there are *two hundred and fifty* people on this list. I don't even *know* two hundred and fifty people.'

Finally, he threw down his pen and stood up. 'What about the cards?' I called.

'I have no idea what to say,' he answered flatly. His bedroom door slammed.

I straightened my biology notes and looked at Claire, hoping my cheeks weren't burning. 'I'm sure my mother will do them when she gets back.'

Claire's eyes bulged. A clear, obvious thought slid across her face.

'*What?*' I snapped. Claire looked down.

When I shifted my books, Claire cleared her throat. 'I saw you getting coffee for all those girls last week.'

I bristled. 'So?'

Claire traced over a star on her notebook, not following the lines. It devolved from a star to a scribble. 'It shouldn't be your job to get coffee for everyone. You shouldn't be their errand girl.'

I clicked my pen on and off, gripped with anger. The girls I got coffee for were the same girls Claire used to be friends with – the girls, in fact, from the back of the bus. I *volunteered* to get coffee for them. It was not like they were holding me at gunpoint.

Claire looked up at me, her gaze unwavering. There was such a sage look in her eye, as if she could see straight through my skin. It made me think of a recurring dream I sometimes had, the one where I had no outer covering. Everyone was able to see right through me to my organs and inside my brain, aware of what I was thinking and feeling at all times. I was called a Visible, and I had to go to a special school with the rest of the Visibles. My mother, disappointed, showed me her high school yearbook and told me that *she* wasn't a Visible when she was my age. It always catapulted me from sleep, causing me to run to the mirror and stare hard at my whole body, making sure my skin was still opaque.

The digital clock on the microwave clicked now from 2:59 to 3:00. I pulled a Christmas card out of the box and held it in my hands for a long time. The pen cap unscrewed easily. I could do them. I had good handwriting. There weren't that many, really.

'What are *you* doing up?'

My father's eyes were squinty slits. He had tied the belt of his robe in a messy knot around his waist.

'I'm doing the Christmas cards.' I made a flourished squiggle on a piece of scrap paper. My mother always used excellent pens for Christmas cards and other correspondence. Fluid ink, fine-tipped, with a gold handle.

My father sat down next to me at the table,

watching as I addressed the first one. It was to a Dr and Mrs Myron Finkelstein. I had no idea who they were. I decided I would just sign my mother and my father's names and not include any sort of holiday greeting. I wrote out their address, slid the card in the envelope, and licked it to seal.

'You don't have to do that,' my father said quietly.

'I'm sure Mom will appreciate it once she comes back.'

'Summer,' my father began. His voice sounded funny, as if there were hands wrapped around his neck. 'Summer . . . Mrs Ryan and I were talking. About . . . this.'

I stopped writing out the address for Dr Melissa Hailey and looked at him sharply, almost punishingly. 'Why did you tell *her*?'

'Mrs Ryan and I are kind of in the same position.'

'No, you're not.'

He folded his hands on the table. I shut my eyes, hoping that he wouldn't say anything else. Finally, I heard him sigh. 'We'll do shifts. You work for a half-hour, and then I'll work on them for another half-hour. We'll get done faster that way.'

I watched as he walked to the living room and stretched out on the couch. The light of the Christmas tree cast pale yellow light over his cheeks, making him look like a kid. Across the harbor, the buildings' lights twinkled sweetly.

I scratched out all the envelopes, trying to keep my handwriting as neat as possible, listening to the

50

kitchen clock ticking. I signed my parents' names on every card. Their names looked so nice together, *Richard and Meredith Davis*. It was so melodic. My father said that when they started dating, there was no one else in the world except for the two of them. She was so beautiful, he said, the kind of beautiful that knocked you down. They walked hand in hand down a street, whispering things to each other, pausing under streetlights to kiss. They fed each other bites of food and talked in the rain for hours. My father made up songs for her. My mother bought him cashmere sweaters. They were the only people each of them had ever loved.

Love like that didn't die. Love like that didn't write a letter and leave.

I tried to envision the love of my life, but there was no one at school who even came close. So he'd have to be new, from somewhere else. He'd come up to me while I was at my locker, put his arms around me and say, 'Summer Davis, forget about all of them. Forget about everything. I'm here for you. I'm all you'll ever need. Never let me get away.'

And I wouldn't. I'd know something good when it was there. Just as my mother should. We were right in front of her, after all. We were here.

The next morning, I teetered through the double doors that led from the courtyard to the school hallways, balancing four cups of hot coffee wedged into a corrugated cardboard holder. A bunch of guys shoved their way in front of me, and I didn't catch the door before it closed. It knocked against my legs, tipping me sideways. I watched helplessly as the coffees dislodged from the carrier and fell to the ground, their plastic lids popping off, the coffee slowly glugging into the cracks in the side-walk. Steam waltzed through the chilly air.

Students stepped daintily around the spilled coffee, barely noticing. I peered into the hall; the girls in my French class were leaning against the water fountains, waiting for me where they always did. By the looks on their faces, I was pretty sure they'd seen the coffee spill, too.

They were tall and straight-haired and pink-cheeked, with perfectly manicured fingernails and bra straps that didn't fall down off their shoulders to mid-arm. Ever since Claire joined them at the back of the bus, I'd watched them with envy. *Summer should have more girlfriends,* my mother had whispered to my father in the kitchen. *Does it really matter?* my father had replied. But yes, *yes* it mattered. It mattered more than he would ever understand. That we were talking, that I was getting them coffee; it all seemed like such a step in the right direction.

The coffee trickled into the sewer grate. The girls' eyes narrowed, their mouths went slack. I turned back to the coffee cart, thinking. I had lunch money in my wallet, but it wasn't like I was eating much lunch these days. I could use it to get the girls new coffees, gratis, to make up for my mistake.

But when I looked over my shoulder to see if they'd like this plan, I saw the girls had turned for the stairs, laughing and wrapping their arms around their shoulders. Slowly, more and more students separated me from them, and after just a few moments, I couldn't see them at all. Something occurred to me, then: What if my mother chose this moment to walk into school, this moment to see me? I was alone. As usual. There was as much chance of her seeing this as there was of her seeing something good. It wasn't as if I had any control.

The bell started to ring, but I didn't move. I wasn't sure I *could* move. As the courtyard cleared out, a janitor emerged from a utility closet, carrying an empty red bucket. He met my eye. 'Don't you need to get to class?' he asked, motioning for the door.

He was an older man, with long gray tufts sprouting out of his oversized ears. There was a name stitched over the right breast of his blue jumpsuit. *Stan.* I liked his functional black shoes, the gold class ring he wore on his right hand.

'If a woman takes off from her family without really saying where she's going, she's coming back, right?' I blurted out before I could stop myself.

Stan blinked his watery blue eyes, just a few feet away. 'Sorry?'

'I mean, she left all her clothes here. And her shoes and her bags and her cat.' I swallowed. 'She left a lot of . . . *other* things, too.'

He didn't say anything, just gave me a sad smile

53

and turned for the double doors. By then, the court-yard was completely empty. I'd never lingered in the courtyard after the bell had rung; I always thought a police officer would appear, pushing everyone where they belonged. I looked around, then took a few careful steps toward the wrought-iron gate. It wasn't locked. When I pushed on it, the gate creaked open easily. No one noticed.

So I left.

And still nothing happened. The gate made no noise when I shut it again. The cars on Lincoln Street swished by, oblivious. To my left, eventually, was the park. I started walking.

I walked up Lincoln and took a right on Eighth Avenue, looking right and left. It didn't take long before I realized who I was looking for. But she wasn't there. She wasn't anywhere I thought she'd be.

Snow began to swirl down. My backpack jostled against my lower back, and my toes prickled with the cold, shielded only by a thin strip of flimsy loafer leather. People streamed past, none of them her. I walked under the Grand Army Plaza arch and crossed the street to the park.

'Summer?'

I stopped, my heart speeding up. But it was Claire Ryan across the road, standing at the park's entrance. She was smoking a cigarette. Her red jacket and jeans were enormous.

I crossed the street slowly, in a daze. 'What are you doing here?' Claire demanded.

'What are *you* doing here?' I shot back.

She shrugged, turning her palms to the sky. 'I don't know. It's snowing.'

An old man in a shiny red jogging suit stamped through the thin layer of snow. A runner stooped to tie his shoe. He was wearing shorts. It was 30°F out. 'You don't go to school,' I pointed out to Claire, as if solving a mystery, even though, in hindsight, it was painfully obvious.

'Yeah.' Claire looked down. 'So?'

'So, wait. You get off the train and, instead of coming to school, you come up here?'

'Uh huh.' She sucked so hard on the cigarette, it crackled.

I blinked furiously. 'And the office hasn't called your parents?'

The smoke mixed with the falling snowflakes. 'That's something I missed about you,' she said. 'You're always worrying about that stuff.'

'But . . . I mean . . .'

'They might have called. My mother hasn't said anything. Or maybe they haven't. Perhaps I'm invisible. Although, I'm not sure *how* I could be invisible.' She let out a bitter laugh, spreading out her arms, showing off her size. I recoiled, shocked by her candidness.

We were quiet for a moment, breathing out cottony puffs. Then Claire said, 'Do you remember when we had that Mega Man tournament at the beach? You did that victory dance?'

'I don't know. Sort of.'

Claire pushed her sneaker into the dried grass. 'I guess life isn't so simple anymore.'

I stiffened. 'What you mean?'

Claire looked at me out of the corner of her eye. My mind started to churn. It was odd that Claire wasn't pushing to know why I'd left school. She knew I was too anal and rule-abiding to ditch, that something must have been really wrong. And yet she hadn't asked.

The realization trickled in. I looked at her sharply, enraged. 'Whatever you think you know isn't true.'

Claire stepped back, startled.

'And anyway, you shouldn't talk.' The words spilled out before I could harness them. 'I know about that French guy and your mom.'

Claire's mouth made a small o.

'I know about her affair,' I went on. 'She ruined a perfectly good marriage.'

Claire slowly shook her head, then ran her hands through her hair. It took her a while to respond. 'My mom didn't have an affair with anyone,' she said, speaking into her chest. 'It was my father. He had an affair with a girl. Like, a teenager. She was barely older than me. But my mother's too proud to take his money, which is why we're basically living in a crack house.'

A garbage truck circling Grand Army Plaza blew its horn. Another runner passed, making crisp footprints in the dusting of snow. I thought about how Mrs Ryan had looked so crumpled and defeated at our house the other day. But I didn't want Mrs Ryan to be the victim. She couldn't be. *Mrs Ryan and I are kind of in the same position,* my father had told me last night, when I was starting on the Christmas cards.

'Why did he do that?' I managed.

'I don't know.' Claire flicked her ashes. An ember landed on her coat and she brushed it off. 'Who knows why anyone does anything? Do you know why your mom left?'

'My mom's on a trip,' I said fast.

Claire scoffed. 'Then why did she resign from her job?'

I stared at her.

'That's why my mom initially came to see your dad. She called her old boss at Mandrake & Hester, to see if he could get her back her old job. And her boss goes, 'Did you hear about Meredith? She resigned. She didn't even leave a forwarding number.''

I took an elephant-like step back.

Claire lowered her shoulders, a look of realization passing over her face. 'Your father didn't tell you this?'

I concentrated hard on the yellow stitches running down the legs of Claire's jeans. Such petite little Vs, for such a wide swathe of fabric.

Claire let out a breath. Her face softened even more. It reminded me of the expression she had two years ago, when she'd come upon me on the bus and realized she'd walked right by without noticing I was there. 'God, Summer. I'm so sorry. But we can talk about this together. About . . . the stuff that's happening to both of us. We need each other.'

I thought of the second-to-last day before my mother left. I'd gotten up in the middle of the night and found her sitting in the living room, staring at the bare Christmas tree she and my father had picked out that morning. She had a nervous look on her face, almost as if she was going to throw up. 'Mom?' I said weakly.

She turned to me slowly and slumped. 'What are you doing awake?'

I just couldn't hold it in any longer. Tears started rolling down my face. It wasn't hard to sense something was going on with her. Admitting it, however, was something else entirely.

'What's happening?' I asked. 'What's wrong?'

My mother looked exasperated. 'Go back to bed, Summer.'

'Can't I help?' My voice was so squeaky, so pathetic. 'Can't you tell me?'

'Just go back to bed. Please.' She didn't get up to touch me or guide me back or give me a hug. She just sat there, wringing her hands. Two days later she was gone.

It was all there, on the surface, waiting. But I stopped it before it could escape out of me. 'She's away on a trip,' I said to Claire. 'She'll be back.'

A long beat passed. The wind picked up, making the snow swirl. 'Oh,' Claire said softly. 'Okay.'

She waited a few more moments, then turned and started walking into the center of the great lawn. Halfway across, she stopped and looked over her shoulder, pausing, maybe giving me another opportunity to say what she knew I needed to say. I stared at a fixed point on the ground, an ember from Claire's cigarette.

When I finally lifted my head, Claire was all the way across the lawn, heading for the snow-dusted trees. The ache inside me was cruel and precise. I stood there for a while, my toes stiffening with cold. The church bell near Grand Army Plaza bonged out the hour. There was nothing to do but walk back. I creaked through the school gate and padded down the silent halls. The classrooms were full and preoccupied. I passed by my biology classroom; the new sub, the one that had taken over for Mr Rice, was showing a filmstrip. After Mr Rice had been asked to leave, it came out that the principal had had his eye on him for a while – there had been reports that Mr Rice had acted strangely in his other classes, too. The principal assured us that none of what Mr Rice taught us that last day – the invisible tethers of DNA, the certitude of science – was true. But I didn't want to believe that. Wherever my mother was – walking on a sun-dappled beach, riding a street car in San Francisco, scampering down a rainy street in London – the tether around her was a literal one, a rip cord. Any minute now, it would stretch taut, and she'd snap back to us.

After school that day, I went home and stared at the buildings across the water for a while, thinking. Then, I sat down at my father's cluttered mahogany desk and wrote Mr Rice a letter. I said I was sorry he had to leave our school, that I hoped he was all right. I wrote that I wanted to know a little more about those magical, unbreakable bonds of DNA he'd spoken about. How exactly did they hold family members together? I was looking for a little more scientific evidence to support this. If he could respond with articles, books, theories, I would be greatly appreciative.

At the bottom of the page, I signed the letter, *Yours in Genetics, Summer Davis.* When my father came home from a rare day at the lab, he noticed the envelope with Mr Rice's name on it but no address. I'd told him a little about Mr Rice – just his theory, not what I believed. Without asking any questions, as if my father sensed something big in me had changed, he picked up the envelope and sealed it with a stamp. He knew the woman in charge of substitute teachers at Peninsula, he said. If I wanted, we could mail the letter to her – she'd know Mr Rice's forwarding address.

It didn't seem possible that my father could know such a person – he wasn't involved with the school and hardly knew anyone outside of people he associated with at the lab. But I chose to believe this, too.

I watched as my father wrote out the woman's

address on the envelope. I watched his head disappear down our apartment building's stairs, and I ran to the window and watched his head reappear on the street below. It was comforting to conjure up this image of him later, after he'd become so very different, so very damaged. I tried to remember him as he was right then, walking to that mailbox, protective and productive and strong.

T hat winter, I would stand in front of Two World Trade and look for you. I watched people go in and out of the revolving doors, thinking you'd be among them. When you weren't, I went down to the underground mall and brushed through the shoe stores, the Gap, Duane Reade. I kept thinking I'd find you among the ribbed V-neck sweaters, the first-aid supplies.

They've asked me to pinpoint pivotal times where things began to really change for me, to reconstruct my life as best I can. I remember we were at a party at the Boathouse in Central Park – a friend of yours from your new job had graduated from business school. I had gotten up to go to the bathroom, and when I was on my way back, I saw you sitting at the table, laughing, drinking, eating cold shrimp with a dainty little fork. And I suddenly realized – it didn't matter I was gone. Maybe it was better. So I started just to walk down the park drive. It was the middle of a Saturday afternoon in May, close to the anniversary.

I stopped when I got to the zoo. Outside the gates, there was a man selling balloons in the shapes of animals. A group of kids ran for the turnstiles, sneakers squeaking. They were so, so young. I sat down on a bench, listening to their high, happy voices, and all the things I vowed so long ago not to think about suddenly throbbed inside of me, way too present. The flashing blue lights. The way Mark looked at me when I told the EMT what I knew. All those years later, and I still felt every ounce of his shock.

And then, suddenly, there you were. You were standing above me, hands on hips.

'What are you doing?' you asked. 'I've been looking all over for you.'

'I went for a walk,' I said.

'Why?' Your face was so red.

I gestured to the zoo's cheerful gate. 'Remember when we took Summer and Steven here?'

'Yes.' You said it very slowly, cautiously, as if I'd told a joke and you were waiting for the punch line.

'Do you think all parents understand how great it is for kids to see animals?' I asked. 'I've been sitting here, watching, and every kid who has gone in is so happy. All parents understand this, right? All kids get to go to zoos?'

You turned your wedding ring around on your finger. 'I thought you were sick. I even had Paul go into the bathroom and make sure.'

We went back to the party and explained that I'd run into an old friend and walked a ways up with him toward the reservoir. Your friends nodded and smiled and drank their drinks. The rest of the lunch, you had a hand on your bare knee, and you kept squeezing, squeezing. When you took it away once,

63

I could see the fermata-shaped nail indentations in your skin.

After that, similar episodes came more frequently. I wasn't where I said I would be. I wasn't as dependable, wasn't as cogent, couldn't carry a conversation, missed days of work, spaced out for hours. Once, you caught me watching a Three Stooges marathon when I was supposed to be getting ready for a party. Another time you caught me on the Promenade, coaxing a baby squirrel toward my lap with a spoonful of peanut butter. I'd said I was going to the lab that day. 'Have you been tricking me?' you asked. 'Have you always been this kind of person, but just hid it all this time?'

'It's hard to explain,' I said.

'Try,' you said.

But it was about the same things, the things I'd already told you. And it was about the things I could only halfway tell – I was so afraid to tell it all. But maybe I should have; maybe I owed it to you. And maybe that's why I waited for you in front of your old office building, that winter after you left – so I could come clean. Or maybe I wouldn't have said anything, if I'd seen you. Maybe it would've been enough to know that you were still here, near us, close.

This is probably the part where I should tell you how I really feel. That I think what you did was terrible, and that you ruined lives, and that I'll never forgive you. But there's room in me to forgive, I think. Maybe, in some ways, I saw it coming. Maybe, in some ways, I understand.

PART II

COBALT, PENNSYLVANIA, JUNE, 1994

twenty-one-gun salute

CHAPTER 4

'Do we have everything?' I asked.

My father and I were standing in the doorway of our apartment, bags slung over our shoulders, the wheels of the suitcase caught on the lip between the door and the hall. Steven had already gone down the street to look out for the car service.

We shut the door and locked all the locks. My father stooped, jiggling the handles to make sure they were truly secure. We heard the shouting on Montague Terrace before we pushed our way out of the heavy wooden brownstone door and clomped down the building's front steps. The bags Steven had brought downstairs were waiting patiently at the curb next to an old diesel Mercedes, but Steven was standing in the middle of the street, his hands on his hips, glaring at Renee Klinefelter, our forty-something neighbor down the block. Renee was in her uniform, jeans cut off at the knees and a slightly-too-small black t-shirt that stretched tight over her paunchy stomach. As usual, her two grumpy-faced pugs flanked her, one on each side.

'Don't pull that amnesty stuff on me,' Steven

was shouting. 'That bomb could have decimated one of our most vulnerable buildings. He should've been shot on the spot.'

'So what do you suggest we do?' Renee shouted back, spitting a little. 'Deport everyone? Take away political asylum as a whole?'

'If that's what it takes.'

'Some people *need* political asylum.'

'And some people who have it like to blow things up.' Steven was moving closer and closer to Renee's face. 'And do you realize you're arguing *for* terrorism? You're arguing *for* people with those ideals to . . . to *infiltrate* here and do this to us when we aren't expecting it?'

He wheeled around, glaring pointedly at Iqbal, who owned the M&J deli down the block. Iqbal had innocently walked into the street to check on the fresh flowers he sold, but when he realized Steven was near, he inched back inside. Steven had gone off on Iqbal a month or so ago – *people from* your *country do this. How does that make you feel?* Iqbal dealt with it quietly, neither calling the cops nor barring Steven from the store – although maybe he should have. During Desert Storm, there were several yellow ribbons affixed to Iqbal's register. He still slipped me loose candy he kept in the plastic bins above the register, barrel-shaped Tootsie Rolls and mini York Peppermint Patties, whenever I went in there to buy a Coke.

'If that van would've been a little closer to the concrete foundation in the basement, both buildings

68

would've collapsed,' Steven yelled to Renee. 'Do you even realize that?'

'Of course I realize that!' Renee shouted. 'But it doesn't mean we should persecute everyone!'

'You should do something,' I murmured to my father, who, as usual, had halted, paralyzed, on the curb. He cradled his right hand in his left, running his fingers over the scar on his right palm he'd gotten a few months ago from the broken snow globe. The deep cut had healed, but he often thoughtfully traced the scar over and over, maybe finding the motion soothing, maybe remembering what happened. I never wanted to ask. A curious, passive crowd had gathered to watch Steven and Renee. People were stepping out of their buildings, heads tilted toward the noise, and passersby had paused, leaning against railings, reining in their dogs, trying to understand what was transpiring.

I moved out to the street and pulled Steven's arm. He wrenched it away without even looking at me. Renee leaned over like a bull ready to charge. My father, finally, pushed around me. 'We have to go,' he said in Steven's ear. 'You've made your point.'

We both managed to pull Steven backwards, returning to our pile of luggage at the curb. Luckily, the car service rolled up then, and I waved it over. We threw our suitcases in the trunk fast, piling them on top of empty water bottles, frayed straps to secure luggage, and a little box that looked either like a tool kit or a small suitcase for a gun. Steven craned his neck to get a look at the driver, a pale man with high cheekbones. When he greeted us, he had a Staten Island accent. Visibly relieved, Steven got in.

As we pulled away, Renee remained in the middle of the street, her stance solid and righteous. A man I didn't recognize approached her, and Renee's mouth started moving fast. It wasn't hard to figure out what she was saying. *Steven used to be such a nice boy, so quiet. And then all that happened, with the mother. What a pity.*

Steven ran his hand over his hair, which he'd recently taken my father's beard clippers to. It was so short, I could see his skull in spots, pinkish and bumpy. 'She started it,' he muttered.

'It doesn't matter who started it,' my father countered wearily.

The car took the exit for the Brooklyn Bridge. There were the mammoth Lower Manhattan buildings from a different angle than how we saw them from our apartment. Looming atop the Municipal Building was the giant Civic Fame statue, a bronze woman holding a shield, a bunch of leaves, and a crown. The World Trade towers jutted up like two prongs of an electrical plug. Out of habit, my eyes drifted to the North tower – last February, terrorists drove the truck into its underground parking garage and set off a bomb. Steven knew every detail of the incident: the bomb was made of urea pellets, bottled hydrogen and various other things. It was supposed to go up the ventilation shafts and suffocate everyone working there. Officials found bomb-building plans in one of the terrorist's suitcases when he entered the country, but he claimed political asylum so they couldn't arrest him on the spot. Because of that loophole, 1,042 people had been injured, and six people had died. The *New York Times* listed the names of the dead, but not all those who had been hurt. Every day, when the paper came, Steven leafed through it, maybe checking, though he never explained.

Since then, whenever he wasn't doing his NYU coursework, Steven read about airplane hijackings, bus attacks, and suicide bombings, most of which take place in far-flung countries like Lebanon, Sri Lanka, Israel. But Steven thought they could happen here, too. We could be walking down the street, he hypothesized, and *boom*. No more street. No more us. There was nothing we could do to control it.

Our car reached the highest point of the bridge. I eyeballed twenty-two flights from the top of the North tower. The entire floor was dark.

My father jiggled his legs up and down as we descended off the bridge and turned onto the looping road to the FDR. 'Are you all right?' I asked.

'I'm fine.'

'Are you sure you're okay to drive?' We were headed for a car rental agency in the Village.

He shrugged.

'I could drive,' I volunteered.

71

'You don't know how to drive,' Steven snapped. 'Neither do you.'

'I'll drive,' my father interrupted. 'I'm the one who knows how to get there.'

He looked longingly over his shoulder for a moment, back toward Brooklyn, pulling in his bottom lip until it vanished.

'It's only three days,' I said in his ear. He nodded quietly, as if this were the vitamin he'd been looking for, as though these few, simple words had made everything better.

Later, my father became talkative. 'We couldn't get that fishhook out of Petey's foot, so we had to take him to the emergency room!'

There was a pause. He swiveled his head around at me, taking his hands off the steering wheel. I realized I was supposed to be paying attention.

'That's funny,' I sputtered.

My father frowned. 'It's not funny, Summer. Petey's dad's car didn't go much above forty-five. It took us over an hour to get to the hospital.'

We passed a truck stop. McDonald's, Arby's, Dairy Queen. We passed a field of cows and then a field of horses. 'This is the real Pennsylvania,' my father yelled, his voice diffused through the open window. His accent had changed between Brooklyn and here, less than a six-hour drive. 'I bet you don't remember this, huh Summer?'

'Not really.' We passed a red-painted barn. Someone had spray-painted *Kill Niggers* on the side of it. There was a big drip line from the base of the *N* to the waist-high grass.

Dear Claire, I composed in my head. *Check this out!* I could send her a photo of the barn. Perhaps she'd find it – what's the phrase she always used? – *très kitsch.*

We passed what I guessed was the equivalent of a 7-Eleven. It was called Unimart, sort of like unibrow. There was a placard out front; faded, plastic interchangeable letters read, LOTTO HERE! MARLBORO $1.29.

'It's so funny, being here,' my father said. 'I feel like I know every tree personally.'

He put on the rental station wagon's turn signal, and we pulled down a street paralleling a river. To our right were closed-up shops, an empty diner called Mister Donut, a crumbling church with ESUS SAVES on the marquee, a Knights of Columbus. Beyond an industrial-looking, algae-green bridge was a hill lined with the kinds of trees I used to draw when I was little: long, narrow triangles, with tiny sticks as the trunks.

My father pointed to the hill. 'We used to pitch our Christmas trees over that.' He swung his finger toward the steel bridge. 'And that's where that movie was shot.'

'What movie?'

'I don't know. The . . . the movie. The one with . . . with the ghost in it. I can't remember the name. Didn't we go to see it?'

He nodded toward a ramshackle house across

73

the hill. 'That's where the Crosses live. We used to sneak over and jump on his trampoline. Once, he came out with a rifle and shot at us.'

'Did he have any kids?' I asked.

'Nope. Hated kids.'

'Then what was he doing with a trampoline?'

My father paused, then slapped the steering wheel. 'You know, I have no idea. Maybe he was in the circus?'

Dear Claire. Guess what my dad had for lunch today? Scrapple. Wanna know what it is? Pig-shoulder pudding.

Suddenly, my father pulled over. 'Stop,' he said. 'Come here.'

At first, I thought he was talking to me. But he was gazing at a wet, dazed-looking dog on the riverbank. It wasn't wearing a collar and had a big piece of fur missing from its side.

Other cars swished past, uninterested. Even here, I worried about them looking. My father turned the car off and stepped out. I shifted, uncomfortable. 'Dad . . .'

He held up his hand. 'I just want to see if I know her.'

'How could you *know her*?'

'All the dogs here, they mate with one another. Chances are I'll know her.'

Steven, who'd been sleeping against the front passenger-side window, rubbed his eyes and stretched. 'Where are we?'

'We're here,' I whispered. 'I think.'

Steven looked around. The dead Mister Donut, a gas station that looked like it had weathered a recent dust storm. Two boys rolled out from behind a pick-up truck, carrying sixty-four-ounce cups of soda. They both had spiky blond hair and gapped, yellow teeth.

My father found the thin red leash and the packet of liver treats he always kept in his knapsack. When he opened the car door, the heat wrapped around us like mummification bandages. *Prepare for record temperatures this week*, the weather reporters had been declaring the whole drive. We'd been able to keep the signal for NPR for a while, but in the western part of the state we'd found nothing but country stations, which my father detested more than Lite FM. He had a whole stack of Jazz CDs to muddle him – and us, by default – through.

My father walked carefully toward the dog. It glanced at him out of the corner of its eye, the pink edge of its tongue darting in and out of its mouth. When my dad reached out, the dog ducked away. 'Come here,' my father whispered. 'It's okay.' He crouched and put the treat on the ground. The dog sniffed the air. When my father made a sudden move, the dog backed away again. It was a dance until the dog ate the treat, trusted my dad enough to come close, and my dad placed his hand on the scruff of the dog's neck. The dog flailed, but my father put one hand on its neck and the other on its belly and it began to calm

75

down. He looped the leash around its neck, walked it to our car and stuffed it in the very back of the station wagon, next to our luggage.

Before he shut the hatchback, my father peered carefully into the dog's face. 'Do you know it?' I called.

'Yep, I know her,' he answered. 'I know her *parents*, anyway. Or her grandparents. Or, I guess it would be great-grandparents. But whatever. She's a Smitty dog.'

I was afraid to ask what a Smitty dog was, for fear it would launch another tale about roadkill or throwing a manhole cover through a car window or sledding down the hill on cardboard boxes, because no one could find the sleds. That was all my father had been talking about the whole second half of this drive.

The dog curled into a ball, whimpering. The car smelled suddenly like wet fur and the chemical that dogs give out when they are afraid. Steven stretched, his t-shirt taut against his chest. 'Are we going to keep her?'

My father didn't answer, but I knew what the answer was: of course we were going to keep her. We had three other dogs in a Brooklyn kennel: Fiona, an Irish terrier, Wesley, a cock-eared Doberman my father had coaxed to him just like he had with this Smitty dog, and Skip, a Beagle who had shown up at our stoop a few months ago just as we were walking out the door, as if it knew we were the people dogs came to when they had nowhere else to go. When my mother left, the apartment was too big for three of us. Now, whenever I entered a room, a dog was there. Whenever I used the bathroom, I found a dog sitting on the bathmat, drooling. If I opened the door to go into our building's hall, a dog tried to come. For a while, we tried to keep things nice, but with three dogs, it was hard. Finally, we just stopped trying altogether.

'So, do you remember any of this?' my father asked. 'Hasn't changed a bit. I can't believe it.'

He navigated over a roller-coaster sized bump. We'd been driving down the same gravel road for about five minutes. The road was uneven, with big pits and puddles, and there were spots where the gravel was strewn out over the shoulder, indicating a spin-out. 'Last time you were here . . . I don't know.' My father scratched his head. 'You were three? Four? It was Christmas.'

'Maybe.' I squinted, pretending like I was trying to remember, but this just looked like a gravel road. A squirrel in a tree eyed us suspiciously as we passed.

'We were only here for a little while, then it started snowing.' He picked at the side of his thumbnail. He was nervous, I realized. 'There's the creek,' he added, pointing. 'It's clean enough to swim in.'

'Since when do you say creek like *crick*?' I asked.

'I didn't say *crick*.'

'Yes, you did.'

He thought for a moment. 'Well, so what if I did?'

I glanced at him, then crossed my arms over my chest. 'I don't think I could swim in a creek. *Or* a crick. And besides, won't we have, like, funeral stuff to do?'

'Yeah, but you're missing out if you don't try it,' he said. 'It's much nicer than swimming in a pool. And Samantha's about your age. You can swim together.'

'I didn't bring my suit.'

Finally, we turned into the driveway of a low-slung house. There were a lot of weeds in the front yard and a very, very old blue pickup truck in the driveway. Off to the left was a white-shingled shed; in front of it was a red, three-wheeled lawnmower, lying on its side. The house had a large, faded wrap-around porch strewn with all sorts of junk – an old television, another lawnmower, a couple of white plastic porch chairs, a dog bed and a fifty-pound bag of dog food, rabidly torn open from the center. There was a dog on the porch, too, eating straight from the hole in the bag. I heard the crick out back, rushing. It could never be clean enough to swim in. My stomach started to hurt.

Dear Claire. Actually, a picture would have said way more than words.

A girl was sitting on the porch swing. She had long brown hair, and her old jeans hung loosely on her hips. She narrowed her eyes when she saw us but made no effort to get up. 'We can't see the body until after three,' she shouted. 'Just so you know.'

My father opened his door and climbed out. 'You remember Samantha, don't you, Summer? She's Skip's sister's kid's kid. Your second cousin.'

'My name isn't Samantha anymore.' The girl didn't move. 'It's Sword now.'

'Ah. Well. Hello, Sword.' My father, surprisingly, didn't miss a beat.

Samantha – Sword – snorted. My father told me on the way here that Samantha's parents died in a fire nine months ago, and she'd been living here with my now-dead grandmother. Stella, my great-aunt, lived here too, having moved from her own house into this one when my grandmother's health began to decline. This, at least, was what Stella told us on the phone a few months ago, when she suggested that my father come see my grandmother before she passed. But my father didn't. This was the first time he'd been back here in years.

My father took a few steps away from the car, squinting into the backyard. 'Where's the boat?'

'Ruth sold it,' Samantha yelled, starting to swing.

He frowned. 'When?'

'I don't know. When I came here, it was gone. She said she sold it to spite you.' Samantha smiled greedily. I expected her teeth to be gnarled, yellow, overlapping, but they were beautifully straight and white.

My father ran his hand through his hair. 'Huh.'

The screen door slammed, and an older woman tumbled out. Her long reddish hair curled around her head, and she wore cat-eye glasses. 'Ritchie!' She had loose jiggle on her upper arms and smeared, orange-pink lipstick. 'It's been . . . my God. How long?'

'I don't know, Stella,' my father answered, hugging her. 'Maybe ten years?'

Stella hit him – hard. 'You're *shitting* me.'

'Nope.'

Samantha swung violently, bumping the porch rail with her feet.

'And who are these two?' Stella turned her over-magnified eyes to me. 'This your girlfriend?' She moved to Steven. 'Who's this big strapping gentleman? You old enough to date, honey? 'Cause if so—'

'We're his *kids*,' I gasped.

Stella sidled very close to us. She smelled not how I thought a great-aunt would – like urine and cats and menthol – but like peanut butter cookies. 'I know that, honey. I know.'

'It's very nice to see you both,' my father said. 'I haven't seen Samantha – sorry, *Sword* – since she was a baby, I think.'

Stella rolled her eyes. 'Sword! Now what kind of name is *Sword* for a girl?' She looked over her shoulder at Samantha. 'If you're going to change it, change it to Trixie. Or Marilyn, after Marilyn Monroe.'

'You wouldn't understand,' Samantha muttered.

'Where's Petey?' my father asked. 'Is he here yet?'

'He's around here somewhere.' Stella pulled out a cigarette. Her cat-eye glasses slid down her nose. She looked at my father. 'Your crazy mother, huh? Had to go and die on us.'

'That's one way to put it,' Steven mumbled.

'And did you hear the latest?' Stella shook her head. 'The Department of Veterans' Affairs gave her a stipend for her funeral, for being in the Army Nurse Corp, you know. And you know what she did? She spent *every penny*. Didn't think, *gee, my sister could use that money to fix up the house,* did she? Nope. Had to buy the best casket and everything. Satin-lined!'

'You're kidding,' my father said.

'Apparently she made these arrangements years ago. So the money had been spent all this time and we didn't even know it. Like she even liked the war! I know for a fact she wanted to be back here, ironing things and baking pot pies. She's even having the military come out and fold the flag and shoot off guns.'

Steven brightened. 'Cool.'

'Mom?' My father scratched his chin. 'Seriously?'

'You would've known this if you visited.' Stella hobbled up the porch steps. 'She probably would've told you. She never told me shit like that.'

My father looked down, not saying anything.

Stella removed her glasses. Her eyes were brown, large, and a little crossed. 'We should go over to the home probably, huh?'

81

'We can't go there until three,' Samantha barked. She and Stella had a funny way of talking, some of their vowels very clipped and thin. *We can't go thirr until three.* 'Don't you remember what that dickwad at the funeral home said?'

Stella looked delighted and punched Samantha softly on the arm. 'Dickwad! Now, *that* is an interesting mental picture. Leon *is* a dickwad, isn't he?'

You'll remember Stella, my father told me on the drive here. *She's a spitfire.* But I didn't remember her. I didn't remember any of this. We used to go to my mother's family's house for holidays. My maternal grandmother lived just two hours from Brooklyn, in a town in Pennsylvania called Bryn Mawr. Her yard was fenced and she had *one* dog – a bichon frise. When she died, there was a closed casket and a small, tasteful service. We had a brunch afterwards, and some great-uncle made me a Shirley Temple with two maraschino cherries. We didn't have to do anything like go see the *body*.

Stella put her arm around Steven's shoulders. 'You'll love it here. It's such a nice little vacation for you. Did your father tell you about the crick? And the river. They have these new things, they're like water scooters. They're called . . . oh, what are they called . . . ?'

'Jet skis,' Samantha sighed.

'Jet skis!' Stella crowed, holding up one finger in *eureka!*

'Jet skis aren't new,' I said.

'A jet ski chopped off Mason's leg last week,' Samantha said.

'It did *not*.' Stella shot her a look.

'How do you know?'

'It's all right,' Steven said. 'I'm not really into jet skis, anyway.'

'Now, have you ever been on one?' Stella asked.

'Yeah,' Steven said.

'No you haven't.' Stella put her hands on her hips. 'These are completely cutting-edge. You're probably thinking of a canoe.'

CHAPTER 5

The front door led into a sitting room with two scratchy plaid couches, a worn circular rug, a dingy fireplace and a very old television in the corner. On the mantle was a large, gold trophy in the shape of a horseshoe. There were gilt-framed, oily paintings on the walls, all of either hunting scenes – dogs majestically pointing at foxes, ruddy men on horseback, a deer, standing dumbfounded in a clearing – or of Frank Sinatra. Frank singing, Frank grinning, Frank with his Rat Pack.

'A sight for sore eyes, huh?' Stella sighed, as if the room were beautiful.

'Looks good,' my father answered quietly.

I passed into the dining room. There was a painting of Frank on navy blue velvet. He was made up to look like a saint, a Mento-shaped halo around his head.

On the table sat a bunch of framed photographs, a little shrine to my grandmother. I leaned down and examined the pictures on the dining table. The first was a black-and-white snapshot of her in a nurse's uniform, standing at the edge of a cot.

Chicken scratch at the bottom of the picture said (I think), *Ruth, Paris, 1944.*

Next was a soft, hand-colored photo. She looked about ten years older, with blonde, neat, bunchy hair, very white skin, no wrinkles. After that was a picture of her with her hands on my father's shoulders. My father, maybe a bit older than me, stood beside her, although I didn't think he intended to be in the picture. He stared off into space, his whole face shattered and fragile.

Something about his face in the photo reminded me of his face the day he threw the snow globe against the wall. Had my father told Stella about that? About the hospital? How had he explained?

My grandmother grew older and older in each successive picture, gaining more weight, her hair receding until it was a fuzzy, bald raft at the crown of her head, her pink scalp shining through. In the last photo, she was in bed. Stella was next to her, wearing the same green stretch pants she had on today.

My father returned from the kitchen, holding a can of beer. It looked strange in his hand; I'd never seen him drink one. He pointed to the photo of him. 'That's me.'

'Duh,' I answered. I motioned to the wall. 'What's with the pictures of Frank?'

My father took a long swallow of beer. 'Yeah. Mom liked Frank. She really went nuts with pictures of him after Dad died.'

85

I stared at him. Samantha, who was sitting on the couch reading a wrinkled *TV Guide,* snorted.

Dear Claire. You know how you're always looking for kitsch? Well, you'd hit the jackpot here.

'Why don't I take your bags upstairs?' my father offered.

We all walked through the kitchen and up the creaky stairs to the bedrooms. The upstairs, way colder than the downstairs, opened into a long, narrow hall with doors on either side. The bathroom door, the first to the left, gaped open. Stacks of books and crossword puzzles balanced on the top of the toilet.

My father tapped the first bedroom door open with his foot. The door was very heavy, with a long crack traversing through its center. 'This used to be my room.'

It smelled musty inside. There was a *From Russia With Love* poster on the wall and a video game console – at least I *thought* that was what it was – on the ground. The television was a tiny bubble. An orange milk crate in the corner held action figures, and a second milk crate behind it was filled with old LPs. *Blonde On Blonde* was up front, a frizzy-haired Bob Dylan pursing his lips at the camera. A plaid spread covered the twin bed.

'Huh,' Steven said, looking around.

'Where did this TV come from?' My father tapped it, puzzled. 'And these video games?'

Steven knelt down to examine the console. 'Atari.'

'I certainly wasn't back here when video games came out,' my father said. 'And I don't remember them here the one time we brought you guys.'

Steven inserted a cartridge into the video game and turned on the television. The words DONKEY KONG flashed on the screen. 'This is, like, vintage. It's never been played with.'

'No one plays those video games,' Samantha scoffed, peering in from the hall. 'They're, like, a zillion years old. I have Sega.'

'I never liked this game,' Steven said, but fired it up anyway. The gorilla pitched barrels down a plank, and Steven's character, a Mario Brother, jumped them.

'Sad!' Stella sang when the barrel tripped up Mario. Then she looked at my father. 'You know who I saw the other day? Georgette Mulvaney. That Kay girl's mother.'

My father's chin jutted up. I watched his eyes carefully.

'I'm amazed they still live here.' Stella gazed out the window. The wind was pushing the tire swing back and forth. 'I thought they moved. I invited her to the funeral.'

My father stiffened. 'What did she say? Is she going to come?'

His face was so splotchy. That name was so familiar, all the years he'd talked about the accident. But I'd always suspected – maybe wished – that he made the accident up, that it had never happened.

'I doubt it,' Stella answered. 'She said she had something to do, I don't know. She thanked me for inviting her, though. And she gives her condolences.'

'Oh.' My father let out a breath. He began running his fingers over the scar on his palm.

'Does the guy still live here?' I asked, searching for the boyfriend's name. 'Mark? The one who was in the accident, too?'

'He lives in Colorado,' my father said quickly. 'Moved out there years ago.' His face had tightened so drastically that I didn't dare ask anything else.

My father shuffled his feet on the shabby burgundy carpet. Mario bleeped as he jumped the barrels on the screen. My father looked around and scratched his head. 'I don't get it. Did someone else use this room? I have no clue where this TV and the video games could have come from.'

'Oh, Ruth bought them for you,' Stella said. 'She bought you all kinds of stuff. I guess she always thought you'd bring Summer and Steven here more often. She bought tons of crap from that space movie, too. It's all in boxes in the closet. What was the name of one of the characters in that movie? The Nookie?'

'The *Wookie*?' Steven fished, after a pause. 'You mean *Star Wars*? Chewbacca?'

Stella frowned, annoyed. 'No. That's not right.'

When Mario died, Steven turned off the game,

bored. He wandered into a bedroom down the hall, and my father and Stella returned downstairs. But I stayed in the old room, looking at the posters on the wall. There was one of a *Playboy* girl, her bathing suit straps sliding down her arms. I couldn't imagine my father looking at girls in that way, let alone taking the time to buy the poster and hang it up, neatly pushing tacks into each corner.

Slowly, I opened the drawers of his desk. In the very bottom drawer, I found a photo of a guy with shaggy, longish hair and sideburns. He wore a football jersey and held up a paper cup to toast. Next to him was a small, pale, freckled girl with a guarded, uncertain smile. Her long blonde hair was parted in the center. They stood in front of the eye-shaped Dairy Queen sign. I turned the picture over. *Mark Jeffords and Kay Mulvaney, (secret!) engagement, 1970.* The handwriting was neat and orderly, definitely not my father's crabbed, crazy scrawl.

I looked at their faces for a long time, especially at her, dead now. Then I tucked the photo back under a bunch of papers and shut the drawer tight. 'This place is really creepy,' I whispered aloud, then went to find Steven to see if he thought so too.

Steven was in the next bedroom, which was done up in green and gold checkered wallpaper. I found him on the floor next to the bureau, his knees bent, his hands behind his head. His cheeks inflated then deflated, and he breathed out in puffs.

My chest knotted. Steven noticed me. His face reddened.

'Why are you doing *sit-ups*?' I burst out.

'I'm in training.' He lowered down.

'In training for *what*?'

'The Marines.'

I couldn't help but laugh. 'Like from your GI Joe days?'

Steven's forehead crinkled and his mouth became very small. After one more sit-up, he stood and swished by me for the bathroom, not answering my question.

CHAPTER 6

My father and Stella sat around the kitchen table and drank cans of beer. Steven closed his bedroom door so I couldn't barge in again. Samantha was smoking on the front porch – Stella just *let* her smoke – and was making a face that indicated she didn't want me to come near her.

The sky was a dirt-brown color, as if it was about to storm. There were no shadows on the road, and the wind blew the leaves on the trees upside-down. I ran my hands over the rusty tin mailbox of my father's old neighbors. The name stenciled on the box said *Elkerson*. I'd seen that name all over Cobalt on our drive in – Elkerson's Grocery, Elkerson's Auto Tag & Notary, Elkerson's EZ Car Wash. In an ad circular on the kitchen counter was an ad for an Elkerson Used Auto dealership, specializing in Dodges and Fords.

The Elkerson house was as slumped and beaten-down as my grandmother's. In the front yard was a large, plastic deer. A smaller deer was next to it, tipped over. There was a rolled-up, waterlogged bunch of newsprint on the gravel driveway. It wasn't a real newspaper, though, just a fat booklet of coupons. On the front page was an ad for Unimart, the convenience store we'd passed on the way in; there was a two-for-one deal on packs of Lucky Strike cigarettes. I considered going down there and buying Claire Ryan a pack; she and her new friends smoked Lucky Strikes by the carton.

After our argument in Prospect Park the December my mom left, Claire and I didn't speak for a while. In the months following, Claire lost some of the weight, settling into an apple shape: bigger boobs, fleshy stomach, flat ass and skinny legs. She befriended a band of outcasts and started dressing in fishnet stockings, short skirts, clunky boots and ripped t-shirts whose obscure band names stretched precariously across her chest. After some time passed, Claire began waving to me in the halls again. By the following school year, she was inviting me out with her and the rest of the freaks. All her new friends hung out at the Galaxy Diner, a greasy spoon on Seventh Avenue, and every time I trailed into the diner behind them I felt unoriginal and out of place. It wasn't that I wanted to hang out with them, I just didn't have anything better to do. Long gone were the days of thinking who I was friends with made any difference. It had been ages since I believed my mother was waiting around every corner, monitoring my every move.

Claire caught up on all the classes she'd failed when she was in France, taking courses over the summer, and graduated with her original grade a few weeks ago. She'd gotten into painting and was going to a summer art program in San Francisco to build up her portfolio. 'I don't like that it's for the whole summer,' she told me the last time I hung out with her. We were sitting in a booth at the diner, waiting for her other friends to show up. 'So don't go,' I answered impassively, gently pushing the tines of a fork into my palm. 'Will you write me?' she asked. I laughed and told her that she should write to the corpses she was friends with instead. 'They're not the types who write letters.' Claire lowered her eyes and tugged at her oversized t-shirt. It bore the name of one of the strange, toneless bands she now loved, Fugazi, and had the words *you are not what you own* printed in small, subliminal letters on the back.

Dear Claire, I don't want to write you. I already told you I don't want to talk to you. You should just leave me alone.

A slightly larger house loomed at the end of the road, a blue light flickering in the front window. As I got closer, I realized it was light from a television. I wasn't sure why, but it comforted me. The main television in my now-dead grandmother's house didn't work, and I hadn't braved the 1970s model in my father's old room.

I stepped closer, gazing at the flickering screen. It was the OJ Simpson thing, yet another recap of the slow-speed car chase that had occurred a few days before. My father and I had sat slack-jawed on the couch, watching the whole thing unfold. I hadn't been clear on why they were chasing OJ, and I still wasn't, not exactly. I felt sorry for him, though, because I'd found him funny in the *Naked Gun* movies.

I had been staring at the screen for a good half-minute before I realized there was a boy on a brown, saggy couch. His posture was so bad that his butt was nearly off the cushions, and his feet stretched almost to the TV stand. He looked about my age, with messy dark hair and an oversized nose, in a baggy t-shirt and shorts.

Surprised, I took a step back, flattening an empty Coke can. The sound made the boy look up. His forehead creased.

I took another step back. He walked to the door and peered outside, scowling. The humid air felt toxic. He gaped at me, seemingly furious. 'How many times are you guys going to do this?' His voice was sharp, impatient.

'I'm sorry?'

'He's not your enemy. It's a completely different religion.'

I blinked rapidly. '*What?*'

The boy paused, moving his jaw from side to side. 'Alan sent you, right?' His tone was more uncertain.

'Alan?' My voice was high-pitched, weak. 'I don't know what you're talking about. I'll go. I'm sorry.'

'Wait.' His expression softened. 'If you're not with Alan, who are you?'

'I'm . . .' I paused. 'I'm Summer.'

'Summer . . . ?'

'. . . Davis.'

He shifted his weight to one leg. 'You don't know Alan?'

'No. I'm not from here.'

'Davis.' He pointed to my grandmother's house. 'You related to those old ladies down there?'

'Yes. I guess.'

'The woman that owns the house died.'

'I know. She had a stroke.'

When he stepped into the light, I realized how good-looking he was. Not in a conventional way, but pleasant to look at. Sort of elfin, with huge eyes. Very messy hair. Perfect teeth. Very nice hands. I wasn't sure I'd ever noticed this many details in a boy before. 'Sorry I yelled at you.'

'It's all right,' I answered.

'I thought you were someone else.' A mosquito landed on his arm, but he made no gesture to swat it off. 'They your relatives?'

'Yes. I said that.'

'They're all right. Who's your dad?'

'Um, Richard? Davis?' I wanted to add that he was in a car crash twenty-four years ago, but instantly realized how absurd that would sound.

He thought for a moment. 'Don't know him.'

'Do you know Kay Mulvaney?'

'Is that your mom?'

The word *mom* startled me. 'No. My mom's not from here. She's from . . . Pennsylvania.'

'This *is* Pennsylvania.'

'I mean Philadelphia.'

He was quiet again. 'Is her name Karen?'

'No, Meredith.'

'Meredith.' He repeated it to himself with such familiarity that suddenly I wondered if he knew what my mother had done. Wasn't that the thing about small towns? Didn't everyone know everything about everyone else?

'She decided not to come,' I said loudly. It was a lie I hadn't told in a while. Honestly, I hadn't explained it much in any way at all.

He looked at me with understanding. 'She doesn't like funerals, huh?'

'Not really.'

The boy nodded, then glanced back at his television, which was still flickering. 'So, guilty or not guilty?'

At first, I thought he was talking about my mom. *Guilty,* I decided. And then, *not guilty.* Then I realized he meant OJ. 'Oh, I don't know. Not guilty.'

He smirked. 'Me too. But you're the only white person in America who thinks that.'

It was strange that he said *you're,* not *we're.* He hadn't included himself. I looked over his pale skin and dark eyebrows and nice, not-too-full but not-too-thin lips.

The boy held a finger up. 'Hang on.' He disappeared back inside the house. In seconds, I heard his footsteps again. A light beamed in my face. 'Take this.' He passed me a gray-handled flashlight. 'You'll need it. It gets dark on this road. Even during the day. All the trees.'

He was right – it was suddenly dark, as if someone had thrown a curtain over the sky. But with the flashlight, I saw all sorts of things on the walk back: two large eyes of a creature, probably a raccoon, huddling under the pickup truck. A big, spindly stick lying in the middle of the road. Someone had spray-painted *Sand Niggers Go Home* on a twenty-five mph speed limit sign. Did that word have to be *everywhere* here? I waved the beam of the flashlight back and forth across the road, then shut it off. Darkness seemed safer.

I thought about my mother. She *wouldn't* have wanted to come to the funeral. She would've made excuses to get out of it – work, a party, a hair appointment. I used to imagine my mother in crazy places – Antarctica, Morocco, the moon. But lately, I was convinced she was still in New York. She was taking the same subways, seeing the same ridiculous subway ads and traveling around the same weekend track-work schedules. Maybe she climbed aboard an uptown 2 train as the doors closed, just as I was passing through the turnstile, watching it pull away.

Sometimes I missed her so much I couldn't sleep. I missed the way the house smelled of cinnamon candles and perfume. I missed how the phone used to ring. I missed how she'd rush into the house with dry cleaning and take-out and shopping bags. But when I tried to think harder about it, I just couldn't – a buzzing noise in my head took over. For a time, I hung on to the story I'd been telling myself, that my mother was away on a trip and would eventually return, that the chemicals deep inside her would pull her back to us, the very thing Mr Rice told our biology class. That, because of science, whether she liked it or not, she was *obligated* to return – it was a scientific rule, as unflappable as the laws of thermodynamics and gravity. Mr Rice never wrote back, but I read everything I could about genetics, trying to find evidence for myself. I read about twins who, even when separated, felt pain at the same time. I read about people who had heart transplants and suddenly had a fondness for oysters, something the heart's old owner loved. Surely this had something to do with DNA, shared or intro-duced? Our world wasn't magical, after all – there was always a scientific theory to demystify what at first seemed amazing.

The last time I hung out with Claire Ryan was more than a year and a half after my mother left. When her friends finally arrived at the diner, they started one-upping each other on how much their families were Nazis – something they often did, even though most of their families were fine, intact, usually nothing more than just a little overprotective. I stood up and walked out, not able to handle them that day. Claire followed me to the street and asked what was wrong. I told her to leave me alone. She asked why. I told her I didn't want to be her friend anymore.

Claire lowered her eyes. For a second, I thought I'd hurt her feelings, which maybe would've been for the best. But then I realized she was looking at me with patient sympathy. 'You have to deal with things some time, Summer,' she said, touching my arm.

For a moment, standing there on the sidewalk, I flirted with Claire's advice. I decided to see what dealing would feel like. The world went silent, and the walls inside my head shifted and opened, revealing new passageways. A sob welled up from deep inside of me, as well as a fizzle of something hot and sharp – maybe loss, maybe anger.

I felt both feverish and chilly at the same time, like I'd instantly contracted a disease. I turned away from Claire, saying nothing, and flew home and ran up four flights of stairs, breathing hard. When I flung open the door, there was my father, lying on the couch as usual. His eyebrows lifted when he saw it was me.

'This is your fault,' I demanded, out of breath. It had to be his fault – if it wasn't, it was mine.

His expression wilted. He sat up, the couch pillows tumbling to the floor. 'What's my fault?'

'You drove her away.' My voice shook nervously – I'd never said anything remotely accusatory to him before. 'You never went to her Christmas parties. You never bought her jewelry – she had to pick it out herself. She wanted to go on that cruise but you refused. You said you hated boats and organized meal times. You said you didn't want to eat dinner with other people.'

My father sank into one hip. 'I didn't want to

go on that cruise because it didn't include you and Steven.'

'You did something wrong.' I pointed at him. 'You didn't try hard enough. And now you don't even care. That's the worst part – you're not even looking for her.'

A thin, shaky noise emerged from the back of my father's throat. I retreated to my bedroom and slammed the door. He was easy to blame because he was there. How could I get angry at my mother? It would be like getting angry at air. I could tear up pictures of her, I could burn the sweaters she'd left behind, but it wouldn't give me much satisfaction.

But then, a few days later, the snow globe incident happened. So I couldn't feel angry at him about any of it anymore, obviously. I just couldn't.

When I returned to my grandmother's, Samantha was still sitting on the porch. The ashtray next to her brimmed with cigarette butts. 'Where were you?' she asked.

'Nothing. Just taking a walk.'

'Were you down at Philip's house?'

'Who's Philip?'

She licked her palm, then stubbed out the cigarette. It sizzled. The butt had blood-colored lipstick marks on it. 'Just this asshole. He doesn't talk to people. He thinks he's too good for everyone. Just hangs out with his family. I hear

100

they're religious freaks.' She stretched her long, denim legs out and considered me out of the corner of her eye, as cagey as the Smitty dog. 'How old are you?'

'Seventeen.'

'So am I. I had sex this spring. With two guys. How many guys have you slept with?'

I looked away.

Samantha's laugh was a bitter, horrid snort. 'You haven't slept with anyone, right? My first time was with this guy David. He's twenty-four. Drives an F-150. We used to fuck in it a *lot*. A big deer stepped out one time when we were doing it. Stared straight at us. It was awesome.'

Her voice did a little dip on *awesome*. I watched her face, expecting her expression to crumple, but her smile became even brighter.

She shook another cigarette out of the pack, lit it, and blew a plume of smoke toward the outdoor thermometer. Samantha's parents used to send us a Christmas card every year. They'd include a letter catching us up on the family's goings-on – a new car purchase, a minor health scare, a vacation to the Grand Canyon. 'Who on earth are Leonard, Ginny and Samantha?' my mother would always say, tossing the letters aside, but I liked reading them. Samantha's family seemed so normal. They went to church, Mrs Chisholm volunteered for a soup kitchen, and Samantha performed in piano recitals. My father told me that when her parents died in the fire, she was in Disney World for a piano competition. Her teacher told her right after she and a few other pianists got off the Maelstrom ride at Epcot.

'So you moved here in the winter, right?' I asked her. 'After your parents . . . you know?'

Her eyes flashed. 'You have a problem with that?'

'I was just asking.'

'I heard stuff about you, too.' Her face was pinched. 'Your mom left you guys. Probably because your dad's a basket case, huh? Apparently he has this big reputation here of being, like, mentally unstable, even when he was younger.'

'That's not true,' I said quickly.

'How do you know?' She put her feet up on the porch's railing. 'That's pretty despicable. A woman leaving her husband. Her *children*.' She said it like she was sitting behind the bench on *The People's Court*. 'Did she leave because your Dad's nuts?'

'No!' I cried.

'Do you think she was having an affair?'

'No!'

She smiled. 'Everyone knows that people only leave marriages when they've found something better.'

'That's not true.'

'So you're not angry? She left you before Christmas! Did you even get any *presents*?'

I shrugged and looked away.

Samantha took drag after drag, her flip-flop hanging off her toe. 'I tried to have sex with that Philip kid from down the street, but he didn't want to. He's not going to have sex with you. His whole family wears special religious underwear.'

'I don't even know him,' I protested. 'And I don't want to have sex with anyone.'

She barked a laugh. 'Sure you don't. That's the dumbest thing I've ever heard.'

CHAPTER 7

'Here you go.' Stella shuffled into the sitting room with a coffee mug. 'Some nice hot chocolate.'

'It's ninety degrees out,' I answered.

'Oh, now. It's good for you. I made it with whole milk. You need to gain some weight.'

My father and Petey had just left to see my grandmother's body. Stella decided to stay home with Steven and me, and no one fought her on it. Everyone, I'd noticed, was being extra-nice to Stella. Perhaps it was because she'd discovered my grandmother was dead when she came into her room to rustle her out of bed for breakfast.

Upstairs, Steven made the floor thump with what sounded like jumping jacks. Earlier, he'd gone running, crunching down the gravel road and disappearing onto the highway. To my knowledge, this was the first time he'd ever run in his life. I pictured him out there, gasping, cars narrowly passing him at sixty miles an hour. I saw him in camouflage, running an obstacle course, out of breath while the other recruits easily scaled a twenty-foot wall.

'So.' Stella sat down across from me. 'Tell me about yourself, Summer.'

'There's nothing to tell.' I looked down at my hot chocolate. It was the kind with mini-marshmallows, which I hated.

'Sure there is! I bet you've got tons of things to tell me about you.'

Her glasses were on crookedly, which made her look a little drunk.

'I'm pretty boring,' I answered.

'That's too bad.' Stella pulled a pack of cigarettes from her front pocket and lit one. She took a drag and eyed me. 'Do you want a little?'

I shifted my gaze in the other direction. 'It's all right.'

'Come on. It'll relax you.'

I lowered one eyebrow. 'There are all sorts of health warnings on the box.'

'These? Nah.'

I took the cigarette from Stella to avoid an argument. She looked overjoyed. As I put it to my lips, I glanced at the stairs, both in hope and fear that Steven would come down and see. 'Thanks,' I said, handing it back to Stella.

'You want your own?'

I shook my head no. We sat in silence for a few moments, Stella smoking. A car horn sounded. Stella cleared her throat. 'Nice day,' she remarked, even though we were sitting indoors, couldn't see out the heavily curtained windows, and even though I was pretty sure it was still overcast out.

'Hope we get a day like this for the funeral. And I hope people bring over a lot of hot dishes.' She leaned back. 'Minnie Elkerson makes the best pierogis. And Marcy makes a good ham. And Liza makes cabbage rolls. You ever had a cabbage roll?'

'Nope.'

'What? No. *Never?*'

'No. They sound disgusting.'

She exhaled. 'Ruth used to make terrible cabbage rolls. She was Suzy Homemaker, but her cabbage rolls smelled like shit.' She leaned back into the cushions. 'At least this holiday, I can make my *own* cabbage rolls.'

'Well, that's good.' It sounded as if Stella really hated her sister. She hadn't said one nice thing about Ruth since we had arrived.

Stella looked at me. 'And you'll come for Christmas this year, won't you?'

'Sure,' I said, but I didn't mean it. Upstairs, Steven made an unusually loud clunk. There wasn't anything wrong with exercising, nor was there anything wrong with wanting to enlist in the Marines . . . at least, I didn't think so. But this had come on so fast, and Steven seemed so *possessed.* That was what made it so scary.

'You got a best friend?' Stella asked.

I thought of Claire. 'Not exactly.'

'What does that mean?'

I sighed. Every time I went along with Claire to the diner, Claire looked at me with pitying, questioning eyes. *Are you having a good time? Are you*

106

having a good time? It was pathetic, how willingly she gave me the benefit of the doubt. All I thought of was how she'd told me my mother had resigned from her position at Mandrake & Hester. How plaintively she'd said, *Maybe we could help one another.* It felt like she continued to say it, inside, every time we were around each other.

'I don't know,' I mumbled. 'We've grown apart. We're into different things.'

'My husband was my best friend when we were growing up,' Stella said. 'But back in thirty-nine or forty – the twelfth grade, I guess – we went through a period of hating each other, too. He thought I was too coarse for him. He liked girls who were quiet, who didn't swear. A year later, when we were nineteen, we fell in love again.' She stubbed the cigarette out on a large, lopsided pea-green ashtray. 'I guess you never met my husband before he passed, huh?'

'I don't think so,' I answered. 'I mean, unless it was when I was really young.'

'His name was Skip. We got married six weeks after we re-met. He was a crane operator in a rock quarry.'

'Like Fred Flintstone?' I blurted.

'Exactly!' Stella grinned. 'Only, working in the quarry didn't make you much money. I had to take on all sorts of jobs to make ends meet. I was an assistant to a lawyer downtown – now *that* was a good job, but then he died. So I became a hair-washer at a beauty salon. It was my idea, you see,

107

and, as far as I knew, no one else was doing it. There should be a girl who does the hair, and a girl who washes it. Now, everyone does it.'

'That's true,' I said slowly. 'The last time I had my hair cut, there was a girl who washed my hair.'

Stella shook her head. 'I should've patented that idea. My life could've been so different. Anyway, I worked there until it closed. Then, I had a friend who was getting into the Jane Fonda workouts. She got me into them, too, and got me teaching aerobics at the Y.' She leaned back into the couch. 'I had a pink leotard and leg warmers and everything. That's back when I was in better shape.'

'What did my grandmother say about that?'

'Oh, you know.' Stella's expression shifted. 'She never came to any of the workouts or anything.'

'But didn't you live here? In this same town?'

She shrugged, ignoring me. 'So anyway, Skip was from a couple towns away. First time we met, we were in ice-skating lessons together. Our mothers couldn't pry us apart. But he thought I was too coarse for him. He liked girls who wore twinsets, who didn't swear. We were friends until twelfth grade, when he started going steady with Muriel Johnson. I hated her – she was a twinset girl. And you know what her yearbook motto was? *She is pretty to walk with and witty to talk with.*' Stella snorted and shook her head. 'I wouldn't speak to Skip when he was with her. Then there was that accident.'

'Accident?' It couldn't have been the same

accident my father was in. She had to be talking about a different era.

Stella nodded. 'Muriel went out on the Doyle boys' pond that November, because she'd bought a new ice-skating skirt that would twirl around when she spun – of *course* she knew how to spin, Muriel. So she was out there, wearing a twinset and that skirt, spinning, and everyone was watching her and saying how *pretty* she was, and then the ice cracked.' Stella clucked her tongue. 'Muriel knew just as well as the rest of us that the Doyles' pond takes a while to freeze all the way through. But she just couldn't wait to start the skating season.'

'What happened?'

'Oh, she fell through.' Stella waved her hand. 'One minute she was spinning, that gray skirt all twirly, the next she was under the water. The boys made a human chain to get her, but by the time they got out to the middle, it was too late. They had to wait to get her body out until the ice thawed – *months*, really. That skirt didn't look quite so pretty, all soggy and covered in frost.'

I gaped. 'They waited until spring? They didn't drain the pond and get her out that day?'

Stella blinked rapidly, as if I'd awakened her from a dream. 'Oh. Well. I don't know, really. It was so long ago. Anyway, I consoled Skip at Muriel's funeral, and the rest is history.' She coaxed another cigarette from the pack. 'We weren't apart until he died.'

The room was starting to fill with blue smoke. In Stella's stories, a story about a girl plummeting through thin ice to her death was on an emotional par with, say, someone waiting in a line at the DMV. I swallowed hard. 'My dad was in an accident a long time ago, right? A car accident?'

'That's right.' Stella turned her neck toward the kitchen, as if she'd heard a noise.

I shifted positions. 'So was he . . . hurt from it?'

'No . . .' Stella didn't meet my eye. 'I don't think there was a scratch on him.'

'He talks about it sometimes,' I said quietly.

Stella extinguished her cigarette in the pea-green ashtray. 'So I bet you miss your mom, huh?'

I sat back. 'Ex*cuse* me?'

She kept grinding the cigarette out. 'I hope you know it had nothing to do with you, whatever it was or wherever she is. But you're okay now, aren't you?'

'Sure,' I said weakly.

'And your father, too?'

'Yeah. I guess.'

Stella smiled. 'Well. Wonderful.'

In some ways, I wasn't lying. Aside from the snow globe incident, my father seemed okay. He went to the lab every day now. He saw a therapist named Dr North, and I had a feeling Dr North had him on some drug. I didn't want to think about it. I didn't want to *have* to think about it. Sometimes Dr North called Steven and me. 'If you ever want to talk, the door is open,' he said

110

if he happened to catch me on the phone, as if he were my roommate and was talking about the door to his bedroom. Several times, I'd dialed the first six digits of Dr North's office number, wanting to ask him if the time I'd blamed everything on my father could have led to what happened. I always hung up, though, before I dialed the seventh digit.

My father still wrote his on-the-fly diaries on cab receipts and phone bills and on the flyers the local grocery delivery service leaves in our mailbox. He wrote one on the day of the snow globe incident, on a slip of paper from a Duane Reade drugstore. *Summer is selling Toblerone chocolate for French class. I took a box into the lab and everyone bought one. They're tearing down the deli next to the lab to build a coffee shop, probably a Starbucks. Four hours' sleep.* Nothing about whether or not I'd hurt him, blaming him like that. Nothing indicating what was to come.

I pored over the receipts like a cryptologist, certain I'd find something that would lead me to understanding him, what he was going through, or if there was something he wasn't telling me. But there wasn't much there. He made a lot of references to drift mines. He sometimes mentioned the name *Jo* or *Josie* or just *J.* He also talked about encyclopedias, Leonard Cohen, Dairy Queen.

One day, a few months ago, he and I went for a walk on the Promenade. It was one of those placid days when all the big buildings across the

111

water had definite, flat edges, Manhattan unfurled like on a map. We leaned against the railing and looked into the oily, black water, not saying much. He took my small hand in his big, rough, squeezy one, the same hand that spliced off moles and held my mother's body close and petted me, cradled me, when I was a baby. 'I hope this never happens to you,' he said.

It didn't take me long to realize what he was talking about. I was my father's daughter.

When Stella placed her mug of hot chocolate on the coffee table, she bumped a stack of magazines sideways. Underneath a *National Geographic* from 1982 was a color photograph of a young girl, about seven or eight, with dark hair chopped to her chin. She stood next to a tire swing and a rusty blue pickup truck. Its right headlight was cracked, just like the truck out front.

'Who's that?' I pointed at the girl. She didn't look like Samantha. And she certainly wasn't me.

A muscle next to Stella's right eye twitched. For a few seconds, she watched me searchingly, as if waiting for me to say something else. When I didn't, she picked up the photo and slipped it into her cardigan pocket. 'It's just . . . you know. A neighbor girl.' Her other hand fumbled for a fresh cigarette. After she lit it, she patted my hand. 'You know what? I have just the thing for you.'

She walked into the kitchen and started to bang around through drawers. I expected her to come back with something priceless – an explanation, maybe. An old slip of paper with my father's handwriting, perhaps an account of his accident. A recording of my mother's voice, the last time she visited here. The answer.

Stella held two small pieces of cardboard and ceremoniously handed one to me. 'Now. I just know you're going to win.'

It was a scratch-off lottery ticket. The theme was 'pot o' gold,' and there was a drawing of a deranged-looking leprechaun with a long goatee shooting rainbows from his fingers. Stella wordlessly passed me a penny, then turned to her own ticket and started feverishly scratching. My windows revealed $5, $15, a pot of gold, a horseshoe, and some kind of unidentifiable blob.

'Nothing for me, I don't think,' I said.

'Me neither.' Stella brushed the rubbed-off debris onto the carpet. She sounded astonished, like she'd truly expected me to win the million bucks.

After a while, my father and Pete, his cousin, returned from the funeral home, quiet and clumsy. I had a feeling they were drunk. My dad opened a beer too fast and sent foam frothing to the linoleum. Pete hit his head on the bathroom door jamb. 'Does it smell like smoke in here?' he asked. No one cared enough to pursue it further.

'How was it?' I asked my dad. I sat at the kitchen table, staring at the place mats, which were a map of the world circa 1954. Most of Eastern Europe was named something I didn't recognize.

113

'Oh, she looked beautiful.' Pete smiled at me. 'Really nice.'

The kitchen's wallpaper was divided into squares. Each square contained a fruit, a vegetable, or a flower, and then the big letter of the alphabet they all started with. A was an avocado, B a banana, and so on. It was all done in pastel greens and browns and oranges. On the butter-colored fridge were heavy, lacquered magnets molded into the shapes of common American dinners, a mini-hamburger and French fries, a plate of pasta, a steak and baked potato.

Stella started on dinner, spaghetti, plopping a big wad of butter on the noodles before pouring the sauce on top. The meat in the sauce looked like little gerbil poops. Pete wafted in and out, a ragged, paperback book in his hand. I'd met Pete a few times – he visited us in Brooklyn after my mom left, driving all the way from Arizona, where he lived. Last summer, my father suggested I visit him there – *Pete lives in a geodesic dome*, he singsonged, as if this were temptation. *He's a nature guide. You could go on some amazing hikes. He raises parakeets!*

Pete drove across the country to get here, too. When he found out Steven and I were good students, he showed us the books stacked in the passenger seat of his old Honda Civic. 'You know how some people eat to live?' he said to us, his eyes wide. 'Well, I *read* to live.' Except Pete hadn't attended college. My father was the only one in the family who had done that.

114

A woman from across the street, Crystal, showed up for dinner, too. She was somewhere between my dad's and Stella's age, and wore a paunchy blue dress that draped all wrong on her bony body. 'I brought you some muffins.' She handed Stella a plate wrapped in tinfoil.

'Muffins!' Stella cried, as if they were some new thing.

We used a slotted spoon to slop the spaghetti onto our plates. The chipped spaghetti bowl had a bunch of bloody grapes painted on the side. Flies buzzed all over the kitchen, landing on the lips of the beer cans, the edge of the butter dish, the tip of the faucet, vigorously rubbing their feelers together in a way that was vaguely sexual.

'So, do you think he did it?' Stella said, winding the pasta around her fork.

'Who?' my father asked.

'OJ! Do you think he killed that wife of his?'

'I think he did,' Samantha said a little loudly. Stella was letting her drink a beer. 'Why else would he run like that?'

'Oh, I don't know,' Pete answered. 'He was the obvious suspect. Even if he didn't do it, maybe he was afraid he wouldn't be able to get out of it if they took him in. Because, you know. He's black.'

I thought of what that Philip boy had said earlier. *You're the only white person in America who thinks that.*

'Oh, that has nothing to do with it.' Stella waved her hand.

Pete sat up straighter. 'The rest of the country thinks it does.'

'He killed her because she was cheating on him,' Stella said. 'She loved someone else. Adultery is a big motivator. Crime of passion and all that.'

I slumped down and stared at the strip of wallpaper under the window. V was for violet. W was for watermelon. Y was for yam. Z was for zinnia. They'd skipped X, the cheating bastards. Part of the wallpaper was peeling. I took the edge of the alphabet wallpaper and pulled. I couldn't help it. It came off easier than a Band-Aid. There was another layer of wallpaper underneath, fat stripes of blue and gold. The edge of it was crumbling as well, so I peeled that back, too. Boyish plaid. There was a gash in the middle of it, and I could see the next layer down. Roses. Perhaps this house didn't have plaster or framing, but was instead held up by wallpaper, hunting paintings, and pictures of Frank.

'So, Summer, have you had a prom yet?' Stella asked.

'No,' I managed, dreading what I knew was going to follow.

'Why not?'

'Our school doesn't have one.'

'What school doesn't have a prom?' Crystal piped up.

'A loser school,' Samantha muttered, taking a healthy sip of beer.

'We're a private school.'

Claire had gone to a senior prom this year with her boyfriend, Terrance, who attended public school. She, Terrance, and her friends ducked out early to see *The Rocky Horror Picture Show*, which was playing at some theater in the East Village. She told me that Terrance's friend, Seth, whom everyone called Moses, wanted to ask me to the prom, which would be great because then we could go together. I stayed home that night instead and played solitaire on my bedroom floor. 'Proms are lame,' I mumbled.

'How about you, Steven?' Crystal asked.

'Um, I'm in college.'

Pete pointed a breadstick at us. 'You've got the right idea, Summer. Proms are capitalist nightmares.'

Crystal snapped her fingers. 'You know who would be perfect for Summer? That Philip kid from down the street.'

Samantha choked up beer.

'He's very thoughtful,' Crystal added.

'I've . . .' I began, about to say, *I've met him.* But then Stella piped up, 'The Arab kid?'

I shut my mouth. Steven looked up, his eyes wide.

'Half-Arab,' Crystal corrected. 'His father's from . . . oh . . .'

'India,' Samantha said.

'That's not Arab,' Pete scolded.

'His father wears one of those towels on his head.' Stella shrugged. 'Isn't that Arab?'

117

That speed limit sign, on my way home: *Sand Niggers Go Home.*

'The boy doesn't wear a towel,' Crystal said, now distracted and subdued. She had an uncomfortable look, as if she'd just realized she had no idea who our family really were. 'Just his father. Philip seems nice. Quiet.'

'Quiet doesn't necessarily mean good.'

Everyone jumped at the volume of Steven's voice. His face had a galvanized glow. 'And India *definitely* isn't innocent,' he went on. 'There was an explosion just last year in Bombay's Stock Exchange building. And tons more bombs that same day. There are all kinds of religious terrorist cells in India, and the father's turban might mean he's Muslim. How old did you say this boy was?'

'*Nice*,' Samantha whispered, excited.

And Stella said, 'Crystal, I can't wait to eat those muffins!'

'He's about Summer's age,' Crystal said, not getting it.

'You guys should watch him.' Steven grew a few inches in his seat.

'Watch him?' Pete repeated.

'Absolutely. We're all caught up in this OJ thing, but OJ is the least of our problems. There are a lot more dangerous people in this country *right now* – a lot of them impressionable teen-agers.' Steven stood up halfway. 'In fact, if you want me to—'

118

'Steven.' My father put his hand on Steven's arm. 'Stop.'

Steven bent his shoulder away from him. His eyes were glassy. 'Nobody's paying enough attention. You guys probably don't even remember that the World Trade Center was bombed. Or, it probably was just something in the news, O*h, that's too bad*, and that was it. You had no connection to it.'

'Steven,' my father warned.

He kept going, his voice arcing higher and higher. 'People want to blow themselves up for crazy ideas. They walk into a market square with people they don't even know and just . . . do it. And here we are, watching OJ, *la la la*.'

'Why would anyone want to blow themselves up?' Crystal looked so lost.

'That's not something that's going to happen here.' Stella made a *tsk* sound. 'It's something that happens in those crazy countries. The ones where people are still riding camels.'

'It *did* happen here,' Steven interrupted sharply, and Stella cowered back. 'You don't *know* what it's like. You just don't *know*.' Steven groaned painfully, scraped back his chair, and stomped to the living room.

There was a long, tense pause. Outside, two squirrels rolled around in the grass, then chased each other up the tree. Finally, Stella said, 'Well!' with a flourish, but nothing else. I poked my tongue into the gap in my mouth where an adult tooth never came in.

119

'Meredith worked in the World Trade tower that was bombed,' my father explained in a low voice. 'She resigned long before it happened, but I think that's why he's worried about—'

'That's *not* why!' Steven screamed from around the corner. 'That's not why at all!'

He stomped up the stairs and slammed a door. Pete's Adam's apple bobbed up and down. Everyone looked at us with sympathy, as if they absolutely understood what we were going through.

'Not that it matters,' I said loudly, breaking the silence, 'but I don't want to go out with that boy down the street, anyway.'

CHAPTER 8

There was one funeral home in all of Cobalt called the Grinsky Family Funeral Home. It was in the downtown area – the downtrodden strip we'd driven past yesterday, with the Mister Donut and the murky river and the Knights of Columbus – in a house that looked similar to my grandmother's. In other words, it was an actual *home,* with a driveway, a porch, an upstairs, and a rotting wooden hatch that led to outdoor basement stairs. I made the mistake of asking Pete what happened in the basement. He said, in a spooky voice, 'That's where they prepare the bodies.'

The home was done up in rose-patterned carpet, heavy, dark-green drapes, and bulky, imposing couches. We all went in very slowly. My father and Steven wore jackets and ties, and Stella had on a teal dress made of featherweight silk. Her orange cat-eye glasses clashed. I wore a corduroy black skirt from the winter and a sleeveless black shirt. Samantha hadn't changed out of her dingy jeans.

An older man with a hooked nose, bug-like eyes and a jowly face greeted us. He could have been a new puppet on *Sesame Street* – some reptilian

121

character, perhaps a lizard. 'You might not remember me,' he mumbled to my father. 'I'm Leon Grinsky. I went to church with your mother.'

'Of course, of course,' my father said. He pointed to us. 'This is Summer. And this is Steven. My kids.'

'Lovely.' Lizard's smiles were more disturbing than his frowns. 'And your wife? Your mother said you were married . . .'

My father looked down. 'I'm . . . we're separated.'

I felt like he'd punched me. I tried to catch Steven's eye, but he was checking out an empty urn. The front door was still wide open, and a snub-nosed little kid circled the sidewalk on a bike. A water gun dangled from his right hand. When he passed again, he turned his head, took his remaining hand off the handlebars and gave me what I guessed were devil horns. '*Naaaah*,' he said to all of us, pointing to the doorway. '*Naaah*.' He waved the gun threateningly.

Grinsky the Lizard led my father and brother through a long hallway to a room at the end filled with more overstuffed chairs, little end tables, a mantel with a painting of pastel roses in a basket. The coffin was at the end of the room. And all the flowers. Luckily, the rest of my family had lined up down the casket, so I couldn't immediately see my grandmother's body.

I noticed Lizard lurking in the doorway. Stella twisted around from the casket and raised an

122

eyebrow. She retreated toward me, the ends of her dress floating behind her.

'Do you want to come up?' she asked.

'I don't know.' I twisted away. 'It's weird.'

She petted my arm. 'Honey.'

I peeked at Lizard, then curled farther into her. 'That guy won't stop looking at me.'

Stella glanced at Lizard, too. 'Oh, he's hideous, isn't he? C'mon. Let's go outside. I could use a smoke, anyway.'

Out on the porch, I felt my head fill with blood again. Stella sat down on the glider and patted the seat next to her. We tried to swing, but the old glider was too rusty. Stella hummed when she took a cigarette out of her leopard-print case.

Separated. We're separated.

It had been a year and a half and I'd never said it out loud that my parents were separated. I'd never heard my father say it, either. But maybe he had. Why, after all, would he decide to tell the funeral director first?

'That Grinsky put on Ruth's makeup,' Stella interrupted my thoughts. 'It makes her look like a hooker. Then again, in some ways, it's nice to see her with makeup on at all.' She took a drag. 'She never wore makeup. Never any sparkle. Same with her clothes, and *definitely* the same with her hair. When I was working at the salon, I told Ruth that Samuel – he was the hairdresser – would style her hair for free. And she refused! Said she was happy with her look! Slammed the door on me and everything, like I'd just insulted her!'

I rubbed my ankles together. After the Trade Center bomb, a counselor came to our school. I was curious, so I made an appointment. The secretary at the front desk gave me a form in a sealed envelope for my parents – I peeked at it; it asked a lot of questions about my mental health. 'We need this signed by both parents,' the secretary explained.

I told her that my mother wouldn't be able to sign the form. 'Why?' the secretary asked, raising an eyebrow. 'Are they divorced? Is your mother . . . ?' She looked up at the ceiling, as if heaven were up there. I gave her the packet back, telling her that, never mind, I didn't need to go to a counselor after all. It was too hard to explain.

Stella was still complaining. 'And that woman was such a germophobe, especially after your father left. Everything had to be spotless. One time, she wouldn't let me in because my shoes looked too filthy! And they were perfectly clean. Nothing wrong with them. She even tried to clean after her first stroke, but finally I said would you *stop*? Life isn't all about cleanliness. Life isn't all about having the dishes stacked perfectly and all the pictures straight on the walls.'

But don't you miss her? I wanted to ask Stella. I couldn't think of anything bad to say about my mother, even though I knew the things were there.

Then Stella looked at me. 'Did I ever tell you I almost cheated on my husband?'

I stared at her, slack-jawed at the inanity of the question. 'Uh, no. I can't say you have.'

'Skip and I were fighting. We fought all the time.'

'Over what?'

She shrugged. 'Oh, you know. Things. It's hard to be married. There was one time though when I really thought things were over. I stormed out of the house and got in my car. I didn't know where I was going. I just drove. I ended up at this bar, the Crest. I don't know what it's like now, but it used to be that you didn't go into the Crest. Not if you were a nice girl, or any kind of girl for that matter – the median age in that place was about fifty. I was only twenty-three or so when this fight happened. I pulled into the parking lot and slammed the door and just walked right in there. Most of the guys nearly fell off their seats when I walked in. There was this man sitting on the last stool, nearest the back door. I walked right up to him and sat down and I ordered a whiskey sour.' She chuckled. 'Have you ever had one?'

'I'm seventeen,' I reminded her.

'They're delicious,' she said. 'You should try one. Maybe I'll make you one, when we go home. Anyway, the bartender said they didn't have any sour mix. He poured me a glass of whiskey, without me even asking. I drank it down. I was so mad at Skip, I remember. So mad. And some man was just staring at me, and he asked what my name was and I told him and then I . . . I slipped my wedding ring into my pocket. It was

125

the craziest thing. But this man stood up and he offered his hand and I stood up too. And we just . . . walked out the bar. He opened his car door. I got in. No words at all. He drove to the Amity – it's not there anymore, because it burned down in the Seventies, but it used to be this motel near the bridge. I just followed him into a room.

'The whole time, all I could think of was my wedding ring in my pocket.' Stella took a breath. 'I was sure it was going to roll out and under the dresser and I'd never be able to find it. And then someone *else* would find it, and they'd see my initials and Skip's initials and our wedding date and they'd know it was mine.'

'How would they know?' I asked.

'Cobalt is small,' Stella explained. 'People know.'

'But what about the guys at the bar? Don't *they* know?'

Stella shrugged. 'None of them would ever say anything. They probably weren't supposed to be at that bar in the first place. It was the middle of the day, after all.'

She stubbed out her cigarette on the porch rail. 'The ring was fine, though. Still in my pocket. And I didn't go through with it, anyway. The man had to pee as soon as we got there. When he shut the bathroom door a little, I left.'

'Did you ever tell your husband?'

'Good Lord, no. I don't even know what we were fighting about. Probably nothing.' She chuckled, then sighed. 'Marriage can be such a

126

bitch, Summer. It really can. It's hard for people to be truly happy together. Some people just can't take it. And that's okay.'

I stuffed my hands underneath me. 'Do you think people that leave their families are despicable?'

'Predictable?' She tilted her ear toward me. 'What'd you say?'

I swallowed hard. 'Never mind.'

The same devil horns kid whizzed by. Truthfully, I was a little astounded to see any kids in Cobalt. The town seemed more like an island of old ladies, all of them as candid and batty as Stella. Then again, there was Samantha. And the kid down the street. The Arab that wasn't an Arab.

I stared at the dirt between the porch's wooden slats. 'So is that kid Crystal was talking about really weird?'

'Kid?' Stella looked at me blankly. 'What kid?'

'That . . .' I searched for his name. 'That Philip kid.'

Stella leaned back, thinking. 'That father of his was getting out of his car once. I was right there, and I was so tempted to ask how he puts his towel thing on. I'm dying to know. Is it a hat, or is it a big long scarf? Does it ever fall off?' She looked off in the distance. 'And why does he wear it all the time, anyway? Someone told me it was because of his religion. But what kind of crazy religion makes you do that?'

'So what's Philip's family doing here?'

'The father has some job, but I'm not sure where. The mother's white. She's a substitute teacher. Her family's not too far away, I don't think. It probably has something to do with that.'

'Have you ever spoken to them?'

Stella ignored the question and stood up so abruptly, the glider swung violently back. She glared at me, her face sprouting thousands of new wrinkles. 'Get up.'

I cautiously stood. She took my hands and started swinging them around. Then she started bending her knees and knocking her hips back and forth. 'What are you *doing*?' I asked.

'Don't you hear Elvis?' she demanded.

I stared at her. She pointed to her temple. 'It's *here*. It's inside of you, too. I know it is. Dance with me.'

'I don't think we should dance at a . . . a wake,' I whispered, peeking inside. My father was still talking to the Lizard. I didn't see Steven. Maybe he'd slipped out back, yelling at some black people he'd mistaken for terrorists. There was a dead person I was related to inside the house.

'You're way too young to be so miserable,' Stella scolded, still dancing. 'You're too much like Ruth. She hated Elvis, you know. Thought he was obscene. And look where that got her!' She pointed through the funeral home door toward the coffin, her movements growing more pronounced. If she swung her back end a few inches to the left, she'd take out one of the potted plants. 'Come on,' she urged.

I moved my hands and bent my knees. I looked over my shoulder to see if anyone, mostly Steven, was watching. 'No looking!' Stella said. 'Shut your eyes!'

So I shut my eyes. I heard 'Rock Around the Clock', a song that was always playing at Claire's Galaxy Diner. Stella made little grunts to punctuate each hip gyration. I couldn't help but laugh.

My father appeared in the doorway. 'Summer?'

I stopped. 'Oh. Hi.'

'You want to come up and see your grandma?'

I hesitated. Stella stopped dancing and immediately lit another cigarette. Her face was flushed and there was a crooked fuchsia smile on her lips.

I followed my father through the long, rose-carpeted hall again, this time to the edge of the casket, which was all ivory, like a birthday cake. No one was standing at it, so I couldn't avoid seeing the person lying inside. There was the jut of her chin and the gummy slope of her profile. Her hair was very white. And then – so weird – a white satin blanket covered her from her waist down to her feet, like she was tucked into bed. The casket was lined, too, like a jewelry box. There was even a little pillow for her head.

I looked at her face last. She didn't look like the woman in the pictures. The corners of her mouth turned down, her eyes were shut, and her skin was waxy. She looked more like a doll – an old-person doll – than a real human. I realized that all of the things just below our surfaces – blood vessels, twitchy muscles, layers of skin, cells; the things that were alive – were the things that made us look real.

All the floral arrangements around my grandmother seemed to have crept in closer, protective. When everyone left, when Lizard crept home for the night, my grandmother would still be lying here with all these flowers around her like guard dogs. What had my father murmured to her, when it was his turn to stand at her head? Had he explained what was going on inside of him? What he'd done to the snow globe? Did he say he was separated?

One of the flower arrangements spelled out the word *Mom*. I picked up the little card that was wedged into the bottom of the first *M*. It was stupid, giving cards at a funeral – it wasn't like the dead person could read them. When I opened it, it said, *Your loving son, Richard Davis*.

I considered taking my grandmother's hands, like Stella took mine, and swinging them back and forth. I didn't want to be morose. I didn't want to recoil from everything. Maybe my grandmother didn't want to, either. But when I reached out, her hand was way too cold and solid and heavy. I dropped it and turned around fast, my heart pounding hard.

CHAPTER 9

That night, I stared at the way the light shifted on the flowered wallpaper, making each flower look like a macabre nipple. As I climbed out of bed, something moved on the floor beneath me. It was the unnamed dog, the one my father picked up on the street. The Smitty dog. I had forgotten about her, since she'd spent all of her time outside with the other dogs. I wasn't sure how she'd gotten in – I wasn't even sure dogs were allowed in the house.

I felt the sides of the walls to get down the stairs safely. The dog followed me to the front door, where we both looked out the glass panels at the street. Light-green pods covered our car. The moon was bloated and glowing. It didn't take me long to get to the house at the end of the road. Most of the windows were dark and there was a nondescript Ford station wagon in the driveway. The same TV flickered.

The dog and I walked up to the same window I was at yesterday and looked inside. The TV cast ghostly blue shadows over the wood-paneled walls. An empty ashtray and a white coffee mug sat on the table. The TV was tuned to that old PBS show, *The Joy of Painting*, where the friendly, frizzy-haired guy blotted the canvas to create spiny trees and blurry clouds. I watched a shot of the canvas, then the painter's lion-like face, then the palette.

'I thought I heard someone out here.'

I turned around, my heart leaping to my throat. Philip sat on the porch, hidden by the shadows. He looked at the dog curiously.

'Hi,' I said.

'Hi,' he said back. 'Summer, right?'

I nodded.

'I'm Philip,' he said. I almost said *I know*, but then he added, 'What's your dog's name?'

'She doesn't have one. My dad found her. She's a Smitty dog.'

'Smitty dog?'

'Apparently it's some local thing.'

He laughed and ducked his head bashfully. 'Well, I'm not really a local.'

He wasn't much taller than I was, but was wearing the clothes of someone who was about six foot ten. His t-shirt fell past his crotch, and his shorts past his knees. He wore no shoes, only white gym socks.

'So you're here visiting?' he asked.

'Yeah, remember, my grandmother died?' I reminded him. 'We have to go to her funeral.'

'Right.' He scratched his nose. 'Did you go yet?'

'No. Today we had to see the body.'

'What was that like?'

132

I paused. 'She looked like she'd been in the freezer for a while.' I pointed to the window. 'You watch *The Joy of Painting*.'

He brightened for a second, although his version of brightening was his mouth lifting just slightly, his muscles tightening. 'You know it?'

'I used to watch it when I was little.'

'My dad used to paint along to the program,' he said. 'He used to put his canvas right up against the TV, and whatever Bob Ross did, he'd do too. He wasn't very good at it, though. All of his paintings just looked flat and empty.'

I wanted him to say more about his dad. When he didn't, I asked, 'So where are you from, if you're not from here?'

'Michigan. You?'

'Brooklyn.'

'Brooklyn,' he repeated, nodding. Thankfully, he didn't say *Brooklyn* in a tough-guy voice, as a couple of youngish older people at the wake today had done, as if everyone from Brooklyn were in the Mafia. Philip pointed off toward my house. 'How are the old ladies?'

'Well, there's only one, now. But she's okay.'

'I know Stella a little. She came over once.' I got a look at his eyes. They were dark and deep set, so lovely.

'My grandmother is having a twenty-one-gun salute at her funeral,' I offered.

'Really.'

'And Aunt Stella, who you met, is living on

133

another planet,' I went on. 'And then Samantha . . . maybe you know her . . . she's downright mean.'

'She's all right. I was like that, too, when my mother was sick.'

The smell of pine was suddenly sharp in my nose. 'Sick?'

'She had cancer,' he added.

He arched his back and looked up at the sky. I looked up, too. I thought that outside New York City, the sky would be perfect and bright and informative, with a legend key telling me which constellation is which. But tonight's sky was murky and dense, the same sky as in Brooklyn.

Philip shifted his weight. 'Want to see something? It's behind my house.'

'I don't know. Do I?'

He thought for a moment. 'Yes. You do.'

I followed him into his backyard. There were flowers planted neatly along the sides of the house, and a bag of K-Mart brand soil propped up at the back. At the back of the house was a huge garden. Everything was in bloom, dewy and green.

Philip pushed past some branches. We were behind the garden now, among a thick patch of trees. The air smelled earthy, like plants and soil and water. The light hit Philip dramatically, bouncing off the angles of his face, making him look romantic, like he was sitting for a portrait. I was hesitant to look at him directly, for fear he'd think I was staring.

'Check it out.' Philip pointed to a small patch

of dirt on the ground. About twenty plants were in neat rows. Behind them were small stones. Each stone bore a name. *Clara. Jezebel. Rufus. Clive.*

'I don't get it,' I said.

'They're graves,' he answered.

'Of . . . *people*?'

He snorted. '*No.* Of birds. See? There's a drawing of one.' He stooped down and wiped away some dirt off one of the headstones; sure enough, there was a crude drawing of a sparrow. 'There are hunters out in these woods. They're hunting for deer, but a lot of times they miss and get a bird. They never collect them. These graves were here when we moved in, though. My mom and I just continued the tradition. Every time we find a bird, we bury it with the rest.'

'Really.'

'Uh huh.'

I looked at the names on the headstones. *Laila. Tristan. Penelope.* Penelope was one of my father's favorite names – it was what he wanted to name me, in fact, but my mother had staunchly refused. 'So is your mom . . . better?'

'She eats now. She didn't eat for a while. Everything tasted like metal.'

'Why?'

'Chemotherapy.'

'That must've been . . .' I floundered for a word. 'Sucky.'

'I'd say it's okay, but I'm sick of saying that, especially when it's not true.'

I thought for a moment. 'Maybe you could say some random word instead. Like *pickle*.'

'Pickle, huh?' He settled against the tree, curling his legs under him, gold stitching along the toe-line of his socks. I leaned up against a different tree about three feet from him. The rough bark cut up my back but I was afraid to move. Philip stared at me for a long time. It didn't feel like an assault, though, just benign curiosity.

'Are your parents getting divorced now?' I blurted out.

He raised an eyebrow. 'Why would they be divorced?'

'Someone told me the other day that marriage doesn't work. That when something goes wrong, people usually bail out.'

Philip scratched his head. 'Really?' He sounded hurt, maybe even worried. I sucked in my stomach, wondering why I'd said something so mean. He'd probably hate me now. He'd probably throw a rock at my head.

'Brooklyn's near the Bronx, right?' he said after a moment.

'Yeah. Close enough.'

'My mom grew up in the Bronx. I bet she'd like to meet you guys. To talk to someone about it.' He glanced at me. 'It's not like she and my dad come from the same background. He grew up in India. And he's Sikh.' His laugh was bitter, embarrassed. 'But you probably don't know what that is, right?'

I wiped my hair out of my face. 'No, I do. A neighbor of ours, Mr Saluja, is that. Sikh, I mean.' It explained, of course, the turban Philip's father wore – it was a religious thing, a religion completely different from Christianity or, more importantly, Islam. Something else occurred to me – Steven knew what it meant to be Sikh, too. He used to shovel Mr Saluja's front walk.

'Why did you show me this?' I asked, gesturing to the graves.

He blinked. 'I thought you'd like it.'

'I do.' It was warm inside my jeans pockets, the denim all soft and worn out.

'I've never shown it to anyone before.'

'Why?'

He paused, considering. 'I don't know. Most people don't deserve to see it.'

And I do? I thought, astounded.

The night seemed to grow darker, quieter, more serious. Philip let out a breath, sort of a sad laugh. Then he stepped forward. In one fluid motion, he touched my hand, and then kissed me. His lips were a quick bloom on mine and then gone. My veins filled with hot chocolate and, for a moment, the world went white.

I must have had a startled expression on my face because Philip broke away fast. 'Sorry. I don't know why I just . . .' He trailed off and stared at the ground.

No, I liked it, I protested in my head. But I felt like I was underwater. If I opened my mouth, I'd

137

drown. There were locusts or crickets or some chirping creatures back in the woods. I clenched and unclenched my hands, wondering if Philip had really kissed me just now, or if I'd dreamed it all up.

Suddenly, I took a deep breath. 'My mother left us a year and a half ago. We don't know where she is.'

Philip turned his head a fraction, saying nothing.

'And then a couple months ago,' I continued, 'we were eating dinner, and my dad took a snow globe that was sitting on our dining-room table and threw it against the wall. And then he got up and picked up the biggest piece and drove it right into the center of his palm. Then he couldn't get it out. It was stuck in there somehow. It just kept bleeding.'

'Was he . . . okay?' Philip's voice was small and tentative.

'I guess. It's healed and everything. The doctors said it was because of stress, but I don't know. It was . . . awful. I'm kind of afraid he might do something like that again.'

I was afraid to say anything else for fear I'd either start crying or tell him the rest – that we took him to the emergency room, that he was screaming and crying the whole time, that he was in the psych ward for three days, that I had to visit him there. How I was certain that it was my fault, all of it, and if only I'd done something differently, it never would have happened. How, even deeper,

138

I felt so angry, anger I had no idea what to do with or where to put.

I shut my eyes. 'Pickle,' I recited. 'Pickle, pickle, pickle.' I opened my eyes again. 'I think it works.'

I looked at him and smiled. He smiled back, but it seemed weak, watered down. I couldn't tell what he was feeling. Perhaps terror. Or disgust. Everything inside me felt like a garbage can tipped over, strewn on the forest floor. *Kiss me again,* I begged him silently. *Please.*

A twig snapped. I looked over and saw a shadow in Philip's driveway. It moved toward us quickly. Steven.

'Oh,' I whispered.

'Who's that?' Philip asked.

'My brother.'

I took a step toward him. Steven stood with his hands on his hips. 'What do you want?' I called to him, my voice trembling.

'Come here,' Steven said, his voice a threat.

I glanced back at Philip. He stood in front of the bird graves, as if guarding them. The wind smelled like bug spray. The creek rushed angrily behind us.

'Get over here, Summer,' Steven repeated, impatient.

'I'm fine.' The words dissolved in the air space right outside my mouth. 'Nothing's wrong. We're just hanging out.'

'*Come. Here.*'

Philip cocked his head, like a dog that heard a strange noise. 'Maybe you should go.'

Steven's shoulders were squared, his legs spread apart. He reminded me of the two-story cowboy statue we saw in front of a restaurant called Round 'Em Up Corral. It was somewhere on the highway, on the way in, and featured an all-you-can-eat buffet for $5.95.

I took a few steps more toward him. 'Just stop it,' I hissed. 'You're embarrassing me.'

'Do you know who you're talking to?' Steven answered, not quietly at all.

'Do *you*?' I asked. Steven blinked. 'You don't! You don't know anything!'

'Summer.' He wrapped his hand around my wrist, guiding me backward.

'Why are you *doing* this?'

'Because . . .' He let out a small whine. It was a noise like a little kid would make, frustrated when he didn't get his way. 'You *know* why.'

I tried to shake him off, but he wrapped his arms around my waist and covered my mouth. I made a muffled cry, vaguely afraid. My brother's body felt solid and warm, and for a second, it was like we were embracing.

Steven continued to hold me to him, his breath hot on my neck. Tears sprang to my eyes. And then he released me, just like that. I spun across Philip's yard. Ten feet away, Steven looked smaller. He held his arms out, staring at them as if he couldn't believe they were his. And Philip was gone. I couldn't feel Philip's lips on mine anymore. When I reached for the memory, I saw my grandmother's dead face instead. The world smelled like driveway tar, thick and black, a smell I'd always hated.

'Summer.' Steven listed toward Philip's mailbox, a cheap steel rectangle on a tattered post. 'It's just that . . .'

'Go away,' I said through my teeth.

He took another step, but I turned around and wheeled back toward Stella's house. 'Just don't,' I screamed over my shoulder, my voice piercing through the woods.

CHAPTER 10

It was raining at the cemetery, big fat drops plopping on the gazebo roof, on the crumbling headstones, on the threadbare mini-American flags around the carious gravesites. We huddled under an umbrella near the open plot, waiting for everyone to arrive from the funeral home.

Steven sniffed behind me. Last night, when I slipped back in the house, I found everyone in the kitchen. 'Are you okay?' my father asked. 'We couldn't find you.' He was crying. In front of everyone, like he always did. Huge tears ran down his face. I hated him for crying. I hated that Samantha was standing there, an entertained little smile on her face, taking it all in. She'd seen where I'd gone and told Steven, I figured. She'd ruined everything just because she could.

And I hated that I'd said something to Philip. It seemed as if the whole world had heard. I was certain my father would next turn to me and say, *So you're sure I'm going to pull another snow globe incident again, huh? Some daughter you are.*

I hated all of them last night. After I kicked my shoes off, I sneered at my blubbering father.

142

'Steven's going to join the Marines,' I spat, tasting acid in my mouth. 'So you'd better do something soon if you want to stop him.'

And then I went upstairs. Steven slid in well after I'd shut myself in my room, gotten into bed, and pulled up the covers. I heard his every step on the creaky, warped wood. He paused at my room, as if he wanted to say something, but then he didn't. Seconds later, the door to his room scraped shut.

One of the biddies that was at the wake floated over to us now, a crooked umbrella over her head. 'It was a lovely service,' she croaked to my father, taking his hand.

'Yes. Absolutely,' my father answered. 'Beautiful.'

Her whole body trembled. 'She's in God's hands now.'

Something indescribable passed over my father's face. 'I'm sure.'

When the seven soldiers ascended the hill, Steven's posture changed. They were dressed in blue suits and carried rifles over their shoulders. They all had hair and expressions exactly like Steven's. I wondered where they'd come from – they didn't seem particularly Cobaltian. More likely, the funeral director had them bused in from some more official town nearby.

They reached us and fanned out in a line. The silence was absolute. Stella shook her head. *Spent every penny,* I bet she was thinking. My brother was rapt, watching as the head soldier or whatever

143

barked out an order and a few of them gathered the flag off my grandmother's coffin and started to fold it up. They folded and folded and folded until it was a compact triangle. Stella balled her fists and kept her eyes on the ground.

The soldiers handed the flag to my father. He took it, befuddled, and finally tucked it under his arm. Then the soldiers lined up again and started shooting. The noise of seven guns shooting all at once was ridiculously loud.

The funeral director hit a lever that lowered the coffin down into the ground, and everyone threw dirt on top of it. Stella tossed in a couple of lottery tickets. One of the biddies dropped a picture of Jesus. My brother threw a yellow ribbon. I threw nothing, and neither did my father. Samantha leaned down and dropped a picture of Frank Sinatra, one in which his eyes were tinted to look extra blue and his skin was all smooth and velvety. At that, Stella began to cry, big, fat tears rolling down her cheeks. Samantha put her hand on her back and walked Stella over to a tree. 'It's all right,' she murmured.

We paraded back down the hill to the car. There would be old biddies coming over to my grand-mother's house for an after-funeral party, if you could call it that, and there would be cabbage rolls and various other things cooked in a Crock Pot. Tomorrow morning we'd go back to Brooklyn and resume our normal lives of ignoring each other.

'So this is Cobalt,' my father said, sweeping his

arm around. He sounded disappointed – maybe because we obviously didn't love it. I walked a little closer to my father. He looked the same as he did before my mother vanished: his face was clean-shaven, his shoulders strong, his legs muscular from – years ago, now – cycling in Prospect Park. If he passed my mother on the street, she would still easily recognize him, but would he recognize her? What if she had really changed?

My father stopped in front of a tombstone. He made a small choking sound and stepped back. I looked down. The grave marker said *Kay Mulvaney, 1953–1970*.

'That's your friend's girlfriend, isn't it?' I whispered.

He nodded. The wind pushed up against our backs. My father crouched down and put his ear to the grass and whispered something I couldn't hear. In a few seconds, he stood back up and brushed the grass and dry dirt off his suit. 'Come on,' he said to me.

I couldn't rightly determine his expression. He started walking toward the others, but I stayed where I was.

'Dad?' I called quietly, my heart pounding. He stopped. 'Why did you say you were separated?'

He stood very still.

'To that funeral director guy. He asked if you were married, and you said you were separated. Is that what's going on?'

He lowered his arms to his side and walked back to me. I watched a hawk circle twice around the graves before he responded. 'What was I supposed to tell him, Summer? The truth?'

'I don't know.'

'It's like when someone says "How are you?" Do you say, "Well, my head hurts and I'm lonely and depressed and I'm worried about everything and the world is collapsing and full of evil?" Or do you say, "I'm fine?"'

I couldn't help but smile. 'You usually go for the longer version.'

He paused. 'I suppose I do, yes.'

'You could've just said pickle.'

'What?'

I closed my eyes, aching again. The memory of the time I'd spent with Philip was slipping farther and farther away with every passing minute. 'Nothing.'

The rain finally stopped. Our feet sank into the wet, loamy grass. We passed a whole section for the Elkerson family. I tilted my head to the sky, expecting to see the thick black smoke from the soldier's rifles. Instead, I saw a rainbow.

'I got a letter from her,' my father said quietly. 'Two weeks ago.'

I gaped at him.

'It said . . . it said she was all right. She asked about you.'

'Where does she live? What is she doing? Are you going to *respond*?'

'Maybe. I don't know.' He picked at a loose thread on his jacket. 'She mentioned a divorce, though. Said she could make it very easy. It's probably the best thing.'

'Did she tell you where she lives? Did she give you a return address?'

He kicked at the grass. 'Long Island. East Hampton. Do you know where that is?'

'The beach, right?'

He nodded. 'But it was only a post-office box. It doesn't mean anything. She could have things forwarded from there.'

'Did you tell Steven?'

'No. But I'm going to. When all this is done.'

A hot, bitter taste rose to the back of my throat. 'Dad, I'm sorry.'

He looked at me curiously. 'What are *you* sorry for?'

I thought of the spiny, crackling snaps under my skin, the day I yelled at him and slammed my bedroom door. How his face had crumpled, how he'd looked so devastated. I shook my head, afraid to say more.

After the snow globe incident, when my father was in the psych ward, he wore a nightgown that stopped at his knees, and then, later, pale green hospital scrub pants. He said his roommate smacked his lips in his sleep. In the ward's lobby was a bulletin board with construction-paper balloons pinned to it. Someone had printed each patient's name in the middle of each balloon. I didn't cry when I saw my dad's hospital bracelet, or the curled-up, mumbling woman in the corner, or the jagged scar on my father's palm. I didn't cry when I asked him what it felt like, suffering with whatever had befallen him, and he replied, 'It's something that's been inside me for a long time. And you fight and fight and fight against it for so long, but then, it just crashes over you and pulls you down.' But when I saw his name written in one of those construction-paper balloons, *Richard*, optimistically, innocently, I had to turn away from him, duck my head into the water fountain as if I desperately needed a drink.

We sat in the common room and he pulled a hand-drawn card from the scrub pants' small back pocket. 'Here,' he said. It was a gelatinous map of the world; he'd penciled in each individual country, body of water, mountain ranges, and even added some fish in the oceans and birds in the sky – birds, come to think of it, that looked a lot like the drawings on the graves in Philip's back-yard. Everything on the map was right: France was next to Belgium, Germany and Switzerland. Japan was to the right of Korea. He even got all of the newly independent Soviet Union countries in the right places: Belarus and Estonia and Uzbekistan. Somewhat arbitrarily, he'd drawn a stick person over Spain, and another over Australia. There was a line between the two of them, linking them together. Inside, the card said, *Me and You.*

We walked now in silence, catching up with the others. 'Hey,' my father said, stopping short halfway down the cemetery's wildflower-strewn hill. 'You know what's over there?' He pointed to a house.

'What?' I asked.

'Old man Cross's trampoline.' He shaded his eyes. 'I wonder if it's still there.'

'It is,' Pete answered. 'I drove by before you got here the other day.'

They exchanged a glance. 'You want to go?' my dad asked.

'Sure,' Pete said.

'Summer? Steven?' My father looked at us. Suddenly, he could be eighteen, the age when he left Cobalt for good. Pete giggled beside him.

'Nah,' Steven said quickly.

'I'll go,' I offered.

'Of course you will,' my father said, and took my hand.

L et me start off by saying that it's all right that you haven't been in touch. I understand how busy your life must be, what with your new job – your sister told me a little about it. For what it's worth, I'm extremely proud.

And I get, too, how life can snow you under so quickly. Even here, I find myself so busy. There are so many activities they encourage us to try, like ceramics, book discussions, tai chi on the front lawn – a whole crowd goes to that, thinking it will work as well as antidepressants. Recently, I took my first tennis lesson. As it gets warmer, I'll be able to practice more and more. There's something very soothing about tennis, especially thwacking the ball against a brick wall all alone.

A lot of things here make me think of you. Not long into my stay, I noticed a starling with only one leg. He managed to get around all right, but it still looked so difficult and painful. I gave him my extra crusts of bread and coaxed him to hop up on my finger. The gray cat started coming around not long after, small and skinny and with a pus-filled eye. I tried to catch her, but cats aren't like dogs – they're slaves to no one. I snagged a can of tuna and an opener from the kitchen, opened it on the lawn, and hid behind the hedges. It took a while, but the cat finally slunk to the can and eagerly began to eat.

Not long after, there was a terrible storm, washing debris onto the walkways, knocking down branches, cutting off our power for a few hours in the middle of the night. I worried about my animals – had they found shelter? Were they cold? I worried so much, I started scratching the skin on my arms raw, and the staff had to settle me down. The following day, the animals were right back in their regular spots, hopping about, begging for food. It made me realize how much tougher animals are than humans. Kind of pathetic, really.

Since then, the people here have helped me understand why I do these kinds of things for animals, why the tug I feel inside is so powerful. I could have swerved, you see. There was time, a few, fat seconds, where I could have gripped the wheel and wrenched it to the right. I remember, all too painfully, the heaviness of the deer's body, the deafening thunk of impact. I will never forget that moment, or the moments that came after.

Maybe it isn't true – maybe there was no time to react. But since then, I've lived my life as though there was. So I wanted to write you to tell you that I understand, I think, what you were going through a while back. The way you felt about the military, about the bombing. How you connected it to other things. I know what it feels like to watch something happen and wish, going forward, that you could do something, **anything**, to change at least your world, the people around you, to keep everything close to you safe. But you don't have to live that way, as you've made no fatal mistakes. You've done nothing wrong. I hope you realize that.

And maybe you don't feel that way anymore, anyway – your life seems so different, richer, at least from what Summer has said. I hope that's the case. I hope that one day, my life will be different and richer, too, but from this vantage point, sitting here in this little room, it's so hard to know.

PART III

BROOKLYN, NEW YORK, JUNE, 1998

acting for beginners

CHAPTER 11

I sat in the waiting room at the dentist's office. It was a new dentist in Lower Manhattan; I'd switched from my old one in Brooklyn when he moved his practice to New Jersey. The office walls were painted lavender, and there were the typical array of *Life* magazines on the coffee tables. A glossy poster across from me asked, What Are Molar Sealants? Another crowed, Let's Talk Gingivitis! The ceiling fan rattled around, its cords swinging. When I came in, the receptionist announced that the air conditioner was broken. She was very defensive, as if someone had tried to blame her for not knowing how to fix air conditioners. The room felt thick and close. It was nearly a hundred degrees outside and only June.

The door to the back opened, and an assistant in a green smock looked around. 'Summer Davis?'

A few fluffy, expectant seconds passed. I knew I should stand up, but I didn't. I wasn't sure why.

'Summer Davis?' the girl called again. She looked at her clipboard, then at the receptionist. 'Is Summer here?'

The receptionist swiveled the phone receiver

away from her mouth and surveyed the waiting room. 'I could've sworn,' she said. I picked at a nonexistent stain on my jeans.

The assistant tugged at her scrub shirt. Down the hall, the dentist turned on the suction device. I heard a tube sucking up someone's saliva. Then, the drill.

'All right,' the assistant said, pausing to look at what must have been a roster behind the door. 'How about Marion Campbell, then? Marion, are you here?'

And Marion, an older woman whose glasses hung on a hot-pink, charm-riddled chain, stood up gratefully. When the door closed behind them, I considered telling the receptionist that I was Summer Davis, and had been all along. Just to see the look on her face. Instead, I asked her for the key code to the bathroom, which was in the office building's hall. She wrote it down on a Post-it and handed it to me wordlessly, her eyes shifting back and forth, as if it were something very dear and private.

In the bathroom, I pulled out the cell phone my father had bought for me for emergencies and called the dentist's office. 'This is Summer Davis,' I said, my voice sounding churchly and impressive in the echoing tiled room. I told the receptionist I was doing lab work and couldn't make my cleaning. The receptionist's voice, just a few walls away, sounded weary but unbothered. 'How about Wednesday?' she said. I thought for a moment – my father's procedure was tomorrow, Tuesday. It was almost impossible to think of something as mundane as a dentist's appointment happening the day after that, but I told her to pencil me in anyway.

When I hung up, I stared at myself in the spotty mirror, trying to focus on both pupils at the same time. But that was the thing – I couldn't do it. I had to concentrate on one pupil or the other. 'This is Summer Davis,' I said to the mirror. But for one brief, beguiling second, it had been sort of nice not to be.

The Greenwich Diner kept its Christmas decorations up all year, so when I passed through the swinging front door, I was greeted by an animated Mrs Claus standing on top of the hostess stand. Her white hair was in a bun, her delicate doll lips puckered into a smile, and she wore tiny, wire-framed glasses. Her legs moved back and forth, making the velvet of her red pantsuit swish. Beneath that, I heard a small squeaking noise: the plastic of her inner thighs brushing together. I felt embarrassed for her.

Dr Hughes hadn't arrived yet, so I slid into the first open booth and took out my notebook. The pamphlet fell out, the one about the fellowship. *Dr Shea is known for his connections to genetic communities around the world,* said a random snippet.

This was going to be the second time I'd met

Dr Hughes, my NYU biology adviser, at this diner. It was the middle of the day, past lunch, so there were only a few old ladies in a booth behind me, all slowly drinking milkshakes. More Mrs Clauses gathered behind the counter, along with Santa and his elves and a toy train. Next to me were a bunch of dog-eared *Time* magazines, including one I remembered on the newsstands over a year ago – Timothy McVeigh in a white sweatshirt and orange prison pants, all ready for his sentencing for the Oklahoma City bombing. He leaned forward, staring at the camera calmly, as if to say, *Why should I feel guilty for anything*? Should He Die? the headline implored.

A waiter leaned down. 'Coffee?'

I jumped. 'Sure.'

'You startling my students again, Victor?' Dr Hughes suddenly hovered over my table.

The waiter pulled her chair back and Dr Hughes sat. We'd met when I was in her junior-level Principles of Genetics class five months ago. Upon entering college, I gravitated to biology, barely looking at the major requirements for English Literature or Art History. It was only natural that I would study genetics, as it had been the only thing that had held my interest for years. The first few freshman and sophomore-level biology classes were simple and basic, but once I got to Dr Hughes's level, things became complicated, full of diseases to memorize, case studies, new technical methods by which to isolate DNA, a lot of genotypes and

158

markers and chemicals and a *lot* of problem sets. At that level, we were learning how to look for mutations in a gene, and that these mutations could lead to dire outcomes, impacting not only our general health, but also our behavior and psychological well-being.

I'd studied harder for her class than I ever studied for anything before, gobbling up the information. A few days after the first exam, Dr Hughes had pulled me aside and told me she wanted to meet me here, at this diner. I had never said a word to her before that.

Dr Hughes had stared at me when I walked down the diner's aisle toward her. I was wearing a long skirt, and so was she. I thought perhaps she might be angry that we were dressed too similarly. When I reached her booth, she said, 'You got every question on my exam correct.'

'Every single question?' I repeated.

'Yes. No one has done that before.'

Not the group of Russian boys who sat up front and answered everything? Not the overweight girl in the back who seemed to have the textbook memorized? Not the pale, fleshy boy named Dieter who wore the athletic-inspired t-shirt that said *Watsoncrombie & Crick, Genetics Department*? I was a little bit afraid of people in the genetics class – they took themselves so seriously.

'I'm sorry.' It was the only thing I could think to say.

'Don't apologize.' She narrowed her small,

brown eyes. 'But how did you get every question right?'

'I don't know. I studied.'

Her mouth fell open. Apparently, this was novel to her. I had paused, still not sure if I should sit down.

Now, Dr Hughes blotted her forehead with a napkin. 'This humidity is killing me. I need to live somewhere dry. Arizona. Or maybe California.'

'My brother's in California,' I volunteered.

'Lucky.' She clucked her tongue. 'What's he doing out there?'

'He's at Berkeley, taking some graduate classes. Or at least that's what he was doing last time I talked to him.' After my father told Steven that my mother had written him a letter, proving she was alive, Steven had dropped his fascination with terrorists, which made me wonder if he truly had linked the two things together. He'd taken off for California that following year. We got letters from him every once in a while – he was taking computer science classes and doing freelance work for various Internet start-ups. Everyone in Northern California, he intimated, was doing free-lance work for Internet start-ups.

Dr Hughes settled down and looked at the menu, pushing up the sleeves of her thick, cable-knit sweater. She dressed more like an artist than a scientist, and had stiff, frizzy, salt-and-pepper hair, a long, thin nose, and glasses that magnified her eyes. She liked to yell at people during class, to

160

give impossible exams, to say, on the first day, while passing out the syllabus, 'We move fast because science moves fast. If you can't keep up, I suggest you study something in the liberal arts.' She called everyone by their last name – *Davis, Cameron, Lorie*. She never specified gender, and admitted to me once that she hated how the science departments were disproportionately male.

'You have any trouble getting down here?' Dr Hughes asked, spreading her napkin on her lap. 'I heard there was a water main break uptown.'

'No,' I said. 'I only had to come across the bridge, from Brooklyn Heights.'

'Ah.' She held up a crooked, bony finger. 'Right. You're in Brooklyn. For some reason I keep thinking you're uptown. So many other students are, I guess.' She leaned forward. 'So. Let's talk about your fellowship application. I got everything. It all looks good.'

I blushed. 'Thanks.'

'You have one more class you need to take to graduate, right?'

'It's just an independent study. I can work on it this summer.'

'Your essays make sense. Your recommendations, of course, are impeccable. As are your grades. If you want to study genetics, Dublin is perfect right now.' She laced her fingers together. 'But there's a problem. You forgot to submit your personal statement. You read the application, right? You were supposed to include one.'

'I read it.' I scratched the back of my elbow, listening to Mrs Claus's plastic body parts squeak. 'I just . . . I didn't know what to say.'

'And so you just didn't include it at all?'

'Yeah. Basically.'

'That's not like you.'

And it wasn't, from what she knew of me. For the remainder of her class, I'd aced every single one of her exams. I loved crossing green flowering plants with white flowering ones and knowing exactly what I would get. I loved locating a mutation on a gene or an indication that a certain gene to code a protein-making enzyme was present.

'*Do* you want to do this?' Dr Hughes inspected me carefully.

'I do. I think I do. It's just . . . I don't know. When I see the words, *Write a personal statement,* I just freeze up.'

She dumped some sugar into her coffee, which had magically appeared before her. 'It's a simple paragraph. Why you like genetics. Why you want to study this before going to medical school. Why this field speaks to you. We're not talking Shakespeare.'

I sighed.

'Perhaps you don't feel comfortable with making a big change like this right now.'

'No, I am,' I answered slowly. Then, realization wound around me. *She knew.*

I knew this, of course. I shouldn't have been so surprised.

When she leaned forward again, the vinyl booth made a helpless, merciful squeak. 'I heard about your father. The type of treatment he's going to try.'

I swallowed very slowly.

'Leon mentioned it to us,' she added.

Leon was my father's partner at the lab. And Dr Hughes's husband was Leon's best friend. That first time Dr Hughes and I met here, she'd asked me if I had any other doctors in my family, and I said my father was a medical researcher, studying melanoma. She let out a note of delight and said what a coincidence; a friend of her husband's did the exact same thing. And then I laughed. 'It's not Leon Kimball, is it?' Dr Hughes's mouth parted and she said, 'Yes, how do you know that?' And it went from there. Afterward, my father told me he had met Dr Hughes and her husband plenty of times – she often came into the office to say hello to Leon, to pick him up so they all could go to lunch. 'Why didn't you mention it?' I asked my father angrily. 'Hadn't Leon told you that his best friend's wife teaches in the biology department at NYU? Isn't that something that would stick out in your mind, considering I'm a biology major?' My father had blankly shrugged, telling me not to be so hard on him, that he had a lot on his mind.

'It starts tomorrow, doesn't it?' Dr Hughes asked gently.

'That's right,' I answered quietly.

'Does it make you uncomfortable that we're talking about this?'

'It's fine.' *Pickle*, I thought – a little sadly.

'Where is he now?'

'He's at . . . home. But, I mean, he's okay. Really.'

'It's just that, I want you to know what you'd be getting yourself into. This is an amazing opportunity for you, if you want it. But it's a lot of money we're giving away, the stipend and the travel and the tuition. Please don't think I'm trying to pressure you, or that I'm not sensitive to the magnitude of your situation right now, but there are other students who could use the scholarship if you're not interested. And it does mean you'd be in another country for quite a while. It would probably be good to know, one way or another, which way you're leaning.'

I'd known this whole time she could only sponsor one student. There were so many other people begging for this kind of attention.

'My dad has help,' I said hoarsely. 'There's a woman there, Cora, who is sort of . . . I don't know. His assistant, I guess. I mean, she cleans the house, she makes sure he's taking things . . . I don't know what else. But she's always there. She lives there. I arranged it. I mean, I'm there, too . . . and I'm going to be taking him to his actual appointments. I guess people wake up disoriented, so . . .'

I began to pick apart my paper napkin. 'It's not

164

as if he's really . . . *ill*. He just gets sad. His brain is resistant to drugs, we think. Apparently they do the . . . procedure all the time. They say he won't feel anything.'

I trailed off. My voice was shaking too much.

'I know that.' Dr Hughes folded her hands. 'It's none of my business. I shouldn't have brought it up.' She drained her coffee, put her napkin on the table, laid down a few crumpled bills, and stood. I followed. 'You know what you can handle. I trust you. Just turn in the essay and the statement and I'll put in the paperwork.'

'Okay,' I said. 'Good.'

'I'm sorry, again,' she added.

'It's all right,' I answered, a beat too late. '*I'm* sorry.' Although I wasn't sure what I was sorry for – showing emotion, maybe.

On that snowy day a few months ago when Dr Hughes and I first made the connection – 'You're *that* Richard Davis's daughter?' she'd asked – her face had registered a small, unrehearsed moment of horror. It was *the* look. The look that told me that Leon had told her all he knew and had witnessed – which included a few of my father's public breakdowns.

I allowed the look to cross her face without challenging it. I pretended not to see it at all, deciding to give her a chance to have a new, more tempered response. 'My father's not doing so well right now,' I'd said, my eyes on the table, giving her space to properly react. 'He has clinical depression.

He's been on disability for a while, but I think he's going to have to resign from the practice altogether.'

And she got to say, 'Yes, Leon mentioned it. I'm so sorry. It's got to be hard.'

Perhaps *that* was why Dr Hughes didn't intimidate me: I loved the fearless way she taught, but I know she was just as impressionable and sensitive as anyone. When I left the diner, that first time, I thought about how I let her reaction pass by without commenting. It was the easiest thing to do, of course – if I had called her out on it and asked her to explain, then *I* would have had to explain, which might have meant admitting everything that scared *me*.

And then, seconds later, I felt somehow responsible – perhaps there could have been a way for me to have warned Dr Hughes, told her who my father was in advance so she could have her moment of horror in private. But warned her *how*, exactly? I felt so uncomfortable with myself and the situation, I stopped in the middle of the sidewalk, closed my eyes, clenched up my fists, and breathed. When I opened my eyes, I was so amazed that the submarine-round windows of the St Vincent's medical facility were still there. And the Two Boots Pizza take-away across the street. The entire city was in its right place. I sort of thought it couldn't be.

CHAPTER 12

Later, when I unlocked the front door to the apartment, all of the dogs – Fiona, Wesley, Skip, and Gracie, the Smitty dog – greeted me. 'Where's Dad?' I asked them, their eyes wet and bright. They ran excitedly into the living room, comprehending. My father was in his usual spot on the couch, propped up on his knees and looking over the back of it at something out the window. Seven glasses of water, all at varying levels, were on the coffee table, along with a bunch of newspapers and the TV remote.

'Hi,' I announced.

He jumped and turned around. 'Summer.'

He was wearing the t-shirt and gym shorts I had given him the Christmas of my freshman year, during one of his active spells when he said he was going to start lifting weights at the Y. And even though I saw him every day, I still wasn't used to the beard, or that his hair was so much longer, or that he wore oversized, square glasses instead of contacts. He had gained thirty pounds from the latest drug he was on. When he took other types of medications, he drooled. Or he twitched, an arm or a thigh, the side of his hip or an eyelid. When he turned his hand a certain way, I saw the mark from the snow globe in the pit of his palm. There were new scars, too, as distinct as tattoos: cross-hatchings on his elbow from the time he broke a plate, the half-moon on his wrist from the hunting knife, the puffy, wrinkled crater near his collarbone from the lit cigarette.

'They towed another car,' my father announced, his eyes bright and wide. The dangerous look. 'The blue Volvo, the bastards.'

'Ah.' I dropped the apartment keys in the bowl on the credenza.

'It was this morning. Three trucks. And the police came this time. It must have been stolen. They surrounded the car.'

He hefted the window open, cold wind swirling in. He put one hand on his hip. 'I'm thinking that white Lincoln might be next. It's got a sticker on it. See?'

I looked at the white car he was pointing at. 'Uh huh.' I stepped away from the draft, leaning against the credenza. I gazed at an old photo of my father and me standing at the top of a snow-covered hill in Prospect Park, wearing snow pants and heavy coats and carrying a single plastic sled between us. We always used to go down the hill using just one sled, my father lying on his stomach, me piled on top of him.

'How do you feel today?' I asked.

'Like shit,' he singsonged, not turning from the window.

'What kind of shit? Cat shit? Dog shit?' I never meant to sound frustrated, but I always came off that way.

In another room, one of the dogs barked.

'Where's Cora?' I asked, trying to soften my voice.

My father pressed his head against the glass of the window. 'I let Cora go. Look! Didn't I tell you? Here comes the tow truck. I thought they'd give that Lincoln another couple days, but I guess not.'

'You *fired* Cora?' I sank into the couch. 'Why?'

'Summer! This is our lucky day.' He pointed at the tow truck. 'Watch how they load it up. Have you ever seen this? It's beautiful.'

'*Dad.* Why did you fire her?'

His shoulders lowered. He turned around and picked up the rain stick that was leaning up against the couch. It was supposed to simulate the sounds of the rainforest; he'd bought it a few months ago when we went into the Nature Store. Sometimes, late at night, I heard him turning it over and over, a million tiny downpours. 'I didn't need her,' he said, sulking. 'She was always here. She was watching me.'

'Of course she was always here! That's her job, to be here!'

'She brought a Neil Diamond CD here. Neil *Diamond,* Summer.'

'I'm sorry.'

169

'Even your mother didn't listen to Neil Diamond.' He shuddered. 'I'm fine. This is so exaggerated.'

'You think so?'

'I feel all right. I've *been* feeling all right.'

At least he was talking today. At least he was watching the cars. Some days, he couldn't even do that. I wondered if I should call up the clinic in the hospital and cancel the whole thing. Because you couldn't do just one treatment and decide, *Nah, I don't like it.* Once you started, you had to do all six. Or eight. Or however many the doctor deemed appropriate. For my father, the doctor had decided on eight. Words repeated in my head: *He will have eight seizures. His brain will be electrocuted eight times.*

'So do you want me to cancel tomorrow?' I asked quietly. 'Is that what you want?'

He didn't answer. Outside, the guy operating the tow truck attached the illegally parked Lincoln to its hitch. My father's shoulders hunched.

'I'm going to call Cora.' I walked into the hall toward the kitchen, all the dogs following. 'She needs to come back. She'll come back, right? You didn't say anything really terrible to her?'

'Summer . . .' My father was behind me fast.

I curled my hand over the receiver. 'What?'

He gave me a pleading, desperate look. Then, without answering, he walked into the kitchen, bumping a stack of mail teetering precariously on one of the island barstools. A magazine fell to the floor. On the back was an ad for perfume: a naked

170

woman kissing a naked man. I turned the magazine over. *Vogue*.

'I thought I cancelled this.' I held it up to show him.

He shrugged. 'I renewed it.'

'Dad . . .' I slammed it down on the island too hard. Some of the subscription renewal forms fell out and slid across the tile.

'What? I might read *Vogue*. Ever think that?'

'You wouldn't read *Vogue*.' I turned it over and looked at the mailing address. RICHARD DAVIS. At least it wasn't in her name. 'I don't understand these magazines.' I held up the cover, Cindy Crawford in a bikini. 'She looks constipated.'

'I think she looks nice. She looks like a woman.' He glanced at me.

'What's that supposed to mean?'

'What's what supposed to mean?'

'That look.'

He flipped through the mail. 'I didn't give you any looks.'

'What, I should go around wearing a bikini like she does?'

'No. Of course not.' He bent back the edge of a flyer. 'Although, it wouldn't kill you to wear something other than jeans once in a while.'

'There's nothing wrong with wearing jeans,' I snapped.

'Except that a dress is more ladylike.'

And a suit is more masculine, instead of pajama pants. 'Got me there. You win. Some day when I go off in the world, I'll wear lots of dresses. Some day when I leave.'

I should have known better. My button: jeans. His: leaving. But who dared press the buttons of someone who was depressed? Someone who could turn on a dime, and – just like he was doing now – start to cry? My father shut his eyes and tried to hold it in. Who dared do this? What dark, evil person?

I crumpled. 'Dad, no . . . stop. Let's not do this.'

'I wish I were someone else. I wish I weren't me.'

'But . . . come on. You're wonderful.'

'No.'

'Dad.'

I leaned into the crook of his neck, but he refused to touch me. 'I can't have you mad at me. You're my good girl.'

'I'm not mad at you.'

'Yes you are. You want to leave.'

I leaned against the fridge. *It's a huge opportunity*, Dr Hughes said about the fellowship. *You'll be away from home*. I had told my father about the fellowship – that it was a prestigious chance to study in my field. I changed one detail, however: I told him it was in New York, not wherever the interesting fieldwork was happening overseas – in my case, Dublin. I didn't know I was going to get this far in the application process. It just happened. Dr Hughes had said, *Apply, you'll certainly get it, we all believe in you*, but I really hadn't thought she'd meant it.

Later, I told myself. *Tell him later. Tell him everything later.* I thought of the flyer I found the other day, the one with her name printed in large block letters, a date, a place, a topic. I'd kept that from him, too.

He looked straight at me. 'I'm terrified, Summer. Of tomorrow. I don't know if I want to do it.'

Then don't, I wanted to say. 'But it might help you feel better.'

'What if it doesn't?'

'It will.'

I didn't want to take him to the procedure tomorrow, either. It sounded medieval. When trying to imagine how it might work, I felt like I was wandering into a wilderness where I had no compass or bearings.

'Are you sure?' he asked.

I nodded furiously. 'The doctor says eighty per cent of patients feel better.' I held on to anything. I held on to percentages, hearsay, catchphrases.

'Eighty per cent? But that means there are twenty per cent that don't.'

'You'll feel better,' I assured him. 'Don't worry about it. So what are you going to do today?'

He shrugged.

'Do you want to do something? Go out to lunch?'

'I don't think so.' He glanced at me. 'You know what you should do today? You should give that coat back.'

I half smiled. I had taken a poncho from

173

someone at a party; I'd told him it was an accident, but he wouldn't let it drop. 'The coat's owner lives in the Bronx,' I said. 'That's an hour away by train.'

He opened *Vogue* to the middle. 'You really shouldn't go around stealing coats that aren't yours. At least you could have taken one with money in the pockets, you know?'

'True,' I laughed.

He leaned in for a hug. He smelled as he always had, like cinnamon gum and soap. It was comforting to think that his smell hadn't changed, even though everything else about him had. If I closed my eyes and breathed in, I could almost imagine him as the man he was when I was eight, the father in the leather-framed picture on the credenza. It had just snowed, and he was standing on a hill in Prospect Park, a plastic sled in hand, a red, pilly hat coming to a point on the top of his head. I was running toward him, burying myself in the soft folds of his coat, and in seconds, we would pile onto the sled and go down the hill together.

There were certain things I wished I hadn't turned my head to see. Once, I saw a car hit a bicyclist head-on, his spandexed body flying into the air and landing jaggedly on the pavement. He did a whole flip in the air. He may have broken his back, maybe his neck. I didn't stand around to watch; enough people already were. Another time, I saw a Chinese man slap his kid, a six-year-old girl, across the face, as she was coming down the slide at a park. All she was doing was sliding.

My father used to make me look at skin cancer photos, to deter me against smoking or drinking or going into the sun without sunscreen or putting anything carcinogenic into my body. A woman had an enormous melanoma on her leg; it had gotten so bad that the black, puckered welt had eaten straight to her bone.

I could have walked right past the flyer last week without seeing it. There weren't any others of its kind on other phone poles or parking signs. But my head turned that direction; I walked by it and saw it and there it was.

The Learning Annex Presents Meredith Heller, it said. *Acting For Beginners.*

And then a description: *Pennsylvania native and stage actress Meredith Heller teaches you the basic techniques of acting. Beginners welcome!*

It gave a date a few weeks in the future. And a location – the Mayflower Hotel, on Sixty-first Street and Central Park West. And a time.

There was no picture, but her name glowed like an isotope. Of course she had dropped 'Davis' and returned to just 'Heller'. And yes, she was from Pennsylvania. But how likely was it that she had become an actress? If a computer randomly came up with a possible fate, it wouldn't have hit upon this.

After my father wrote my mother back,

permitting their divorce, he attempted to hold it together. But eventually, something inside him just gave up. He stopped going to work entirely. He made the couch his permanent residence. And then he couldn't do much of anything. He wanted to die, he said over and over again. Time felt painful. Every second felt painful. Like needles, like a branding iron singeing his skin. He was sick of things hurting.

I brought him cold washcloths and tried to listen. I filled out the medical disability leave paperwork and submitted it to his office. I knew the people at his NYU lab personally. Leon Kimball. Bethany the lab assistant. They smiled and patted my shoulder and all signed an over-sized Get Well Soon card of a cartoon cat with a plaster cast on its leg.

I stared at the Acting For Beginners flyer for a long time. People passed by. Some of them bumped into me. I was standing in the middle of the street in the East Village, near a bus stop. I tried to imagine the people that would go to an Acting For Beginners Learning Annex seminar: gray-haired, jowl-faced East Village types, the kinds who lived in rent-controlled apartments but still solicited for roommates. They would come and take off their shoes at the door and sit in a circle on the linoleum and get into the guttural humming exercises and the role-playing. And where would my father and I sit? In chairs? On the floor? We might stand at the back of the room, in the shadows. We would hide and make small noises and not participate.

I came home and didn't tell him. We made spaghetti and I was the only one who ate it and I didn't tell him. We watched television and my father moaned softly and I didn't tell him. The secret beat in me like a second heart. *Meredith Heller, Meredith Heller.* Perhaps she did climb up on a stage and change completely. That was what she wanted, wasn't it? To change?

The next day, I met my father at his psychiatrist's office at New York Presbyterian, the whole way up on Sixty-eighth Street – I was going to take him out to a quiet dinner afterwards. Dr North popped his head into the waiting room, a weary smile on his face. 'You want to come into my office for a sec, Summer?'

My father sat on a leather couch, and Dr North settled at his desk. When I sank down into a leather chair adjacent to the big picture window that looked out onto York Avenue, Dr North said, 'So. We're thinking of treating your father with electroconvulsive therapy.'

I looked searchingly at my father. 'Are you serious?'

My father shrugged, then looked at Dr North. 'Are we?'

'Now, we talked about this,' Dr North encouraged him. He turned back to me. 'Medication isn't working. We need to try something else.'

'I don't want to feel this way anymore,' my father volunteered.

So don't, I wanted to say. *Just turn it off.*

'ECT has come a long way. It's very humane,' the doctor said.

Dr North proceeded to explain how it would work: they put a patient on muscle relaxants and administered a shock that produced a seizure in the brain. The only way the doctors could see the seizure was through a tiny twitch in the patient's foot and by a computer recording of the patient's brainwaves. Once the brainwaves settled down, the seizure was over.

It was like rebooting a computer, Dr North said. Afterwards, many patients felt better.

'How?' I asked.

'How what?'

'How do patients feel better? How does it happen?'

Dr North scratched his head. 'Well, it's not definitive. We think that the shock releases neuro-transmitters in the brain, which helps to lift the depression.'

'I've heard it's because it causes brain damage,' I said.

My father shifted on the chair, making the leather crinkle.

'It doesn't.' Dr North slid his platinum Rolex around his wrist.

'Will he feel it?' I asked. 'What happens when he's done? Are there . . . scars?'

'He won't feel anything. When he's done, he might feel sleepy, or calm, or sometimes anxious

178

. . . it can vary. And no, there aren't scars.' He chuckled. 'The major side effect is memory loss, especially right after. Just bits and pieces, though. Little things. Nothing important.'

My father said he had to use the bathroom before we left, so I had a few moments alone with Dr North. 'Is this really necessary?' I whispered to him. 'I mean, he's gone to the hospital a lot, yes. But isn't there some other medication he could try? Something . . . else?'

The doctor fiddled with his burgundy tie. 'Nothing else is working.'

'But he's not even that *sick*,' I protested. 'Not always, anyway.'

The doctor looked at me very evenly. 'If you're worried about how it might affect his mind, it won't. And believe me, it's safe. It's not cruel. He won't even feel it. And as for memory, he might forget simple things, like names. But not permanently.'

'How do you know that?' I asked.

'Experience and research, Summer. We're professionals, and it's a difficult decision, one that I know is hard to hear. But having diagnosed your father with the best of our ability, we think this will help him.' He cocked his head. 'He'll need support through it. You have to believe it will help, too. You have to have faith.'

That was what it came down to – faith. I had to believe, just like people believed when they went to church. But I had believed – I'd believed

179

in the medicine and the psych ward and the therapy and time off and staying here in my child-hood apartment instead of living in NYU's dorms. I had believed in not seeing friends, not having a boyfriend, rushing home after classes in order to make sure he was all right, keeping things even and steady. It went back as long ago as the day of my grandmother's funeral, when I wanted to run back to Philip's house and apologize for Steven pulling me away. But I didn't. I hated, too, that I'd told Philip about my mother and the snow globe incident, that I'd let him see such a flawed side of me. Then again, sometimes I wondered if I'd done it as a defense – so he'd know I was messed up, so he'd know to stay away.

'Is this kind of thing genetic?' I asked Dr North.

He looked uncomfortable. 'Well, there are some findings that say it might be. But it's hard to tell. But even if there are genetic links, a combination of environmental factors have to be at play, too. One generally doesn't work without the other.'

I leaned against the wall. Was this all curled up in his DNA? If I studied hard enough, would I be able to decipher and treat it? As much as I tried to forget about Mr Rice spouting out nonsense to my tenth grade class, I couldn't – not quite. Wouldn't it be nice if our DNA explained everything? Wouldn't it be nice if I found one of my mother's stray hairs, clinging to a sweater she'd left behind, put it under a microscope, and suddenly understand what had driven her to leave us? I could swab the inside of my father's cheek and decipher why he had crumbled. I could inspect my own blood and absolve or convict myself.

What else was possibly genetic? Messiness? Laziness? What about abandonment? What about duty – what, exactly, kept me here in Brooklyn, while my brother was okay with leaving? Perhaps my actions really could be attributed to a malformed piece of DNA that wasn't coding for the right protein. Perhaps genetics controlled things as minute as my dreams and my day-to-day actions, and I was bound to my decisions long before I made them. If I saw all that under a microscope, at least I'd know it was something deeply set inside of me, something I couldn't change.

'What am I supposed to do if this doesn't work?' I asked Dr North.

'What are *you* supposed to do?' Dr North repeated.

'Yes. What am I supposed to do?'

'We'll cross that bridge when we come to it. For now, try not to let this take over your life. I know it's sometimes unbearable. But it's not your fault. It's really not.'

The day after that was a Friday. I went into a sporting goods store on lower Broadway and asked an overweight, sloppy woman behind the counter if I could see a stun gun. It was smaller than I expected. 'Is it on?' I asked. She nodded. I hit the switch, watching the metal prongs toss the blue sparks back and forth.

I held my hand out. A hot snap went through me. 'Jesus Christ!' the saleswoman screamed. Two boys who had been looking at hunting rifles gawked. The surprise of the jolt had caused me to drop the gun to the floor. 'What the hell is wrong with you?' the saleswoman said.

I picked up the Taser and handed it back to her. My heart was racing, probably from the surprise. My thumb and pointer finger felt blue and numb from where I'd shocked them. It took only a minute or so, though, for the feeling to come back.

CHAPTER 13

On the morning of his first procedure, my father and I sat together on the subway, legs touching, even though there was hardly anyone else in the car. He pretended to be very interested in the Captain Morgan ad across the aisle. In the ad, people leaned on each other, holding half-empty tumblers of rum. All of them had fluorescent-green, swirly mustaches penciled in above their upper lips. Captain Morgan peeked out from behind a lamppost, girlish in his frilly shirt. *The Captain was here,* said the slogan in slashed, green, graffiti-like print.

My father turned to me. 'Now, if something happens, I want you to at least keep Wesley. I've contacted a rescue organization for the others. The number's on the fridge.'

'Nothing's going to happen to you.'

'I'm just saying.'

An Asian woman came through the car selling batteries, little plastic noisemakers, plastic key chains, Seek-And-Find word puzzles, Skittles candy. The loot was in a large box strapped to her chest. She waved the noisemakers in our faces and pantomimed a light show with a laser pointer. Something about the laser pointer reminded me of the statement I had tried to write this morning for my fellowship. *Explain your inspiration for pursuing a scientific career.* I had sat at my laptop, eating pretzels out of the bag, thinking and thinking and thinking. *I knew I wanted to study DNA when a substitute teacher stood up in front of our class and told me that all of our secrets, every single thing about us, is coded within our DNA, and if we look hard enough, we'll be able to figure it out. He was asked to leave after that, and later we found out he'd doctored his whole résumé. Still, what he said had a huge effect on me, greater than anything any other teacher taught me before or since.*

I had erased it and started over.

Although I would like to take this fellowship, I probably can't. I shouldn't, in fact, pursue medical school, either, because my father likes to drill pieces of glass into his arm and that takes up a lot of my time. I'm sorry.

My father had dressed up for the occasion, wearing a button-down shirt and carefully ironed khakis. His loafers were shined and his fingernails were clipped and he put his contacts in, although he was blinking furiously, not used to them yet. He hadn't shaved or gotten a haircut, but his hair was combed, his beard a bit less scraggly. At first, he came into the kitchen wearing a tie, but I told him to take it off. I couldn't imagine him lying there on the bed, electrodes hooked up to his temples, wearing a *tie*.

184

'Tell me something,' my dad said.

'Something what?'

'Something about your life. Did you give that coat back yesterday?'

I sighed. 'No.'

'What were you doing yesterday, then?'

'Nothing. Reading. I don't know.'

He made a clucking noise with his tongue. 'My daughter, the thief.'

'I didn't steal it. It was an accident.'

'Uh huh.'

The train's doors opened. The echoing sounds of a platform performer rushed in; a black man in dirty jeans and a brown, tattered sweater strummed a guitar and belted out 'Redemption Song'. He was good, but everyone was ignoring him. I could still hear him as the train pulled away.

'Well, tell me something else,' my father goaded. 'Just talk.'

I flared out my hands. 'I have to write a statement,' I blurted out. 'For that fellowship, the one I told you about.' *The one I didn't tell you everything about.* 'They want me to write an essay about why I want to be a scientist. And . . . and just about me, in general.'

'And?'

I wrapped my hands around my knees. 'And I don't know what to say.'

'Why not?'

'I don't know. I just . . . I'm not good at that sort of thing.'

My father settled back against the plastic seat. 'Aren't you becoming a scientist because of me?'

The subway rocked and rattled. Across the aisle, Captain Morgan whispered into a girl's ear. He looked like a transvestite. 'You?' I repeated.

'Well, sure. I always wanted you to study science. Your mother always wanted you to go into liberal arts, something like English or journalism or maybe even PR, like she was doing. But you picked science. I'm glad you did.'

It was that he just *assumed*. Like I didn't have a mind of my own, like I couldn't come to decisions for reasons unrelated to my past. The anger was palpable, like a paper cut slicing into my finger. I thought about what he'd said years ago in relation to his sickness: *I hope this never happens to you*. He just assumed we were coasting on the same fixed path in every regard, and there was nothing I could do about it. On one hand, it was what I believed in, but on the other, it was exactly what I fought against.

I looked away. 'It's not like I want to go into dermatology.'

He looked away, too, and I knew I'd hurt his feelings. Why didn't I just say yes, he was an influence? Yes, I liked science because he did?

'I probably won't even take the fellowship, anyway,' I mumbled. 'What's the point of writing anything?'

'Why wouldn't you take it?'

It's in Ireland. Which is a million miles away.

'You're lucky you have the opportunity to succeed, to go out into the world and do things,' he said. 'You're so lucky you can just go and do that.'

I suppressed a groan. *You can get up and do things, too. Stop making me feel bad about it.* 'It's just not very good timing.'

We faced front. The same Asian woman with the plastic toys barreled through again. A young girl across the aisle bought a hot pink plastic gun. She pointed the gun at her little sister. When she pulled the trigger, a firing noise sounded. My father shifted his weight. 'I told you about how when I got in that car accident, I looked right into the deer's eyes before we crashed, right?'

'Yes. I guess.'

He stared straight ahead, speaking out of the side of his mouth. 'I actually didn't realize Kay was hurt when I first saw her. I thought she was just sleeping.' He let out a small, aching laugh.

I peered at him, waiting. I never knew what to think when he brought up the accident – he only gave little pieces of it at a time, and I never was sure how to read them. The unsettling smell of urine floated through the air, then disappeared. In the next car, a baby began to wail. My father leaned his head on the window and closed his eyes, apparently choosing not to say anything else about it.

It was getting so hot in the car. The train ground to a stop, more people stuffed on, some of them

187

leaning over us with their sweaty armpits to read the subway map. I had the urge to dart through the gaping subway doors, up the stairs, and through the turnstile. Maybe I could run through the streets and hide in a doorway or a dumpster. I could nest by the recyclables. New York was so big and complicated, it would take a while to be found. I pressed my feet more firmly into the floor, ready to stand up and do it. But then the doors wheezed shut, and the subway took off again.

'So tell me something else,' my father said after a moment. 'Tell me about your friends.'

'What friends?'

'Your friends from school, I guess. The ones that live in the apartment building in the Village and are all in love with one another.'

I looked at him blankly.

'One of them is named Monica?' he reminded me.

I squinted, finally getting it. 'Wait. *Really*?'

He nodded, excited.

'Okay,' I said slowly, thinking. 'So . . . you know the one guy who had that part in that soap opera? Well, this girl started to stalk him. She thought that the soap was real, and that he was the doctor character.'

'Oh dear,' my father said, as the train rocked forward. 'A stalker.'

'Right. She was pretty nuts. And you know the zoologist guy's monkey he had to give up? He found out that the monkey is in town because he had a

188

part in a movie. So he went to visit him on the movie set. It was at the Central Park Zoo.'

'I love the Central Park Zoo,' my father exclaimed. 'Did the monkey recognize him?'

'Y-yes,' I said, hesitating, not really remembering.

'Good,' my father said. 'I'm glad monkeys recognize people, too. Dogs certainly do. Even if you're away for a long time, a dog won't forget you.'

These weren't people I knew. It was a plot synopsis of an episode of *Friends* I had watched two days ago. When my father had an earlier incident like this and asked me to tell him something, I'd told him about another episode of *Friends*, saying it was on TV, but he still didn't get it. He was TV illiterate, and always had been. I didn't have the heart to tell him the truth.

A battery, discarded on the floor, rolled from one side of the car to the other. The lights flickered on and off. And then it was Sixty-eighth Street, us. We got off, walked to the stairs, and climbed them.

The Saturday after I learned my father was going to have ECT treatments, I went to a party up at this girl Nadine's house in the Bronx. Nadine was part of NYU's biology program, too.

On my way there, I passed a Key Food grocery store. There was a kid on the crimson electronic rocking horse, screaming his head off. He tossed some Game Boy handheld thing on the ground every few seconds, and his mother stooped down to pick it up. When the horse ride ended, the boy whined that he wanted to do it over again. 'Why don't you ride the whale?' his mother suggested, pointing to the lower, smaller whale ride right next to the horse.

'I hate that whale!' the kid screamed, and took off into the store. His mother picked up his hand-held thing and followed him.

I tried to pass as quickly as possible. Every Key Food in the city had the same horse and the same whale in the front of their store. And every kid in the city loved the horse and hated the whale. But I loved the whale. He was so round and blue and happy. I worried that since he wasn't making enough money for Key Food, they'd take down the whales and replace them with something else – machines with a claw-grabber and toy prizes, maybe, the ones toddlers always climbed inside. And then where would the whales go? To some warehouse? To a junkyard, to be destroyed for scrap? As I passed, I imagined finding a ceramic shard of a whale's smile in some dumpster some-where. It would be heartbreaking.

The party was in a high-ceilinged, crumbling brownstone. By the time I got there, the place was already humidly stuffed with people. Nadine had moved her rickety, thrift-store furniture to one wall and set up a couple of folding tables for plastic bowls of chips and jugs of liquor. Nadine's black miniature poodle, his coat clipped so low you could see its black skin shining through, yapped from behind a baby gate.

I sat on the back of the couch and mixed equal amounts of rum and Pepsi into my cup. Then it became a splash more rum, and then hardly any cola at all. As I talked to people, a strange, soothing calmness came over me. *So this is what drunk feels like*, I thought. So this was why people got drunk so often. It felt like sliding into a pool on a hot summer day. So I drank more.

And then, it began to turn. At one point, I talked to Nadine herself. I'd always thought Nadine was kind of dorky – she'd entered NYU as an English major, and had part of a Yeats poem tattooed on her stomach. Our conversation started out normal, but then the whale ride popped into my head. While I was at this party, the whale was sitting in front of the grocery store, unused, unwanted, alone. My father was alone, too, sitting in the apartment in Brooklyn. He'd encouraged me to go to this party, saying I should get out more. I pictured him staring into an empty microwave, looking out the window, picking up a book and putting it down again. My eyes began to fill.

Nadine stopped mid-monologue. 'Summer,' she whispered, 'are you OK?'

'The whale . . .' I said. 'No one wants to ride him.'

She paused for a moment and lit another cigarette. 'Did you take those pills Randall was handing out? I swear to God, they were laced with something freaky.'

I shook my head. 'I'm not on anything. It's just that, the whale's all alone, and I don't know what to do.'

Nadine looked away uncomfortably. Then she smiled and laughed at some guy break dancing in the middle of the carpet, and moved toward him, done with me. I pushed my way past her and ran for her bedroom, knowing I'd given away too much.

Nadine's bedroom was empty. I climbed into her canopy bed, which was piled high with everyone's coats, and pulled the curtains around the sides to conceal me completely. I had never been on a bed like this before. It reminded me of Ebenezer Scrooge's bed, the one he sleeps in when the various ghosts of Christmas visit.

I burrowed under the coats, inhaling their owners' separate smells – cloying perfume, cigarettes, shawarma. The rum zoomed through my veins and my skin heaved, rising and falling like the bellows of an accordion. I heard the doorknob to the bedroom turn once, but someone said 'oh' and quickly shut it.

And then I didn't want to be under the pile of coats anymore. I slid out and opened the canopy's curtains. The sound was everywhere again. I considered climbing out the window, but there was no fire escape. I opened the door a crack and peeked out. Everyone had gathered in the main room. I had an easy shot to the door. I wouldn't have to say goodbye.

I did one more thing before I left: I looked back at the pile of coats and picked one off the top. It was a fringy poncho with tribal designs, jagged edges, and a drawstring neck. I didn't know whose it was; I couldn't imagine anyone at this party wearing something like this.

I put it on and cinched it tight. I wasn't me anymore. I was someone who wore ponchos. I was Native American. I slid out of the room and I dived for the door. No one said anything. No one was looking.

The ECT clinic was also at New York Presbyterian, a few buildings down from Dr North's office. The waiting room wasn't nearly as plushy or nice, though, but instead trapped in the Seventies, with gold patterned carpets and green, fake-leather couches.

A thin, pasty doctor motioned me into the hallway behind a door. His name was Dr Frum, which I immediately changed to Dr Frown, due to his humorless expression. 'This won't be too long,' he said. He went through the same thing Dr North had told me last week: they would give my dad a sedative to put him to sleep, attach electrodes to his head and one to his foot, and then put over a hundred volts of electricity into his brain. They tracked the seizure's progress by the twitching of his big toe. When the twitching stopped, the seizure was done. Then they just waited for him to wake up from the anesthetic.

'We make a printout of the brain activity during the seizure,' Dr Frown said.

'Can I have it?' my father asked hopefully, listening too. As if it were something he'd hang next to his diploma from the Pennsylvania State University medical school.

Dr Frown looked alarmed, then said no. He turned back to me. 'He'll be in and out in no time.'

A nurse took my father's arm. My father pumped a closed fist in the air, like he was pulling on a tugboat horn. *Toot toot, I'm off.*

'Can I watch?' I called after them.

Dr Frown and his nurse exchanged a look.

'I'm serious,' I said. 'I'm a biology student.'

The nurse smiled at me. Dr Frown was already leading my father into a small room. The door shushed shut, and I turned around, temporarily unsure of my bearings. As I retreated back into the waiting room, the receptionist caught my eye. She tilted her head and clucked her tongue. She was short and round, with square fingers. There were packages of unopened bags of pretzels, cakes, chocolate-covered raisins sitting by her phone. She had one of those soft, lovely faces; people probably noticed her all the time and thought, *You could be so beautiful, if you weren't so heavy.* I could feel her trying to meet my eye, but I looked away.

I faced a window that looked out onto York. Down seven flights was a Tasti D-Lite, a liquor

194

store, a small hovel that made duplicates of keys but barely had room for anything else. Next to the shops was a park, which consisted of a few benches and a basketball court. Six or seven guys were playing a very loud game of basketball. Even from this high up, I could hear their hip-hop music blaring out of the boom box they'd set up on one of the benches.

I heard a small clicking noise coming from the back of the office and looked up. What were they doing now? Were the electrodes hooked up to his head? Had they given him the anesthetic? How did electrocution erase depression, anyway? Was it like spraying on disinfectant and wiping away the grime?

The basketball players liked to scream at one another, saying things like, *throw it here, you fuckin' pussy, nice one.* There was one guy with semi-greasy blonde hair and a moustache who dominated the ball, springing up to the hoop and sliding it in. I watched as he pranced around with his chest puffed out, guessing he was probably one of those self-assured assholes who harassed women out his car window simply because he could.

'Those basketball players,' the receptionist said, making me jump. 'I have to apologize. It's a new thing, them playing here. We've had a lot of complaints.'

'It's all right,' I said. 'They're not bothering me.'

'No really, they're animals.' She rolled her eyes. 'Why aren't they working? Middle of the day.'

'It's fucking out of *bounds*,' said a voice from the basketball court.

The receptionist pursed her lips. I gripped the seat, her tension suddenly infectious. They *were* annoying. All of a sudden, I wanted to shove something through the window to make them shut up. A brick, perhaps, something heavy. I wanted to hurl it at the loudest player down there – the shirtless guy with the scraggly moustache – and scream, *Have some respect. Do you know what's* happening *up here?*

I pictured the brick hitting his head and cracking it open. I saw him falling awkwardly, a pool of blood running out from his head, his greasy face contorted, the other men flocked around him. My vision narrowed. My thighs trembled and knocked against the arms of the chair. The zigzag designs on the carpet blurred.

When I opened my eyes a few seconds later, the waiting room was still and bright. The receptionist marked something in her book and absentmindedly placed a pretzel on her tongue like it was a pill. The basketball game continued. When the ball hit the hoop's rim, it made a loud, clattering sound like a piece of the earth splitting open.

And then the nurse was touching my arm. 'Miss Davis?'

I shot up.

'Do you want to see your father? He's done.'

Her expression was bland, almost obtuse. He was done? How long had it been? 'Do I?'

'He would like you to, I think.'

She led me through the door to a long, fluorescent-lit hall. Near the window were two people in wheelchairs. I could see my father's hair poking up over the wheelchair's back, his hands curled over the arms.

'Why is he in a wheelchair?' I whispered. 'Can't he walk?'

'No, he's fine. It's just for recovery, so he feels more comfortable.'

They'd made him change into a faded, worn hospital gown. I had a foolish thought, although I didn't realize until later how foolish it really was: my father's hair wasn't standing on end. And his ears weren't bleeding. I wasn't sure what I had expected, but maybe that. When I got a few steps away from him, I coughed, thinking he'd turn, but he continued to look out the frosted-over window, blinking and blinking, his teeth gnawing at the middle portion of his bottom lip. I peeked at the person next to him, a woman in her thirties. Her head lolled to one side, her eyes remained closed.

'Dad?' I said softly.

He still didn't turn. I walked around to face him. His face contained no expression whatsoever. His eyes followed me, then landed on me. I felt him taking me in. He was looking at me like he was watching television; anticipatory, with no idea what would happen next, but not really so concerned either way.

I had no idea what to do. Sit down, continue to stand? Tell him who I was? Wait?

'Summer,' he finally said, his voice dry.

'Yes.' It came out like a gasp, like a release of air. 'Dad. Yes. Hi. It's me. I'm here.'

'Summer.' He swallowed hard.

'How are you doing? Are you okay?'

'I . . .' His movements were slow, his mouth opened and closed like a goldfish. *It's just the sedatives*, I told myself. *They haven't worn off yet.* But there was something else, too: a void. It was like his whole past had been wiped away. Like he had no idea who he *was*.

The alarm on his watch started to go off. He looked around, puzzled, then located the sound on his wrist. He stared at his watch, then at me. Desperately. He coughed, moved his neck from side to side and then slowly, so slowly, edged his hand toward the watch. He tapped the face gently, as if he feared he might break it. When that accomplished nothing, he tried pressing a button. When the beeping continued, he looked at me again. I shrugged back at him, just as desperate. We were two different species trying to communicate.

'I don't . . .' he said, then looked down and tried another button. The alarm stopped. He stared at it for a while, perhaps wondering if it was going to start again. The woman in the wheelchair next to him still hadn't moved. The silence was louder and more penetrating than the beeping. My ears rang and rang.

'How do you feel?' I asked.

He put his hands back on the wheelchair's arms.

Every movement seemed tentative. The lines in his forehead were gone.

'My neck hurts, I think,' he said. 'And my arms. And my jaw.'

'So it hurt, then?'

'Did what hurt?'

'The . . .' A nurse walked by a few yards away. She glanced at me. *Is this normal?* I wanted to ask her. *Is any of this normal?*

'How do you feel?' I asked my father again.

His eyes moved up toward the ceiling as he tried to think. 'Feel? I don't know.'

'Do you feel sad?'

'No. I don't think so.'

'Do you feel . . . happy?'

'Happy?' He ran his hand over his chin. Was his chin unfamiliar, too? His hands? When we went home, would he look in the mirror and not know himself? 'I don't know,' he said, with a certain amount of fatigue, but also a certain amount of wonderment. 'I don't really feel anything.'

He made a groan and put his head against the wheelchair's back. 'I'm going to close my eyes for a minute.'

'Okay. That's fine. Take all the time you need.'

While I sat there with him, I composed a commentary in my head, as if this were a documentary about ECT and I was the narrator and I already knew how the story would end. *This was Richard Davis's first appointment, and by far the toughest. After this, he began to miraculously recover.*

Says Lawrence Frum, the doctor who administered the treatments: 'This is the best outcome from ECT I have ever seen in my practice. This man has a new lease on life. It is simply astounding.'

I changed my high, thin voice to a deep, assured one. *Faith*, I thought. Yet again, I turned everything over to faith. I revised the documentary script a few times to make the outcome better and better. My father would eventually practice medicine again. He would eventually run a hospital. My mother would wash up as something plain and somewhat pitiful, maybe a telemarketer or sales clerk, her drama career hitting a dead-end. We would get through this, and he'd come out a hero. It made me feel better. It really did.

CHAPTER 14

The computer's screensaver drew fractal-like scribbles. Once the image became an impossibly tangled ball of yarn, it dissipated and a new drawing began. I watched it for a while. I touched the monitor and there was static. The keys on the keyboard felt like teeth.

In the past two months, I have hidden under a pile of coats at a party and not gotten up when they called my name at the dentist's office. I have also given a fake name when a woman from a marketing survey called home and, just yesterday, I bought a postcard off the street and addressed it to my great-aunt Stella in Cobalt, PA. I wrote about horses and windmills and signed it Beatrice A. Haverford.

I stared at the sentences, astounded that my hands had created them. I pulled the cursor over everything and hit delete.

When someone is severely depressed, he often doesn't want to take his medicine. But you cannot be angry at him. You cannot blame him and you cannot blame yourself. You just have to accept it and realize that it is something out of your control and not get angry. Except it is angering, so you find yourself getting angry at other things, like strangers, or garbage bags that don't open properly, or your purse, when you can't find things at its bottom.

I looked out onto the Promenade. There was the typical lineup of nannies with strollers, old people leaning over the railing, the resident homeless woman with her shopping cart of junk. She was splayed out on one of the benches, her head rested on a carefully tied garbage bag of empty Coke cans. There was a little smile on her lined, dirty face, as if she was terribly pleased with her makeshift pillow. It jolted things into perspective – it was unclear when this woman had last slept in a real bed or eaten a real meal, and yet she seemed more grateful and content than I was.

It was the day after my father's first treatment. He and I had come home from his first ECT appointment in a cab – I didn't want to subject him to the subway. At home, he lay on the couch, staring at the wall. After a while, he started crying. 'I can't *think*,' he kept saying. 'This is horrible, I can't *think*. What the hell happened to me?'

I tried to tell him what happened. He signed the papers, I said over and over. He agreed to this. But I can't *think*, he kept repeating. I can't *feel*.

In the end, I called Dr North; he prescribed a sleeping pill. I begged the pharmacy to send someone to deliver it; I was afraid of leaving my father out of my sight, but also knew he wasn't capable of leaving the house.

If I went to Ireland, I could study genetics with Dr John Shea. He was working on finding genetic markers for all the important things in the world, or at least was linked to those who were. He was looking for links to certain cancers, multiple sclerosis, ALS. He was associated with those who were looking for a link between our genes and depression. I could study that. I could study whatever I wanted.

But if I went to Ireland, my father would be alone.

I didn't know if he was supposed to be left alone; doctors hadn't told me one way or the other. Perhaps there were terrible side-effects of ECT that hadn't shown up yet – other than, of course, the memory thing. Something else I'd learned: doctors were often loath to mention the staggering side-effects of medications. They said, *just take this, it might help,* but they so rarely explained that you might not sleep or you might see things or that it might make you more depressed or gain weight or lose weight or stop eating or not be able to produce natural tears. There were no instructions that came with ECT, just a pamphlet, *What Is ECT?* featuring a smiling blonde woman in a pink sweater, proffering a teapot to the camera.

Just do it! her smile said, but it seemed coerced, like someone was pushing a gun to her back. *Your life will be as carefree as mine, really, honestly! Would you like some tea?*

I picked up the phone and called the number I'd written on the little slip of paper last week, the number from the flyer in the East Village. It rang a few times, and a woman answered. 'Learning Annex.'

I cleared my throat. 'Hi, I was calling about the talk that's in two weeks, the one with Meredith Heller at the Mayflower Hotel? Acting For Beginners?'

'Yeah. And?'

I gripped the phone. I hadn't rehearsed past this point; I'd expected them to say *Meredith Heller? Who?* 'What will Miss Heller be speaking about?'

She flipped some pages. Sighed. 'Um, acting?'

'Right. And . . . is she around forty?'

'I don't know. Harold?' She moved her mouth away from the phone. 'Do you know anything about Meredith Heller? . . . I don't know, she's speaking next week, or . . . yeah. That's her. Yes. How old is she, roughly?'

There was mumbling. 'Harold says she's fortyish, yeah. If you want to buy tickets, though, you should call back tomorrow. I'm just manning the phones because the regular person is sick.'

'Okay,' I said weakly.

'You can buy them at the door, too, Harold says. The day of.'

She hung up without saying goodbye. I held the phone at arm's length, worried for a moment that it had recorded the conversation in its little plastic fiber-optic parts, storing it for a later time when my father could rewind it and hear everything. Did my mother have any idea what things were like with us? Surely she assumed we might find out about this lecture and come to see her. It was possible – it was very possible – that she had no idea what had happened to my father. Perhaps she thought we would show up, happy and well-adjusted and completely forgiving, ready to hum or pantomime or pretend we were dead or whatever it was people did in acting classes. But all this was waiting for her. She didn't even know it.

It was late afternoon; the sky had faded from gold to lavender. I sat on the back of the couch, rubbing one foot against the other. After a while, I looked up the Mayflower Hotel on a map of Manhattan. I imagined us walking into the lobby and seeing my mother. I imagined my father healthy and my mother dumpy and silly, teaching a Learning Annex class to make ends meet. We wouldn't want her. We'd laugh. We'd leave the lobby without taking the class, without paying the twenty bucks.

CHAPTER 15

As we were pulling into the Brooklyn Bridge station, on our way to his fifth appointment, a 6 train had already pulled into the station across the platform. A good sign, I decided – my father hated waiting on the platforms lately, as they were too hot or smelly or loud. Lately, I'd been looking everywhere for good signs. I enlisted the documentary voice again: *On the fifth appointment, Richard Davis is showing marked improvement. He has moved off the couch and back to his old bed, and he has started eating with vigor, amazed because food suddenly has taste again. Dr North said this was very, very encouraging, very positive progress.*

After we found seats on the train, my father glanced at me sideways, like a fish. 'Why don't you have a boyfriend?'

'Dad!' I exclaimed, instantly embarrassed.

'What? You're pretty enough.'

I immediately thought about Philip. Which was silly – that was four years ago. There had been crushes here and there, but I'd never had a real boyfriend. No one felt right. I always gravitated to Philip, the fleeting kiss in his backyard. I liked to think that some of Philip's skin cells fused with mine; that, even for a moment, a little bit of his DNA was mine and a little bit of mine was his. But it was embarrassing. It reminded me of the Missed Connections ads on the back page of the *Village Voice*, a boy longing for the girl who smiled at him on the crosstown L train, a girl eagerly wanting to reunite with the boy who stood in line in front of her at the bank, certain that they'd shared a special moment.

'I can't remember the names of the layers of skin,' my father suddenly said.

'What?' It was hard to switch gears, especially from Philip.

He held his palm outstretched. 'Wait. So. It's the stratum corneum, then the stratum lucidum, the stratum granulosum.' He lowered one finger with each layer. 'But then what?'

Even I knew this. The stratus spinosum. Then the stratum basale. Then the dermis. I waited a few seconds, but he still couldn't think of it. *Doctors said memory loss was a common side-effect,* the documentary voice intoned. *The patient forgot words, details, what day it was, what had happened the day before. Sometimes, Summer would come upon him and he'd just look so lost, a stranger in his own skin. She made a list of the words he forgot: orange, handkerchief, Broadway, placemat.*

I'd begun to be able to sense when he was struggling with his lost memory, trying to hide what he had forgotten. Yesterday, there had been smoke coming out of the window of an apartment

207

building across the street. 'It looks like it might become a fire,' my dad said, turning to me. 'Do you think we should call that number?'

'What number?' I asked.

He snapped his fingers, trying to tease it out. 'You know. That emergency number.'

'. . . You mean 911?'

'*Yes.* Thank you.'

He always acted like it was something on the tip of his tongue, simple things everyone forgot. But I knew it bothered him. Each time, a flare of worry passed across his face.

'So what do you think your mother would think of all this, if she were still here?' he asked, the subway jerking forward.

I sat up straighter. 'Why are you asking that?'

He looked away. 'No reason. It just makes me wonder. I don't know what she'd say.' He chuckled. 'She'd probably just throw me into an institution.'

'That's not funny.'

'I didn't say it was funny.'

'You shouldn't think about her,' I said angrily.

He shrugged. 'I don't know, maybe this treatment is working. I don't feel so bad about her. I don't mind thinking about her. What would I say if I could talk to her right now? I would probably tell her about you. Not about me.'

I faced him. My father in his pressed chinos, his scraggly, tawny hair, that crazy beard. 'You wouldn't tell her anything about . . . this?'

'That's a big bomb to drop on someone,

Summer, don't you think? If I had cancer, do you think that would be the first thing I'd tell someone on the phone? *How are you? Well, I have cancer, how are you?'*

I narrowed my eyes, angry at his sarcasm. 'You wouldn't be able to keep it a secret. I know you.'

Surprise flashed across his face. I clamped down hard on my tongue. 'I'm sorry,' I muttered, even though I knew it was true.

He crossed his arms over his chest and did the thing he always did when he was upset: pulled at the loose skin on his elbows, stretching it out. 'This is my fantasy, Summer. Don't go and ruin it.'

My *fantasy.* He was fantasizing about her.

Only, we could get real answers. The acting class was only a few days away. Our mother might open her arms, overjoyed to see us. Or she might take one look at my father, horrified, and cancel the class entirely.

The subway stopped and the doors opened. People bounced around the platform like electrons. A large black woman sat on a bench, a baby carriage next to her. Except there wasn't a baby in the carriage, there were newspapers.

My father snapped his fingers. 'Stratum spinosum!' he cried, loud enough so that everyone else in the subway car looked up. 'I just remembered! Stratum spinosum!'

As if he'd just split the atom.

★　★　★

A couple sat in the waiting room. I only saw the man briefly before the nurse took him back, but I could tell he was youngish, perhaps in his thirties. The woman stayed behind, sitting in the chair, knitting.

She noticed me and smiled. 'Hi.'

The receptionist picked up her phone and dialed.

'Hot outside, isn't it?' the girl pressed.

'Uh huh,' I muttered.

'The air conditioning in the subway car I was in was broken, too,' she added.

'It's nice and cool in here though, isn't it?' the receptionist chirped, hanging up the phone, not having said anything into it.

'Sure is.' The girl's needles were metal, and they clicked together when they touched. The conversation was so small and mundane it made me itchy. It was as if we were waiting for a bus. As if near-death experiences weren't happening just a few feet away.

The door opened. Dr Frum stood in the hallway, staring at me. He moved forward without picking up his knees, and then his hand was on my arm.

'Your father is still in the recovery room,' he said quietly. 'He had a bit of a bad reaction this time. So it'll be a little longer before you can see him. He's resting.'

I shot up. 'Bad reaction . . . how?'

'Some patients are fearful when they wake up.' He smiled at me kindly but absently.

It broke my heart to hear he was *fearful*. I imagined him curled up in the fetal position, thinking the jar of cotton swabs is a monster. *It's because of our argument on the train*, I thought. He had entertained the idea of talking to my mother again, and I'd fought him on it. *It's because of something I've done*. The doctor slipped back into the hall, and I clutched the arms of the chair and lowered myself back down.

The silence settled back into the waiting room, like a parachute that had been momentarily airborne but was drifting back down to earth. When I looked up, the knitting girl's eyes were on me, a simpering, pitying smile on her face.

'What are you making?' the receptionist called to her.

'A sweater,' she answered sweetly.

'In this heat?'

'I know. But the speed I'm going, I'll be done by December.'

They both laughed.

I couldn't be in the room anymore. I stood up and staggered to the door, my arms outstretched like a mummy. I walked to the end of the hall for the stairwell and descended one flight. Doctors whirled by. Some of the doors to the patients' rooms were open; I looked in and saw a woman lying in a bed, picking at her lunch. There was a man sitting on an orange plastic chair next to her, quietly talking. In another room, there was a whole group of people laughing, inspecting someone whose leg was in traction. 'I can't go back to work for six fucking weeks,' the patient whined. 'Don't worry,' his mother/sister/girlfriend/some anonymous family member said. 'We'll take care of you.'

Ahead of me was a closet marked *Janitor*. I fumbled for the doorknob and wrapped my hands around the cool metal. It opened, amazingly. Inside were a bucket, a few brooms, and some cleaning products. I stepped in and bent down, curling my knees into my chest. Then I closed the door. It was so dark in here. Quiet.

He was fearful. I put my head down on my knees.

Suddenly, the door whipped open. A man was standing there, staring irksomely at the broom and the mop. I screamed. He looked down, at first not having noticed me, and jumped.

'Jesus,' he said. 'I thought this was the bathroom. What are you . . . ?'

He squatted down. He was dressed in brown pants, work boots, and a brown work shirt. It wasn't until he got very close that I realized it was the loudest basketball player from the court across the street, the one with the greasy blond hair and mustache. The one I was sure harassed women just for the hell of it.

A small smile appeared on his face. 'Are you stuck?'

'No,' I said quickly.

'Then what are you doing?'

I couldn't answer. His smile grew larger, more sinister. It occurred to me that he was a dangerous man, capable of violent things. During my father's last appointment, I'd watched him and another basketball player get into a shouting match. It had quickly escalated into grappling on the pavement. I watched this man clench his jaw, the cords of the muscles ropy and straining. He hit the other man again and again and again. People just walked by. It both thrilled and disgusted me that rage could be so plain and obvious, in the middle of public, genteel York Avenue.

Now, here he was. He stood back. 'You want to come out?'

'I guess.'

He held out his hand. There was dirt caked into his palms. As I took it, my ears started to ring. He pulled me up fast and with so much force that I tipped in the other direction, staggering into the hall. He wrapped an arm around me to help me catch my balance.

'Thanks.' I dropped my hand from his.

'You're welcome.' He paused, looking me over, starting at my feet, then to my knees, then to my skirt and shirt and breasts and neck and head. My heart pounded.

'Do I know you?' he asked.

I frowned. Could he have seen me watching, eight flights up? 'No.'

'You sure? You look familiar.'

He looked at me carefully, with certainty. Perhaps he was able to see deep inside me, under my skin and muscles. Maybe he saw everything I wanted, everything I felt, even things I didn't want to admit to myself.

'I'm not familiar,' I insisted.

He shrugged. Then, right in front of me, without breaking eye contact, he reached down and rubbed his crotch. Up and down. Cupping it completely. Scratching sounds. There was nowhere else for my eyes to look. It was like the hall had lost air pressure. His eyes danced, enlivened.

'I should go,' I said, taking a step backward.

'Bye bye,' he teased.

But he was the one who turned and walked away. As he glanced over his shoulder, my mouth dropped open. It wasn't the basketball player anymore. It was some other guy, a man with straight, limp hair and a wide, pear-shaped ass. A hand had come down and switched them. I rubbed my eyes, not believing it.

And then I bounded up the steps, passing a window that overlooked York. The basketball court was empty. When I turned a corner and burst into the ECT hall, there was my father, standing in the middle of the corridor. His face was so pale, his expression so lost. His gown gaped open at the front.

'Dad!' I bleated.

He looked through me.

'Dad.' I took his arm. 'Why are you out here?'

His mouth parted. Little strings of saliva hung between his lips. 'Where's Dr Frum?' I cried. 'I thought you were supposed to be resting.'

214

My father blinked. He registered me, finally, his eyes fixing on my face. 'There's a secret I never told you,' he whispered.

'What?'

'I hid it.' His voice was half an octave lower than normal. 'I hid it so you won't find it.'

'Oh Jesus, there he is.' The overweight receptionist burst out the door, followed by Dr Frum. 'He ran through the waiting room before I could stop him.' She looked at me. 'I think he was looking for you, but you weren't there.'

'Richard?' Dr Frum said loudly into my father's face, as if he were deaf.

'You let him walk off?' I asked them.

Now a nurse was behind the receptionist. '*You* should have been waiting.'

I looked back at my father. He had a secret he never told me? Was that true or . . . not true? *He's so sick*, I thought. *And he might not get any better. What if he never gets better?*

My father put his hand on my arm. 'Summer!' he cried, as if I'd just arrived. 'Oh, Summer, Jesus. What's going on? Where the hell am I? Am I dead?' He slurred his words.

'Dad.' I took his hand. 'You're in the hospital. You just had a treatment.'

His eyes widened. 'A treatment? Do I have cancer?'

'No . . .'

'What treatment, then?'

I told him.

He ripped his arm from me. 'No. *No.* Who's making me? Why?'

'Dad, you signed the papers.'

'Mr Davis.' The nurse took his arm.

'*Leave me,*' he screamed at her.

I looked pleadingly at the nurse. She pressed her lips together but didn't look that surprised. This wasn't even unusual to her.

My father careened to the window and crouched next to it, trying to heft it open. 'What are you doing?' I called out.

'If I just . . . it's so . . .' he grunted. 'I need to get out before they find me.'

'Richard,' Dr Frum said wearily.

'Dad, stop it,' I pleaded. So many people were staring at us. Even people from other offices. 'Dad, please.'

He didn't listen. He just kept straining at the window, his hospital gown now completely open at the back, the knobs of his spine poking through.

'*Dad.*' I managed to get between him and the window and pushed him a little, back toward the office door. He wagged his head stubbornly, lunging for the window again. I pushed him harder, spinning him sideways. He lost his footing, stumbled, and collapsed to one knee. Someone by the door gasped. My father gaped at me in disbelief, then turned away.

'Dad . . .' I started.

A man moved toward us, a big guy with dark hair and thick eyebrows that grew together. 'Mr

Davis? It's Michael. Do you remember me?' He had a German accent.

'I didn't sign any papers,' my father shouted, still on the ground. 'And I'm *Dr* Davis.'

'Dr Davis,' Michael corrected fast. 'I apologize.' He helped my father up. 'It's much cooler back in our office. The air conditioning works better in there. You need to get some rest, okay?'

'You aren't taking me back in there.' My father's protests were wearier.

'You'll be safe. You'll just rest.'

His hospital gown was completely undone. As he turned, I looked through the slit in the side. He wore something strange underneath it, something made of plastic that went the whole way around him. My hands twitched with instant realization. It was a *diaper*.

Michael helped my father back into the hall. They passed by me without saying anything.

'Thanks, Michael,' Dr Frum said. Michael shrugged, as if he had to do this all the time. Perhaps he did. Perhaps tonight, he'd go home and recount this story. 'We had a guy today who was an extra nutcase,' he will say, laughing over a beer. 'And his daughter was something else, too. Shoved him hard, the bitch.'

The nurse glanced at me, her eyes cold. I wanted to tell her – I wanted to tell all of them – that I loved my father. That I felt constant terror and guilt and pain for him. I wanted to tell them that we played cards together, we watched the boats on the East River, we went for walks. And all of those things were, in their own way, wonderful.

But instead I pressed myself against the radiator next to the window, watching as they coaxed him into submission. And then I walked away.

CHAPTER 16

I dreamed I was in Dublin, walking over the brick-lined squares to work. The buildings were stately and old. Red buses whizzed by. Men wore top hats. When I came to a park and walked the whole way around a large, smooth pond, my skin started to pale. It became translucent, so much that I could see straight through my hands to my bones and my veins. When I moved a finger, tendons and muscles flexed before my eyes. And my heart was a black knot. Then, my brain slipped into focus. My father was trapped inside my head, sitting on a rocking chair with a blanket thrown over his legs. He stopped rocking and peered out at me. 'There's a secret I never told you,' he said. 'All you have to do is find it.'

I woke up sweating.

My room was dark and cold. Two dogs were snoring at the foot of the bed. I heard my father's voice through the wall and sat up, cocking my head toward the living room. And then I remembered: he wasn't sleeping on the couch anymore, but in his bed again. His last appointment, the bad one, was two days ago. When he came home, he slept for eight hours, and since then, he'd been quiet and peaceful. We had decided to skip today's session and resume next week, giving him some time to recuperate.

I tiptoed to the edge of my room. At first, his voice just rolled up and down like waves, and I couldn't pick out individual words. But when I walked into the hall, I heard him clearly. There was a slice of golden light spilling from the gap at the bottom of his bedroom door. He was talking into a tape recorder Dr North had given him to help with his memories. He was supposed to explain to his future self exactly what he was doing in a particular moment so he could go back, listen, and remember.

I heard a crinkle of paper. 'There are certain things I don't remember, but I have a list,' he said.

I ran my tongue over my teeth.

'I don't remember how she and I met,' he said. 'I don't remember the place. Was it a football game? In a hallway? Was it Dairy Queen? No, wait. That was . . .'

He paused.

'And . . . what's next,' he said. 'Oh. What was her mother's maiden name?'

He went through little things. Her favorite meal at the Italian restaurant in Park Slope was risotto. She loved Hall & Oates and Lionel Richie, much to his chagrin. A good friend from the gym was named Marissa. He talked about words they used to say to one another. Nicknames they used.

Gifts they got for each other. Gifts they got for Steven and me.

It shocked me that he'd lost this much. Then I heard him bumping through the box he kept at the end of the bed, looking through the receipts. 'I don't think I wrote it down anywhere,' he mumbled.

He sighed. 'There's so much I don't remember,' he said, louder. 'There's so much I need to clear up. It's like . . . I have emotions but sometimes I'm not sure *why* I have them. Everything reminds me of everything . . . and at the same time, nothing.' After a pause, he continued. 'Like today, I was looking out the window and saw this man on the street. A neighbor, maybe, but I couldn't remember his name, and I had no idea what he did or how long I'd known him. The only thing I knew was that I had a strong feeling about him, but I didn't know what that feeling was – friendship? Hate? Irritation? If I'd have run into him today, I would have ignored him. But what if he's a good friend? What if I pretend the wrong thing?'

I walked back into my room and retrieved my journal. *I should be writing this down*, I thought – but for what? Posterity? Still, I took it back to the hall and opened to a fresh page.

'But Summer,' I heard him say.

I wrote down my name, waiting.

'This is so much better for Summer,' he said. 'This is what I have to do. It's not worth putting her through . . . all the . . . I was so . . .'

This is what I have to do. Maybe he knew I was listening. Maybe he was saying this – that he was making a sacrifice – because he knew I was on the other side of the door.

It felt as though there were ping-pong balls jumping inside my stomach. When I went back to my bedroom, I climbed under my desk. The computer above me hummed. I could smell the remains of the apple I had eaten for lunch. In the darkness, it probably seemed like I wasn't even there. *Hide and seek.* Now, all someone had to do was come and find me.

There was a vase of flowers on the table in the little waiting room outside Dr Hughes's office at NYU. Out the window, I watched as a girl in a red dress ran down University Place. Her mother followed, yelling at her to slow down.

The door opened, and Dr Hughes stuck her head out. 'Hi, Summer.'

I stood up. 'Hi.'

Her calico dress had pockets meant for spatulas and wooden spoons. 'Do you have something for me?' she asked.

I looked down at my bag. 'I'm not sure.'

'Not sure?'

'I have something, but I'm not sure if you want it.'

She leaned against the door. There was a sign taped up in the hall talking about guidelines on locking up at night. *There have been many theft's,* it said in sloppy handwriting. There was an unnecessary apostrophe. 'I was cutting you some slack for a while,' Dr Hughes said. 'But I don't know. Maybe you don't want me to.'

She held out her hand. I ran my fingers over the edges of my leather bag. This morning, I typed out my journal. Some of it wasn't even complete sentences, just lists of drugs and symptoms. I even included the scribble from when my father was talking into the tape recorder. I found another flyer for Acting For Beginners and put it in there, too. The date printed on the flyer was today's date; the class was starting in less than an hour from now. I stapled all those things together and wrote, at the end, *If this can happen to a person, and if this is genetic, I want to be able to fix it. Except I can't. I can't take this fellowship. I'm sorry.*

But I also typed out a perfectly normal essay. One that talked about my love of genetics, how I'd like to find the cause of the things that went wrong inside of us, because I was certain that so many of them began at the smallest level, at a mistake in our gene sequences. I wrote about my father, saying that he had an influence on me when I was very young, encouraging me to excel in science even though I was a girl and people expected girls to do better in things like English and art.

My hands curled around the normal essay. I pulled it out, leaving the crazy one in my bag. I passed it to her, wincing.

223

'I should go,' I said, as soon as the papers transferred hands.

'Wait.' She caught my arm. 'I'll read it right now.'

'Don't. Please. Just . . . read it later.'

Dr Hughes's phone rang. She glanced toward her office, disappointed. 'I want to talk to you, at least. Can I talk to you?'

I paused. The phone rang again.

'I should take that.' Dr Hughes gestured to the waiting-room chair. 'Sit. Don't move.'

But as soon as she turned her back, I crashed through the front door and down the stairwell. The exit sign burned into my retinas. Out on University, I looped around people and bus kiosks and phone booths. A cab was parked at the curb outside the deli. The door was open, and the driver was just sitting at the wheel, his eyes closed. I wobbled on the sidewalk, and then threw myself into the back seat. The cab driver opened his eyes and glared at me. He was a large black man in a blue work jacket. He had a beard but no hair on his head; there was a small roll of skin at the back of his skull, leading into his neck. 'I'm not on duty,' he said gruffly.

I didn't answer.

He shifted in his seat, making the leather crinkle. 'Are you going uptown, at least?'

People briskly passed. NYU students, with book-filled backpacks. Dr Hughes was probably reading my essay right now.

'Well?' the driver demanded.

'Yes,' I heard myself saying. 'The Mayflower Hotel. Central Park West and Sixty-first.'

He sighed and started the car. A jazz station, the same one my father listened to, came on the radio. The driver glanced at me in the rear-view mirror, then yanked his door closed. We started up University, stopping at the light at Union Square. People paused in front of a shoe store, walked in clumps, edged around a man in an electric wheelchair. The insides of my elbows wouldn't stop sweating.

We paused at another traffic light; more people crossed. A man wheeling a hot-dog cart. A couple with their arms around each other's shoulders. The guy looked like Steven. It was amazing, suddenly, that Steven and I hadn't really spoken for years. After my grandmother's funeral, he disappeared back to NYU, finishing school, applying for a graduate degree in California, then going. The times he flew home were perfunctory and businesslike: he cleaned out his bedroom, he helped Dad with tax returns. He had an excuse to stay away for both holidays that following year: a hiking expedition in Chile over Thanksgiving, a cabin with friends in Martha's Vineyard from Christmas to New Year's. Only, two days after Christmas, I had gone into the city to tour NYU's library, already knowing I was going to attend there the following year. When turning onto Broadway from Waverly, there was Steven, standing in front of the Astor Place Barnes &

Noble. We stared at each other two whole green lights.

'You should be going to the beach,' the cab driver interrupted my thoughts. I jumped.

'Sorry?'

'The beach. In this weather. One of the first real warm days, you know? Everyone should be going to the beach today.'

I ran my hands over my bare legs. 'Yeah, well, not me.'

The cab driver glanced at me in the rear-view mirror. The whites of his eyes had a yellowish tint to them, or maybe they just looked that way because his skin was so dark. 'Maybe you're not a beach person, huh?' He gripped the wheel tightly. 'My wife's not a beach person, either. Likes climbing mountains, camping. Me, I like the beach. You'd think I'd want something quiet, like my wife. Out in the middle of the woods. Especially after driving through this city. But I'd rather drown myself in noise and just . . . drift off, you know? Places that are too quiet make me nervous. I get to thinking; and when I get to thinking, it's not always good.'

He chuckled. I tried to smile back but I could feel the outer edges of my eyes and the corners of my mouth doing strange things.

'You gotta take a break once in a while, though,' he went on. 'I mean, you have to. I have a daughter, you know. She's a little older than you. She had a baby that died. It's tough, man. It's tough.

My wife's having a hard time getting through it. We all are, I guess. But sometimes, I say, 'You know what? Let's just go to the beach.' And they say, 'Carl, are you nuts?' But we go. We go to Long Beach.' He met my eyes again. 'You know Long Beach?'

I could barely move.

'It's nice enough,' he said, putting on his blinker to switch lanes. 'Better during the week, when you don't get the crowds. But sometimes, you know. You just have to do it.' He shook his head, turning onto Broadway. 'Sorry I got into all that. You probably want a peaceful trip up, and look what you get. Well, that's what happens when you get in when I'm not on duty.'

I swallowed. 'How did it die? The baby?'

An air-freshener Jesus spun from his rear-view mirror. 'She drowned. In a neighbor's plastic swimming pool. It was a Memorial Day party last year. Beautiful day. Not a cloud in the sky.'

'I'm sorry.'

'Anyway. It just happened so fast . . . the pool wasn't even *deep*.'

'That's terrible,' I whispered.

'Well, it happened, you know? And there's nothing we can do about it now. You can blame and blame yourself, thinking of the things you might've done differently, or ask if maybe it was her time, and ask if this has something to do with *God*, maybe, but sometimes, I think things just happen. There's nothing you can do about it – you just gotta deal with it. Sometimes life really sucks. You know? Sometimes it just sucks.'

He cleared his throat. 'But then, there's the beach. Right? There's the beach.' He eyed me. 'Or maybe, for you, there's something else.'

We passed the flower district, the garment district, the glittering lights of Forty-second Street and its surrounding craziness. A group of tourists – one of them staring perplexedly at a New York City guidebook – stood in front of an enormous electronics store, holding giant Barnes & Noble shopping bags. That day I saw Steven outside the Barnes & Noble downtown, I finally crossed the street to meet him. He had a Barnes & Noble plastic bag in one hand and an Other Music bag in another.

'I thought you were at Martha's Vineyard,' I said to him.

'Plans fell through.' Steven zipped up his jacket.

'So why aren't you staying at home?'

'My friend's away for the holiday. He's got a place on Ninth and First.'

I gawked at him, amazed that he'd avoided the question so cavalierly. He wouldn't meet my eye. 'You guys have a good Christmas?' he asked.

Our Christmas dinner had been lonely, pointedly quiet. We imagined Steven doing wonderful things in Martha's Vineyard: sledding, eating an enormous dinner with his friends, exchanging brightly wrapped gifts. After dinner, my father curled up next to our small Christmas tree and cried.

I rubbed his head, sending the Swiss men down the plastic ski slope again and again.

I tilted my chin up to Steven. 'Do you remember that ski slope Mom and Dad got for us when they went to Switzerland?'

He glanced at me warily. 'Huh?'

'You know. The little Swiss skiers? You loved it when they got it for us. You played with it constantly. It was your favorite toy.'

The wind had turned the tip of Steven's nose red. 'Sorry, no.'

Years of words lodged in my throat. *Please just tell me something real*, my mind clawed desperately. *Anything.* I wanted Steven to answer the same questions I had always longed to ask my mother: how did he manage it, suppressing everything, detaching so completely? Had that terrorist obsession been it – had he gotten his emotions out of his system, vowing never to explore them again? I had never felt so lonely, standing on that corner. How was it that a cab driver, a stranger, could unburden himself far more than my own brother could? How was this so backward?

'Here you are,' the driver said after a wall of silence. 'Mayflower Hotel, right?'

We were in front of a modest hotel with a few stone steps. The bellhop opened a door for an old lady. Across the street was Central Park. A magazine vendor rearranged a stack of newspapers. I gave the cabbie money and, just like that, he peeled away up Broadway, cutting off another cab as he changed lanes.

The hotel's lobby was shabby yet stately, with old wooden fixtures and gilded details, the carpet worn, the chandelier missing some crystals. A tired-looking Indian woman hunched at the front desk, sleepily taking my money. The flowers in the vase next to her were slightly wilted. A placard by a conference room said, *Acting For Beginners here!* Someone had propped open the conference room's double doors with a dictionary. Inside were five rows of folding chairs. A few people were already sitting. They weren't the East Villagers I imagined, but jowl-faced old ladies, Upper East Side to the core in their stiff suit jackets, their brooches, their magenta lipstick. Two women sat at the front, whispering. An older man wearing a hound's-tooth cap slumped at the back, doing a word-find puzzle.

I wanted there to be a bigger turnout. If I stayed, she'd survey the crowd and recognize me. Or would she? I was taller, older, my oval face thinner, and I wore mostly oversized black sweaters and black jeans, a far cry from the bright, preppy colors I'd worn in tenth grade. But it was still my same green eyes, my dark hair that couldn't hold a curl, my petite ears, features that were half hers. She would look out and know.

A few more people walked in and sat down. There was a youngish guy with tattoos on his neck, a woman in a tall, African-style head wrap. After a while, someone emerged onto the stage. The crowd broke into applause.

My hands shook so badly I couldn't bring them together to clap. The woman wore a long patchwork skirt and a white blouse. Her brown hair fell down her back. She faced the wall, taking items out of a box. It looked like her back, I thought: straight and thin and strong. Older, a little, and she'd started wearing rings. In just seconds, she would look out into the crowd and see me. And then what? Would the talk stop? Or would she keep going? I had a horrible thought: *She will keep going. It won't matter.*

But when she turned around, her eyes were brown, not green. Her lips were small and pinched. Her skin was sun-baked and wrinkled, raisin-like. She wore large turquoise earrings in her ears, and when she smiled, one of her front teeth was gray, possibly dead. This woman had large breasts and a sweet, motherly smile and a low, raspy voice that was nothing like my mother's mid-range, clear one. This Meredith Heller wore no makeup, and looked out in the crowd at me and smiled. And then she smiled at the women next to me, and the man with the flat head. She smiled at us. 'Welcome,' she said. 'Thank you for coming.'

I stayed anyway. She made us hum, just as I thought she would. We stood up and let our shoulders go and bent over and started shaking. 'Loosen up,' she demanded. We space-walked around the room and gathered in a circle and held hands. We sculpted one another into feelings; when a woman made me 'angry', she jackknifed me at my waist and curled one of my arms over my head.

And then we did an exercise called 'Find Your Mother Like a Little Baby Penguin'. People on the left side were designated the mother penguins; people on the right were the baby penguins. Meredith Heller matched mothers and babies together, and the mother was to come up with a unique sound that only her baby knew. I was on the right, a baby, paired with an older lady who hadn't stopped smiling. She whispered her sound to me – it was like a dove, *cooo*. She said it a few times so I would remember it. *Coo, coo, coo.* Her breath smelled like violet candies.

Meredith Heller pulled us baby penguins to another part of the room. 'Pantomime your feelings as a lost baby penguin,' Meredith Heller instructed. I shut my eyes, trying to feel feathery and small, but the only thing I saw was that basketball court, those angry players. I held a brick over my head, and slammed it against the basketball player's skull again and again, cracking it like an egg. Someone to my right whispered, 'What is she *doing?*'

'Mother penguins, make your sound so your babies can find you!' Meredith Heller cried. And I heard it from across the room – *coo, coo, coo.* I fumbled my way toward it, the basketball player lying dead and bloody on the ground, my eyes spotted with tears. I imagined other things, too – my mother, alive and beautiful and interested, my father, strong and healthy and smiling. I reached the mother penguin and she kept cooing, flapping her penguin wings and jumping up and down. I nestled my head into her, just as all the other little penguins were doing. And then, filled with glee and purpose, I broke away from her – from all of them – and made a circle into the wide expanse of the room. I fluttered around the row of chairs and the projector screen. I squawked past Meredith Heller. I skipped past the door and the windows with the heavy blue curtains and the ladies' discarded old-lady purses. I danced next to the man in his wheelchair, feeling free and wonderful. The class just let me do this. It was as if they understood without me having to say it. It was as if they knew, somehow, that it was something I had to do.

CHAPTER 17

A month and a half after his last appointment, I was walking up the stairs to the apartment from my Driver's Ed class. I took Driver's Ed that summer because, basically, I didn't have anything better to do. Accelerating and braking through the streets and trying to merge into one lane of bridge construction traffic seemed as productive a way to spend my time as anything else.

My father was sitting on the couch, his hands folded in his lap. We met eyes, and then he looked at the coffee table. There was a pamphlet there, next to a full glass of water. It was for something called the Klein-Stochbauer Psychiatric and Wellness Center of Connecticut.

He'd already paid the deposit, he told me. They were expecting him there the following day. There were two women on the pamphlet's cover, both wearing flowing white skirts, both drinking tea. It reminded me of the *What Is ECT?* pamphlet we had received before he started treatment. What the hell was it about mental health products and people drinking tea? And the place's nickname was simply 'the Center'. The center of what?

We took a cab up instead of the train. The pamphlet described the place as a hospital, but it looked more like an old manor, with turrets and limestone masonry. There was a winding stream in the front yard and a labyrinth garden on the side. I saw a badminton court set up in the back-yard, a wishing well next to it. My father told me about a few of the Center's high points on the drive up: everyone got their own room, appointed with the 'highest-quality' sheets, carpeting and light fixtures. Everyone was given their own personal therapist, tailored exactly to their needs. And they didn't make you do group, one of the things my father hated most at New York Presbyterian.

My father refused to let me carry his bags into the lobby. A round, cheerful woman in bright red lipstick wheeled out a cart and he piled them on it himself. Since the ECT, he'd aged even more. His back was stooped. His shoulders slumped. His legs no longer seemed sturdy – the thirty pounds he'd gained from past medication had fallen off him once he'd begun ECT. After he had completed all eight treatments, he worked for exactly three days, trying to organize his files and catch up on the developments, medications, and scientific find-ings he'd missed. There was so much. On the last day, he came home and went back to the couch. He said, bravely, that he needed a day off. 'Take all the time you need,' I told him.

He looked at me with scared eyes. I could see

how desperately he wanted to be better. And then he said to me: 'Summer, you should go.'

And I said, 'Go where?'

'Ireland.'

I stared at him dumbly, my lips dry. 'You don't think I know?' he said. 'I'm not stupid. I know they awarded you that fellowship. They want you to go in September, right?'

'I know you're not stupid,' was all I could think to say.

'I think you should go,' he said again. 'Please, go.'

'But I don't want to go,' I said after a while, but it was only for show, only because I felt I had to.

'This is beautiful,' I said as my father and I walked now through the Center's lobby. It had a beamed ceiling like an old hunting lodge, and the air smelled like apple cider. 'You were lucky to find this.'

'They have a celebrity chef,' my father boasted. 'Can you believe it? Or, someone who studied with a celebrity chef, anyway. I don't know which one. Someone on PBS.'

'That's wonderful.'

'I bet I'll be just like that guy in *The Magic Mountain*,' my father joked when they showed him his room, which had a terrace. No one pointed out the bars on the terrace's perimeter, which seemed to be the sole difference between this place and, say, a resort. 'You ever read that book, Summer? This guy has tuberculosis, so he goes into a sanatorium, and there are the kookiest of characters, people you really wouldn't want to be around for days at a time, but then, over the course of it, he begins to fall in love with the place. All the regular meals, all the blankets. He can't imagine living in real society again. He stays there for seven years. And then he gets out because the war starts, and he goes to war, and he dies.'

I told him I hadn't read it.

I had dinner with him, spaghetti eaten with plastic utensils, orange soda from a pitcher. The patients were all well-groomed and had a WASPy, wealthy look about them – as they should, considering that the Center didn't accept any form of health insurance. My father was paying for it out of proceeds from several patents he'd helped develop, plus money saved, plus cashed-in stocks I'd never known about. He assured me that he could afford this, and that I shouldn't worry.

As we ate, I stared out the window at the endless green lawn. The posters on the walls in the hallways were also of green lawns, except the lawns were in places like Scotland and Pebble Beach Golf Course. Extra dinner portions sat on a stainless-steel table in the corner, warmed by a long column of hot lights.

After dinner, we sat in the TV room – with its marble fireplace and built-in bookcases – and watched an episode of *Friends*. My father smiled at the funny parts, picking at a scab on his ankle bone. Another patient, a girl about my age, walked in and said, 'I've seen this one', and left. Someone crossed the room wearing a familiar t-shirt that said *you are not what you own* on the back. It took me a while to place it, but then I remembered Claire.

Not long ago, I found an old roll of film stuffed under my bed and had it developed. There were generic pictures of Paris: the Arc de Triomphe, quaint road signs in French, the Chanel storefront. Then, I came to the last photo on the roll: Claire Ryan and I were standing awkwardly together, neither of us smiling. Behind us was the same tile-and-mahogany console table that was still wedged into the corner in our Brooklyn apartment, and I was wearing my favorite purple polo shirt, the very last thing my mother had bought for me.

It was obvious when the photo was from – the pain was stark on both our faces. I'd forgotten about stealing the Fun Saver camera the day Claire came over for biology tutoring, but the emotions of that time suddenly snapped back to me, an old, unhealed wound. As I stared at the photo, I was startled to see that Claire wasn't even fat. A bit pudgy, maybe, certainly larger than she had been, but not *obese*. She still had her beautiful blonde hair, her lovely round face.

Looking at it, I thought about the summer my grandmother died, when she and I were friends again and she'd wanted us to correspond while she was at her art program in San Francisco. When

I'd arrived home from Cobalt, there weren't any letters from Claire waiting for me in our mailbox. None had arrived, either, the remainder of that summer. That fall, I caught a few glimpses of her at the diner with those same friends, but she never acknowledged me, perhaps giving me what I wanted – anonymity. I heard rumors about Claire over the years – that she was a hotshot artist in Baltimore, that she begged some guy to marry her, that she was a lesbian in San Francisco. But I would probably never know the truth about any of them.

I spent five minutes watching TV with my father before I had to leave the TV room, hiding in the Center's white, plushy-toweled guest bathroom, crying. I wasn't sure when I'd last cried – it seemed like years. And yet, the tears felt almost perfunctory, offering me no release, no fade to black then credits, no epiphany or happy ending. I felt like something was missing, like I'd taken off a ring I'd been wearing for a long, long time, so long that it had become part of my finger. The bathroom smelled like someone's floral perfume. An old woman, perhaps a patient, had left a gaudy costume jewelry bracelet on the edge of the sink. I slid it on my wrist and, for the rest of the night, pressed its bumpy surface up to the side of my cheek, feeling like I was, in a very small way, someone else.

I talked to my father on the phone a few hours before my flight to Dublin. I had cleaned the house, I had packed my things, I had taken the dogs to their new owner, a woman down the street my father and I screened together – she loved dogs, and had a lot of room and a lot of time to exercise them. We wanted them to remain in this neighborhood – the smells would be the same for them.

When it got to that winding-down part of the conversation where it was obvious we had nothing else to say and should probably get off the phone, my father made this sigh. In it was the smallest of whimpers. 'Have a wonderful time,' he said. I stared out the window, watching the kids rollerblading up and down the Promenade. One World Trade glimmered across the water. Squinting hard, I tried to accurately count twenty-two floors from the top, but the building seemed too far away, the distance between floors too ambiguous. It made me wonder if I had ever been able to tell which office was my mother's, or if I'd just convinced myself I could.

At the airport, I tried calling my father from the pay phone near the security line, but a nurse answered. I hung up fast.

I sat in front of the arrivals and departures board outside the international terminal. I hadn't gone through security yet; my bags were still with me, unchecked. The big schedule board said another flight to Dublin would leave a few hours later – it was on Air France, with a stopover in Paris. I flirted with the idea of not going to Dublin at all, but to somewhere else entirely. Madrid, maybe, or Johannesburg – both were leaving at the same time as the Dublin flight. If I hung out for a while, there were late-night planes to Reykjavik or Lima or Geneva. I traced the tweed pattern on the edge of my suitcase. From the bar just past the security gate, someone spoke in what I decided was Finnish. Someone else said, *Would you* stop *it?* Someone else laughed.

And then, my flight to Dublin was boarding. I heard the attendant call for first class over the PA, then rows twenty-five through thirty, then rows twenty and higher, then rows fifteen and higher. I imagined the people lining up at the gate: two old ladies, a couple with a baby, a man in a wheelchair. A beautiful boy I might be sitting next to.

All rows for Dublin, the flight attendant called. I pictured old people pressing their hands to their knees and, groaning, standing. The flight attendant would be smiling with all her teeth as she ripped their tickets. She called my name over the PA once, then twice. But I had suddenly become so sure of something: this wasn't how it was supposed to work. I wished it were, I wished I could have gone, but I knew I couldn't.

The flight attendant called my name for a final time. I watched the departures board. After a while, the status of the flight to Dublin changed from Boarding to Departed. I ran to the window, dragging my bags. There it was, a big Aer Lingus jet. The massive, capsule-shaped contraption backed away from the gate, the old people and the children and the cute boy inside, their luggage packed in like Tetris pieces. Eventually, it pulled to the runway, hovered there for a while, warming up, and then with a splintering, white sound, it took off, screaming faster and faster, higher and higher, until it was rushing over Manhattan, until it was indistinguishable from the stars.

They encourage me to write letters to everyone I know, even if I'll never send them in a million years. They say if I'm stuck, I should just start writing. Just go for it, they tell me. Dive right in. Talk about anything.

So I guess you'd be out of school by now. Maybe in grad school, if you've gone that far, or maybe out of that, too. Perhaps you didn't go to grad school, or even college. Which is perfectly okay. Sometimes I'm not sure how much I learned in college, really. There was an awful lot that was just filler.

You might have a job now, or perhaps even a family. Your house might have a view of those enormous mountains. I admit the only mountains I've ever seen are pretty pathetic in comparison, mere hills stuffed with coal – although, I suppose, they were the first mountains you saw, too. What did you think when you first laid eyes on the real ones, all purple and capped with snow? Was the wind knocked out of you? Did you cry?

And what do you go by? Jo? Josie? Just J? Or maybe you have a fabulous nickname.

One day, maybe I'll work up the courage to write

a real letter to you, one with substance and explanation. Sometimes, it doesn't even feel like you exist. You're so far away, almost nothing. But some days, when I'm feeling very brave, I admit to myself that I don't want you to be far away, not anymore. Some days, I think I want to know the truth about you, once and for all.

PART IV

COBALT, PA,
SEPTEMBER, 2001

**it will kill you
if you're not looking**

CHAPTER 18

Samantha pulled into the driveway in a deep gray Mercedes SUV. Stella and I watched her through the dingy curtains in the front room, the one with the pictures of Sinatra and the television. 'Well, isn't she fancy?' Stella said in an awed voice. 'I bet that car has that wonderful, leathery new-car smell. You know that smell?'

Samantha parked, slid out of the front seat, and grabbed a brown snakeskin purse from the back. When she rang the doorbell we snapped the curtain closed, as if we hadn't been watching. Stella settled back into the chair, and I answered the door. Samantha's head was bent down as she keyed something into her cell phone. 'Hi,' I said.

She looked up and broke into a five-alarm smile. 'Hello, Summer! So nice to see you!'

Her blazer and skirt were the same iridescent gray as her car. As she pushed her sunglasses up on her head, I tried to make myself presentable, standing taller and wriggling my toes around to conceal the hole in my sock. I quickly tried to think up excuses for my disheveled appearance: I was wearing pajamas so Stella wouldn't feel so self-conscious.

247

I hadn't washed my hair because we were trying to conserve water. And anyway, Samantha had told us she'd be coming yesterday.

'Sorry, I got tied up yesterday,' Samantha said, as if reading my mind. 'I was waiting for paperwork from a seller and it took for*ever*.' She pushed her way into the door . . . and then stopped. I watched as her knuckles gripped her bag and then released. It was pretty obvious what she was looking at.

'Hi, Sam,' Stella cried in a voice louder than mine. She sat up straighter on the couch, adjusting her black satin gloves and straightening her magenta wig.

'Well, Stella!' Samantha cried, returning to herself, as polished and as unsnagged as her nut-colored pantyhose. She gently rested her purse on the worn corduroy couch, glided over to Stella and gave her a delicate, uncertain hug. 'Are you cold?' she asked, her eyes falling to the blanket around Stella's legs and the other blanket around her torso.

'Not really,' Stella said. 'Nice car out there!' She attempted a whistle.

Samantha rolled her eyes. 'Well, you know. It was a present to myself. For closing on six houses in one month. In the real-estate world, that's tough – that's more than a house a *week*. I worked like a dog, though.' She sighed and panted, as if she'd just finished not only closing on the houses but building them, too. Then, she looked around, frowning. 'You could use some more *light* in here.'

She walked to the window and pulled back a curtain. The sunlight barreled its way in, showing off every crack in the windowsill, every stain on the carpet, every yellowed blotch of water damage on the ceiling. I watched as Samantha gazed around the room, taking in its pieces. I'd done the same thing when I had come to live with Stella over a year ago, trying to match the room to the mental image I'd been carrying around for years. The living room was smaller. There were more pictures of Frank Sinatra. I hadn't recalled the curio cabinet above the mantel with the little crystal figurines – a leaping dolphin, an owl, a turtle – or the complete set of encyclopedias from 1965.

Samantha gingerly crossed her legs. I sat down on the poky blue upholstered chair near the dining room, which smelled like stale cigarettes and root beer barrel candies. 'So I have been so, *so* busy,' Samantha sighed. 'It's been constant work since I've started, which is a really good thing, of course. The Northglenn area is absolutely on fire. Everyone wants in. They just built a new hospital, they're splitting the schools in two, and there's this wonderful gym up on the hill that just opened, too. It's just so . . . *chill*. I got them to teach yoga classes there!'

'Yoga!' Stella repeated. With some difficulty, she raised her arms into a Y, like she was doing a cheer. Gimme a Y for Yoga.

'There are adorable little developments,'

Samantha went on, the words tumbling out of her fast. 'That's mostly where I'm selling. To young couples, like Chris and me. Neighbors of ours, in fact! The houses that have cropped up around us are just lovely. They have built in barbecue grills and side basketball courts. They're brand new. I always tell customers that a new house is the best. You can put your own stamp on it, you know?'

Stella gave her a dippy smile, seeming perplexed.

'Where is Northglenn, anyway?' I asked.

'It's just past State College,' Samantha said.

I drew a map in my head. 'So it's not that far away,' I said slowly, so perhaps Stella would get it.

'Yes, but it's not the best highway,' Samantha said. 'Lots of accidents.'

And then she started up again, taking a deep breath. 'So Chris sends his regards, of course. He would have loved to come but he couldn't spare the day, obviously. It's busy, busy, busy with all the building he's doing.' She pantomimed wiping the sweat off her brow. 'He comes home so bushed every night.'

At the word *bushed,* I stood. Samantha's eyes lingered on me for a split second. We'd only talked on the phone before this. Each phone conversation had been the same: Samantha reiterated how badly she wanted to see us, but she was just so *busy.* First, because she and her husband, Chris, were buying a new house. Then, because she was studying for her realtor's license. Then, because she was selling houses. And more

250

houses. And more houses. For some reason, I couldn't quite imagine Samantha selling real houses – little plastic green ones from Monopoly seemed more plausible. People came to her real estate office, all prepared to look for a three-bedroom, two-bath, and Samantha held the little game piece between her hands and said, *You don't want* that. *You want* this.

At the end of each phone call, Stella loomed in the kitchen, weakly reaching out for the receiver. I told Samantha that Stella wanted to talk, but Samantha always said she had another call coming in. Or a client had just walked into her office. Or Chris needed something, *urgently.* When I went to hang up the phone, a little flurry of hurt crossed Stella's face, but she quickly distracted herself by scratching the skin under her wig, or digging through her box of cassette tapes for something by Elvis, or tickling her slobbering pug, Nelson, on his belly.

'I've gotten Chris on this vitamin program,' Samantha went on. 'There's a health store that opened across town, too, which I tell my clients is a really, *really* good thing because that indicates wealth in a community, you know? The whole McDonald's phenomenon – the poorer people are, the worse they eat. Because, you know, McDonald's is cheap. And . . . fattening. If people want to eat better, it means they have more money.'

'But vitamins aren't food,' I offered. 'They're . . . pills.'

251

Derailed, Samantha scratched the edge of her chin. 'Well, anyway. They have the most amazing selection of vitamins and herbs, and I've told Chris that if he's going to be working such long hours and feel so stressed, he should get his body into balance. I'm trying to get him to yoga too but you know, he *is* a man.'

'I've tried vitamins,' Stella piped up.

Samantha's forehead creased. '. . . Really?'

Stella's eyes gleamed excitedly. 'They were the size and smell of a horse's asshole. I practically couldn't swallow them. Made the inside of my mouth smell like a barn. Now, what if I wanted to kiss a man? He wouldn't want to come near me, my mouth smelling like manure.'

Samantha's mouth dropped open a little.

'It's true!' Stella looked at me. 'Tell her, Summer. Tell her about the men that kiss me.'

'There are lots of them,' I said. Stella liked to kiss men on TV, crawling up to the screen and suffering through a few moments of static to get her mouth close to their faces.

'Chris takes vitamin E, vitamin A, and vitamin C,' Samantha said. This person she'd become. 'And then he takes a multi. I think it's really been working for him. I take them too, of course. And calcium. Do you take calcium, Stell?'

'What were the things I took, Summer?' Stella asked. 'The asshole pills? It was a vitamin that wasn't a letter.'

'Well, I mean, you take lots of vitamins,' I

explained, searchingly. 'You're supposed to. I think you're thinking of the herbs.'

'That was right around when I did that walk for breast cancer,' Stella said. She glanced at me, sheepish. 'Or, well, *started* that walk for breast cancer. There were too many people to finish. I thought it would be more like . . . oh, I don't know. A *parade*. Everyone was walking so damn fast! I would think you'd want everyone to *look* at you, not just whiz right by.'

The cuckoo clock in the dining room chimed out the hour. The truth about the breast cancer walk was that Stella had been in terrible pain that day. She'd stood at the start, all ready to walk, but then went pale and grabbed my hand. 'Honey,' was all she needed to say. We moved to the sidelines fast. Children stared at us. Other people looked away. Shortly after that, the doctors put her on a low dose of morphine.

Samantha ran her hand through her hair. 'I brought you a present, Stell.' She pulled out a fat romance novel. There was a woman on the cover, her breasts tumbling out of her corset. She had windswept hair and a troubled, I-have-to-make-a-huge-life-or-death-decision-about-my-kingdom expression. 'You used to love this series, remember?'

'She's not reading that much,' I butted in.

Samantha looked at me sharply. 'Well, why not? It's probably good for her.'

'It's true, I'm not reading much,' Stella

admitted. 'TV is far more interesting these days. My favorite show is *Road Rules*.'

Samantha wrinkled her nose. 'Really?'

'Oh, it's so good,' Stella said. 'We'll have to watch it later – it's so deliciously nasty. It's just the kind of show you'd like.'

One of Samantha's eyebrows shot up. 'I don't *think* so.'

Stella pursed her lips. 'Well. Maybe not anymore.'

There was a catch in her voice. Samantha looked startled, as though she'd been slapped.

My gaze ping-ponged from Stella to Samantha, not sure what would happen next, but hoping, maybe, for an altercation. But Samantha just stared down at her purse, running her fingers along its brass grommets.

According to Stella, Samantha left Cobalt when she turned eighteen. Just disappeared. Stella had a lot of excuses for it. *She* was like that when she was young, after all – *she* never played by the rules. Then, during the time my father was suffering through the worst of his depression, Samantha called Stella out of the blue. She was working as a legal secretary, she said. She'd just gotten married on a cruise ship to a man named Chris; he developed townhouses in Central Pennsylvania.

I asked Stella if she'd seen Samantha since she took off, and Stella shrugged and said Samantha had only come back once to retrieve her savings bonds from the safe-deposit box and haul away

254

the rosewood chest that had belonged to her parents. When she visited, she dropped off a few wedding photos, and, after enough pestering, Stella finally showed them to me. I was stunned to discover that all of Chris's family had attended the wedding ceremony, boarding the cruise ship for the afternoon when it docked in Miami. Stella slowly pointed out each family member, saying both very little and so very much. 'Here's his mother, his father, his grandmother, his great-aunt,' she recited. She squinted viciously at the great-aunt. 'Good Lord. What idiot wears *black* to a wedding at sea?'

'Do you want something to eat?' I asked Samantha, heading toward the kitchen. 'A sandwich? A soda?'

'Oh, goodness, Chris forbids me to drink soda,' Samantha said quickly, desperate to break the conversational void. 'Do you have any fruit?'

'We have grape jelly.'

'I want a glass of wine,' Stella called from the living room.

Samantha ran her hands over the crystal candy dish, which had a fine layer of dust on its bumpy edges. 'I don't really drink wine, either,' she said quietly. 'It gives you wrinkles.'

'Sweetie, you're so pretty, you have so many years until you get wrinkles,' Stella called out. 'Summer, get us wine, okay?'

'We don't have any.'

'Break out that bottle on the top of the fridge.'

255

I walked back into the living room. 'You can't have wine. You can have an iron pill. That's it.'

Stella rolled her eyes. 'I'll sip. Slowly. Give me a thimbleful.'

I turned back for the kitchen. There was the same peeling alphabet wallpaper that had been here when I visited for my grandmother's funeral. The same lopsided cabinets, an even bigger accumulation of thermometers and bags of charcoal and garage sale crap on the back porch. There was indeed a dust-covered bottle of wine on top of the fridge. I pulled it down and searched the silverware drawer for a corkscrew. Samantha hovered near the kitchen table, pulling her cell phone's antenna in and out. I could hear Stella grunting in the other room, and hoped she wasn't trying to come in here. It always took a huge effort for her to move from room to room. 'Are you okay?' I called to her.

'I'm fine, fine,' she said.

'We'll be there in a second.'

This morning, Stella had been so excited Samantha was coming. Samantha had finally carved out a niche in her busy schedule to see us! How fortuitous that she had a conference in Ohio, and that the drive took her right by Cobalt! 'I hope she remembers how to get here,' Stella said, worried. 'Do you think she'll remember to look for the McDonald's off the interstate? The one with the really high golden arches?'

I helped her put on makeup. She pulled on

256

her gloves and slid her feet into her green high heels and dug out a set of blue plastic dumbbells to keep on her lap, perhaps to make Samantha think she'd just been working out. And then, after she was ready, I found her on the living room floor, clutching her side. 'Again?' I asked. 'Again,' she said.

She insisted that she didn't want to take something that would completely knock her out, so I suggested she take a bath to relax. I filled up the tub with bubble bath, laid out her red and black robe, and spritzed Charlie perfume, her favorite, around the bathroom. She told me that when she was younger, she used to take bubble baths all the time, with Skip perched on the toilet, admiring her. She would smoke cigarettes, he would drink Scotch, and sometimes he would climb into the tub with her. 'Those were the good years,' she sighed.

I pulled the wine cork out of the bottle. A cough of dust came up as well. I poured a shot-glass-full for Stella, and found chipped tumblers for Samantha and myself. 'We don't have any real wine glasses,' I said, noticing Samantha looking at the tumblers with disdain.

'Well, you should get some,' Samantha insisted. 'Wine glasses aren't very expensive.'

'They'd go to waste.'

'Every house needs wine glasses.' Samantha returned to the living room and perched daintily on the couch next to Stella. 'I always send my clients wine glasses when they move into their new home. It's such a chill way to celebrate, you know?'

I eyed her carefully. I wasn't sure I'd heard the word *chill* used so often in such a small span of time, not even when Andy Elkerson came over to repair the air-conditioning unit. But as she and I continued to nervously watch one another, I wondered if Samantha was smarter than I thought. Even though Stella and I had never talked about it, Stella very well could have told Samantha about my father and the hospital. It was possible, too, that Stella had theorized with Samantha why I was really, truly here, caring for her. Every time Samantha glanced in my direction, I thought I could see it in her face – the pity, the self-satisfaction of how her life had turned out so differently from mine.

I handed Stella the tumbler, and she belted it back fast. I felt like I should go and clean something, or prepare something, or hide Stella's medications. 'I didn't know every house needed wine glasses,' Stella said, picking up on the conversation. 'I'm trying to remember if I own any.'

'I'm sure you do,' Samantha cooed.

'Then where are they?' Stella wondered aloud, adjusting the Magic Bag on her belly. It was a bean-filled cloth bag that we kept in the freezer. We'd recently bought a new cover for it, a scene of the night sky, complete with cartoonish planets. 'I don't recall owning a single wine glass.'

Samantha slapped her knees with her palms.

'You know what? I think we should have an outing. Go get you some new wine glasses.'

'Samantha . . .' I whined.

'That sounds like a good idea,' Stella said creakily.

'We could go to the Wreston mall,' Samantha suggested.

'Oh, honey, no,' Stella said. 'That place burned down.'

'Really?' Samantha scratched her head. 'Well, where else is there?'

Stella and I looked at each other. 'Well, there's Wal-Mart,' Stella said. 'They have everything.'

Samantha winced – Wal-Mart probably wasn't what she was imagining. But what did she expect? This was Cobalt. 'Well then.' Her tone was brisk. 'Wal-Mart it is.'

'Do you feel well enough?' I asked Stella.

'Of course,' Stella said sharply, weakly making a muscle with her arm. 'Fit as a fiddle.'

I resisted laughing. 'Maybe we should go to Wal-Mart tomorrow. We should just rest today. We could go before we take off on our trip.'

'Where are you going?' Samantha asked.

'Summer's taking me somewhere so I can smoke grass!' Stella cried.

Samantha looked startled. 'No, I'm not,' I reminded Stella. I faced Samantha. 'I told you about this on the phone, remember? I'm taking her to this . . . doctor, sort of. Near Lancaster.'

'He's a drug dealer!' Stella announced. 'He smokes with you!'

259

'He makes you *breathe in* things,' I corrected her. 'Healing things. Not . . . marijuana. He's Native American, I think. His name is Cheveyo. It means "spirit warrior" in some tribal language.'

Samantha pursed her lips and turned her wedding ring around and around on her finger.

'And before we go, we're also going to see the jackalope,' Stella added.

'*Maybe* we'll see the jackalope,' I said. 'If we have time.'

'. . . jackalope?' Samantha asked weakly.

'Oh, it's amazing,' Stella gushed. 'You'll never see anything like it in your life.'

Samantha blinked furiously. Finally, she pointed at Stella's black satin gloves. 'Why are you wearing those? You *are* cold, aren't you?'

'Not at all, dear.' Stella turned her wrists under.

Samantha pursed her pink lips. 'What are those even *made* out of?' She reached and pulled at the very tip of the left glove's thumb. Stella made a pained noise.

'Samantha, don't,' I said sharply.

The glove bagged around Stella's thin arms, so Samantha barely had to pull to get it off. Stella slithered around to hide her arm, but we all got a good look at the bruises. There were the green spots in the crook of her elbow, the purplish-blue welts by her wrist, the black blotches on the top of her palm, not from any recent hospital visits – she'd finally given in and gotten a chemo port – but from *months* ago. *Not unusual, for all the treatments she's had,*

260

the doctor assured us. *Chemotherapy makes you bruise very easily.*

It was as if a curtain had been ripped back. Samantha fell silent, letting the satin glove drop to the table. I snatched it up and handed it back to Stella, who shoved it on her arm as quickly as she could, which wasn't as fast as she'd have liked.

'I just like the gloves,' Stella said stubbornly. 'I think they're pretty. All right?'

'Of course,' Samantha said quickly. It seemed like she was becoming less whole before our eyes, the way a photo bleached out in the sun. She cleared her throat. 'You know, if we want to go to Wal-Mart, we should go today. Because I really should leave later this evening. My conference starts really early tomorrow morning, and I should get there as soon as I can.'

'But we have your bedroom ready for you,' Stella protested. It was true – we had been under the impression that Samantha was going to stay the night.

'No, I was always leaving today. I didn't say that?' Samantha smoothed her hand over the lacy doily on the coffee table, avoiding looking at us. 'They really need me at my conference. And I'm up for an award.'

'An award!' Stella weakly clapped her hands. 'Well, then! What kind of award?'

'A . . . real-estate award.' Samantha looked at me, her eyes pleading.

I could tell she'd just tacked this on in a panic.

261

Stella had probably caught on to this already, I realized next. But we both gave in. What was the point of arguing? 'Well, all right,' I said. 'I guess we could go today. Stella, you up for going to Wal-Mart today?'

'I think I could manage,' Stella said, putting a gloved hand to a yellowish cheek.

'Good,' I answered. I raised my wine glass and looked at Samantha. 'Cheers.'

'Cheers,' Samantha answered, snapping back to her new self. In a few minutes, she carried her wine glass to the sink and poured it down the drain.

CHAPTER 19

My father hadn't seemed that surprised when I gave up my fellowship two years ago, and he hadn't pushed me to explain why I'd stayed. After I watched my flight to Dublin take off, I'd come home and picked up the dogs from Mrs Church, the woman down the street who'd volunteered to adopt them until my father was back from his 'rest cure' – his description, not mine. Mrs Church seemed so relieved when I showed up at the door, saying that as soon as I had left, the dogs had eaten a shepherd's pie that was sitting on her kitchen counter, knocked over a coffee pot, and lapped up the coffee. Only Wesley greeted Mrs Church when she returned to the kitchen, leading Mrs Church to believe that he either had some remorse for what he'd done, or that he possibly wasn't involved at all.

That Christmas of 1998, the first Christmas he was at the Center, he and I celebrated in the facility's common room with some of the other patients. There was a fir tree in the middle of the room, a roaring fire in the fireplace, and six inches of glittering snow outside. My father squealed when he saw I'd brought Wesley with me, which only reminded me that he never squealed when he saw me.

Bing Crosby was on constant repeat on the Center's stereo. There was a marathon game of Scrabble, the aides making sure no one used any words that would upset anyone else. Everyone ate with plastic utensils, and the pecan pie was eschewed because everyone seemed to have a nut allergy. It didn't really feel like Christmas.

When Christmas came around again in 1999, I helped my father move into the Center's 'rehabilitation' property, an old manor at the corner of its grounds. Merewether was built for patients who could handle more space and freedom but still wanted day-to-day treatment. My father wanted to move there on Christmas Day – it was his present to himself.

The day was icy and bright, and we had to be careful carrying my father's bags up the slippery front steps. I felt charmed by Merewether's cozy Craftsman-style detailing, dusty Mission furniture, upholstered window-seats and drafty farmhouse kitchen. There was a big fir tree in Merewether's living room, too, only this one felt more appropriate. Sweeter. Not many residents were around – most had gone to visit family, as Merewether patients were allowed to leave the Center's premises for a few hours each day. There was an older woman who was a wonderful painter; she gave paintings to the other housemates as Christmas gifts, even one to my father, though he'd just moved in. There was an overweight man who spoke very softly and cried when we sat down to Christmas dinner, prepared for us by some of the aides and the chef they'd brought over from the main building. There was an emaciated girl in her twenties, barely older than me, with dark hair and translucent skin. They were nice, though, and grateful for a celebration. I didn't mind my father living with them.

My father laughed and joked with the aides. Wesley came again and sat on everyone's laps. We talked about how this might be the last Christmas of our existence – Y2K was upon us, and there was a lot of half-baked talk about water pipes exploding, massive floods, planes falling out of the sky, and bank accounts dissolving into rows and rows of zeroes. There was even a round of singing, the thin girl banging out Christmas carols on the house's old piano.

That winter, my father and I set a time every night to talk on the phone, but suddenly, I would call and he wouldn't be there. When I did catch him, he was often distracted, getting off quickly. We'd agreed to read a John Irving novel together and conduct an over-the-phone book group, but when I asked him about it a few weeks later, he admitted he hadn't started it yet. A good chunk of the winter went by when I would call, leave a message, and it would take him days to call back. When we spoke on the phone, he asked me such small and generic questions, as if I was a distant relative, or perhaps a friend's child: How was my new job? How was the guy I was dating? I began answering in monotone, insulted.

Or was I just being sensitive? Was he just busy, or was he avoiding me? Perhaps there was something he wasn't telling me. Perhaps there was something I'd done. The paranoia mounted through the spring, creeping up without me quite knowing it, until I realized three weeks had gone by and I hadn't called him – nor had he called me. Who had not called first? Who had started this?

I finally visited him in early August, more than eight months after he'd moved into Merewether. I took Metro-North, got a cab at the station, gave my name at the security desk at the Center's front gate, and a golf cart picked me up and drove me to Merewether's doorstep. Merewether didn't allow any cars on its premises; everyone got around by golf cart or bicycle or on foot, not unlike a retirement community.

My father opened the door to Merewether himself, announcing that the others in the house had gone to see the new *Austin Powers* movie at the big theater in town. I stepped into the house tentatively, unsure of how to greet him. We awkwardly hugged, then moved away from one another. I looked around. The front room's furniture was lumpy and comfortable, the pillows missing some of their batting. A Big Mouth Billy

266

Bass – the electronic novelty that sang 'Take Me to the River' – was propped up against a credenza across the room. There was plenty of evidence of the other housemates – a pale blue cardigan hanging from one of the coat hooks, a wrinkled copy of *The Stand* by Stephen King face-down on the front room's easy chair, a pair of eyeglasses on the round table. Next to the glasses was a large note that said, *Without speaking, without silence, how can you express the truth?*

My father noticed me looking at it. 'We sometimes write koans for each other.'

'Koans?'

'Philosophical sayings. For meditation. Leahanne is a Buddhist. She got us into it. It's really useful.'

I assumed Leahanne must have been another Merewether resident. 'So . . . you like everyone in the house?' I asked.

'Sure,' he answered. 'They're very nice. They love animals as much as I do. I'm trying to see if we can get an indoor cat.'

I laughed. 'Right.'

'What?'

'You're not a cat person, Dad.'

His face clouded, offended. 'I like all animals.'

My father took me out to Merewether's backyard and showed me the apple tree, the plot of dirt for flowers and vegetables, the wheelbarrow. 'I have a new job,' he declared. 'I'm replanting the garden, weeding and mulching and making sure that the bulbs are evenly spaced.'

'Why aren't you in the office anymore?' Last year, his doctor told me that once the patients graduated to Merewether, the hospital staff gave them small jobs. They'd assigned my father to the accounts office; he was to update pertinent information into the Center's database.

He shrugged. 'Because I'm doing this now.'

'Did something . . . happen in the office?'

He stiffened. 'I just didn't want to work in the office. It was my decision.'

I held up my hands, surprised by his defensiveness. It was unusually brave of him. 'Okay, okay,' I said. 'I got it.'

My nose filled with the earthy smell of mulch and dirt. When my father first went to the Center, his therapist told me that breakdowns were very likely within the first two months. When that didn't happen, he told me that if the patient doesn't have a breakdown in the first two months, he is almost *guaranteed* to have one in the following six months. He said I shouldn't be alarmed if my father had to move back into the Center's main facility for a while – it was actually a sign of progress. I was confused. A breakdown was now progress?

Yet my father looked strong. He told me on the phone a few months ago that he'd begun playing tennis. An instructor came out on Tuesdays and Saturdays, and a group of them were talking about holding a tournament later in the summer. I was happy for him, but I didn't want to say it out loud or even feel it too strongly in case that might jinx it.

268

My father made sandwiches for lunch and brought them out to the patio, remarking that the tomatoes were from the garden. 'So how's work?' he asked, taking a big bite.

That generic question, yet again. 'Fine.' I noticed a big blob of tomato on his cheek, and leaned over and mopped it up.

'Doing anything in the lab?' he mustered.

'I'm not licensed to do that, Dad. I'm just the office assistant.'

'You're smarter than everyone that works there. Are you going to apply to grad school?'

'It's too late now. I missed the deadline for fall.'

'Apply for spring. It would be a waste not to go, if they're paying for it.'

Dr Hughes had found me a job at NYU's genetic counseling office. When she introduced the possibility, she kept apologizing for its meagerness – 'It's like a glorified assistant's job. I'll see if I can get them to give you some more challenging projects, and it's a great way to go back to grad school, because working for NYU means they'll comp your tuition, but still, it's awfully menial' – to the point where it annoyed me. *Maybe menial is all I can manage,* I wanted to say.

Most of the counselors at the genetics clinic were sweet, soft-spoken, adequately educated women, there to gently explain the details of Tay-Sachs disease and sickle-cell anemia and spina bifida to couples who were either already pregnant or thinking of conceiving. A guy named

Alex, 25, was in charge of the billing department, gathering people's insurance information and asking for upfront payments and making sure bills weren't outstanding. The women in the office loved Alex in a mother-hen way. The first thing people noticed about him was his size: He was six-five, broad, with ham-like arms and powerful legs. And he was a fan of wearing the same color tie and dress shirt, like Regis Philbin. One day, as we were both leaving the office at the same time, he'd asked if I wanted to get a cup of coffee. It was the way most people started dating, I realized. Not after years and years of tempestuous pining – as I'd done with Philip – but casually, curiously.

My father stood up and carried our dishes into the house. When he came back out, he asked me if I could help him put up a chicken-wire fence around one of the trees. I was to hold the posts steady and upright, and he would hammer them into the ground.

The sledgehammer had an awkward center of gravity; it took my father by surprise. The first time he swung it, he missed the top of the post completely. The second time, he hit the side. I watched as his hands shook, probably a side-effect of his medication.

'Maybe you should let me do it,' I suggested.

'It's pretty heavy.'

He finally hit the top of the post, but it was a tentative, ineffectual little tap.

'You have to give it more force than that,' I said with a laugh.

My father dropped the sledge to the ground. It fell heavily, the wooden handle tipping into the dirt. The air was absolutely still. He trudged over to the graying, splintered picnic table and sat down. When I lifted my head, he was staring at me peacefully.

'What's going on with you, Summer?' he asked. He didn't sound wounded or fragile, merely curious. 'I haven't heard from you in a long time.'

A bird let out a very long call. My heart pounded. *You haven't heard from* me? I wanted to say. *You're the one who doesn't answer your phone!* 'N-Nothing,' I stammered, stunned. There was a tinny buzzing in my head where thoughts should have been.

'You seem different,' he said, cocking his head to the right. 'I'm not sure how, but you do.'

I blinked, flummoxed. *I* seemed different? And I wondered if I somehow *did* seem different to him. 'Is it because of that guy you're dating?' he went on, almost sounding hopeful. 'Alex?'

Alex? My heart sank; my father and I really *didn't* talk. Alex and I had fallen into a pattern with which I was mostly unfamiliar but pretended as best as I could that I'd had plenty of practice. He took me out to eat and to the movies, always paying. Things hadn't moved too quickly or too slowly, but rather followed a very proper timetable, as if he'd read about when to do what in some sort of manual.

But I knew my relationship with him wasn't going anywhere. One night, while we were lying in bed, he'd propped himself up on his elbows and told me he loved me. It was like he'd flung himself from a tall tower. His face was flushed, his pupils huge. He asked me if I loved him back, but I couldn't say anything. I just stared, dumbstruck. How could he love me? What had I done that was so incredible? I wanted to say that I loved him, too, but I knew I didn't mean it, so the words wouldn't come. I wasn't sure if I was equipped to love anyone.

Moreover, Alex knew nothing about me – I'd told him nothing about my mother leaving, my father's condition. It was amazing, actually, that he didn't know, considering that Dr Hughes had ties with the office and had probably said something to someone there. But he believed what I told him – my father lived across the country, and we didn't speak.

I poked my finger into the chicken wire. 'You seem different, too,' I said, my voice a childish whine.

My father stretched his arms to the sky. 'I guess I am different. I feel pretty great. Better than I've felt in a long time.'

'You . . . do?'

He nodded. 'I've been seeing a great new doctor. His name is Walter, and he's a million times better than anyone else I've seen. I feel so much . . . clearer.'

I hadn't been told he was seeing a new doctor. 'You call the doctor by his first name?'

'He asks that we do. And I've been on meds I haven't had to change for months. It's like, after all these years, I finally got the right combination. I feel like I've finally emerged from a cave. I've even thought about leaving here soon.'

'You mean to come back to Brooklyn?'

One corner of his mouth curled up. 'It's where I live.'

I stared at him for a few long seconds, silent.

He crossed his arms over his chest, still smiling. 'Don't act so ecstatic.'

'No, I mean, I'm happy,' I said quickly. 'Of course I'm happy. It's wonderful that you're feeling better. But, I mean, are you sure?'

I wanted to ask him if he was thinking of leaving soon. What would he do, back in Brooklyn? Would he try to find a job?

He gazed out at the farmland beyond Merewether's split-rail fence. 'You know I'll always love you.'

I started up. 'I love you, too.'

There was a pause, and then he said, 'The accident I got in years ago. I told you about the girl that died, right? Kay? We saw her grave in Cobalt?'

I rubbed my eyes. 'Yeah. Sure.'

He stared off at the woods. 'She was in a coma for weeks after the accident. They kept her alive, but not because they thought she'd live. Because . . . she was pregnant.'

Far off, a car door slammed. A few birds took off from a nearby tree. 'She was pregnant?' I repeated.

'It was unthinkable, really. They knew she was going to die, but they also found out she was pregnant. They wanted to see if they could save the child.'

'Were you there?'

'Well . . . no.'

'Why not?'

'Her fiancé was there. Her family.'

'But you were her friend. You didn't see her?'

He took a sip of water and stared at the outdoor thermometer, mounted on a post next to the house. 'No.'

I tried to process this, to make sense of why he'd chosen this moment to tell me. 'So I guess the baby died?' I asked. I tried to remember if I'd seen a smaller headstone beside Kay's. I couldn't remember one, but then, I hadn't been looking.

'What?' my father asked.

'The baby. It died, right?'

He bent down and picked up the sledge, and then leaned it against a tree. 'I'm thirsty. Do you want more water? Or another tomato, maybe? It's good with just a little salt and basil. I think I'm going to get one for myself.' He started for the door.

I glared at his receding back. He was always like this; he hated discussing things that had died, adults or children, even animals and trees.

He couldn't watch nature programs because they always involved something strong killing something weak. By the time he came back outside, the other housemates had returned from the movies, bumping around the house noisily, saying Austin Powers catchphrases like 'Yeah, baby!' and 'Danger is my middle name' in swaggering British accents. The conversation quickly veered somewhere else.

On my way home, pressed against the window on the Metro North train, I felt unsettled, as if I'd left something behind. I started planning the next time my father and I would talk. It would be better. I would be better. I would ask him about gardening and tennis. What was bothering me, anyway? Didn't I want a father who played tennis and gardened and *interacted* with society? Didn't I want him to be well?

At work, I watched patients in the waiting room. There were pregnant women with fretful looks on their faces, pale couples trying desperately to conceive, mothers who already had a child die from leukemia and were mining their chromosomes to see if something inside of them had caused it.

Was I missing out on something, living this way? Where would I be now, if I'd have taken the fellowship in Ireland? What would I be studying, how would I fill my days? There were so many times I wanted to correct the counselors here for mispronouncing easy scientific terms, dumbing down processes until they were basically incorrect, mixing up easy genetic markers for certain ailments. And yet I couldn't say a word – I was simply an assistant with no rights. A cruel thought occurred to me: Perhaps this was what my mother felt like, before she left us. Stifled like this, compromised, angry that she wasn't living her life according to exactly what she wanted. But, as soon as I thought it, I felt so guilty and small. So I wasn't doing earth-shattering research. I could be doing a lot worse.

The dogs followed me as I walked through the apartment I grew up in, sifting through my father's big leather box of receipts and tickets and take-out menus and Post-its and packing slips. I read a few again. *Today, there are only two pigeons sitting on the ledge across the street. What did they do to the other one?*

What had my father alluded to in the hospital, during that bad ECT treatment? *I've hidden something from you,* he'd said – or something like that, anyway. Would it unlock why this had happened to him, who he was – or was it ridiculous to think that way? I wandered into his closet and stared at the button-down shirts and blazers he'd left behind. Some of them were moth-eaten or out of style; he'd have to buy new things, if he was considering going back to work. Some of my mother's clothes were still in there, too, relics of the late Eighties and Nineties: three black dresses from

Ann Taylor. A suit from Brooks Brothers with shoulder pads. Some pink blouses, a light gray cashmere sweater. I pressed in the rivets of a pair of pale blue jeans. I'd never thought to look through my mother's pockets before – I hadn't thought she was the type to leave things in there. But I found a faded receipt stuffed into the fifth pocket, the purple ink still crisp and legible, for a dozen donuts from the bakery down the street. My mother used to have to go to the bakery and buy them for my father because he had an inexplicable fear of standing in the bakery line.

And there was a business card in the next pocket for Karen Keyes, MSW. I'd never heard my mother mention anyone named Karen Keyes. The items appeared staged, like someone had snuck in and filled my mother's pockets, planting the seeds, waiting for me to uncurl the mystery.

I didn't know how much later it was that the phone rang. I let it go to the answering machine, expecting to hear Alex's voice again – he'd already called several times, but I hadn't had the energy to talk. Instead, my father's voice floated out. 'Summer? Are you there?'

I leapt up and ran across the bedroom to grab the extension. 'Dad?' I gasped it out, like he was a ghost I'd just encountered around a corner. 'Why are you calling me?'

'No reason,' he said. 'I just wanted to call. To talk.'

I cleared my throat. 'I'm sorry about our last visit.'

'. . . Why?'

'I don't know. I just felt like it was . . . weird.'

Silence followed. 'It was fine,' he said.

I stared out the window blankly, my heart beating so fast it felt it might rip out of my body. A tugboat skidded down the East River; cars zoomed up the FDR.

'You want me to be happy, right?' my father asked, sounding almost afraid.

I cupped my hand over the head of one of the dogs. 'Of course I want you to be happy. That's a silly question. Why would you ask that?'

'I just wanted to make sure.'

'I want you to come back to Brooklyn,' I said quickly. 'I'm excited that you feel better. I hope that you didn't misunderstand me, when we visited. I was just surprised, is all. We just haven't talked that much, and—'

'I know, Summer,' he interrupted. 'I appreciate what you've done for me. I don't know what I would've done without you.'

The sun broke through a cloud, sending splendorous light across the faces of the buildings across the water. I felt wonderful. He still cared about me. And he was coming home. He was better. The dogs would be ecstatic. They'd remember him immediately – they'd bowl him over and lick his face. We could go to the park and let them swim in the lake and buy each of them a hot dog from the cart.

I was about to tell him that I thought he'd been

acting strangely, lately, and how I'd felt a little left out, maybe, a little excluded from his life, but it was okay now because he was coming back, because we would know everything about each other again. But then my father coughed. 'Summer, I've met someone.'

The air conditioner kicked on, sending a cold blast down my back. 'Pardon?'

'I met someone.' His words came out rushed. 'Someone I think I've fallen in love with.'

There were a lot of people out on the Promenade. Two little girls in frilly dresses ran down the length of the walkway, scuffing up their shoes.

'Her name's Rosemary,' my father galloped on. 'I met her here. She's an aide.' He swallowed something noisily on the other end of the line. 'She's really helped me. She's been an amazing friend. I wanted to tell you when you visited, but there wasn't time. The movie ended sooner than I thought.'

I looked at my left hand. I had been pressing my nails into my palm so hard, there were four white half-moons in my skin.

'I'm coming back to Brooklyn in two weeks,' my father said. 'I – we – decided today. I've asked her to come with me.'

I laughed. It just slipped out. 'What, as your nurse?'

A stiff silence followed.

'I'm sorry,' I backpedaled. 'I just . . . I don't

quite understand. This is all a little sudden. I mean, what, you couldn't have met this person – she's, what, an *aide*? – more than a month ago, right? That's the last time we really talked. Don't you think it's a little soon?'

His voice was low. 'Well, I met her almost a year ago.'

I went limp.

'I didn't want to say anything to you until I was certain. My new therapist, Walter? He thinks it's wonderful. He really supports us, and thinks what we're doing is perfectly healthy.'

'*Healthy?*'

'You'll really like her. She's very kind.'

'Did I already meet her?' I demanded. 'Was she there at Christmas?'

He was quiet for a moment. 'Yes, she was. She helped cook the dinner.'

I had spent so much time passing judgment on the patients – the anorexic girl who wouldn't stop petting Wesley, the grandmotherly woman who worked a jigsaw puzzle of kittens in a basket. I thought *they* had been the ones to watch.

'Okay,' I said slowly. 'Okay. Well, wow. Huh. I don't exactly know what to say.'

'How about that it's great? How about that you're happy for me?'

'No, it is great. Really.' I didn't know how to word this. 'You've been in the hospital, Dad. For a long time. I think . . .'

'You think what? That because I've been here,

280

I've . . . I've turned into a child? That I don't understand relationships? That I'm not worthy of anyone loving me back?'

'I didn't mean that at all!' Tears of surprise burned my eyes.

'That's what it sounds like. You assume these things about me, Summer, and I've lived with it long enough that maybe I assume them about myself. But I'm not that way. You don't even know.'

It hurt, like a pickax driving into my side. '. . . *What?*'

'This is my chance at being happy. I need a chance to grow, Summer. I had that here, and I don't want it to end. I need a chance to live my life, and you need a chance to live yours. There's enough room for all of us in that big apartment, don't you think?'

The sentiment was so familiar. 'I'm keeping *you* from living *your* life?'

He let out a frustrated breath. 'I have to go. Someone else needs the phone.'

And then he just hung up. I stared at the receiver, the dial tone like a siren. I tried to call back. The phone rang and rang, but no one answered. Something hit me, then: everything he said, especially his retorts, seemed like it'd been rehearsed, like he'd traced it over and over in his brain, committing them to memory, knowing that if he didn't get them out quickly and word-for-word, he wouldn't be able to say anything at all. I had never heard him speak so eloquently or succinctly about his feelings, especially if they might hurt someone else. Usually, he stumbled, backtracked, realized what he was trying to get out much, much later.

It made me feel both proud and horrible at the same time. He had, it seemed, truly turned a corner. But at the same time, it also meant my father had possibly sat in this new therapist's office and discussed how certain people in his life were preventing him from growing as a person. Maybe he'd prepared for when he would break the news, make his feelings known.

An unidentifiable feeling fluttered deep, but I didn't allow it to surface. *I'll make dinner*, I thought, standing up. I opened the fridge. Eggs. No cheese or butter. Grapes, a wilted head of lettuce. Some milk and some Diet Coke. When I looked around, the apartment was the same as it was just minutes ago, before I'd answered the phone. The bedspread still rumpled. The dogs still muddy. I breathed carbon dioxide out, plants sucked it back in. Everything I took for granted still acted as it should. Almost everything.

I thought about my father and this new woman, coming back to the apartment. Maybe he'd carry her over the threshold, stamping happily down the hallway to his old bedroom. I'd begun sleeping in his giant bed, the twinkling skyline as my night-light. I was glad for my father, that the darkness around him had lightened, but I wasn't particularly glad for myself. The emotion was sore and embarrassing. I no longer had any idea what my place was. I couldn't bear to think of climbing into my old bed, pulling up the heavy pink quilt I'd always secretly hated.

And then there was the phone call I received a few days later, when coming home from work. A woman identified herself as a nurse from St Geraldine's hospital in Wrightsville, Pennsylvania. She said that Stella Rogers had been in a car accident. Could I come by the hospital and pick her up? Stella was fine, but she wasn't in any condition to drive.

I started laughing. I told them I was in Brooklyn, New York – perhaps they could call someone who lived closer? The nurse on the phone said that I was Miss Rogers's in-case-of-emergency contact – the *only* in-case-of-emergency contact. Stella had demanded they call me.

I was looking for an excuse to leave. I packed some things and took a cab to LaGuardia. The next flight to Pittsburgh was on American. I walked up to the counter and bought a ticket. The plane was boarding in a half-hour.

When I got to the hospital, Stella was sitting on a hospital bed, watching television. I gasped when I saw her. I didn't even try and mask it. She looked like she'd lost about forty pounds and aged a hundred years since I'd last seen her six years earlier. The first thing she told me was that she had just watched the 2000 Summer Olympics women's triathlon. 'I think I might do a triathlon,' she said. 'I used to be quite the swimmer in my day.' I glanced at the old woman sleeping in the bed next to her. There was a tube in her nose and a wheelchair next to her bed. Stella rolled her eyes. 'That's Agnes,' she whispered. 'She's pathetic.'

The hospital gave me papers to sign, and then the doctor came to speak to me. He was so tall he had to stoop through doorways, and he had large, fingernail-shaped teeth. He said the reason Stella came in here – her car accident – was nothing. The problem, however – and he bent down to tell me this – was when she said that, as long as she was already here, she might as well mention the blood in her stool. And that she was – he twisted up his lips when he said this – 'defecating up a storm.' I had a feeling Stella would have used a more colorful word for 'defecating'.

'The red flags went up for me, just looking at her,' the doctor said. 'So I ordered a colonoscopy. I'm glad I did, considering.'

He finally told me that Stella had locally advanced colon cancer. They had taken blood samples and biopsies. God knows what they told Stella to get her to prep for the colonoscopy. The tumor was localized in her rectum, the doctor said, but perhaps not localized enough. It may have spread through the colon wall and possibly into her lymph nodes. This type of cancer was curable, but only if caught quickly. If it were up to him, he would get her in here to start treatment immediately.

I laughed. I thought of my father and this new woman, Rosemary, preparing to come back to Brooklyn. I thought of Alex, of Steven, even of Claire Ryan. They were living their own lives, simply, right now eating potato chips straight out of a bag, walking a dog, watching a baseball game, buying something on the Internet.

I drove Stella home in my rental because her car had been towed. I didn't know what to say to her; I hardly *knew* her. Halfway to her house, Stella turned to me and said, 'That doctor of mine is cute, isn't he? Do you want me to give him your phone number?'

'What, my number in New York?' I snapped.

'Oh, you were dying to come,' she said, putting her hand over mine and squeezing. For a moment, I was afraid that she knew really, truly, why I was here.

Stella navigated me back to the old house on the gravelly road. I felt like I was falling into a billowing dream. The tire swing had fallen off its tether and was now lying on the ground beneath the tree. Next door was the Elkerson house. Down the street was Philip's house, but it was too dark to really see it. A buzzing glow filled my stomach – surely he wasn't still living there. I was terrified to find out – if he was, that would be disappointing, pathetic. But if he wasn't, it would be equally disappointing, just for different reasons.

Stella opened the flimsy, rusting screen door. A strange smell wafted out – a mix of mildew and plug-in air fresheners. 'Are you coming?' she asked me.

I stood next to the handprint my father had put in the front walk's cement. RICHARD, it said, in very straight, neat letters. I could have stopped the arc of what was happening. I could have called someone, a caretaker, a nurse, hospice. The little I knew of Stella, I was pretty sure it wouldn't be easy to cajole her into months of surgery and treatment – the doctors had said, for instance, that she might end up needing a colostomy bag. It wouldn't even be easy to get her to admit there was anything wrong with her. I looked up at her in the door. Stella wore a shrunken neon-blue t-shirt underneath her hooked cardigan that said DIVA in sparkly rhinestones across the chest. She mentioned she was thinking of starting a website. I pictured a dark, noxious mass inside her, sitting on top of her bowel the way a kid perches on top of a carousel horse.

I stared at my bags. I had packed enough clothes. The dogs were at a kennel called the Doggie Day Spa, the only one my father said they could go to if I had to travel anywhere, because the ratio of dogs to daycare workers was four to one. Maybe being a caretaker was inscribed into the very fiber of me, meaning that if I looked at myself under a microscope, this was exactly what each of my individual cells would say. Why else was I always finding myself in these situations? Perhaps in Cobalt, I could succeed, where elsewhere I had failed. I wasn't here because of fear or anger. I was here because of, well, scientific destiny.

In the year between then and now, Stella and I would get to know each other through our habits. I would take comfort in her banal routines: her morning hour and a half of primping, the copious amount of sugar in her tea. I would relish the more significant moments, too. We would walk along the creek bed, cutting through Philip's old backyard – his family had moved after all, just a few years after my grandmother had died. We would stumble upon the bird graves Philip had shown me years ago. The headstones would be washed clean by rain, and the handwriting on the tiny slabs would be so hauntingly, painfully familiar. Neither Stella nor I would say anything, but we both, in our own ways, would know who'd buried most of the birds there, long before Philip was born.

I would learn that she couldn't go to bed without watching the Lottery, even though neither of us played – she simply liked the way the ping-pong balls blew around to and fro. And that she loved her dogs desperately, and gave each dog a song. She was like my father in that way, in many ways. She would tell me many stories about her husband, Skip, sometimes full of confessions, but I would never confess anything back. In the year since I came, Stella would ask only once what my dad was up to, and I would answer, 'Oh, he's doing his thing.' She wouldn't delve further. There would be a lot of things I wouldn't ask her – if she was angry this had happened to her. If she asked why. If she was afraid. The closest we would get to a conversation about heaven was the time I found out that Stella believed the afterlife was an episode of *The Price Is Right*. Those who lived fair lives would be able to come on down the aisle and play the pricing games with Bob Barker, those who were very good got to climb up on the stage and play Plinko and the shell game and Cliff Hangers and spin the big wheel, and those who were criminals or pedophiles or sold drugs to children got to sit in the audience, waiting for the rest of eternity for Rod Roddy to call their names. When I would ask her what she thought she'd get to do in *The Price Is Right* Afterlife, she would reply, 'Oh, I might not be in the Showcase Showdown, but I'd definitely get to spin the wheel.'

Maybe I knew all this was coming, standing there in Stella's gravel driveway, still fresh off the plane from New York. Maybe I convinced myself that she needed me instead of admitting what I couldn't bear to think about back home. Whatever the case, I swallowed hard, lifted my bags, and threw them over my shoulder. Stella's old dogs regarded me tiredly; none of them got up. 'I'm coming,' I said. Of course I was.

CHAPTER 20

The Cobalt Wal-Mart parking lot was packed with Saturday shoppers. Samantha parked her Mercedes in one of the very back spaces to avoid any potential parking lot accident: 'Look at the way some of these people are taking up three spaces!' she cried. 'In an enormous pickup truck, no less!' I unfolded Stella's wheelchair from the cavernous back area and helped her into it.

The double doors swished open into a wall of gumball machines. Beyond that was the store. The vastness of the place, after the corner delis and economy of city space I'd grown up with, had been remarkably easy to get used to. As soon as we hit the cart corral, Stella struggled to stand up. 'I'm fine,' she muttered.

'No you're not,' I said.

'I'm *fine*,' she said again.

'What do you want me to do with this?' Samantha looked at the empty wheelchair.

'Stick it by the carts,' Stella suggested.

Samantha looked suspiciously at the people ambling through the lobby. The room echoed with beeping cash registers and screaming kids.

Something told me Samantha didn't spend much time in her town's Wal-Mart. 'Someone might take it!' she whispered.

'We could put it back in the car,' Stella said.

'But don't you *need* it?' I asked Stella.

Stella shrugged. 'I need to start walking more anyway. I'm pretty sure the Jackalope Museum isn't wheelchair accessible. It's not much more than a shack.'

I gave her a weary look. 'We might not be able to go. It depends on how long it takes to get to Cheveyo. He lives in the middle of nowhere.'

'Near the *Amish*,' Stella stage-whispered, sinking into a seat at a snack-bar table. 'I'm not sure it's right to be around Amish people when you're ill.'

'Where'd you hear that?' I demanded.

'Oh, it's around. It's everywhere. The Amish people are carcinogenic.'

I thought of the pamphlets I'd gotten in the mail about Cheveyo. *Miracle healer,* the cover of the first pamphlet said. There sat Cheveyo, a wise, hippie toad in his tie-dyed t-shirt, his face the color of a worn-out saddle. Next to him was a young woman who had cervical cancer. That was how she was described in the caption: *Cheveyo with Jane (31, cervical cancer).* Cheveyo did something with stones. Or feathers. Animal spirits. Aromatherapy. Peace pipes. No one was very specific about his practices. 'It's hard to describe,' said Jennifer (*59, rheumatoid arthritis*). 'It just worked. I felt better immediately,' said Lori (*42, lupus*).

290

'Cheveyo could really help you,' I told Stella, drumming my fingers on top of the laminated snack-bar table. 'He was on *Oprah*. Remember when we watched it together? How he helped all those people?'

'I was sleeping.'

'Maybe she doesn't want that type of treatment,' Samantha piped up.

My whole body tensed. 'She wants to go. We're going.'

'Which means I need to practice walking, then.' Stella pointed vigorously at the wheelchair, as if it was the cause of all the problems.

At that exact moment, a boy next to us decided to fart very loudly. His parents barely noticed and continued eating their hot dogs. Samantha thrust her purse higher onto her shoulder, the disgust on her face apparent. She eyed the wheelchair. '*I'll* put it back.' She turned around and wheeled it out of the store, losing control of it for a moment or two, the front wheels lifting off the ground and the seat tilting backwards. I wondered if she'd figure out how to remove the wheels and fold it up, or if she'd just stick the whole thing in the back of her SUV intact.

Stella surveyed the store, straightening her wig. I knew she was searching for acquaintances, people who wouldn't expect to see her in a wheelchair. Her oncologist was in Pittsburgh, only an hour's drive away, but Cobalt was so insulated and separate from Pittsburgh that Stella felt like her secret was safe here. She felt like no one in Cobalt would ever guess how many times we'd gone to her doctor – first for the surgery to remove the portion of her rectum, then to prepare for the bigger surgery in her colon, then for the chemotherapy and radiation treatments, then for the various surgeries to remove more and more pieces of her colon and to probe parts of her intestines and inspect her lungs, which had suspicious spots on them, too. Then for the CT scans, more chemotherapy, experimental drug chemo pills that she could take at home. We were in the middle of radiation to shrink the tumors in her lungs, staving off the disease's possible progression to other systems, especially her brain. Her doctor warned that the various treatments Stella requested were far too aggressive for someone her age, but Stella squared her shoulders and said, 'Bullshit. I can take it like a man.'

Stella went to great lengths to keep up as if nothing had changed. She still played euchre with her friends, a scruffy bunch of women of varying ages who had lived in Cobalt their entire lives. I tagged along, sitting in the lumpy, overstuffed, chenille chairs that seemed to live in each of their living rooms, reading a magazine or the same racy parts of the romance novel they all seemed to own. Stella told everyone I was her 'chauffeur' because she temporarily couldn't drive – a small squabble with the police, she explained, rolling her eyes, making out like she was an outlaw.

Although she never missed a euchre day, those days were always hard on Stella; after one euchre game, as soon as we had climbed into the car and rolled out of the driveway, Stella had made me pull into the wooded part of the cul-de-sac so she could open up her window and vomit.

'Why don't you just tell them?' I pleaded with her. The women had to know something was up; Stella showed up every week in those satin gloves, formal attire for a Tuesday afternoon. She declined glasses of iced tea on sweltering summer days because her treatments made her sensitive to cold drinks. At five-six – tall for a woman her age – she weighed one hundred pounds. And that was an improvement – when I'd picked her up after her car accident, her chart had said that she weighed eighty-eight. 'Then at least they'll cut you some slack,' I had gone on. 'Then you can lie down between hands.'

Stella wiped off her mouth with the roll of paper towels she kept in the car for exactly that kind of emergency. 'There's no way I'm admitting that I had a bout with cancer of the ass. And anyway, this isn't because of that. It's probably from that foul food Esther always serves. Those cookies are about a million years old!'

'They were sealed,' I argued. 'They're from the grocery store.'

'They taste like metal.'

'You know what that's from.'

'Perhaps I'm pregnant!' Stella suggested. 'You

ever think of that? This could be morning sickness.'

'Some people don't mind sympathy from their friends.'

The street ended in a T; straight across was a steep hill that looked over downtown Cobalt. It had been dusk, and Cobalt's one bridge had been lit up, making a soft, green reflection on the river. The little houses that lined the bank looked sweet and quaint that night; you almost couldn't tell they had stability issues and peeling paint and junked-up porches.

Stella sank into her seat, looking at the view too. 'Cobalt used to be a wonderful place to live. You might not believe it, but it really was. Your grandmother and I used to do so much shopping on that main drag when we were teenagers.'

'It sounds like you guys were such good friends when you were younger,' I said. 'What happened?'

'Oh, life,' had been Stella's answer.

If it turned out the cancer took Stella, I was to handle the announcement in the papers. She didn't want me to mention anything about her illness. If pushed or struck with a burst of honesty, I could only say she died of natural causes. But if she had her way, I was to tell the Cobalt papers that she died rather fabulously. For instance: A ten-point buck had attacked her. She wrestled it to the ground but its antlers bored her through the heart. ('Which part of the heart?' I asked. 'The left ventricle,' Stella said quickly, as if she'd been thinking about it for a while.) Or: she was giving a phone interview on CNN and had gotten so wrapped up in her answer that she'd accidentally driven her car over a cliff. ('An interview about what?' I asked Stella. She looked at me sternly. 'Does it matter?' 'I just want it to sound real,' I said. 'Fine.' Stella stared at the television. On the History Channel, a man in a tweed jacket was strolling among a bunch of enormous stone heads. 'They were interviewing me about Easter Island.') Or that she went down with a sinking ship. ('On what body of water?' I asked. 'The Allegheny River.')

'You go get me the wine glasses,' she instructed now. 'It'll be like Christmas. I'll just sit here by the hot dogs and wait for my gift.'

'Are you sure?' I asked. 'What sorts of glasses do you want?'

'Whatever, sweetie. Have Samantha pick it. She knows about that sort of thing.'

Stella had Christmas on the brain, lately. The night before, when we were preparing for Samantha's arrival – which amounted to, basically, cleaning the toilets, doing the dishes, going through Stella's closet to decide which robe she would wear – Stella remarked that the air seemed full of yuletide excitement. 'It's Samantha Eve,' she proclaimed. The real Christmas holiday would be here in three months. Last year, Stella had been well enough to come with me to get a tree, and we decorated it together, pulling out old ornaments of my grandmother's that Stella had found years ago in the basement when she took over ownership of the house. It wasn't lost on me that my father's hands had probably touched each and every ornament, the glass balls and Styrofoam cones and ancient garlands. There was even an ornament of my father's young, smiling face in a heavily gilded frame. There were his eyes. There was the crooked incisor. The smattering of freckles on his forehead. *Your life will be uncomfortable and often sad*, I said to my six-year-old father's faded image. *Your daughter will run away from you. This is the first Christmas the two of you are apart.*

On that Christmas Day, Stella and I exchanged gifts – among other things, she gave me a small, cloth voodoo doll that had little afflictions and hardships written across its body, words like *paper cut* and *audit* and *depression*. I stabbed five white pins into the doll's head over the words *good hair day,* but put the black pins aside in a dish on the credenza. We watched *White Christmas* and *Holiday Inn.* She was so healthy a year ago, so whole. She'd gained back some weight, her latest CT scan had been clearer, and she wasn't on any treatment for a month. What would Christmas be this year?

Samantha swooped back through the double doors, wheelchair-less. We snaked through Wal-Mart to the Housewares section, leaving Stella behind. Samantha ran her hands over fabrics as she walked – first an entire row of plaid shirts, then pink bathrobes, then black blazers with brassy buttons.

'I haven't been in a Wal-Mart in a long time,' she said. 'Northglenn has these darling little shops that are much better. A woman I recently sold a house to has a knitting store in town – a*dor*able. The store, I mean. It's *so* chill in there.'

She flicked her hair over her shoulder. 'The house I sold her was adorable, too. One of those brand-new ones Chris built – the walls totally white, everything pretty and new, nothing damaged yet. You can just put your stamp on it, you know? Make it your own, much easier than an older home.'

'So, is it weird being back here?' I interrupted, making a turn at a vacuum-cleaner display. One of the vacuums was tipped on its side, and someone had abandoned a sixty-four-ounce plastic Coke cup on the edge of the platform.

Samantha shrugged. 'I can hardly remember being here, it was so long ago. Oh! Do you guys have a Foreman grill?' She pointed to one on display, lifting its plastic lid.

'We're not big grillers.'

She clunked the grill top back down. People watched her as she strutted through the store, her skin luminous and healthy, her heels tapping against the linoleum. I wondered what really happened at real-estate conferences. Did they honestly get awards? Last year, Stella and I were leaving breakfast at Mr H's, a restaurant connected to a hotel about fifteen miles outside of Cobalt. There was a corporate award ceremony taking place in the hotel's only conference room. Stella peeked in and said that everyone was just sitting there, morose, like they were at a funeral. 'What do you think they would do if I ran into the room and did a somersault?' she whispered giddily. 'Do you think anyone would laugh?'

'So is it shocking to see Stella?' I asked Samantha.

'Do you think she would like these ones?' Samantha talked over me, holding up a box of Oneida long-stemmed wine glasses. She noticed me glancing at the price tag on the shelf. 'I can pay, of course. It's totally my treat.'

She looked at me as if I were as poor as all the other patrons of the Cobalt Wal-Mart. For a while, I had been. A few months after coming to Cobalt, my savings had depleted down to almost nothing. I couldn't draw from anything in my father's account – it was all going to the Center. Medicare paid for Stella's hospital costs, but I'd had no idea how she paid for anything else. Finally, I'd broken down and asked her. 'The Internet,' she told me.

She walked me to my father's old room. Inside the closet were piles of unopened boxes of toys. A lot of it was *Star Wars* paraphernalia, action figures and the X-Wing fighter and comic books and statues. 'Ruth used to buy Richard all kinds of crap, long after he left,' Stella explained. 'I put one of the things on eBay last year just to make some space in the closet, and some dumbass paid five hundred dollars for it. Can you imagine, for this crap?' She held up a box; inside was a Yoda figurine. 'Now, what the hell is this thing? Why is he so hideous?'

She was slow at using the old computer she'd bought from one of the Elkerson boys, but I wasn't. I was able to list plenty of things on eBay every week. And people bought them. I couldn't believe how many toys were in that closet, sealed up and in mint condition, ready for my father or Steven or me to come home and play with them.

'Stella's happy you came.' I tried again now, standing close to Samantha's straight back. 'She always talks about you. She wishes you'd come more.'

'You know . . .' Samantha turned the box over and inspected the bottom. 'This one looks like it's been tampered with. Do you think it was a return? I don't like the idea of someone *else* drinking from my glasses.' She peered into the shelf. 'Do you see any more like this?'

'I think she's nervous about going to the healer tomorrow,' I went on.

'Well, I can see why.' Samantha sniffed. 'And I wouldn't expect you, of all people, to buy into a crazy person like that. I thought you were into science and medicine. Didn't you go to school for biology?'

My insides warmed. So she *did* know a little about me. 'Medicine isn't exactly working, is it?'

But I'd asked myself this same question. Yes, I believed in science, but maybe we could believe in Cheveyo, too. Just this once. And maybe it would work, just this once. 'Anyway, Stella would love it if you came with us.'

Samantha turned to me, lowering the box to her waist. 'You know I can't, Summer. I have my conference.'

'You don't have to go.'

Something skipped across her face, and then submerged. 'Yes, I do.'

'Stella's afraid of the Amish. And you could be a big help to us – you know all about health, what with your vitamin routine and all.'

Samantha stared fixedly at a picture of a woman and man toasting on a box of margarita glasses. The woman looked like her, with shiny chestnut hair and dark pink lips. I hated myself for sucking up to her.

We stood there for a while, looking in opposite directions. Back at the snack bar, a line of people waited for food. The place was crammed with teenagers, the girls in heavy makeup and tight jeans, the boys in baggy, oversized shorts. It was possible that Wal-Mart was the cool place in Cobalt to hang out.

After a while, Samantha looked up. 'I meant to tell you. Philip was asking about you.'

I looked over at her. 'Philip . . . who used to live down the street?'

She nodded.

300

'You . . . know him?' I felt like my heart might stop.

'I went to high school with him. So yeah.'

'I mean, do you know him *now*?'

'We're on the same high school reunion email list. I wrote an email to the list saying that I'd gotten married, and then I wrote another one that Chris and I bought a house. He wrote me back about two weeks ago, asking how I was, congratulating me, you know. Then he asked if I still spoke to you.'

Philip was a ghost in my head; I couldn't even remember what he looked like. A new couple had moved into Philip's old house, a pie-faced young man and woman with an enormous red pickup truck.

'He's in New York,' Samantha volunteered, as if aware of my thoughts. 'Or he was, two months ago. He works for an architecture company. I don't remember the name.' Samantha rooted through the other shelves of glasses. 'Wouldn't you know it? This opened box is the only one.'

'How long has Philip been in New York?' My skin prickled. Perhaps Philip went to New York because I lived there. Maybe he thought he'd find me. But I pushed that thought quickly away, mortified that I'd even considered it.

'Um . . . he went to college there. I think he never left.'

'What school did he go to?'

Samantha straightened up, exasperated. 'I don't

know, Summer. I didn't really ask him that many questions.' She picked up the tampered-with box of glasses. 'I guess we'll have to go with this one and wash them really well.'

I was jealous that Philip had written to Samantha. If only he knew the truth – I still thought Steven showing up the night Philip and I were talking had been because Samantha had told him to. Then again, maybe Philip wouldn't care. Maybe Samantha had already told Philip, and he'd found the whole thing amusing.

'I have Philip's email address if you want it,' Samantha said. 'And his phone number.'

I cocked my head at her, wondering why she was being so charitable. 'That would be great.'

'Remind me. I'll write it down for you.'

'Thanks.'

'So we're getting these?' Samantha handed me the box of wine glasses. I took them. The box felt so substantial in my hands. Heavier than Stella, maybe. My head was suddenly cloudy, and it felt like Wal-Mart's overhead fluorescent lights were giving me sunburn. I couldn't remember the tilt of the conversation before this. I opened my mouth to tell Samantha yes, we were getting them, but she was knifing through the aisles, already on her way to the checkout.

CHAPTER 21

For the rest of the gray, weary day, I felt lost in Philip. Samantha wrote down his email address and phone number on a piece of her *Samantha Denver, Realtor* stationery. Philip's last name was Singh, a detail I'd never known.

It was folded up in my pocket, it was sitting in a crumpled blob on my desk, it was unfolded and stared at. I tried to imagine what Philip was doing. Was it truly possible that he and I had walked down the same city streets, climbed aboard the same subways? It was Friday, so perhaps he was at work, at this mythical architecture company Samantha said he worked at.

Most likely, Philip's life had evolved, changed, grown. My life in Cobalt, on the other hand, had stagnated – I had designed it that way. Each new day unfolded exactly as the last: I ate white toast with unseeded strawberry jelly. I read the encyclopedias, trying to live as if it were 1965. The Betamax video recorder was an amazing new invention, AIDS was unheard of. Watson and Crick had laid out their 'Central Dogma' of DNA, explaining the links between DNA, RNA, and

303

proteins, but there certainly wasn't any DNA testing, engineering, or even much understanding yet. I tried to avoid any news of current-day New York City, as well as references to it in movies, TV shows, magazines and books – every time I saw an image of New York, I was reminded of my father.

It hurt that I didn't just call my father. It hurt that he didn't call me. Surely he knew I was here – certainly Stella had let him know. Or what about Dr North, whom I'd called shortly after I'd arrived in Cobalt? Dr North had assured me that he'd keep tabs on my father – in fact, my father had already called him, saying he was coming back and needed someone to manage and monitor his medications. Surely Dr North had immediately turned around and told my father that I'd reached him. But maybe my father was so fine with Rosemary and Rosemary alone, he had no need for anyone else.

Certain images of my father and Rosemary together were manageable – them sleeping in the same bed, for example, as long as they didn't touch. The two of them riding in the car together, as platonic as brother and sister. But did he draw greeting cards for her, like the one he'd drawn for me when he'd been in the hospital for the snow globe incident? Did he lay his head in her lap and make up songs for her? I thought of Rosemary wandering the rooms of our house, running her hands against the top of the credenza, against the refrigerator magnets, along the muzzles of the dogs. My father was probably trying to make his life hers – showing her how to tell Wesley to roll over, demonstrating how to achieve the right blend of hot and cold with the shower taps, *walking her through the box of memories.*

Philip probably had roommates, a girlfriend. My memories of him hardly amounted to more than a few sharp, painful fragments – the look on his face when I left him, the feel of his lips on mine, the heaviness of the moment when I told him about my father and the snow globe. It was inconceivable that what I'd constructed in my mind about him even remotely resembled the person he was today. And anyway, Philip had more than likely forgotten about me as soon as I left Cobalt; I was just a girl from out of town who needed some sympathy. He had asked Samantha about me out of politeness, nothing more.

After we returned from Wal-Mart, Stella made her way into the downstairs den, which was now her bedroom. I sat on the living room couch, leafing through the H encyclopedia's layered tracing paper overlays of the human body (first there was the leaf with the skin, then the muscles, then the bones, then nerves, then organs, and then the organs beneath those organs, until you turned the page and it was just text again). It was comforting to know that the people of 1965 saw the human body exactly as we did today.

I flipped to the front of the book, searching. Not

long ago, wedged between the pages for the entry on Handwriting was a photo of a young girl of about eight with freckles and short, dark hair. She stared seriously into the camera lens, standing next to a tire swing and a pickup truck with a cracked right headlight. After a moment, I realized I recognized it: I'd seen this same photo when I visited for my grandmother's funeral. I turned the picture over, but there was no inscription. The next time I opened the H encyclopedia, the photo was gone.

Samantha walked into the room, coming to a stop in the exact center of the round, ropy rug. 'I should go.'

I closed the book. 'You're not even staying for dinner?'

She fiddled with a strap on her purse. 'I should get on the road.'

I ran my fingers over the encyclopedia's bumpy cover, trying to remain expressionless. 'Thanks for stopping by.'

Samantha looked over at the box of wine glasses, unopened on the dining-room table amid un-folded towels, empty pill bottles, a big box of disposable wipes. The wine box showed one of the glasses full of some thick, blood-colored wine, perhaps cabernet. It was the type that stained your teeth and lips, the kind – Stella would say – that dyed your shit black. We would never use them.

'You should really clean up around here,' Samantha finally said, her eyes still on the dining-room table. 'All this might not be . . . good . . . for her.'

I slammed the encyclopedia on the coffee table, hot with rage. For a moment, I was positively tongue-tied. 'You know, I hear the highway you're taking to the conference has lots of accidents on it, too,' I blurted out. 'Just like the highway from Northglenn to here.'

She crossed her arms and looked away. 'Summer.'

I gestured to her car out in the driveway. 'And are you sure SUVs are reliable enough? I had a good friend who was in an accident in one. Rolled right over.'

A vein in Samantha's neck pulsed. 'Really?'

My insides felt blackened and thick. I didn't even know what I was saying. 'No,' I admitted, staring at the floor.

'Do you feel overworked here?' Samantha asked. 'I might know someone out here who could do something for you. Cleaning, odd jobs, any of that.'

'We're fine. We don't need anything.'

'I'm just trying to help.'

'You could've fooled me.'

'Look, if you're going to *guilt* me into coming with you to this miracle healer and seeing this jack-apoo or whatever it is, maybe I can change things around, but it's really not the best time . . . I mean, it was tough even taking *this* day away . . .'

'I'm not forcing you to do anything.' I crossed my arms over my chest. 'I know your job is important.'

Samantha opened and closed her mouth, like she was chewing gum. Her cell phone started to ring. Her face blossomed. 'I should take this,' she said.

She started for the door. 'Good luck with your excursion tomorrow. I'm sure it will go well.' And then she unfolded her phone. 'Hello?' she chirped into the receiver, her voice like a ballet dancer, straightening up and snapping into position as the music began. 'Oh, David! Yes, of course. No, it's wonderful to hear from you – I thought I would! I saw that look on your face when you saw the house on Currier Court!'

She put her hand on the doorknob, turned it, and crunched through the gravel path to the car. I could hear her high, happy voice the whole way to the road, and I was sure Stella could, too.

CHAPTER 22

Things started badly on our journey to Cheveyo. Stella kept coming up with excuses not to go. Each was wilder than the next: She wanted to stay home and watch *Survivor*. She had a horrible feeling aliens were going to abduct most of the East Coast this weekend, spanning as far as Lancaster, where we were going, shutting off roads and prohibiting us from returning to Cobalt.

We had a hard time locking the house's front door, something we usually never bothered with. The lock kept sticking, and the barrel wobbled. Stella told me just to leave it, and eventually we did. This annoyed her, though, and she fidgeted in her seat as we rumbled up the gravel drive to the main road. It got to the point where if she would have just said, *I don't want to do this. I don't feel well*, I would've turned around the car and taken her back. But she had to make it outrageous.

The day steadily declined from there: our cones from the Dairy Queen just outside Cobalt tasted funny, like sawdust. Stella tossed hers out the window after just one lick; it splattered against a car's windshield behind us. The driver laid on his horn, then pulled over. 'Maybe we should pull over, too.' I glanced at the rear-view mirror. The ice cream had dripped down over the other car's windshield, onto the hood, and into the grille. The driver had definitely gotten our license plate by now.

'Just drive!' Stella screamed, as if we'd just robbed a bank. 'Keep driving!'

Late afternoon, we pulled over at a Bob Evans. Our waitress had pink streaks in her hair, a pierced nose, fishnet stockings, and combat boots, well-worn even though she'd never see battle. She sat us in a booth.

'So.' Stella removed her silverware from the napkin. 'I'm pretty sure the Jackalope Museum is on this road somewhere. I say, tomorrow, we head over there first thing.'

'But we're on a time schedule,' I told her, for about the fiftieth time that hour. 'You have Cheveyo at one tomorrow. I don't want to be late.'

Stella rolled her eyes. 'Maybe this should just be a sightseeing trip instead.'

I gave her a pleading look. She gave me a sulking one back. 'I'm not sure I want to smoke grass anymore,' she said.

'He's not going to make you smoke grass. I promise.'

'He lives in a *log cabin*,' she whispered, leaning forward so I could see the fine, pale hairs that

310

grew above her upper lip. 'There probably isn't any plumbing.'

'I'm sure there's plumbing.'

'But the jackalope is a feat of nature!' Stella cried, the lines around her mouth pronounced. 'You'll be *amazed* when you see it. It's . . . it's miraculous, is what it is. And they have a nice display of the various animals that live in this part of Pennsylvania.'

'How about this?' I took a sip of water. 'We'll go after Cheveyo.'

'What kind of name is Cheveyo, anyway?' She narrowed her eyes.

'Native American.'

Stella made a noise through her nose.

I dug my nails into my palms. 'He was featured on *Oprah* a few months ago, don't you remember? We watched it together. His patients came on the show to show everyone how much better they felt.'

Stella leaned forward. 'I don't know if you've noticed, but that Oprah woman is *black*.'

'What's bothering you?' I demanded. 'Are you upset because of Samantha?' Yesterday, when Stella emerged from the den after her nap and found Samantha gone, there was a very obvious look of disappointment on her face. She wiped it off quickly, saying nothing, asking what I was going to have for dinner. She liked the routine of dinner, even if she didn't eat. I wanted to scream at her, *Get upset! You can, you know! You have the right to be pissed off at Samantha!*

Stella shook her head quickly, taking the smallest sip of her water. 'No, no. Samantha was lovely. She's so pretty, isn't she? So driven.'

I poked my pinkie finger into a small tear in the middle of the vinyl booth. 'But don't you think it was weird that she left while you were sleeping?'

'Well, she's a busy girl. She's got a busy life.'

I pictured Samantha at her real-estate conference, glancing at her cell phone discreetly while someone gave a presentation. 'Remember when we saw that conference at Mr H's?' I asked. 'I wonder what Samantha would say if you did a somersault at her realtor thing.'

'I wouldn't do that,' Stella snapped, astonishment in her voice. 'That would embarrass her.' She leaned over the table. 'And honestly, Summer, you could've been a little nicer to her.'

I blinked quickly. '*Me?* Nicer to *her?*'

But Stella's attention had wandered elsewhere. The waitress led a group of young men in military uniforms past us. They had freshly shaved heads and wide, blue, scared eyes. Unlike the waitress's, their boots were polished to a high shine, one that matched the mischief in Stella's eyes. Stella scooted forward in her seat.

'Hello, boys!' she cried, waving at them.

The army boys glanced at her and smiled. 'Ma'am,' one of them said.

'Keep up the good work,' Stella trilled, as if there were a war on. She gave them a salute. By now, everyone was staring at us. The army boys saluted back.

Stella's satin-gloved fingers wrapped around mine, as though we were on a date. 'They're adorable,' she whispered. 'Why don't you go talk to them?'

'I don't want to talk to them.'

'You're not committed, you know. Loosen up. Chill.'

My face flushed. I would kill myself if I ever heard the word *chill* again. 'I'm sorry I'm not as fun as Samantha is, okay?' I shook my head slowly. 'And I can't believe you said I should've been nicer to her!'

'Well, you should have. You weren't friendly at all. You were very . . . cold.'

I stared out at the red and white Bob Evans sign, too stunned to think. 'Samantha doesn't need me to be nice to her.'

'Of course she does. Everyone needs people to be nice to them. She's probably more afraid of you than you were of her. And anyway, life's too short to be nasty.'

I clutched my water glass so hard, I thought it might shatter in my hands. The muzak groaned on, a dirge. An old woman across the aisle gaped at us, her mouth full of eggs.

The lights in Bob Evans dimmed, then brightened. The muzak changed to something else equally dour and life-denying. Abruptly, the military boys got up without ordering. They unconsciously formed a line and strolled past us again, their boots squeaking virginally. After watching them pivot past the dessert refrigerator and out the exit, Stella turned to me, peeled one end of the wrapper off her straw, and blew it in my face. It hit my nose.

I sighed and removed one end of the wrapper from a spare straw at the table and blew it back at her. It missed her, and instead careened across the aisle onto the old woman's plate of eggs. The old woman jumped back, as if a tarantula had climbed onto her plate. Her husband, who was sitting next to her and not across from her, leaned over to inspect the straw. He put on his glasses for a better look.

The waitress with the pink-striped hair stared at us from the register. Stella looked at me and I looked at her and we both burst out laughing.

The key card that opened the door to our squat, stale-smelling motel room had an advertisement for Dunkin Donuts Munchkins on the back. Inside the room, heavy green curtains blotted out the light.

I unzipped my bag and pulled out all Stella's medicine. The day's doses were doled out in one of those Monday through Sunday plastic organizer kits. There was Ondansetron and Dexamethasone for nausea, various medications for pain including morphine, and vitamins. Stella wordlessly unscrewed the top of her Mountain Dew bottle and swallowed Saturday's pills one at a time. I sat down on my bed and pulled out the Cheveyo pamphlets. On the cover was Cheveyo himself, and the Verdana-font words *The Magic of Healing. As the true healer is God himself, Cheveyo acts only as a mediator. Visa, MasterCard, Discover accepted.*

It wasn't a scam because he accepted credit cards. Because he'd put together glossy pamphlets and a professional-looking website. And anyway, Western medicine had turned out to be a scam itself, doing nothing to halt Stella's cancer, which had proceeded stubbornly on. Why not try something else? The only thing we hadn't been scammed out of was time – when I rescued Stella from the hospital after her fender-bender, her doctor gave her a year to live, and we'd already outlasted that prognosis. A nurse once tried to turn it into something positive as she stuck yet another needle into Stella's arm: *At least you have time to say things you need to say.* As the nurse turned away, I saw a flicker of outrage cross Stella's face.

I helped Stella settle into her bed. The evening stretched before me, blank and dull. Stella shut her eyes, nestled under the covers. 'Skip and I visited the jackalope together. We hadn't meant to. We just stumbled on it.'

Here we go again, I thought.

She took a breath. 'It's beautiful, Summer. I remember going in there with Skip and just thinking, *Well now, this is what life's all about.* Beautiful and strange. A huge mess, everything

315

smashed together. Real and crazy and worth believing in.'

'Mmm.' Stella had done an amazing job keeping the nature of the jackalope a surprise. Whenever I closed my eyes, I had a different mental picture of what a jackalope was. A jack-o-lantern skull, maybe, its head pumpkin-shaped and its teeth scraggly. A type of plant that swallowed dogs whole. A rock that had naturally formed in the shape of a deer. Perhaps it was all those things, depending on what we wanted, or depending on the day we visited. Maybe the mutability of the jackalope magically altered everything else around it, too, like an activator ray in a science-fiction movie. Cancer would walk into the room as a mass of purple, pulsing, murderous cells but then, after seeing the jackalope, it would morph into a long, intricately woven carpet. Or a truck full of diamonds. A piece of anise-flavored candy, about the size of a Nerd.

I changed the TV channel. On the screen, the two Williams sisters were playing in the US Open final. Mid-set, the program broke to a commercial for a Lincoln Navigator, a commercial for American Express, a commercial for a Mercedes SUV – Samantha's car. The car navigating the twisty California roads was even the same battleship gray.

'Has Samantha ever seen a therapist?' I asked.

Stella's sheets rustled. 'A what?'

'You know. A shrink.'

'Why on earth would she do that?'

'For her parents. To deal with it. Or something.'

'Now, do you honestly think that nonsense works?'

We watched the TV in silence. I felt confused. Stella's question seemed to end in an ellipsis. Was she waiting for me to say something? Comment, perhaps, that therapy had worked for my father?

After a while, Stella curled her legs into her chest. 'I think I might take a nap.'

'Okay.'

She turned. 'I want to go see the jackalope tomorrow morning.'

The US Open was back on. The blimp circling Arthur Ashe broadcast a view of the New York City skyline. I felt the familiar ache. There was my mother's old office. There were the jutting buildings on the Upper East Side – somewhere up there was the hospital where my father had had his treatments. My father was somewhere in the city, and so, apparently, was Philip. My whole past was compact and bite-size, fitting in just one TV screen shot.

'All right,' I whispered into the darkness. 'We'll try and squeeze it in.'

'Good. You'll love it. I promise you will.'

A few minutes went by. There was a splash in the outdoor pool. A door slammed. 'Stella?' My voice sounded pitted, small. 'Aren't you angry at Samantha? She could have said goodbye. I don't think that was very nice of her. Surely she was meaner to you than I was to her, right?'

No answer.

I turned on my back and stared at the ceiling. 'But maybe I am mean, sometimes.' And then, even quieter: 'Once, when my father was getting those treatments in the hospital, he sort of lost it in the hall. It was . . . embarrassing, I guess. Everyone was looking. And I shoved him.'

I glanced over at her. Still nothing. 'I never talked to him about it, either,' I whispered. 'I never said I was sorry. But I didn't do it to be cruel. I just didn't know what else to do. I just felt . . . he's my *father*.' I closed my eyes. My cheeks felt hot. 'He's supposed to . . . he should . . . I'm his *kid*.'

Stella let out a snore. I opened my eyes, very aware of my surroundings. The room looked the same as before that had spilled out of my mouth.

I walked to the window, pulled up the shades, and then clutched both sides of my head. The rattling of the A/C penetrated my bones. I wanted someone to recognize this moment with me. To tell me that I was right – he *was* my father, and I was his daughter. These roles usually had different responsibilities and expectations. That I wasn't a terrible person to think this, and no one would condemn me for saying it out loud.

I turned off the air conditioner, found my key card and slid out of the room. The paisley hallway carpet smelled overly deodorized, like the staff were trying to mask something. In the lobby, I made a left and went through the revolving front door. A group of Mennonites stood around a long, white van. One squatted down, checking out the front tire.

I watched them for a little while, leaning against a small green bench. We'd had a whole unit about genetically closed communities like the Mennonites and Amish in one of my college classes. Because of inbreeding, so many Amish children were born with incredibly rare diseases that didn't exist anywhere else in the population. But instead of understanding that their own restrictions and bodies had done this, they simply said it was God's master plan. I realized, though: my old belief in DNA – that it immutably set your course for life, that you were only the sum of its parts – wasn't really that different. A master plan was a master plan, after all – it hardly mattered who or what was behind it.

The Mennonites had honest, plain faces, and I wanted to tell them everything. But then, as I took a step toward them, they noticed me and froze. Silently, they nodded in unison, climbed into the van and drove away.

CHAPTER 23

The humidity skulked about the room, making us stick to the threadbare bed-sheets. I woke up cramped, Stella woke up ornery. She complained that everything hurt; I assured her that Cheveyo would help her. I saw her rolling her eyes at me in the mirror. She complained about the coffee in the lobby and I snapped at her that she shouldn't be drinking it, anyway. She complained that there weren't any Amish people here, that she'd wanted to see an Amish person. I reminded her that, just the other day, she'd told me Amish people were carcinogenic.

And she looked at me as if I'd just told her I was planning to marry a potted plant. 'Now, why would I say a dumbassed thing like that?' she spat. 'You must have heard me wrong.'

In the car, Stella put on her pink cat-eye sunglasses and held the Pennsylvania road map a foot away from her face so she could read it. 'So, we have to take this squiggly road here. We'll run smack into the jackalope.'

She pointed to a red line. The lines mingled with other lines and reminded me of veins on a leaf.

'There's no marker that a Jackalope Museum is there,' I told her. 'Are you sure?'

'Of course I'm sure. It's a little building on the side of the road – they wouldn't want to mark it on a map because then too many people would know about it. I remember that day clear as anything. Skip and I were trying to find Punxsutawney, but that's right here.' She pointed to a town almost a finger's distance away. 'We were quite lost.'

'Why were you looking for Punxsutawney?'

She glared at me. 'Because of the *groundhog,* of course.'

Of course.

'The groundhog's name was Phil,' Stella added haughtily. 'Or perhaps Philip. I don't remember.'

Philip. I looked away. It was a Sunday in the middle of Pennsylvania, the day already too bright and hot. The only things that marked distances here were telephone poles. New York – and Philip – might as well have been on another planet.

People savored Sundays in New York. They shopped at the overpriced stores, they rode their bikes, they ate ice cream. My father used to take the dogs to the dog park in Park Slope, loading them into the car we used to have and driving them all there, circling Grand Army Plaza a million times before he found a parking space. He'd sing on the drive, his head hanging out the window like he was a dog, too. And I remembered thinking, *He's fine. He's completely*

321

fine. The dogs made him so happy – sometimes, I thought they understood him better than people did. They always sensed when he was about to go back into the psych ward – they'd lie around the couch in a tight circle, guarding.

Philip probably had a million friends and a crammed schedule. A fantastic life.

I clicked on my seat belt and pushed the car into drive. 'All right. If you're sure.'

The road was dry and sparse. We passed a few signs for Amish delicacies, shoo-fly pie and funnel cake and fresh soft pretzels. Stella instructed me to leave in the dust a car with a bumper sticker that said *USA: Love it or leave it.*

'So why were you going to see the Punxsutawney groundhog, anyway?' I asked, because the silence between us was thick and pointed. I wanted to blame it on Samantha – before she'd visited, everything between us had been fine.

Stella shrugged. 'It was something to do. We needed to get out of Cobalt. Clear our heads. Our lives were getting complicated.'

'Why?'

She mashed her lips together and made a few *tsk* noises. 'Oh, you know. Normal things. Fights, affairs.'

'Your almost-affair? That thing in the hotel room?'

She glanced at me, horrified. 'How did you know about that?'

'You told me. During my grandmother's wake,

322

remember? You told me when we were on the porch at the funeral home.'The story was so weird, I'd never forgotten it.

'I most certainly did not.' Stella's eyes bulged. 'I never told anyone about that.'

'You said you put your ring in your pocket,' I reminded her. 'And when he went to the bathroom, you left.'

Stella's jaw became even more sharply pronounced. 'Well.' She ran her hands along the cords of her neck, then pinched the flap of skin beneath her chin. 'Well,' she said again.

'It's okay. It's not like I said anything to anyone. I mean, I didn't tell my father, or Samantha, or anyone like that, if that's what you're worried about.'

'I did that because of what Skip did,' Stella blurted out. 'I was driven to do that . . . with that man. I never would have, otherwise.'

A few signposts went by. There was a fan-shaped tree alone in the middle of a field. 'What did Skip do?'

Stella sighed. 'Oh, you know. The usual. Classic soap-opera story. I found him with someone else. They were in the park next to the fire station. You know it, the one with the tire swing? They were there. Sitting on the tire swing together, she on his lap. Kissing. It was so stupid, I was driving by, just going . . . I don't know. To the market, maybe. To the florist's. And I just looked to my left and there they were. In front of everyone. I marched

323

over to them and started screaming something, I don't even know what, and then the fire whistle started blaring. That crazy air-raid fire whistle, you know, blotting out the sound. I kept screaming though, even though they couldn't hear me, and the fire truck comes out of the garage but they can't get past because my car is there, and I'm still screaming and Jack Baker, you know Jack – or no, I guess you don't, he's dead – he tried to get me to calm down but I couldn't, I just kept screaming, and finally someone moved my car for me and the fire truck got out. I think, actually, it was an ice cream parlor that was on fire. The one that later became the Dairy Queen; the one we stopped at on the drive out of town.'

She made a small hiccup on the word *town*. 'Can you believe that? An ice cream parlor on fire? Now, that's just about the last thing I would imagine. A bar and grill, maybe. A . . . a . . . store that sells wood and matches, certainly. But an ice cream parlor? Now, that just shouldn't happen.'

'I'm so sorry,' I whispered.

'Oh, don't be.' She waved her hand, stifling a sniff. 'This is a silly thing to talk about. I don't know why I'm going into it. Maybe it's because I think this Chevrolet man or whatever his name is will rape me. Maybe I want to confess things, like you're a priest.'

I drove for a while, thinking. 'So who was it?'

'Who was what?'

'You know. Who was the woman Skip was with?'

She stared straight ahead at the flat, unimpressive road. 'He was . . . well, he was with Ruth.'

I squeezed the steering wheel tight, paying careful, careful attention, because I was certain I was going to wreck the car. 'My grandmother?'

'Yes.'

I took a breath. 'He was with my grandmother.'

She sighed, teenager-like. 'That's what I *said*.'

The highway rolled on, endless. A green sign popped up, telling us that the Spring Mine Road Exit was ahead. The exit sign loomed in the distance, seemingly suspended in air. The road beyond it was desolate and empty. 'This is us.' Stella's voice broke.

'Are you sure? This looks like it goes to nothing.'

'I remember this road. This is us.'

I put on my turn signal and we slowly eased into the exit. None of the other cars was getting off. A bright yellow arrow sign told us we had to turn left or right. 'Which way?'

'Right,' Stella said.

I turned right. There were cornfields on either side of us. Stella sat next to me, her posture perfect, her gloves pulled up over her elbows, her patent-leather purse sitting on her lap.

'Do you still think about it much?' I asked her.

'Think about what?'

'The . . . you know. What we were talking about.'

She blew air out of her cheeks, making a neighing noise. 'Nah.'

'Really?'

'What's the point?'

A few anemic trees slid past. Then a shack with a few trucks parked out front. A red barn. On its side was an advertisement for chewing tobacco; the words weathered from the years. There was a sign for a McDonald's thirty miles ahead. The giant hamburger's sesame seeds were as big as boulders. 'Did you ever say anything to your sister about it?' I asked.

Stella shrugged. 'Not to her.'

'*Never?*'

'Nope.'

'Why not?'

'Oh, I don't know.'

'But she's your *sister*,' I protested.

'And?'

'You two didn't talk much. You weren't friends. It was because of that, wasn't it?'

Stella looked at me sharply. 'What do you want me to say, that it was? That if I would've patched it up, acted like it didn't bother me, we could've become best friends? She was different. And she wanted different things than I did, and one of those things was a husband that provided, a picture-perfect marriage. I wanted love. And look where that got both of us. And there's no law that says you have to get along with your siblings. It's not like you get along with Steven.'

My ears felt tinny, shunting closed. A bird flew very close to the windshield, almost running into us. 'How do you know I don't get along with him?'

Stella turned and stared at me. It felt as if she'd unzipped me and was feeling around at my bottom, looking for loose change. I could tell there was something she wanted to say. 'What?' I demanded.

She lowered her eyes. 'Nothing.'

'*What?*'

Stella's face was firm, almost young. 'I don't want to go to this man today.'

'Did Samantha say something to you?'

'No, she didn't. I just don't want to go.'

'But what if he helps you? What if there's a miracle?'

'It's not *real.*'

'How do you know that?'

'Because I just . . . know. It's not real. And you know it's not real, too. You with your degree in science, you with your big, wasted brain. Don't treat me like an idiot.'

'But you don't know until you try it! I really think this is reputable. I really think this could *be* something.'

Stella leaned her head against the window; the trees whizzed by. 'I think it's probably time for you to go back to New York.'

I lifted my foot off the pedal. '*What?*'

'I don't need to be saved, Summer. I don't need to be taken care of . . . not like this. I'm fine – I'll *be* fine. But what about you? What are you doing here?'

My mouth was wide open, a chunk taken out

of my face. I blinked once, twice. I heard 'The Star Spangled Banner' in my head, deafeningly loud. *Oh, say can you see . . . ?*

Stella looked out the windshield, then down at the map. She frowned. 'You know, I don't recognize any of this.'

I couldn't respond, gripping the steering wheel until my hands were white. *What so proudly we wave . . .*

Stella turned around and looked behind us, then ahead again. 'No . . . this isn't right.'

I let out a groan and pulled into a parking lot to a hillbilly 7-Eleven of sorts; there were faded NASCAR and Mountain Dew posters in the window, a sign for propane and worms, a plastic newspaper dispenser near the door, its contents depleted.

'I guess it was the next exit instead,' Stella sighed.

I set my jaw and stared fixedly at the cracked sidewalk outside the market. 'We're on a time schedule. Our appointment is in an hour, and it's still a half-hour down the road.'

Stella clutched the passenger door and, after a few seconds of fumbling, managed to push it open. She swung her bandy legs onto the pavement and hefted herself up, using the door as leverage. 'Where are you going?' I cried.

'I'm going to ask for directions.'

I didn't know what else to do but sink back down into the seat and watch her stumble toward the door. The general store's windows were murky, so I could only see a few shapes inside. There was nothing around here; it was more desolate than even Cobalt.

I think it's probably time for you to go back to New York.

After a while, I checked my watch. Stella had been in there for six minutes. She was probably chatting to someone at the counter, perhaps about the jackalope. Or perhaps she was talking about me. That I wasn't as accomplished as her other grand-niece, Samantha. That I was testy and lazy and not married and that I didn't have a job. *That I was using her as an excuse.*

I don't need to be saved. That was what I got. If I didn't save her, if I didn't do these things, who would? And what did she think, I was *running away*?

I hit the steering wheel, annoyed, and turned the car off. The ground was crunchy beneath my feet. Dust swirled. But then I wondered, *why bother?* If Stella didn't want to go to Cheveyo – if Samantha had said something to her, if she wanted to give up, whatever – then why was I pushing for it so much? Why shouldn't I just let her be?

But then the fear took hold of me again, the fear of so many things. I pushed my way through the market's door.

Bells jingled. An older woman behind the counter looked up. Beneath her were different coffee cans full of fishing worms. In the back of the market were a few refrigerators full of beverages, and to my right were aisles stuffed with candy and chips. A dilapidated hot-dog machine squeakily rotated in the corner. Stella was gone.

My heart started to pound. 'Help you?' the old woman behind the counter asked. There was a large wad of something in her mouth.

'Did an older woman come in here?' I asked.

The woman lazily pointed a bony finger toward the back. 'Bathroom.'

The door to the bathroom was unmarked, but I could see a key with a fish-shaped keychain hanging out of the knob – I assumed Stella had unlocked it and then forgotten to pull it out. 'Stella?' I knocked on the door. With the store's country music blaring, I couldn't really hear anything. 'Stella?'

She didn't answer. I thought of her stubbornly in there, waiting it out until she knew we wouldn't be able to go to Cheveyo. *I don't need to be saved.* The words washed over me again and again, like a hose that sprayed down a criminal upon entering prison.

'Open the goddamn door.' I pushed against it. And then, it gave. She hadn't even locked it. I half-fell inside, taking in the yellowed toilet, the cracked sink on the far wall. There were Stella's high-heeled green shoes, cockeyed on the tiles. There was her hand with her boysenberry-red nails – always painted, because chemo had turned them black – curled inward in an awkward pose.

330

Her purse gaped open, and a few of her pill bottles had spilled onto the floor. Their tops all said *Charles Kupka's Drugs, The Finest Apothecary in Western Pennsylvania.*

'Oh my God,' I whispered, sinking down to Stella. Her cheek was pressed against the dirty tiled floor. Her wig had fallen off, revealing a fluff of thin hair underneath. And underneath that, I could see her skull, transparent and vulnerable. A noise came from somewhere, something that sounded like an animal wail. I didn't realize for a while that it was me.

Strong arms lifted me up. A man in a plaid shirt and a beard pressed me against him. 'It's okay,' he said, patting my shoulder. Behind him stood the woman at the counter, her mouth a straight line, her fingers dancing nervously against the hem of her t-shirt. 'It's okay,' the man repeated. I tried to find something to stare at, to fixate on. There were cheerful posters for Pepsi, M&M'S, a promotional deal between Willie Nelson and Marlboros. As they pulled Stella out, I reached forward and touched the edge of her wig, adjusting it so that it was straight again. Her arms hung down limp, bathed in her satin gloves. From this angle, if I squinted, with the gloves and the hair and her pale profile, she looked like she could be a vamp in a big-screen musical, carried on the shoulder of an adoring male fan, ready to revive and break into her big show-stopping, tap-dancing number. Any minute now, she'd do it. Any minute now.

CHAPTER 24

The nearest hospital was a half-hour away, back in the direction from which we'd come. I rode with Stella in the ambulance, answering the ER medic's questions about what medications Stella was taking, what treatments she'd undergone, how advanced her cancer was. After we pulled into the ER entrance, I was directed to a hospital waiting room. The walls were pale blue and there were a lot of scratchy couches, old magazines, broken kids' toys, and a television was stuck on a channel that played *Home Improvement* episodes non-stop. When no one was around, which was almost all the time, I threw balled-up Kleenexes at the screen.

Stella was in and out of consciousness for most of Sunday. Late that afternoon, the doctor gave me the report of her scans and blood work. Afterwards, I went down to the ground floor. A rainstorm blew through, cracking and grumbling overhead, sending sheets of water on the parking lot, the tops of the ambulances, the nearby farmland. I stood in the lobby, watching, and called Samantha, wondering if she was still at her conference or had driven back by now. The call went straight to her voicemail. Her message was perky yet efficient. Samantha said she could be reached at two other numbers besides her cell phone – her office and her home. 'Call me anytime, really,' she assured. 'I'm available day or night.'

I watched as the rain turned from deluge to drizzle to nothing. The hospital was on a hill and overlooked a cornfield-strewn valley; everything smelled fresh and wet. I looked at my phone again, not satisfied. I felt a pull to call someone else. In my pocket was Philip's number.

I dialed it quickly, without thinking. It went to voicemail, too, and there was Philip's voice, gravelly and deep and not quite what I remembered. I waited for the beep and blurted out, 'It's Summer Davis. I met you once years ago, and I'm in Cobalt because my great-aunt Stella has cancer, and Samantha Chisholm came into town, which is how I got your number. And anyway, I started this message without knowing what I was going to say, except that it's funny to look down Stella's street and see your house and think that it's not your house anymore. And I guess you're in New York, and I hope it's nice there right now. It probably is . . . it's always nice in the fall, except for the smell. And—'

I was cut off, abruptly, by a loud *beep* in my ear. I held the phone back. I hadn't even given him my phone number or any other way to contact me. Did all phones have Caller ID? Would he even *want* to call me back, after my message? I couldn't even remember what I'd just said. There was no way to edit the message or record it over again.

Taking a deep breath, I redialed. It rang; Philip explained yet again that he wasn't available. 'This is my number,' I blurted out quickly. I gave it to him, then hung up fast.

I cupped my phone in my hand, suddenly feeling brave. My fingers wanted to dial the old number in Brooklyn. I typed it in and stared at it for a while. If I hit SEND, would he answer? Would we talk about the weather, about New York? Or would we talk about something serious, real? Maybe I could ask him something easy first, perhaps a memory from his big leather box. I could ask if he remembered the time I'd stayed home from my classes at college and he'd (obviously) stayed home from any remaining work that he was doing and we'd watched a videotape of *Bedknobs and Broomsticks*, the old Disney movie with Angela Lansbury. Maybe I could ask him if he remembered the *first* time we watched that movie together, when I was about six. After the movie was over, I ran to my parents' bedroom and climbed onto the bed, touched my hands to the post at the end of the bed, and asked it to fly. It had worked for the kids in the movie.

My father had noticed what I was doing, and climbed in bed too. 'Where do you want it to go?' he said. 'Spain,' I answered, just picking anywhere. And then he called for Steven to get on the bed.

And then my mother stood in the doorway, asking what we were doing. 'We're going to Spain!' my father announced. I thought she might say it was just silly and demand that my father get up and do something useful. But, to my surprise, she lowered her shoulders and smiled and climbed on the bed, too.

I slowly closed the phone and put it in my pocket. It felt heavy against my hip, like it was full of secrets, waterlogged with things I hadn't said but probably should. We would never be like that again, my father and me, so we'd have to be something else. No matter how much I had done for him, I wasn't what he needed right now. And I *was* angry with him for that. Really, I'd probably been angry for years, for other things too. But as the wind shifted, I just felt tired. All I wanted was for him to put me into bed and tuck me in. Maybe even Rosemary could be there.

After a while, I went back upstairs and down the hall to Stella's room. I could see her face through the little window in the door. She was in the far bed, connected to various machines. Her head was bent off to the side, her eyes fluttering fast. At my request, the doctor and nurses had left her gloves on, rolling them down so they bunched up around her hands. There was a small smile on her face, like she was having a good dream.

Stella woke up early on Monday morning, just as the sun cracked over the horizon. I was slumped just outside her hospital room, reading a *Cosmopolitan* someone had left behind. There was an article inside that read, *Daddy's Girl: Is it true that we go after men who resemble our fathers?*

I heard Stella cough and went into her room. For the first time, her eyes were open and she was looking around as if she understood where she was. She saw me, smiled, and then shrugged at the tubes running out of her arm and the IV bags alongside her bed.

'You weren't feeling so great.' I sat down in the little orange chair next to her bed. 'How do you feel now?'

Stella cast her eyes off to the side. 'If I had a martini I'd probably be great. You think you could sneak me one?'

'I doubt it.'

'Come on.' Stella hit me weakly on my arm. 'I bet you could.'

I played with the hem of my t-shirt. 'I got you this.' I held out a little stuffed hedgehog I'd found in the gift shop last night. When I squeezed it, the hedgehog squeaked. It was either a dog toy or a baby toy. Stella grinned and reached for it, pressing it to her nose and then to her chest.

'They did some more scans, didn't they?' she asked.

I nodded. 'A few.'

'So is the needle not working for me? Do we need another kind of needle?' She called the IV chemo treatments 'the needle', as if she was a rock-and-roll heroin addict.

336

I looked away. It was always more chemo after her setbacks – it meant the cancer had advanced somewhere else, and they were going to try the drugs again to hold it back for as long as possible. Except this time. I wasn't sure what would be worse – if I told Stella the truth, or if I let the doctor do it. The doctor was from Haiti – dark-skinned, with lovely eyes, thick, black hair and a funny last name that I couldn't remember but knew it sounded like a magic word. If I left it up to the doctor to tell her, Stella might slap him and say something terrible, like that people from Haiti couldn't be doctors because they were uncivilized voodoo-worshippers. Instead of treating her with normal medicine, the Haitian doctor would probably want to sacrifice a chicken and spurt its blood over her forehead. We'd watched a PBS report about voodoo in Haiti the week before.

'What were you doing, going to the bathroom in a place like that?' I asked.

'I had to pee. But then I fell, I guess. I don't know. Is that what happened?'

'Pretty much,' I said. 'You shouldn't have gone into that place, though. It was scary.'

'Oh, nonsense. It was fine. The woman behind the counter was very nice. I didn't get a chance to ask where the jackalope was, though. Had to go so badly, I felt dizzy.'

'I thought it was scary in there,' I said.

'Oh, I'm not afraid of anything anymore.' Stella held up her thin arms, marred with needle tracks.

337

'You were afraid of Cheveyo,' I said quietly.

Stella eyed me. I looked back at her, then stared down at my lap. 'Sorry. But I mean . . .' Something caught in my throat; I had to look into the rectangular overhead light and wait for it to pass. I wanted to tell her that I didn't have an agenda, trying and trying to save her. That I wasn't using her as an excuse. But I wasn't sure I should lie to her, if she was right.

'I said that for your own good,' Stella said gently, understanding without me having to say a word. 'I'm not angry. I'm just saying. We'd have a much better time if we just, I don't know . . . Smoked grass just for the hell of it, not because it might be some miracle cure.'

I balled up my fists and pressed them into my knees. 'Who's going to save you, if not me?'

'No one.'

'Well, then, I'll save you.'

She let out a laugh. After a while, she took a deep breath. 'I didn't tell you everything about Ruth. You were right – of course I was angry at her. So angry, in fact, I told her husband what I saw.'

I widened my eyes. 'What did he say?'

'He just got really quiet, nodded his head, and said, *I see*. I knew what I'd done. But I wanted to ruin Ruth's life – I thought she'd ruined mine. The thing was, she *hadn't* ruined mine. We got over it, Skip and me. We talked about it. Who talked back then? But we did, as best we could.

338

But Ruth and Gerald . . .' She pulled at her bedsheets. 'What's done is done. You make mistakes and you learn from them. Everyone does. It's just what happens. You probably wouldn't be alive if you didn't. The thing is, I have a feeling that if either of us would have just broken down and apologized, Ruth and I would've been okay. But it's so hard to *start*, isn't it? To say it. You carry this anger around about someone, and they carry different anger around about you, and everybody's secretly so angry at everyone else, and we're all hurting one another. It's not like anyone's innocent.'

'Maybe,' I said.

She smiled sadly. 'I tried to apologize to Ruth, almost at the end. She was lying in bed, snoring, and I had come over to wash some stuff for her – it was after she was too weak to go down the stairs to the washing machine in the basement. I stood over her bed and told her that I was sorry, and that we'd been acting like assholes for years. She didn't hear me, though.'

'But that counts, though, right?' I asked in a small voice. 'Just saying it aloud?'

Stella's dim eyes met mine. 'I can see why your father depended on you. He always needed someone. The way he was with his mother . . . he looked to her for everything. Every decision.'

I stared at the rising and falling lines of Stella's EKG. *He doesn't need me much anymore.*

Stella ran her fingers over the folds in the

bedsheets. 'Ruth never cared about Gerald – before Skip, after Skip. Their marriage – well, they should've gotten divorced after he found out. It would've been so much better for both of them. He was so cold, so emotionless, even before he found out. I forgave her, in a way, for going after Skip, faced with a lifetime with that man. She needed some warmth and intimacy. But she ended up pouring that love into your father. She cared so much about him, sometimes too much. She wouldn't let him breathe. 'Get a girlfriend,' I always said to your dad, always behind his mother's back. 'Live a little.' 'I'm fine,' he always said. I always told him there were plenty of pretty girls in Cobalt – I even tried to fix him up with some of them, girls whose hair I used to wash, that sort of thing. He never went out with any of them. Until the one. The important girl. I saw them together, once. He never knew. He always thought he was being so stealthy, but I saw them taking a walk near the train tracks, and I could just tell.'

The clock on the wall was too loud. The second hand skipped like it had tremors. 'What girl?'

'And then she was in that coma,' Stella went on, as if she hadn't heard me. 'After all that time in the hospital, although everyone knew she was going to die. Even if she'd lived, her life wouldn't have been much of anything. We talked about how tragic it was for her boyfriend, but no one talked about your father, what he was going through.

340

No one could. Even if people knew, it was indecent to talk about it, with the boyfriend standing by her while she was supported by those god-awful life-support machines. Your father left Cobalt shortly after that and never came back. If people knew why, they never said anything. They pretended like it hadn't happened.'

The weight of what she was saying began to take shape. 'Wait. Stop.'

Stella hesitated.

'Wait.' My voice cracked. 'You're telling me that the girl who was in the car accident with my dad, Kay Mulvaney, she and my dad were . . .' I waved my hands, trying to understand. '. . . *together?*'

Stella nodded just slightly. 'It destroyed him when she died. Especially because he'd been the driver.'

I sat up straighter. '*He* was the driver?'

She shifted in her bed. 'He never told you.'

I ran my hand over the top of my head, trying to remember. He'd never said one way or another. It was always *we* hit a deer, *we* got into a crash.

'The boyfriend was dead drunk,' Stella explained. 'If he'd have been the driver, he would've been arrested. Or they *all* would've died.'

It took me a while to catch my breath. 'Why didn't I know about this?'

'I guess it wasn't the right time to tell you. And I don't know what your father's going to think, if I tell him that I've told you. Maybe I shouldn't. Maybe I should just leave it up to you two to talk.'

341

There was a laminated sign near Stella's door that said PAIN CHART. Patients could describe their pain based on different facial expressions, numbered one through ten. I searched through them, but none of the faces rightly described what I felt. 'Have you been talking to him?' I sounded out slowly.

Stella looked away. 'A little, honey. Here and there.'

The fluorescent light flickered and shivered. Outside, two elderly people were walking up the sidewalk into surgery. A man in an electric wheel-chair sat by the curb, waiting for a ride. I looked up, recalling what my father had told me the last time I saw him. 'Kay was pregnant.'

Stella clucked her tongue. 'It was a big deal for the time. Especially for Cobalt. That boyfriend of hers married her while she was in the coma. There was a ceremony and everything.'

I tried to hold on to a single thought, but my head felt like it was caught in a windstorm. Things were whirling everywhere. This was like working for sixty years on a scientific theory and discovering that the principle underlying your idea was incorrect, so your research was useless. It couldn't be possible, any of it. My father couldn't have been the one driving. He would've wrapped the car around a tree rather than hit a deer. And Kay Mulvaney was in love with Mark Jeffords. They were going to get married; my father was their friend. He met my mother in college; that was when he fell in love. That was where his story started; he escaped Cobalt because there wasn't enough here for him. There wasn't anything more. There couldn't be.

I stood up, banging my knee hard against the edge of the bed. 'That's just some stupid rumor.'

Stella's lips parted, startled.

'He would have told me. He wouldn't have kept something like that a secret. It's an easy thing to speculate, anyway – girl dies in car accident, my father leaves town – let's blame it on misguided love, on him feeling *responsible,* or whatever you said. Let's blame it on loving the wrong person. They were *teenagers.* They couldn't have been in love. That doesn't come until later.'

Stella looked amused. 'It doesn't?'

Her mocking tone of voice scratched against me. I plucked the hedgehog from her chest and hurled it across the room. It hit the wall so hard that it squeaked.

'I know my father,' I said in a shaky voice. 'And that never happened.' I thought of the picture I'd found all those years ago: *Mark Jeffords and Kay Mulvaney, (secret!) engagement, 1970.* I thought of Kay's round, pie-like face, her button nose.

'I can understand if it's hard to accept,' Stella said.

'There's nothing *to* accept. I know my father. It didn't happen.'

'Summer . . .'

'I know my father.' As I said it again, a little

voice needled me. *Do you?* The voice sounded like Stella's, but her face was blank, indicative of nothing.

I slumped back down in the chair and put my head in my hands. When I looked up, Stella's eyes were closed again, but she wasn't asleep. I moved to the other side of the room, picked up the hedgehog, and put it back on her chest. 'Thank you,' she said.

I answered by letting out a little groan. I pressed my palm onto her bare leg.

'Your hands are cold,' she said, her eyes still closed.

Outside, a black van pulled up, a ramp mechanically lowered, and the man in the electric wheelchair motored inside. Far off in the distance, a dog barked. Stella smiled, hearing it too. I was sure she missed her dogs, who were roaming around the house without us, who were swimming in the creek without an audience.

'So how's my dad doing?' I asked quietly.

'He's good,' Stella said, opening her eyes a crack. 'You know he and Rosemary are living in Brooklyn, right?'

I nodded silently.

'She sounds like a good person, Summer.'

I swallowed hard. 'I know.'

I plucked the hedgehog off her chest once more and squeezed it. It made a small, dying wail. I shut my eyes, about to cry, but nothing came out.

Stella pressed her thin, papery fingers against

344

one of the IVs in her hand. 'So. Tell me straight. It's in my brain, right?'

I looked over at her. Thankfully, they hadn't taken her wig off. I could still see the flaking remains of the temporary heart tattoo we affixed to her chest, right under her chemo port. A chill ran through me, and I got a horrible fear that I was either going to pee my pants or throw up. 'Yes,' I whispered.

'I thought so,' she said. 'So what do we do now?'

I sat down next to her on the bed. She was so small that there was plenty of room. She smelled the same way she had the day I met her – like peanut-butter cookies. It was a scent that emanated from her pores, even when her insides were rotting. *We reschedule Cheveyo*, I wanted to tell her. *We try meditation. We could go to Tibet. We don't have to stop.* So what if I was trying to save her? She deserved saving. I wanted to be able to save someone.

The following day, I would wake in the same hospital waiting room and see a crowd gathered around the television. What they thought was a small plane had crashed into a building in New York City, and I would soon find out which building it was. I would stand there as a jumbo jet hit the building next to it. Someone – many people – would scream. More things would happen, more things would fall down, people would run, and the whole view I remembered from my Brooklyn apartment window would

345

immediately change forever. A minute would morph into a half-hour, but I wouldn't move. People around me would be slack-jawed in the middle of the hospital hall.

'Can you believe what they put on TV these days?' Stella would demand, as soon as I entered her room. 'It's for some movie, right? It's in poor taste, blowing up the World Trade Center . . . but then I stopped understanding Hollywood after the Fifties.'

And a nurse would turn halfway, looking at me with terror. *I don't have control of this, do you?* I would tell Stella that yes, it was for a movie. And that she shouldn't worry, that television did all kinds of horrible, manipulative things these days, just like *War of the Worlds* on the radio years ago.

Samantha would show up that day, too, her face pale, her lipstick in need of reapplication. At that point, her arrival wouldn't even seem shocking. 'Do you know anyone . . . ?' she'd whisper. And, 'Didn't your mom . . . ?' and I'd tell her that probably not, almost definitely not, but I didn't know.

Later, Samantha and I would drive back and pick up Stella's car from the parking lot of the general store. The people inside would run out and ask how Stella was doing. I'd tell them fine, and they'd give us candy, silly things like Now and Laters and Reese's Pieces and Blow Pops, their eyes big and round, full of charity. The physical world would be surreal, bursting with blueness and late-summer leaves and chirping birds and a

346

cloudless sky. Samantha and I would return to our own separate cars, on our way back to the hospital, listening to the endless radio broadcasts. We'd crane our necks out the windows, searching for falling planes, a falling sky. Instead, we'd see a little wooden shack on the side of the road. Samantha would pull over into the parking lot and roll down her window. 'Is that?' She'd point a care-fully painted nail at the sign.

The words would be inky black, striking against the gray-blue weathered sign. *Come on in to see the World-Famous Jackalope.*

The door would swing open easily, as if hanging by one rusty hinge. The room would be dark and cool, and there'd be an old woman sitting behind a makeshift counter that bore a few pamphlets, some magnets that said *Jackalope* and a picture of something unidentifiable, on sale for $1.50. She'd be watching the news, too, like everyone else. The turquoise sky, the burning buildings, falling again, one floor then the next then the next, collapsing into dust. People running, screaming.

'Excuse me,' Samantha would say very softly to the woman at the desk, 'can you tell us where the jackalope is?'

The woman would look up and study us for a moment, as if she couldn't understand why we were there and what we wanted. Then she'd point and say, 'There. Right there.'

There would be a glass case across the room. Behind the glass, we would make out something stuffed: a large, fat, brown and gray rabbit standing on its hindquarters, its head turned jauntily to the side. On the base of its skull would be two large antlers, almost as big as the rabbit itself, the ends of each tapering into two sharp, curving points that almost touched one another. There would be an old sign underneath, printed in a small, dated, Sixties font, that said, *The Jackalope (*Lepus temperamentalus) *is one of the rarest animals in the world. A cross between a now-extinct pygmy deer and a species of killer rabbit, they are extremely shy unless approached. It is written that you can extract the jackalope's milk as it sleeps belly-up at night. The milk is believed to be medicinal and can be used to treat a variety of afflictions. Many do not believe in the jackalope's existence, but do not be swayed! It will kill you if you aren't looking! These dangerous creatures ARE REAL!*

Samantha and I would stand there for a while, not saying anything, admiring the jackalope like we were looking at an artefact in the Smithsonian. The jackalope's eyes would be glassy, and I'd see the clear lines of glue where the horns had been attached, the piece of fur on its back that was torn back, as if a dog had recently been playing with it. But, despite this, I would grapple for something magical. I would want to believe it was real, that everything was real – Cheveyo, miracle cures, loving someone I'd met seven years ago and had only briefly kissed. But believing that the jackalope was real would mean I had to believe what was going on behind me on television – the planes, people screaming – was real, too. And that cancer was real. And that my father truly loved a girl that died, desperately loved someone before he desperately loved my mother, and that perhaps he desperately loved Rosemary, too. That he had changed, leaving me behind, and that it was probably the best, healthiest thing he could have done.

My fingers would graze my phone in my pocket. I knew I would call him, at least to see if he was all right.

There would be nothing else in the shack, except for the jackalope and a few books of jackalope lore and a few suspicious photos of the jackalope in the wild. After a while, Samantha would begin to talk. 'I'm selling the most wonderful houses in Northglenn right now.' Her voice would be low, shaky. 'All empty. You walk through the rooms and they echo. They smell like new carpet and fresh paint. The garage is so clean, the closets don't have dust in them. There's enough room for a big refrigerator in the kitchen and a sectional in the living room. There are rooms for nurseries and for kids' bunk beds. The master bedrooms are gorgeous, too. Vaulted ceilings. Whirlpool tubs.'

She'd stop, then, for a moment, and glance at me. Her lips would quiver, and I would notice that, for whatever reason, she wasn't wearing her wedding ring. But I wouldn't ask.

'Tell me about the backyard,' I'd goad her.

She'd exhale and relax. 'The backyard is beautiful.'

All that was going to happen the very next day.

In just twenty-four hours, what we were going to do and what we would worry about would change, and the distance between us would change, too. But in the hospital, sitting on the edge of Stella's bed, that all seemed impossible, unimaginable. We were still, for the most part, innocent and okay.

'What do we do now?' Stella asked again, hugging the hedgehog to her chest.

I touched her hand. 'We have fun, just like you said. We go get you some pie. And that martini, too.'

She smiled. 'With three olives?'

'With *four*, if you want. We'll have a martini-drinking contest.'

She sighed decadently, already imagining it. 'Sounds like a plan.'

The first time I saw you, you were wearing a flowered smock and pink cotton pants. Terrible shoes: those white nurse things. Orthopedic. I didn't think much about you the first time I saw you. You were a new aide, one of the many aides that cycled through the place. The aides didn't do much, just tried to keep us comfortable and entertain us and do all of the things that the nurses didn't have time for. Some of the aides volunteered, in fact, and weren't even making money at it. They were just doing it because . . . I don't know, I guess they saw it as charity. Maybe it made them feel less crazy.

You were younger than most of the aides. You didn't have that cropped-short, old-woman hair helmet, but shoulder-length, wavy hair, wavier in some spots than in others. You had delicate hands, red-raw skin, sensitive to cold, dry temperatures, a long, sloped nose with a little bulb on the end, and a wide smile, although you withheld your smiles most of the time, almost as if you worried smiling too much might upset us. When the other aides and nurses went out to smoke, you read all of the pamphlets near the meds room, the ones that were titled **What Is Anxiety?**, as if any of us didn't know. Perhaps you read them simply to look busy, to pose as if you were perfectly fine with not being included. I liked you for that, because the other aides acted like bitchy hens out there, smoking together. It's obvious they were talking about us, the patients.

Then there was the morning I had the episode. According to some, I started screaming. I pulled the couch cushions off the floor in the TV room, and I kicked Thatcher in the shin and upturned Ursula's and Kevin's chess game. They don't even play chess, they just sit there staring at the pieces and talk about how indecisive they both are, so I didn't feel bad about messing up their game. I don't remember any of it, though. All I remember is waking up and seeing Kay hovering above me. Her wavy hair hung around her face, her gray eyes slanted down with concern, and she kept pressing her full lips together, just like she always did when something worried her. I was certain we were in the back room of Dairy Queen, just waking up from a nap.

I said Kay's name. Kay smiled tentatively. She put her hand to my forehead and then glanced somewhere I couldn't see. Then Bev came into the picture. 'Just lie there,' Bev said.

I looked around to see where Kay had gone. I didn't understand what Big Bev the nurse was doing at Dairy Queen. 'Bring Kay back,' I said.

'Shhh,' Bev answered. 'How about you have some water.'

'Don't let Kay leave!' I said, frantic. 'I haven't seen her in so long. I want to talk to her.'

Bev put the pitcher back down on my nightstand. 'You've had a confusing morning.'

I tried to sit up, but Bev wouldn't let me. 'I just saw her here,' I said. 'She was looking at me. You said something to her.'

'The only other person in here was Rosemary,' Bev answered.

Then I heard your voice in the hallway. 'Bev? What? Do you need something?'

'No, Rosemary, it's fine.'

You walked into the room anyway. And it was you, Rosemary, not Kay, with your stubby blonde ponytail and your — I'd never realized it, until right then — haunting gray eyes. I stared at you hard. I didn't quite believe it. 'How are you feeling, Richard?' you asked.

Bev settled me back down and looked over her shoulder. 'Can you watch him for a second?' she asked. 'Make sure he doesn't try and get up again.' I knew she wanted a cigarette.

'Of course,' you said.

Bev shut the door. You immediately started straightening my sheets. 'Feeling better?'

'What happened?' I asked, so groggy.

'You . . . got up. Ran around a bit.' You looked at me curiously. 'You don't remember?'

I shook my head. I looked at you and told you that, a few seconds ago, I swore you were my girl-friend from high school. You still looked like her, if I squinted.

353

You looked embarrassed, but then said, 'Well. That's nice.'

You pulled a chair over and sat by my bed. 'Do you want to talk about this girlfriend?' you asked. You probably weren't supposed to ask, being just an aide. 'What was she like?'

'It was so long ago,' I said. 'And we hadn't told anyone we were together. It was wrong, really. She was with someone else. My best friend. They were engaged.' I glanced at you out of the corner of my eye. Your Kay essence hadn't fully worn off yet.

'And what happened to her?'

I took a deep breath. 'She was in a car accident,' I said. 'She broke her neck, and was in a coma for four weeks, on life support. Then she died.'

'Oh gosh,' you said quickly. 'I'm sorry.'

My mouth felt electrified. There was a strange humming in my stomach. For the first time, I felt I could keep going. I felt I could talk about it and not stop.

We had been at a party. I had something to tell her, she had something to tell me. The thing that I had to tell her was that I had been awarded a college scholarship, a full ride. I would be leaving Cobalt, where we both lived.

I found Kay in the hallway. I knew she'd be happy for me – she was always so encouraging, saying I was so smart and that I had an amazing mother, for it was my mom who'd found out about the scholarship in the first place. But when I told her, Kay's face fell. She looked like I'd just punched her.

'I'm pregnant,' Kay blurted out.

I didn't mean to burst out laughing, it just happened. 'It's not a joke,' Kay said. 'I'm really six months pregnant.'

'Are you sure? How the hell can you be six months pregnant?' I stared at her stomach. At her boobs. At everything that changes in a pregnant woman's body. She was wearing a gauzy, flowing top, the same sort all her girlfriends wore. They hid a lot – only, I knew what her body felt like, and I hadn't felt anything. It was inconceivable.

'I've gained twelve pounds,' Kay said. 'It's low, but the doctor says I'm okay. He says that, sometimes, women gain a bunch of weight at the very end.'

I felt tricked. Bamboozled. I kept staring at her body and trying to figure it out. Where were the twelve pounds? 'Why didn't you say anything before?'

'Because I only found out last month,' she whispered. 'I didn't get my period for a while, but I often skip a few months, so . . . I don't know. I thought it was normal. But then I went to the doctor.' She gave me this look that said **Please don't kill me. Please be happy.**

'Are you sure it's mine?' I asked.

Her mouth got very small. 'I know how to read a calendar, Richard.'

People streamed around us, not paying any attention to what we were talking about. 'It's an honest question,' I said quietly. 'Six months ago . . .'

'. . . we were together,' she answered quickly. 'One of the first times.'

'You've been with Mark, too.'

She smashed her mouth together. Her eyes began to water. I looked around fretfully for Mark, for Andy or Jeanie, someone who might notice. 'I knew this would happen,' she whispered. 'I knew I would tell you this and you would want to leave.'

'Wait, did you plan this?' I asked.

'Of course not!' Her eyes flickered back and forth, trying to meet mine. Have you ever noticed that, though, that your eyes can't completely meet someone else's? You have to look at one pupil or the other. We're never truly looking at one another at all. 'What are we going to do?'

'I don't know!' I blurted out. 'Why do you think I would know?' I was getting angry now. This was my day, my big news. And I wanted to be having this conversation anywhere but the hallway of Jeff's parents' house – the sounds of Leonard Cohen drifted out of the stoner room, and people were dissecting 'Suzanne' for its sexual implications. I wasn't ready for this to be real. I wasn't ready to have to deal with things like this.

'I'm so scared,' Kay said. 'You're going to go away. You're going to abandon me.'

'I'm not going to abandon you,' I said. 'But we have to think rationally. You're going to finish your senior year here. Break off your engagement. And then you're going to join me at Penn State. That's the way it's supposed to work.'

'Well, I guess we'll have to rethink that.'

I let out a small whimper. 'Those are our plans.'

She widened her wet, already-round eyes. 'What are you saying?'

'I'm just saying . . . I want things to be the way they were ten minutes ago.'

'Well, they're not!'

More people rushed by. A few looked at us warily. Someone in the stoner room turned up 'Hey, That's No Way to Say Goodbye'. 'I want this scholarship,' I whispered.

'I can't believe you,' Kay said quietly. It annoyed me. And it hurt. I didn't know what to say to her. This was how it happened to plenty of guys around here: they were bound for better things, but then they knocked someone up and did what was honorable. They married her. They got some job, any job, and they raised the kid that neither of them particularly wanted. When I thought about our future together, I had never factored in this. It had never entered my list of possibilities.

Kay turned away then, pressing her back along the wall. The pot smoke formed a thick, blue halo around her. 'Maybe she's Mark's,' Kay said. She had given the baby a gender already – I never got to tell her, later, that she had guessed right.

Mark came up. 'What are you two talking about?' he asked, clapping a hand on my shoulder and the other on Kay's. He touched Kay's boob and squeezed. She let him. Her eyes were on me the whole time, as if to say, See, your chance is gone.

Jimi Hendrix came on the stereo. I stormed across the room into the kitchen. After a few minutes, I felt

Kay's hand on my arm. 'Mark wants to go,' she said, 'but he's . . .'

We both watched as Mark tripped over the edge of a round braided rug. Beer sloshed over his cup. 'Give me the keys,' I said, cruelly sober. I hadn't even made it to the keg yet.

On the way out to the car, Kay said, 'Mark? Why don't we get married this summer?'

'Your parents would kill us,' Mark answered sloppily, wrapping his arm around hers. 'We're supposed to wait until you're done with high school.'

'Not if we had a giant wedding,' Kay cooed. 'We could invite everyone. I want to be a married woman my last year of high school. It sounds so romantic.'

'Sounds good to me,' Mark slurred.

I threw myself into the front seat. The shell around me grew thicker and thicker. Kay got into the passenger seat and looked at me, but I made a big deal out of putting the key in the ignition, shoving the car into drive. Kay looked at me for ten whole seconds, and then blew the air out of her cheeks and turned around to check on Mark, who'd lain down in the back.

I wove around the cars haphazardly parked on Jeff's lawn. Mark made a gagging noise, as though he might puke, but then rallied. He started talking about fixing up an old dirt bike with Andy Elkerson next weekend. 'You want to help?' he asked me.

'I don't know,' I said in monotone, my thoughts sloshing, my emotions tangled. 'Maybe.'

'Elkerson's so lucky, out of school and all that,' Mark said.

'We only have a couple more weeks,' I told him.

'I don't know if I can do it, man,' Mark said. 'Fucking Mr Tole.' He turned to Kay. 'Did I tell you how this guy bought dope off of that guy that works at the gas station? Barney something?'

'You told me,' Kay said quietly.

I forked onto Wyndell, which is full of thick woods and blind turns. 'We should tell the PTA, don't you think?' Mark was saying. 'How can these drugged-up bastards teach at our school and get a paycheck? I mean, at least hire someone who isn't shit-faced all the time. Like hire me.'

'You're not done with school yet,' Kay pointed out.

'I will be soon enough.'

'You wouldn't want to teach here,' I said. 'Teach somewhere else, if you want to teach. Just not here.'

'There's nothing wrong with teaching here,' Kay said.

'It's easy for you to say, Rich,' Mark talked over her. 'You're getting out of here. You've got it all. Me and Kay, it's different.'

'It's better,' Kay said, her voice gnarled and abrasive, like steel wool. 'Real people stay in Cobalt. Honest people. They do what they have to and they stay.'

'Shut the fuck up,' Mark said. He often thought people were making fun of him when they weren't.

But I knew better. 'Shut up,' I said, too. I met her eyes, finally, right across from me. Then she faced

359

forward, screamed. There was the deer, long legs, wide eyes, erect ears. A thick-antlered buck. He stared at the car, and I stared back at him. His eyes glowed blue. For a moment, right before we collided, the expression on the buck's face looked almost human, startlingly cognitive. It was like he understood what was happening – not just with the car in front of him, but also with me. He looked straight into me and saw what I'd said to Kay, what I'd given up.

Then there was the crunch, and a long few seconds of nothing.

When the noise stopped, it was so quiet. Like death. The wind brushed peacefully through the trees. There was a far-off swish of another car going by on a distant road. When I sat up, some of the window's glass had shattered into the inside of the car. It was all over the seats, glittering in the moonlight.

I saw clearly, then, I realized I could defer the scholarship. I could go in a year or so. Kay and I could live in married students' housing with the baby. Maybe she could even go to school there, too. My life wasn't ending – it was just starting a little sooner than I'd planned.

I pushed out the car door. It crackled with more broken glass. I saw the deer lying on the ground, enormous and immobile. I turned back into the car and looked at Kay. I wanted to tell her. But then . . .

I told you this in a series of visits you made to my room. It was like I was a serial novel, or perhaps a soap opera. You were tuning in for the next episode of Richard Davis's tragic, young denouement. You knew nothing about me except for this – and, ironically, doctors knew everything else about me except for this, in this kind of detail. By the time I got to this part in the story, your eyes were very wide. 'But then . . . what?' you asked.

I looked down. Kay was covered in blood. She wasn't scrunched up or cockeyed or bent in an unnatural angle or anything, though – it seemed more like she was just sleeping. When the ambulance came, I grabbed an EMT's arms and told him he should be very careful with Kay; she was pregnant. I heard a gasp behind me and turned – they had pulled Mark out of the car and laid him on the pavement. He had come to, and was staring right at me. In the back of my mind, I'd always wondered if he'd suspected what was going on between us. Maybe I'd hoped that, deep down, he had always known. But he hadn't, that was obvious. He hadn't known a thing. It was the last time Mark ever looked me in the eyes.

I told you about how, a few days after that, I had lain on the carpet in the living room, the TV blaring. I told my mother I wouldn't be taking the scholarship for college. 'But we worked so hard,' she said, astonished. And it was true, it was we. She'd pushed me into taking the accelerated courses, she'd bought me the encyclopedias, she had filled out the paperwork for the scholarship and ridden me until I finished the essays. You need to get out of Cobalt, she always said. **You're destined for better things.**

'I'm sorry,' I told her, sprawled out on the floor. 'I can't do it. I can't go.'

My mother stood there for a long time. All I wanted was for her to lean down and tell me the right thing. She was so good at telling me the right thing, bolstering me up, making me feel like I was okay. But she just quivered at the edge of the room, her face growing redder and redder. 'Fine,' she said finally. 'Stay here, then. Ruin your life.'

'I really need to talk about this with someone,' I said. 'I feel like I'm coming apart.'

'What's there to talk about?' she snapped, twisting a hand towel around in her fingers. 'It was an accident. People hit deer all the time, there's nothing you could've done. Think about your friend. Think about what he has to face now.'

'Maybe he needs to talk to someone too,' I moaned.

She rolled her eyes. 'Get off the floor. Go get a goddamn job.' **Goddamn** was razor-edged; she'd never used that tone with me.

The phone rang. My mother stomped over to get it. I knew right away it was my father. My mother's voice drooped, a wrung-out washcloth. 'Well, just come home,' she said. She slammed the phone back into its cradle. She didn't know I was watching when she put down the hand towel and glared at the portrait of Sinatra she kept by the telephone and stuck her thumb right in his smarmy face, as if blotting out his shiny, optimistic existence.

I saw her differently, then. How cornered she felt, how purposeless. My relationship with Kay was the only thing I'd ever kept from her. Perhaps that was why she didn't come to me when I was lying on the floor in despair – because I'd concealed it, because she thought she'd been replaced.

'I'm sorry,' you whispered, when I finally finished.

I looked up at you then. Really looked at you. 'Why are you an aide here?' I asked.

You looked startled. First, you touched your throat, as if checking for your vocal cords. Then you turned the little silver chain you wore on your wrist around. 'I like helping people,' you said. 'And I was here once, myself. A long time ago. When I was nineteen.'

'Why?'

'I used to do this.' You pulled up your sleeve and showed me scars up and down the insides of your arm. Then you pulled up your shirt and showed me similar ones on your stomach. There were more on your calves, the insides of your thighs. 'I used broken glass.'

'Are you better?' I asked.

'Yes,' you said. 'No. I don't know.'

We kept things a secret for a while. When we met to play tennis, we were both very businesslike. If it seemed like I talked to you a lot during meals or spent more time with you when we drove upstate into Rhinebeck, no one said anything. So we got bolder. You would slip into Merewether while the others were watching TV. I would pull you up to my bedroom and we would hide under the covers of the twin bed and listen to Coltrane on my Discman, one earbud in your left ear, the other earbud in my right. It was exciting, knowing that Paula, who watched over us, might walk in at any time. What can I say? That I felt alive? That I felt understood? Sometimes you said you still felt crazy. I told you I had a brownstone apartment in Brooklyn Heights, and that I wanted you to come home with me. You were hesitant – you'd had difficult relationships in the past. 'Life's not as easy as that,' you said. 'You should know that by now.'

I told you I did know that. But even if things got hard, I wanted to deal with that, too. I've run from a lot of people when things got too hard, I told you. I ran from my mother, I ran from Kay, I ran from my cousin and my aunt and my friends and my daughter. I'm tired of running. I don't want to do that anymore.

'Your daughter?' You stopped me. 'You didn't run from Summer. She's in Brooklyn.'

I looked away. I hadn't been clear. But there was time to explain all that later. There was time for everything.

I want to be idealistic about you. I want to be hopeful, as hopeful as I'd been with Kay. I am still me. We are the worst of ourselves and also the best. They can try and shock it out of us but it doesn't really go away, not entirely. And that's okay. It made me feel great to realize that. It made me feel almost whole again.

PART V

BROOKLYN, NEW YORK, FEBRUARY, 2003

blizzard

CHAPTER 25

The family met for dinner in Park Slope, at an Italian restaurant on Fifth Avenue. The restaurant didn't have a bar, so we had to stand in the alcove by the door to wait while they cleared a table for us.

The alcove's heavy plastic walls kept buckling in from the wind. Rosemary stood next to me, wearing a long, sweeping skirt, pointy boots with a bunch of tiny eyelet buttons, and an oversized plaid coat. Her dirty blonde hair was pulled back into a ponytail, but many strands had broken free, spiraling around her face. Philip was talking to my father about the apartment. Structurally, it seemed very sound, he said. However, there were ways to maximize the space that might appeal to buyers. He could knock down the wall that separated the kitchen and the living room to make it one large room. The kitchen would get more light that way.

My father ran his hand over his chin. 'I wonder how long that would take . . .'

'Not long, once you get the permit and a contractor,' Philip said. He knew a contractor who

367

owed him a favor, actually, from when he lived in New York. He could call him, if my father wanted.

'Richard,' Rosemary warned, 'we can't knock down a *wall*. People are coming to see the place in two days.'

'True.' My father nodded slowly.

'But, for the record, I was always telling him that we should open up the space between the kitchen and the living room,' Rosemary added, snaking her arm around my father's elbow.

'You have been,' my father said, leaning into her. 'I should have listened to you.'

I looked away.

I left your bedroom untouched, my father had written in the email that announced he had decided to sell the old Brooklyn apartment. Logically, selling it made sense – it wasn't as if anyone were living there, as my father and Rosemary were in Vermont, and Philip and I were living in Annapolis, Maryland. He'd probably make a killing on it, too, the way the apartment values in Brooklyn Heights had gone up since he'd bought the place.

The realtor had scheduled an open house for this Monday and Tuesday, which was why everyone had to come into town this weekend and get their stuff out. It was also an excuse for us to come back to Brooklyn and hang out together; a 'family gathering', as my father called it.

The talk transitioned to tennis, whether Roddick was the real thing or just a flash in the pan, that Hewitt was an asshole, and who were these

Russian girls coming into this country and using our trainers and playing in Florida but still competing under the Russian flag. I had no idea Philip knew anything about tennis. Sometimes, he just came out with these random facts about things – famous mountain ranges, American history, the Dalai Lama. I could see the corner of his eyelid twitching, which happened whenever he was nervous. In the year we'd been together, I'd told him plenty about my father, but this was the first time they'd met. I wanted to tell Philip he didn't have to try so hard.

'Summer, I wanted to show you this.' Rosemary pulled a binder out of her enormous handbag. Inside were photographs, notes scrawled on lined paper, and more notes and drawings on Post-its. 'It's the general premise to my book.' She pointed to the photographs. 'I featured twelve gardens in Vermont, and interviewed each of the people who cultivated them. I tried to vary them as much as possible, to give people a lot of options. If it ever gets published, maybe we could sell it at my store. Anyway, I thought you might want to take a look.'

'It's nice,' I said, leaning over, feigning looking. 'Very pretty.'

'You should see the things Rosemary's doing for that store,' my father butted in, just as the frizzy-haired maître d' announced that our table was ready and that we could sit down if we wanted, even though Steven and Angie, his girlfriend, hadn't arrived yet. 'They raise llamas on the neighboring property, right? Well, now they don't only just sell plants at Carson's. Rosemary is buying some of the llama yarn to sell there as well.'

'And you should see *him* with those llamas.' Rosemary jutted a finger at my father. 'There's this one mother who was completely ignoring her baby, and Richard was so worried. He thought maybe *we* should adopt it. Had all these plans of how we could build a little llama barn off the garage.' She rolled her eyes good-naturedly. 'Your dad and his worries about karma.'

I recoiled, horrified she had so nonchalantly referred to what I thought she had referred to – my father's accident, his guilt over hitting the deer, his loss of Kay. My father had surely told Rosemary, and maybe Rosemary had assumed he'd discussed it with me. Only, he hadn't. Not once. I wasn't even sure if he knew I knew.

'I think it's nice he saves animals,' I said, unable to suppress the snip in my voice.

Philip touched my arm.

'Well, I know.' Rosemary sucked in her bottom lip. 'I mean, so do I.'

I clamped down on the insides of my cheek. I was trying. I was trying to try.

'You really should come to Vermont, Summer,' Rosemary said gently as we all sat down. 'It's so beautiful there right now, with the snow.'

I turned away, pushing my tongue to the roof of my mouth. All in all, it was a relief that Rosemary was who she was. Before I met her, I'd pictured her as this exuberant, carefree woman, the kind that wore short A-line skirts and was always the first to get up to dance at a wedding – like Kathy Lee Gifford on those Carnival Cruise commercials. Rosemary had come to Cobalt with my father to organize Stella's things and make the funeral arrangements. She was a godsend – she cleaned Stella's house top to bottom, sorted through a good deal of her things, braved places I didn't want to go, like the basement or Stella's closet or the kitchen pantry. Pete drove across the country to attend the funeral, too, and Rosemary cooked for everyone. She hung out in the living room doing a cross-stitch while my father and Pete caught up in the kitchen and I walked up and down Stella's gravelly street, talking to Philip on my cell phone.

'She's just so . . . ordinary,' I had told him. At this point, Philip and I hadn't actually seen each other yet, but we were talking to each other on the phone every night.

'Does she seem nice?' Philip asked.

'I don't really know,' I said, passing the old speed limit sign. I could still make out *Sand Niggers Go Home*, although the paint had faded almost white. 'She hasn't really said anything.' Not that I'd exactly said anything to Rosemary, either.

The third night in Cobalt, when my father and Pete were yet again drinking beer on the de-cluttered back porch, Rosemary started to brave a conversation with me. She did the talking. She told me she was working at the Brooklyn Botanical

Gardens. And that she wanted to start a gardening business and write a gardening book. Rosemary had created a gorgeous garden on the Brooklyn apartment's roof deck, and a few neighbors who had seen it from their roofs hired Rosemary to come over and make over their spaces, too. She told me she'd been working on the roof deck the day the terrorist attacks happened, and they'd put a big, jagged tear in her memory for life. She wanted to move my father out of the city – to Vermont, she was thinking – as fast as she could. She said this with a lift at the end of each sentence, like a question, although I doubted she was asking my permission.

'We should both go up to Vermont,' Philip said now, his hand on my arm again. 'We could learn how to ski. Or snowboard.'

'Mmm.' I dove into the bread basket as soon as the waitress placed it on the table. In Vermont, Rosemary worked at an organic plant store/coffee shop; they held folk concerts and poetry slams Sunday nights. My father didn't do anything for a while, but then began to renovate their farmhouse. He bought how-to books and just started . . . doing it. My father, who used to fear doing the laundry, now knew how to plumb and do electric work and hang windows. He knew how to frame a door and check if things were level. After he finished the farmhouse, he'd taken a job at an artist colony, repairing the studios and cottages. Apparently, Vermont was full of artist colonies, places where artists went and just . . . existed. Writers took over run-down barns and cabins. Painters climbed uneven steps to slanted lofts and marveled at the windows and light. My father, the once-dermatologist and cancer researcher, a holder of not one but several advanced degrees, wandered around with his tool belt, making sure the windows opened properly to vent out turpentine fumes.

Now, Steven and Angie stood awkwardly over us, smiling and holding hands. Angie had her purse slung across her chest like a postal worker, and Steven's hairline was receding, which I still found shocking and funny but also sad. 'Hey!' Steven cried.

My father stood up. 'You're here!' He wrapped his arms around Steven. Rosemary hugged Angie, who was petite and Asian and had the smallest teeth I had ever seen. The two of them sat down and shrugged off their jackets and bags. 'So happy you made it,' my father beamed. 'You get in okay?'

'Oh, sure, for once.' Angie rubbed her red hands together. She and Steven rolled their eyes in the understanding that frequent travelers had. They both worked at an Internet company in San Francisco. The website, which had something to do with on-line music reviews, was getting bigger and bigger, so they frequently flew around the country, attending events to promote it. This past summer, Steven had scored my father and Rosemary third-row seats to see Dave Brubeck at the Newport Jazz Festival, the musical zenith of my father's life.

'Who knows about our return flight, though?'

Steven added. 'All we've heard all day is talk about this snowstorm.'

'They're saying three feet,' Angie said.

My father lowered his eyes, looking distraught. 'They're wrong,' Rosemary assured him.

'You think?' my father asked.

'I'm sure,' Rosemary said.

'Actually, I'm pretty sure it's true,' I piped up. 'The meteorologists are usually right about blizzards.'

'Oh, I have a feeling it won't,' Rosemary said.

'It's not like you're God,' I said. I'd meant it as a joke, but it had come out so harsh and mean, and the whole table paused for a second.

'I'm Philip.' He reached across the table and shook Angie's hand, breaking the silence.

'You're here with Summer?' Steven asked.

'That's right.'

'Do you guys live near each other in Annapolis?'

'We live *together* in Annapolis,' Philip said, slowly, glancing at me.

'Oh!' Steven and Angie looked at each other in surprise. Philip kept his eyes on me, twirling a fork around in his fingers.

Steven nodded toward Philip. 'You look familiar.'

I clenched my butt in my chair. Philip was going to say that he had lived in Cobalt, or Steven was going to ask how we knew each other. I didn't want to talk about Cobalt now, or ever, not with Steven.

'Well, I lived in New York,' Philip said.

Angie snorted. 'Meaning he's completely *not* familiar.'

I began to relax; perhaps the dangerous moment of opportunity had passed. Steven leaned back and regarded our father. 'So I have to sort through my old room, huh?'

'That's right,' my father answered.

'I can't wait to see his high school bedroom,' Angie giggled maliciously, wiggling her hands like Gargamel about to muzzle a Smurf. She looked at us. 'Have you guys been by there yet?'

'Actually, we're staying there,' Philip said. 'In Summer's bedroom.'

'You're staying there?' My father sounded confused. 'You didn't get a hotel?'

I shrugged. 'My bed's a double. We can both fit. And we'll be out of there before the open house. Then we're going to stay in a hotel.'

My father scratched his thick hair. It was short now, tamed, and his beard was gone. His skin was red with either windburn or sunburn, and he wore a thick, cream-colored wool sweater, dark green corduroy pants, and complicated hiking boots, the kind that probably insulated against Vermont's snow and ice. 'And . . . how long are you going to be in town after the open house?'

I chewed slowly. 'We're staying same length of time as Angie and Steven. Until Tuesday. Then we'll drive home.'

'Tuesday morning or Tuesday afternoon?'

I breathed out, sharp and cold. 'Do you have plans or something?'

'No . . . I just . . . well, yes. I mean, I wish you

would've told me,' my father said, his eyes darting back and forth.

'What's the matter, Richard?' Rosemary looked concerned.

'It's just . . .' My father fiddled with his napkin. 'Never mind. Sorry.' He smiled tightly at us. A few seconds passed.

The waitress arrived and took our order. I got the risotto. Rosemary ordered vegetarian pasta, my father got duck, and Steven and Angie both ordered steak. I wondered if they were both doing Atkins together; they seemed like a couple who conquered things as a team. When they came to Cobalt to help sort through Stella's house – I had been astounded when Steven showed up, and even more astounded when Steven seemed normal, friendly, calm, and with a *girlfriend* – they had Rosetta Stone tapes in their rental car, and at night, I heard German words filtering out from underneath the old bedroom door. I wanted to say that Angie was a good match for Steven, but I really didn't know who Steven had become. So what if I neglected to tell him that I was bringing Philip today, or that he and I lived together in Annapolis? It's not as if Steven and I ever talked.

'So how are things going in Annapolis, guys?' my father asked us.

'Well,' Philip said. 'My job is great. We're designing a new apartment high-rise in Eastport.'

'And how about you, Summer?' Rosemary smiled at me.

'Oh, you know. Still at Chow's. The cooking store.'
Everyone blinked.

'We have our summer stock already,' I continued, because it seemed like they were waiting for me to say something else. 'Margarita blenders, champagne buckets, mini-grills. It's so cold, I can hardly imagine summer right now.'

My father frowned. 'Have you given any thought to going back to school?'

'I've told her that, too,' Philip interjected, way too excitedly. 'Johns Hopkins isn't far.'

'I'm not going to get into Johns Hopkins,' I hissed.

'Isn't the University of Maryland close, too?' Rosemary suggested.

'*And* there's that job,' Philip added.

I cut my eyes over to him. 'I couldn't get that job.'

'You don't know that.'

'What job?' Steven asked.

'It's nothing,' I said, stomping on Philip's foot.

'It's a research associate job,' Philip said excitedly, ignoring me. 'A friend of mine's wife works at a biomedical institute near Baltimore. They help develop drugs and treatments by doing genetic research. I told him about Summer's degree, and he said she should apply.'

'That sounds wonderful.' There was a frozen, hopeful smile on Rosemary's face.

'It's working with fruit flies,' I said limply. 'It's not *that* wonderful.'

'So?' my father said. 'You worked with plenty of fruit flies in college.'

'It's . . .' I shook my head. 'I'm not going to get it, okay?'

I glowered at Philip. He tilted his head, lifted his shoulders to chin level.

The waitress gingerly set down our dinners, warning us that the plates were hot. My father smacked his lips and said *mmm*. I could feel Philip's eyes still on me, but then Angie asked him a question about digital cameras, something else he knew a lot about. I let the warm, soothing risotto wash over me, trying to savor this moment – I was in Brooklyn, which I'd missed ever since I'd moved to Cobalt and then Annapolis. Only, the restaurant was dingy and small – I was practically sitting in the lap of the diner next to me. Outside, scattered trash and chicken bones lined the gutters. A cab honked its dissonant horn when an SUV paused too long when the traffic light turned green. I felt hypersensitive to the smells and noise, as if I'd never lived in the city at all.

Between dinner and dessert, Rosemary stood up and checked the vibrating phone on her hip. 'Ugh, work,' she groaned.

'I'm going to get some air, too,' my father said. And Philip slid back his chair, heading for the bathroom. Angie and Steven remained, draining their wine glasses. Steven flagged down the waitress and asked for another carafe of wine.

I watched Rosemary weaving around the tables for the door. 'Don't you think it's strange that she has to check in with work?' I mused aloud.

'It's just a plant store. And it's not like she even *owns* the place. She's just an employee.'

Angie twisted up her mouth. 'I think she's nice.'

'I'm just saying it's silly, is all.'

Steven simply didn't react. I watched as he took Angie's hand. It still astounded me, the tender way he touched her. I'd had no idea Steven had it in him.

Steven leaned forward. 'Was Philip in your grade? I can't place him.'

I grabbed my wine glass and swallowed the rest, rallying. 'He's from Cobalt. He was Stella's neighbor. That's probably how you remember him.'

I watched the realization drip down his face. 'Ah.' He laughed, then smiled, then gave me a look of disbelief. 'He was still living there? Down the street? That's how you know him?'

I shook my head. 'Samantha was in touch with him. We emailed and talked on the phone for a while, and then I visited him. He was living in New York at the time, actually, but then his job transferred him to Annapolis.'

Steven sat back. His eyes were on the ceiling, and I could tell he was reliving that night he confronted me in Philip's yard. I felt embarrassed, as I knew I would. 'So I guess it's serious, huh, if you moved in with him?' Steven finally asked.

'Not necessarily.'

Angie and Steven exchanged a glance, their eyebrows raised.

'It's not like we're engaged,' I said hurriedly. 'I

mean, who knows, right? We might not marry anybody, Steven, with the models we had for parents. And, I mean, we were into some pretty weird stuff as kids. It's not like we had a normal childhood.'

Steven just stared, aghast.

'Well, he seems really nice,' Angie said quietly. She picked up her messenger bag and stood. 'Excuse me.'

We watched as she slipped out the front door, found my father, rooted through her bag, and lit up a cigarette. Then, Steven dumped the rest of the first carafe of wine into his glass. 'I would appreciate it if you didn't discuss some of the things I used to be into,' he said quietly. 'Like, you know. That time in Cobalt. All that crazy stuff I used to say. I mean, Angie doesn't really know about any of that. She wouldn't get it.'

I crossed my arms over my chest and felt my heart knocking against my wrist. 'These days, I thought you'd be saying I told you so.'

Steven's Adam's apple bobbed. 'Look.'

But I was on a roll. Here he was, finally in front of me. 'I thought you'd be saying that we should've sent every foreigner out of the country when we had a chance. That we should've screened everyone, whoever they were. That this was bound to happen – everyone was saying it wouldn't, but they were too stupid to pay attention. You would've found Muhammad Atta and killed him with your bare hands. You would've snuffed out every last one of them, and then we wouldn't be in this mess.'

'Summer,' Steven warned, 'that's not fair.'

I raised an eyebrow. My cheeks felt seared. 'It's not?'

Something I'd been holding in for years was now wafting around the room, vaporous and spectral. I wasn't sure if it felt good or not. I didn't even know what I was angry about, exactly, and what chances Steven had taken from me. Philip and I had still ended up in the same place, after all. Hadn't we?

But it was more than that – Steven could have been a better brother to me. And maybe I could've been a better sister to him. We hadn't really tried hard enough, neither of us. We had both a lot and very little to work with.

'It was just a phase I was going through.' Steven ran his hands through his thinning hair, making it spike up. 'It was just a thing, okay?'

I sighed, suddenly out of energy. 'Yeah. Okay.'

He pulled out the collar of his shirt. 'Jesus. I feel like they turned up the heat, huh?' Steven twisted around and looked at Angie, who was leaning against the front window. We couldn't see her cigarette, so it looked as if there were a thin curl of smoke rising up from the center of her palm.

Then, I noticed something else. I leaned forward. 'Is Dad *smoking*?'

My father stood next to Angie. He put a cigarette to his lips, breathed in, and blew a smoke ring toward Angie's head. Angie laughed.

'I guess he is,' Steven said, his voice flat.

I sighed. 'Dad keeps all kinds of secrets.'

Steven frowned, uncertain. 'I doubt he does from you.'

'Ha.' It came out hard, sharp.

'I'm serious. You guys are, like, the same. You always were. I always felt so jealous, actually, how easily you understood him.'

An incredulous laugh caught in my throat, but there was no trace of mockery in his face anywhere. 'Well, I don't understand why he's smoking,' I finally said.

For one moment, even though we barely knew each other, we were connected. Steven and I held the same past that started everything, that made everything flip. Once Angie and Philip and my father and Rosemary returned, we'd be splintered apart again, but right then, it was just the two of us, The Schnoz, spying on our mysterious father. Back then, we'd been so certain he was a super-hero, and thought that since we looked like him, we'd grow up to be superheroes, too.

It was amazing how the old Brooklyn neighbor-hood had remained crystallized in time. There was Mrs Delaney walking one of her many yellow labs, still wearing that big purple parka that made her look like Grimace from the McDonald's commer-cials. There was Mr Gould, still dancing in front of the window – he never could figure out how to close the curtains. There was Mrs Fry's same collec-tion of pinwheels, trapped under a film of ice.

I put the key in the lock, anticipating the dogs' jingling collars until I remembered they were in Vermont. The apartment looked as I had expected it would – boxes everywhere, most of the furniture gone, a big hole in the kitchen where the fridge used to be. New granite countertops and dark-cherry cabinets in the kitchen. A new coat of paint on the walls, and new light fixtures in the kitchen and living room. My father had taken the curtains off the windows and stripped the freshly sanded wood floors of their rugs, making the whole place seem enormous.

We went to my bedroom. There was a poster of The Smashing Pumpkins on the wall. Pairs and pairs of Gap jeans in the closet. My old *Babysitter's Club*s from elementary school were on the bookshelves, as were my biology textbooks. I opened a random drawer; inside were things I hadn't thought about in years. The pale pink leotard and iridescent tights from the year my mother urged me to try ballet. A little crystal box someone had given me in a Secret Santa exchange. A Nintendo Game Boy, without batteries. I shut the drawer again.

Philip swayed in the doorway. 'So this is it.'

'Only for a little while longer, I guess.'

'I used to imagine you here, you know,' he said. 'When we were young.'

I smiled into my chest. 'What did you imagine me doing?'

'Just . . . being you. Lying in your bed. Looking

in the mirror. I imagined you thinking about me, maybe.'

We'd had this conversation thousands of times by now – that the time we met in high school during my grandmother's funeral was more significant than either of us had ever dared to let on, but we'd both felt silly, afterwards, for holding onto it. But I guess it wasn't silly, after all.

Over those first long phone conversations, me in Cobalt, helping Stella through the last few months of her life, Philip in New York, before his company moved him to Annapolis, I could connect to him in a way I had never been able to connect to anyone. I could tell him things I'd told no one else. Maybe it was because we weren't face to face, or maybe it was because he told me things about himself, too – that he had been teased all his life for his father's religion and appearance. That he'd had an obsession with the ThunderCats cartoon when he was young, and wished that he could just become a ThunderCat to escape harsh, confusing preadolescence. That one girl he had dated had called him too feminine and sensitive and had cheated on him. He didn't seem sensitive like my father, though – he just seemed willing to talk. And willing to accept what I had to say.

With that connection, though, came a vulnerability I'd never really felt before, and with that vulnerability came paranoia. I was stunned when he asked me to move to Annapolis with him after Stella died. I waffled over it for a few days, wondering if I really should go. I was afraid that, soon enough, Philip and I would discover the hateful things about each other, and our relationship would recede into alienation. Or we'd realize that there was no plausible way two people who met once as teenagers would actually end up together. There were some days where I didn't think about it, but most days, I did, at least a little.

I pulled the quilted comforter back and sat down on my old bed. 'You didn't have to kiss my dad's ass like that, you know.'

'I didn't kiss his ass.' Philip looked surprised.

'Yeah you did. How you loved his shirt? How you loved *Vermont*? You've never been to Vermont.'

'I didn't say I'd been. I said I wanted to go. And anyway, what's wrong with wanting him to like me?'

The back of my neck ached, the same way it used to after I played Steven's video games too long. I always played so clenched and tense, afraid that an enemy would come out from the pixelated ether and disintegrate me with his mace or sword or three fire-breathing heads. 'My dad was really nervous tonight, wasn't he?'

'Well, he was seeing all of you again. It's been a while, right?'

'No, I think there was more than just that.' I thought about my father's fluttering hands, how he'd gone outside to smoke. I had confronted him about it afterwards and he'd shrugged, saying it wasn't a habit or anything, just something he picked up during his boring days at Merewether.

'Maybe he's tense about selling the house. Or maybe he's tense about me. It's not like I've talked to him much.'

'You talk to him all the time.'

'Yes, but not *real* talk.'

'So have a real talk with him.'

I wandered out into the hall, made a right, and entered my father's bedroom. There was a bleached mark in the wood floor at the foot of the bed, the leather box's old spot. There were no curtains to frame the big square windows, and the Lower Manhattan skyline spread out before us, missing a couple of its most essential buildings. Tiny lights strung on the tops of the South Street Seaport clipper ships twinkled and danced. Headlights drifted up the FDR.

'What are you doing?' Philip asked, scaring me. He'd changed into his pale blue hospital scrub pajama bottoms. He'd had them since his mom had cancer, when he was a teenager.

I didn't turn. 'Why did you tell them about that research job?'

I could tell Philip was smiling. 'I think it's a great job for you.'

He had brought a printout to me a few weeks ago. *The Developmental and Molecular Pathways division is looking for talented, self-motivated scientists interested in using drosophila as a genetic model system for the elucidation of disease-associated pathways and identification of target genes and compounds.* As I studied it, he stood back, arms crossed over his chest, an exuberant smile on his face.

'I didn't want my father to know about that job,' I answered now. 'I didn't want anyone to know.'

'Why? I know someone. You would at least get an interview.'

I glared at him. I'd known about RNA interference, which was what the job was mostly about, for a while. It was a process where a group of very tiny molecules stopped pieces of RNA from doing damaging things, like letting virulent viruses take over a cell and attack the body. The action the molecule performed was called 'silencing' – I always imagined that they were clapping a hand over the RNA strand's mouth, telling it to shut up and stop making trouble. The protein that cleaved the RNA strand in two was called a 'dicer', which made me think of the complicated gadgets we sold at Chow's. Perhaps, one day, an RNA interference dicer would be packaged and on the shelves next to the Cuisenarts. I'd be the only one with the knowledge to sell it.

In private, uncensored moments at work, I considered the research job. I could see the clean, raw lights of the lab, the cool, quiet flutterings of the people working, the drosophila in their little vials, their bodies so tiny they made no audible sound when they tapped against the glass. But then a customer would come, or one of the oven mitts would fall to the floor, and I'd think about the other applicants' résumés in the Human Resources administrator's inbox. Their illustrious education, their previous work and research experience, the fellowships they'd taken.

Philip looked small and shadowed in the empty room. 'Just stay out of it,' I said. 'I don't need help.'

His face fell. As he walked out of the room, his pant legs dragged on the floor. Outside, a siren howled. The wind pressed up against the windows. Someone's high heels clacked against the sidewalk below. I wondered what Rosemary and my father or Angie and Steven were doing right now. They were probably lying in their hotel beds, being nice to one another. I heard Philip sigh as he sank into bed. Something broke inside of me.

'I'm sorry,' I said, entering my bedroom.

'It's all right,' he mumbled, his face to the wall.

I sank down in the wicker chair. Philip and I slept side by side each night in the little downtown apartment in Annapolis, clinging to each other, safe under our down quilt that we had bought at a nearby mall. But then Philip woke up in the morning and left for long, empty hours. I'd begun to talk to the plants around the house, just to hear my voice. I made small talk with the regular barista at Starbucks. At work, I chatted with customers unnecessarily.

Once, Philip had been later than usual, and I'd been looking out our apartment's window, reflecting on how the neighborhood, which was close to the Naval Academy, looked at night, quiet and calm, the streetlights making soft circles on the sidewalk. Philip had appeared right then, bounding up the concrete steps and waving at me through the window. When he came inside, he said, 'You looked like a little puppy, waiting for his owner to come home. It was so sweet.' I knew he'd meant it affectionately, but I'd curled up inside. It cut too close to the bone. I needed him too much.

I crawled into bed, and Philip turned to face me. His eyes were so dark and thoughtful. The first time we saw each other again, he picked me up at the BWI Airport, the closest Amtrak station to Annapolis – I took the train from Pittsburgh, eight long hours. When I got in the car, I couldn't stop staring at his hands. I didn't remember them. They were so perfectly shaped, not knob-knuckled or Yeti-hairy or spider-fingered. I watched everywhere his hands went – as they opened doors, shifted the car into park, drummed nervously on his knees when he searched for answers to my questions.

We stopped at a little park off the highway. There was only a picnic table and a parking lot, and I didn't understand why this park was so special. 'You'll see,' Philip said, getting out of the car. 'We just have to wait.'

The air had a savage bite to it. We sat on top of the picnic table, the feeling seeping out of our legs and hands. Suddenly, there was a small, distant roar growing from the horizon. A spot emerged in the sky. 'Lie down,' Philip said. Suddenly, a plane was above us. *United*, it said on the side. It flew right over us, so low that I thought we might get caught in its propellers. We shaded our eyes. The wind was so strong, it felt like it could lift us into the air. When we sat back up, we accidentally bumped hands, except it wasn't an accident, at least on my part. 'Were you screaming?' Philip asked. 'I think you were screaming.'

'I wasn't.' I patted my hair back down. I tried to be as poised as I could, as together as I had been during our phone conversations. Philip knew everything that had happened in my life, but in a tempered, elegant way. I didn't want to ruin my chances. I was already starting to feel vulnerable.

'It's okay,' Philip said. 'I screamed the first time, too.'

Outside my old Brooklyn bedroom, a siren howled. The moon spilled in through the window, and I watched Philip close his eyes. His hand was still wrapped around mine. Often, I tried to get back the feeling of being underneath those airplanes, the loud noises they made, the big shadows they cast.

'We've been together for a year,' I murmured.

'Mmm hmm,' Philip said back.

'Isn't that scary to you?'

'Mmmm.'

In two more minutes, he was asleep.

CHAPTER 26

Philip had a computer in the spare room of our apartment, an old thing from his college days. It had dial-up Internet access, same as the computer that Stella and I used in Cobalt. A few weeks after moving in, I began to look up people on-line. First, Dr Hughes. Then some girls from the NYU biology department. I looked up Alex, who was still working at the genetics clinic, and I looked up Samantha, although she wasn't lost to me. Samantha had her own web page, with her picture in the upper left-hand corner. She wore a blue blazer and a large smile, beckoning people to shoot her an email about any of the houses listed on her site.

And then, finally, I looked up the person I really wanted to find: Claire Ryan.

It hadn't been easy to find her. Claire hadn't contributed information to the Peninsula alumni website about her education, marriage or career, as many others had. She wasn't listed on Classmates.com, and she didn't appear to have a blog. I found plenty of other Claire Ryans, including lawyers, track stars, physicists, and a

391

soprano in an ensemble musical group. I finally found her, though, in a Craigslist post: someone had found three kittens in a vacant lot. She was looking for good homes for them, preferably families that didn't have dogs. The contact email was Claire's first name and last name at something called Howell United, which I later found out was an environmental action group. When I clicked on the Craigslist ad's accompanying picture, there was Claire, holding a squirming, orange kitten in her arms. The straight smile, the teal eyes, still beautiful. It was hard to tell if she was fat or thin.

She had posted on the Washington, DC Craigslist page. I couldn't believe our close proximity, and I wrote her immediately. A few nail-biting days went by, but finally she wrote back. Not that you could gauge emotion from how someone wrote an email, but part of me had anticipated an ecstatic response, so I was startled when Claire seemed almost blasé that I'd found her. We decided to meet at her office near the Smithsonian after she finished work and take it from there.

I took the Metro into DC and got there way too early. Since I had a few hours to kill, I walked around the Mall, which was strangely empty, perhaps because it was a weekday and the middle of winter. My footsteps rang out on the marble floors of the Air and Space Museum. I bought a Bio-Dome habitat in the gift shop, which promised to house four separate species under one plastic shell. It even came with a little magnifying glass so that I could take in the action up close – the ants burrowing through tunnels, presumably. It reminded me of my father's snow globes.

I sat on a dried-up fountain outside Claire's office building. I saw her come out right away; she walked with a few other women, deep in conversation. She recognized me immediately. 'Hi, Summer,' she said. 'Good to see you.'

Her voice sounded so smooth, so adult. She sounded as though she meant it. She wore no makeup, had big red earmuffs on her ears, and there was still something substantial about her size, but in a comforting, Mother Earth way. Her blonde hair stretched down her back, nearly to her coccyx. She reminded me of the women I used to see in Washington Square Park, wearing tie-dyed shirts, banging on bongos and singing.

We looked at each other for a moment, the cold wind swirling around us. 'Hi,' I answered, my heart pounding hard. For a moment, I couldn't remember how old I was, or where we were.

A convoy of policemen on motorcycles passed, going around the traffic circle like they were on an amusement park ride. I expected a big fanfare, a light shining down from the sky, indicating that reconnecting with Claire was good, was right. Claire touched my arm. 'Do you mind if we stop back at my place? It's not far from here.'

She lived in a block of apartments with spindly terraces, rickety carports. The walls were drab blue cinderblock. Music thumped behind one of the closed doors, and another had a big flag bearing the Virginia Tech football logo draped over the little peephole. Claire unlocked the apartment door and walked in first. A young girl, probably a college student, sat on the bare floor, her legs outstretched. A little blonde girl of about kindergarten age sat next to her, making a tower out of gigantic Lego blocks. 'That's beautiful,' the college student said, handing the kid another block. When the kid saw Claire, her eyes lit up and her mouth spread into a wiggly smile. 'Hi!' she screamed, then ran over to Claire and wrapped her arms around Claire's legs.

Claire looked at me. 'This is Frannie. Frannie, this is Summer. Remember how I told you that you were going to meet someone named Summer today?'

Frannie stepped back from Claire and looked at me solemnly. 'Hello,' she said.

'She's yours?' I asked Claire, flummoxed.

Claire nodded. 'Indeed she is.' She picked up Frannie and put her on the couch. I took a tentative look around the apartment. The furniture was a warm butter yellow. There was a Greenpeace poster of a snow leopard and a framed black-and-white Ansel Adams print on the far wall. A red milk crate filled with dolls, plastic tools, and more blocks sat in the corner. Next to the crate was a battered rocking horse whose white, ropy mane had been arranged into four fat braids. There were at least twenty photos of Frannie on the TV stand.

A pair of manly-looking shoes lay next to the coat closet door. I glanced at Claire's left hand. It was bare.

Claire thanked the girl and gave her some cash. The girl silently stood up and shrugged into her coat. When she left, Claire turned to me. 'Jen has been a godsend. Most of these kids, they won't baby-sit for less than ten bucks an hour. I mean, seriously. That's like two hundred dollars a week! And so many of them come in here and smoke pot. That's the last thing I need.'

'What about day care?' I asked tentatively, not really sure if I had the right to give an opinion. This whole thing struck me as so weird, suddenly, Claire complaining about something so adult and with such familiarity, as if we hadn't been apart for years.

Claire shrugged. 'There are so many kids at day care. Maybe we'll try that later. But Emmy likes Jen for now, don't you? You guys built that big Playmobil village, remember?'

Frannie had migrated to the other side of the room and was feverishly drinking from a plastic sippy cup. 'And then the hurricane knocked it down.'

'She loves hurricanes,' Claire stage-whispered. 'She was named after one.'

'I was named after a tropical *storm*,' Frannie said sharply.

Claire started to put Frannie's toys back into the milk crate. 'So you were. I was in labor during

Tropical Storm Frances. Even though she never became a hurricane, she was still powerful. She caused five hundred million dollars' worth of damage in the South, after all!' Claire rolled her eyes good-naturedly.

'Are we going to go to the pool now?' Frannie sounded bored.

'Well, I don't know.' Claire took off her coat. She wore a long turtleneck sweater, made with variegated red yarn. 'Do you have any interest in going to the pool, Summer? We could have coffee after.'

'There's a pool?' Out the window, the sky was steel gray. It was cold enough to snow.

'It's indoors, obviously, and just down the street,' Claire said. 'Frannie's obsessed. You and I can swim, too, if you want. The water's warm. I have an extra suit.'

Going to a pool seemed as good as going anywhere else. Claire packed a bag quickly, and we walked back down to the street. Frannie ran ahead of us, dodging around people walking their dogs, and piles of leftover slush. 'So, this is kind of crazy, right?' I said. 'You and me. Walking down the street like this.'

'It is.' Claire grinned, but really didn't seem that surprised. 'That's the Internet for you, though. Everybody finds everybody.'

'So what happened to the kittens you found?'

'Oh, some lady took all three of them. She was one of those cat people.'

'How long have you been in DC?' I asked.

'I went to school here for a while, at the University of Maryland,' Claire explained. 'One summer, I got a job with Greenpeace. I thought I was really going to be doing something good, you know? But basically, I was stationed at intersections, accosting passersby about the environment. If they walked on without saying anything, we tried to make them feel guilty – if all the icecaps melted, it would be their fault.' She sighed. 'I hated it, but I did it all summer.'

'Why?'

'Well, because I needed the job, for one. And because Frannie's father worked there. Or, I guess, her future father. Thomas. He accosted people, too.' She glanced at me and smiled. 'I work for a different environmental group now, and so does he. We're not yelling at people on the street anymore. We both work behind desks. I do the graphics, design the website, that sort of fun stuff. It's nice, actually.'

'My brother does web work, too,' I volunteered. 'Steven.'

'Steven!' Claire's mouth dropped. 'How is he? Still obsessed with math and the military?'

'Not really,' I said with a laugh, touched that Claire remembered.

Claire ran ahead and grabbed Frannie's hand before she swept across the street. As she pulled her daughter in closer, wrapping her arms around Frannie's tiny body, she looked at me knowingly.

'Thomas and I aren't married. I saw you checking, earlier.'

'I'm sorry,' I said haltingly. 'It doesn't matter . . .'

'It's okay,' Claire assured me.

Frannie tapped Claire's arm. 'Are we going to go off the high dive?'

'Maybe. If you're good.'

'Can I try a flip?'

'No.'

Frannie stomped her little foot. Claire ignored her.

'So what about you?' Claire asked when the light changed. 'What are you doing in Annapolis?'

'My boyfriend lives there,' I said. I felt funny volunteering this, remembering how Claire had offered up potential boyfriends for me in high school, always people in her clique, and I'd turned them down. I felt younger than her, without responsibility or anything to show for myself. It was the same way I always felt around Claire. 'We live together.'

'So it's serious.'

'Well . . . I don't know.' What *did* I mean? I didn't know.

The Y's lobby brimmed with kids. There was a big poster behind the desk with information about swimming lessons and participants. The swimming lesson skill levels were divided by types of fish: those just learning to swim were the Pike class, then Eel, Starfish, Polliwog, Guppy, and Shark. Frannie noticed me looking.

'I'm a Starfish.' She pointed to her name on the poster. 'I can tread water for ten minutes.'

'That's wonderful,' I told her.

'She's the youngest Starfish in the group.' Claire fished out her membership card. 'It was terrifying when I first saw that they just *let* them swim. Without swimming arms and whatever. I thought for sure she was going to drown.' She handed her card across the table to the girl behind the desk, a teenager wearing a woolen hat with earflaps. 'Now she's going off that crazy platform diving board and everything.'

'So, do you like it here?' I asked Claire as we proceeded to the locker room. 'In DC?'

'Sure,' Claire said, plunking her nylon bag down on one of the locker room's benches. 'There's a lot to do here. My job is good.'

'Do you ever go back to Brooklyn?'

Claire looked down. 'Not really. My parents both remarried, did you know? My mom lives in Virginia. So she's close. It's nice.'

In a flash of guilt, I remembered the Fun Saver camera I'd stolen from Claire's mother. I opened my mouth and shut it again.

Frannie had migrated across the locker room and was talking to another little girl who was taller than her. She put her hands on her hips bossily and whispered something in the girl's ear. When a new cluster of girls came into the locker room, Frannie started waving. 'Madison! Heather!' She broke away from the first girl and ran to the new ones.

Claire snorted. 'We call Frannie the mayor of the pool. She talks to anyone. She's not afraid of anything.'

'Kind of like you,' I said.

Claire ducked her head, and I got the feeling it was something people hadn't said about her in a long, long time. She handed me a faded green suit. 'This is for you.'

We changed with our backs to each other. The straps of the suit were stretched out and thin, and the belly area sagged. I tried to press it flatter to me, embarrassed that my body didn't occupy it completely. Claire wore a black and white Speedo, showing off her apple-shaped torso, prominent chest, skinny legs. With her hair pulled back off her face, she was truly beautiful.

'So where's Frannie's dad?' I asked. 'Work?'

'No, he's down in Louisiana, with his father.' Claire slung her towel around her shoulders. 'He's sick. At first, they were just thinking it was Alzheimer's, or Parkinson's. He was so twitchy, I guess. But it's something else, apparently. Sort of a degenerative thing. It starts with an H.' She thought for a moment. 'Hunter's?'

'Huntington's?' I asked.

She snapped her fingers. 'Yes.'

I stared at her. 'He has Huntington's?'

'Yes. Well, maybe. They're running tests. It looks pretty likely.'

'And this is Frannie's grandfather,' I stated.

Claire's brow creased. 'Yeah. And?'

I let out an exhale of disbelief, then walked to the sink and bent over the basin. 'It's a serious disease, Claire. And it's genetic. He could've passed it to Thomas, and Thomas could've passed it to Frannie. There's a fifty per cent chance, and if you have the gene, you eventually get it. It's fatal. Someone told you this, right?'

Fear and surprise flashed across Claire's face. She looked away, turning on the warm tap of the sink and running the water over her palms.

'No one told you?' I goaded. 'So Thomas hasn't been tested?'

Claire shook her head slowly. 'They're just testing his dad right now.'

'Claire, you have to do something about this.'

'What? What am I supposed to do?' Claire tried to laugh, except her mouth bent at an unnatural angle. 'What am I supposed to do with this information? Jesus!'

She walked over to Frannie, taking her hand and speaking into her ear. I leaned up against the cold, hard sink. I didn't know what she was supposed to do with the information, but I felt I had to share it, knowing what I did, having worked at the clinic, having taken the genetics classes. And who didn't know about Huntington's? Who, when faced with a disease or even the possibility of a disease, didn't immediately go on the Internet and read everything they could about it?

401

I caught Claire's arm as she headed for the pool. 'I wouldn't worry about Thomas or anything. Or Frannie.'

'I'm not going to,' Claire said stiffly. 'Thomas's father has lived a good life. He plays in a bluegrass band. He has a boat. He taught Frannie a lot of songs. He's a good person.' She watched as Frannie pushed through the sunshine-yellow door into the pool area. 'It doesn't change who he is, and it won't change who Frannie is, either. I couldn't imagine my life without her. I couldn't imagine the world without her in it. It's not like I'm going to feel guilty, now, for having her. I got enough of that already. It's not like we had any idea.'

I gazed at her, briefly confused. 'I wasn't trying to make you feel guilty,' I said. 'But the test would be really easy. It's a tiny blood sample, that's all. Frannie wouldn't even feel it.'

Claire stared at me, exasperated. 'That's up to her. It's her choice, when the time comes.'

'But don't *you* want to know?'

Her hair fell over her face. 'Would *you* like to know how you're going to die? Or how your daughter's going to die?' Then she laughed bitterly. 'Maybe you would, actually. You always wanted to know the answers to everything. You'd be much happier if your whole life was plotted on a perfect course and went exactly to plan, no surprises.'

'I'm just saying—'

'Some things aren't like that,' Claire said. Her

402

face was getting redder and redder. 'It's not always black and white, yes or no. Thomas, Frannie's father? He's gay. He's down there in Louisiana with James, his boyfriend. They've been together for two years now. He came out shortly after I got pregnant. I should have known, really – I sensed he was unhappy, even when we were dating. I've heard enough from people about how this was a selfish decision, how I shouldn't be bringing a child into the world without a proper father. You wouldn't believe what people said to my face. But he's a good guy, Summer. He's a great father. James is a good person, too. He's a lawyer – he set up a trust fund for Frannie, for when she gets older. So how's that for things not being black and white?'

She whirled around, storming into the pool. I followed her, feeling like my head was detached from my neck. The pool air smelled humidly of chemicals. The lifeguards sat on their high chairs, twirling their whistles. The pool was large, with twelve lap lanes, a shallow swimming area, and a diving well. There were normal-height diving boards as well as two higher ones, the highest one seemingly grazing the skylights in the vaulted ceiling.

Frannie was already in the shallow end, bobbing with a few other girls. Claire dropped her towel onto a plastic chair and pulled jerkily at the strap of her suit. My nose and eyes stung with chlorine. I walked over to her and touched her arm. 'I'm sorry.'

She sighed and rolled her eyes. 'It's all right. I probably would've found out some time, if that's what his father's got. But God, Summer. Is this some sort of complicated revenge? Did you come here just looking for a way to ruin my day?'

'. . . Revenge?'

Claire wagged a finger in my face. 'You were the one that found me. I was cautious about it, but I thought, Jesus, we've been out of school for years, we're different now. But maybe you aren't. I mean, maybe you want revenge for . . . for I don't know, everything I knew about you, when we were young.' She stared me down. 'It's not like I wanted to know any of that stuff, Summer. It's not like I sought it out.'

'What are you talking about?' I whispered.

Claire shook her head. She concentrated hard on a flyer for synchronized swimming classes that was taped up on the wall. 'That one summer, when we were at Long Beach Island? You were going into eighth grade, I was going into ninth? We were such good friends. And then when school started you just . . . stopped speaking to me. The same thing happened when we were older, too.'

I stood up straighter, astounded. '*I* stopped speaking to *you*?'

'Yeah, you did.'

I let out a barking laugh. Finally I said, 'You could have introduced me to your friends, you know. The first set of friends. The people that were on the back of the bus.'

404

Claire wrinkled her nose. A long moment went by. 'Why didn't you just *ask* me to introduce you?'

I stared at my bare feet, coughing out a laugh. 'You don't *ask* about that kind of thing, Claire! At thirteen years old? The last thing you do is ask! And besides, you stopped speaking to me, too. After that.'

Claire took her bottom lip into her mouth. 'You're right. But I thought I was bothering you. You always seemed so . . . *irritated* when I said hi.'

I turned away. How could our rift have been even remotely my fault? She was the one who ignored me when we started school. She was the one who shunned me after our argument in Prospect Park, avoiding me for months. She was the one who didn't bother writing from San Francisco and turned away from me that following autumn.

I ran my hands up and down the lengths of my arms, feeling a headache coming on. Was it possible I'd pushed her away first? I considered eighth grade. Whenever I saw Claire coming down the hall, surrounded by her sparkling, captivating friends, I always pretended like I was busy. I pointedly looked in the other direction when she waved to me; I feigned deafness when she called my name from the other end of the hall. Why did she need me, after all, when she had all of them? A few years later, when we'd sort of become friends again, I said to her, *leave me alone,* and eventually, she did.

I'd been ashamed by her pity, yes, but I might have turned away from her for other reasons, too: maybe I hadn't wanted to invest anything in her. Maybe I figured that if I did, Claire would eventually abandon me, just as my mother had. The past suddenly twisted, making me feel uncomfortable and a little breathless. I wondered who else I had pushed away. Who else I was *still* pushing away.

'Do you think about school a lot?' I blurted out. 'Peninsula?'

Claire shrugged. 'I do, I guess. But not any more than I think about anything else.' She rested on her heels, assessing me. 'You think about it a lot, huh? Of course you do.'

There was no way I could deny it. 'Probably too much.'

She kicked off a flip-flop. 'I don't know. It happened. It sucked. School sucked. End of story. There's nothing we can really do about it. And who knows who I would've been if it wouldn't have happened the way it did. I would've been really different, I think.'

'But do you think you would've been better? Happier?'

'Are you suggesting I'm not happy?' A furtive smile crept onto Claire's face. She laced her hands over her thick stomach and let out a breath of air. 'This is quite a conversation to have, after years of not seeing one another. I mean, I was hesitant – I *wondered* if it would come up – but I thought

406

maybe we'd start out a little slower. You know, what you think about DC, what you like to do for fun, if you know what anyone else from Peninsula is doing. Not, like, serious shit. I deal with angry people who think big business is poisoning our water supply every day. I need some lightness in my life.' She looked at me carefully. 'And you probably do, too. You shouldn't let everything scare you. You should let go a little.'

'I'm sorry,' I said, my voice choked.

'For what?'

'Just, you know. For things. Everything.'

Claire snorted. 'Stop it. Forget what I said. I was being ridiculous. And so are you.' She said it in such a motherly, confident tone, I immediately stood up straighter.

Frannie barreled for us, water spraying off her tiny arms and legs. 'Dive!' she screamed, grabbing her mother's arm. 'High dive!'

Claire looked at me. 'She loves the platform.'

'You let her go on that?' I pointed at the highest diving board, aghast. The ladder just kept going. 'She doesn't get hurt?'

'Nah. I was scared when she first did it, but we watch her. I had to sign a release, though, allowing her to go off. She never jumps without me watching. That's our rule.' Claire started to follow Frannie, her long hair swinging. She looked over her shoulder. 'It's actually really fun, Summer. You should try it.'

Afterwards, we went to a diner down the street,

ordering heaps of breakfast foods as if we'd just swum for miles. Claire ordered blueberry pancakes, I got an omelet, and Frannie got a Belgian waffle with whipped cream on top. When Claire's coffee ran low, Frannie marched to the checkout counter and rang the bell for service. When she came back, Claire said, 'Let's pretend we're French,' and the two of them took small bites of things and said *Oui oui* and pretended to blow smoke rings, using coffee stirrers as cigarettes. They nuzzled noses and giggled at each other. Frannie even made up a song about me, about a girl named Summer who had a dog named Winter and liked to eat peapods in the spring. 'Peapods?' I asked her. 'Yes, peapods!' Frannie looked at me crazily, like I was the stupidest person in the world. Claire sang too. All of a sudden, I felt so sheepish for questioning Claire's happiness.

And when they walked me to the Metro station afterwards, Frannie gave me a hug and told me in a very adult-like voice that we would be seeing each other again soon. When she pressed her head into my knees, a warmth came over me, something I hadn't felt in a long time. I felt like I did after crying – exhausted, and a little foolish, but cleaner. 'It was very nice to meet you,' I said to Frannie. I pulled the Bio-Dome habitat I'd bought at the Smithsonian from my purse and handed it to her. I could just see her marveling over the little ant colonies, loving it. 'I hope to see you soon, too.'

CHAPTER 27

A Muppet-like woman on the Weather Channel announced that atmospheric conditions were unusually favorable for a blizzard, with air circulating off the Carolina coast, moisture feeding in from the Atlantic Ocean, cold air damming down south. 'It's going to be a big one,' she said, waving her hands around a map of clouds and arrows. 'So stock up now. Hit the grocery store. Be ready.'

'Oh dear.' My father took a bite of eggs.

'It'll be okay.' Rosemary patted his leg. 'Don't worry.'

It was Saturday, and we were at a diner near the Brooklyn Botanical Gardens, one of Rosemary's old favorites. The only things on the diner's walls were clippings from newspapers that had reviewed it over the years. Someone from *Newsday* in 1986 thought the egg creams needed some work but that the grits were passable, and someone from *New York* magazine thought the service was slow, but in all, it got four out of five stars. I stared at the serifs on the word *York* for so long it didn't look like a word at all.

Steven, wearing a zip-to-the-chin navy sweater and jeans, checked his cell phone messages. Philip flagged down the waitress for more coffee. He tried to take my hand, but I pulled it away. He looked at me questioningly, but I couldn't return his gaze. Angie and Rosemary were talking about Rosemary's gardening book. 'So you see, I wanted to make the gardens as varied as possible, to give people a range of what they can do.'

'Will your book talk about things that will grow in California?' Angie asked. 'Steven and I have a little back garden plot that I'd love to find a use for.'

'I'm sure,' Rosemary said. She pulled out the binder, which she must have carried everywhere, and flipped through the laminated pages. 'I have an example somewhere in here.' Although I wondered how – every garden she was featuring was in Vermont.

Angie patiently waited, patting her bangs, which were cut bluntly across her forehead. She had a fifties vibe about her, and today she wore saddle shoes, cherry-red lipstick, and a pink twinset – it made me think, startlingly, about Stella and the twinset sweater-wearing girl her husband had once dated, the one who'd fallen through the thin ice. I couldn't imagine what Steven had told Angie about our family. Whatever it was, maybe it hadn't been the truth – she didn't seem the least bit awkward or uncomfortable.

'Really, artist colonies are just like mental hospitals or rehab facilities,' my father was saying to

Philip. 'Only people don't go there to dry out, they go there to . . . I don't know. Juice up. But they spend a lot of time in little rooms, thinking about themselves. They gather around a central television. They play ping-pong. They eat the carrot sticks they give you at every single lunch. It's really no different. We sometimes have silent dinners, where no one speaks. At first, it's strange. You think you're *supposed* to talk, that it's awkward not to. And you laugh and you don't make eye contact with anyone and you gobble up your food as fast as you can. But after a while . . . I don't know. It becomes nice. It's like this huge weight is off you. You don't have to talk. You can just exist.'

'Wait a minute,' I said. 'You eat dinner at the colony?'

My father shrugged. 'The chef there is great – except for the carrot stick obsession, that is. Rosemary goes too.'

I looked around aimlessly for a while, until my eyes landed on Rosemary. 'Hi,' she said, beaming.

'Hi,' I answered, not quite as enthusiastically.

'You tired?' she asked.

'Something like that.'

My father said a few more things, then excused himself, heading down the narrow corridor for the front door. The others acted like it wasn't a big deal, but I got up and followed him, wondering if he was going to light up another cigarette.

There was a line outside for tables; about a half-hour before, we'd been standing in it, too. Every

411

so often, a waitress served people coffee in oatmeal-colored mugs. Another waitress handed out orange slices and cookies. I followed my father a few doors down, where he stopped in front of a hardware store. And, sure enough, my father pulled out a Marlboro from his pocket and fumbled with a pack of matches.

'I can't believe you're doing that,' I said.

He glanced at me. 'I know. Bad habit.'

'Bad habit?' I clenched my fists. 'You used to make me look at the scariest skin cancer photos to keep me away from cigarettes.'

'Skin cancer photos?' His face clouded.

'The woman with the . . . the hole in her leg? The guy dying in the hospital bed? You tortured me with them.'

'Oh. Right.'

His eyes still looked faded. I wondered suddenly if this was a gap in his memory, an old wound from ECT. 'Do you . . . not remember?'

'Sort of. I guess. It was a while ago.'

When my dad and Rosemary came to Cobalt to help clean out Stella's house, I checked his toiletries bag to see if he was still even on medication. He was – a different antidepressant, the same sleeping pill, and another prescription I'd never heard of, maybe something for anxiety. The prescribed daily dosages were still quite high. There was a time when I knew every detail of my father's drug regime, perhaps even better than he did. It was a long time ago, now.

'It's weird being in the apartment,' I blurted out. 'It's weird that you're going to sell it.'

My father put his hands in his pockets and leaned back. 'We can't just let it sit there.'

'It's just . . . even if I have some strange memories from there, it's hard to think that it's just going to *go away*. That it won't be ours anymore.'

'I know.'

We stood facing the street, our breath coming out in translucent puffs. I felt him looking past me – but for what? 'What if I bought it from you?'

He smirked. 'At market value?'

'No. What if I . . . I took over your mortgage? I could probably manage that with a job, right?'

'They would have to do a credit check on you,' my father said slowly.

'I have good credit, probably.'

'Would you and Philip buy it together?'

'No, just me.' I felt a rush of euphoria, followed immediately by a stomach-gnawing surge of doubt. I imagined living in the apartment alone, sleeping in my old bedroom.

My father pulled at the edges of his hat. 'New York City is going to be nuked. It's dangerous to live here these days.'

'You don't really believe that, do you?'

He shrugged.

'I mean, seriously, Dad,' I said. 'You're going to come back to New York eventually. Don't you want somewhere to live once you do?'

He stared at me. Suddenly, I wanted my father

413

to tell me something important. Anything. Something that indicated that someday, maybe we'd be normal around each other again.

But instead, he said, 'There's a new subway line, you know. The V. It's part of the Sixth Avenue train. I saw it on the subway map on the way over. I guess it's an alternative to the F, although not in Brooklyn. The end of the line is Second Avenue and Houston.'

I eyed him carefully, but his face was blank. This was who he was now, at least for me. The crack between us had instantaneously sealed after September 11, because it had seemed petty to fight about anything. I never mentioned anything about the things I'd said, and he never mentioned anything about the things he'd said. Our conversations remained superficial, usually arts-and-culture related, or about things Philip and I did on the weekends, or about llamas and Vermont – because, I supposed, it was easier that way. Sometimes, when we were talking about nothing on the phone, I wanted to tell him all Stella had said to me about his accident. All those secrets. I also wanted to ask him where his rehearsed speech years ago had come from. Had his new therapist told him to get on the phone with me and tell me that I was hindering his growth as a person? Or had he come to that conclusion on his own?

A tall, slender woman with a fur-lined hood walked on the other side of the street. After a moment, she stopped and peered at us. The hood was tight around her head, so it was hard to see her face, but I could tell she was in her thirties or forties. Her black down coat extended past her waist, ending in two thin, dark, denim-clad legs and tall black boots. She was sophisticated in a different way than the ghetto-fabulous girls of Crown Heights, the neighborhood the diner bordered. To my astonishment, the woman held up a gloved hand and, with some uncertainty, gave my father a little signal.

'Do you know her?' I asked. My father's face grew pale. His hand was at his chest, and his fingers were curled. I wasn't sure if he had been waving back. The woman slunk down the block, in the general direction of the Brooklyn Museum, pulling her expensive-looking black leather purse close to her side.

'We should go back in,' my father said, turning back for the door. I didn't know what else to do but follow. On my way past the line of customers, I got a big whiff of the plate of orange slices a waitress was passing around. They smelled so ripe and tart, they brought tears to my eyes.

Stella had remained in that Central Pennsylvania hospital for a few more days until she was stable enough to travel back to Cobalt. After that, there was really nothing we could do. We had to accept this. Stella's oncologist had pushed hospice pamphlets into my hands. They referred to this as *the death process*. Hospice professionals made *the death process* as comfortable for the patient as possible. Hospice professionals were available around the clock, because patients often fear going through *the death process* alone.

I imagined the spots on Stella's brain that the latest MRI had detected. They were palpable and writhing. After a while, I would enter her room and she would think I was someone else, often her sister. 'So did you talk to him in study hall?' she babbled. 'Who?' I asked. She rolled her eyes. 'Tommy Reed. Jesus, Ruth! You've been talking about him all week.' Her hands fluttered open and closed, like she was a little squirrel digging in the ground.

And one time, she glared at me and said, 'It's been three years, Ruth, and you've said nothing to him.' She wagged her fingers in my face. 'Get over it. So he made a mistake. The baby is healthy. You think the world knows, but who cares if they do? The only one who really cares is you.'

'What are you talking about?' I'd asked. 'What baby?'

Stella snorted. 'Always in denial.'

Stella made less and less sense. I worried she would die in her room alone, so I set up a cot in her room. Once, in the middle of the night, she sat up in bed and stared at me.

'Your father was in a mental institution,' she screeched, witch-like.

'I know that,' I said.

'And he's got something in hiding.'

'What is he hiding?' I asked.

'Like the Nazis,' she announced.

'What?'

She flopped back down on the bed, exhausted.

A few days later I spoke to my father on the phone, telling him about Stella's worsening condition and how he should probably come to Cobalt soon. 'Stella says you're hiding something,' I wanted to add. 'She told me everything about your past. Sometimes, she thinks I'm your mother. Will you help me understand this?'

But I didn't. Instead, I went to the old chest of drawers in the living room and pulled on the brass handles. I had moved the secret engagement photo of Kay and Mark from my father's old desk drawer in his bedroom to the top drawer in the chest, next to the deed to the house, Stella's insurance information, and the pamphlets for the hospice. Kay's center parting was so finely etched. *I know something about you,* I whispered to her. I wished she could talk back, tell me what she knew, too.

CHAPTER 28

I shot up in bed. The moonlight pooled across my lap, white as milk. There was an art project I made my junior year in high school propped on my old desk. It was a self-portrait of me, done in blues and greens. I had cat eyes and a scaly neck. In the darkness, it seemed alive.

'It was my mother,' I whispered, partly to the portrait, partly to Philip. 'It was my mother across from the hardware store, down the street from the diner.'

'Huh?' Philip shifted. He'd been lying in an awkward position, scrunched up against the wall with one arm over his head. He noticed that I was awake and opened his eyes wider. 'What's going on?'

My pulse was fast, and my veins were hot, as if coffee were flowing through them. 'You know how I told you this woman was waving to my father from across the street? And my dad waved back? I think it was my mother.'

'Did you see her face?' Philip sat up, too. A horn blared outside, even though it was 2 a.m.

'Well, no. She had on a big jacket, and the hood

was pulled tight. But of *course* it would be, right?' I slapped the bed for emphasis. 'I mean, she doesn't want me to know that it's *her.*'

'I don't know if that makes any sense.'

'It makes perfect sense,' I answered quickly. 'My dad told me the two of them talked after the terrorist attacks. He said she called to see if he was okay. He tried to pass it off like it was a one-time thing, but I bet they kept talking after that. Maybe they're both on the apartment's deed. He'd have to settle that, at least. He'd have to make her part of this sale. But maybe they've been talking about . . . other stuff, too.'

Philip squinted. 'Wouldn't they have settled that in the divorce?'

I shrugged. Who knew? 'My father has been so nervous this whole time he's been up here. Did you see the way he couldn't even form a sentence at breakfast? How he kept looking over his shoulder? How he kept *checking his cell phone?*'

'He said he was just looking at the time.'

I pressed my hand to the windowpane, which was thickly frigid. 'Do you think they've communicated a lot? It's not like he and Rosemary are married. They could end things at any time, no strings attached.'

Philip looked at me carefully. 'But your mom . . . she . . . would you really *want* her back?'

There was a thin layer of dirt on the windowsill, the city soot that permeated everything. I pressed my thumb into it, then stamped it on a clean piece

419

of wall, leaving behind a black print. 'You wouldn't get it,' I said.

'Maybe I would.'

Philip's parents had been together all this time. They'd overcome lots of things – his mother's cancer, a relocation for work, people's backlash about his father being a Sikh, especially post 9/11. Their lives had been far from easy, and yet they'd prevailed. 'It's just . . . I think about her a lot,' I said.

'What do you think about?'

'Where she is. What she's doing. That sort of stuff. It's weird to think she's out there, living. Putting on clothes in the morning. Drinking coffee. Having dreams at night. That's all.'

'So, if that was really her across the street, and you see her again, what do you think it would be like?'

'I don't know.' What *would* we talk about? Who had I been, when she left? How much of me had changed? It might be more like meeting a potential employer in a job interview. I'd have to describe my strengths and weaknesses, where I went to school, that I was a good multitasker and a team player. *And another bonus is that I share half of your genetic material. So please hire me.*

'It will probably be awful,' I whispered.

Philip moved his legs around under the covers. It made a soft, comforting swishing noise. 'I have something to tell you,' he said. 'Promise you won't get mad.'

420

I pushed my hair out of my face. 'How can I promise that when I don't know what you're going to tell me?'

'Okay.' Philip sat up. 'I sent in your résumé for that research job.'

A bus swished down the BQE. Mrs Guest, who had lived below us for years and had always been an insomniac, switched TV channels. The new channel was much louder than the previous one, and I could hear very clearly it was some man shouting about something called Kaboom!, which pulverized stains on tile, tubs and showers.

'When?' My stomach jumped around.

'Last week.' Philip took my hands. 'I just . . . I think you *could* get it. I don't think you give yourself enough credit. You want to do something in science, right? Why not try for it?'

'Jesus.' I shot off the bed and walked across the room to the closet.

'I'm sorry,' Philip said. 'I thought . . . I don't know. I thought you'd be happy.'

'Why?' I didn't turn around. 'I've been telling you over and over again that I *don't* want to apply for something like that. And you didn't even *listen* to me! You just . . . just did it anyway!'

'I just wanted to give you a push.'

'You should've asked.'

'What are you so afraid of?'

'I'm not *afraid*,' I spat.

'You know what I think?' Philip said quietly. 'I think you don't want to apply for it because it's

421

easier just to have the job at Chow's. Because you can quit it at the drop of a hat, and it won't really . . . I don't know, affect anything. It's not like it's going to go on your résumé. It's not like you're making big connections there. It's easier not to commit to something real, because then you'd have to admit to *wanting* something, to feeling something.'

I whirled around. 'That's not true.' But I could feel the blood creeping into my cheeks.

'You've been like this for months now,' Philip said. He was still sitting on the bed, saying this so calmly, rationally. 'Maybe the whole time we've been together. If you just want to leave, then leave. Don't make me keep wondering.'

'What are you talking about?'

He curled his hands around his knees. 'Tell me how you feel about me. Right now.'

I laughed uncomfortably. 'You know how I feel about you.'

'No. I don't know if you've ever said it.'

'Of course I've said it.'

'So say it again, now.'

I opened my mouth, but my eyes got distracted by the crown molding, the old bronze radiator, the heavy plaster windowsill.

'That time we first met?' Philip's eyes shone. 'Years ago, when your grandmother died? Sometimes I think that was the last time you were truly honest with me. When you told me about . . . about your dad, and how scared you were.'

'That's crazy!' I exploded. 'How about everything I tell you every day? None of that matters?'

'Of course it matters,' Philip said. 'But it's also like, you just get to this point, and then you just . . . stop. It's like you have your comfort zone – and if you leave it, you've given up too much of yourself.' He trailed off, but I understood where he was going. 'Shouldn't you be able to tell me more? Why can't you just say it? And why can't you tell me how you feel? Is it because you feel nothing?'

'You know that's not true!'

'Well, then, why can't you say it?'

I shook out my hands. What did he want me to say? My relationship with Philip was scarier than caring for my father and Stella combined. I wasn't here just to listen to Philip's problems and to take him to doctor's appointments. I had no real utilitarian purpose, in fact, besides taking up space in his apartment . . . and being his girlfriend. What were the requirements for that job? Perhaps I'd entered into this too quickly, after losing Stella. Who knew why I'd entered it at all? I thought about what Stella had said all those years ago at my grandmother's funeral: relationships could be a bitch, and it was hard for people to be truly happy together. Some people couldn't take it, and that was all right. I thought she'd been talking about my mother, but maybe she sensed something about me, too.

Only, *why* was I one of those people who

couldn't take it? Was it because of my parents' relationship or my mother's abandonment or my father's descent into illness, or was it because of something deeper than that? Perhaps the problem was in my blood, right down to the tiny little things I couldn't see. The little coiled pieces of DNA pulsing inside me that very moment, tracking precisely how I behaved, whether I wanted them to or not, just like crazy Mr Rice had said. It was all neatly spelled out in chemical code – why we waited, why we took care of people, why we always had to be the one who needs taking care of. Our sense of direction, our taste for bland pasta or for Belgian waffles, or why love – real, unconditional love – scared us.

If I could just get to the genetic core of myself, I could solve all my problems – and fix them. I could fix my father's, too, and my mother's, and Steven's. I could glue things back together, build things back from nothing, stitch in the right piece of DNA and remove the wrong one. It was all there before our eyes, both too small and too big to understand.

Philip waited, pumping his foot up and down. *Yes, I have a hard time admitting it*, I wished I could say out loud. *Because doing so would mean I want something, I need something.* When Claire told me at the pool to not let things bother me so much, to let go, I thought it could be possible. But despite what I knew, it still felt like something I couldn't do.

The early morning light began to drip into the apartment, first gray, then pink, then orange. I lowered my eyes, hardened. 'I think I need some room right now, okay?' My voice wasn't particularly friendly.

He blinked. A car outside had its hazard lights on, making the room strobe light and then dark. 'Okay. Fine.'

He stood up, then, and pulled on his jeans. He put his shoes on slowly, tying them in a neat, double-loop bow. 'Where are you going?' I asked.

'Well, I have the car. I can drive home.'

I breathed in, knowing that this was the moment when I should tell him that he was being silly, and that he shouldn't go. Philip paused a moment, looking at me, maybe waiting for me to say it, too. His face was lit up by the moon. There was either a mole or a pimple on his smooth, right cheek. We both silently counted to three. I just let it go by.

He looked past me, then, and pointed to the window. 'You should close that.'

I turned around. The window was slightly ajar – no wonder it had been freezing in here. When I hefted it closed and turned back around, Philip was gone.

'Where's Philip?' Rosemary asked, coming into the apartment with a bag of groceries.

'He . . . he went back to Annapolis,' I said. It was the following morning, and I was still stunned

425

Philip had left. I thought he might come back in the middle of the night, curling into me and apologetic. Had he really driven the whole way back home? What would he do the rest of the weekend?

Rosemary looked startled at my answer. She searched my face, trying to gauge a reaction. 'He was worried about the blizzard,' I said quickly, before she could ask.

'Oh, the blizzard.' Rosemary walked down the hall and plopped the grocery bag on the new island. Inside were pretzels, bottled iced tea, and apples. It made me ache a little, seeing Rosemary navigate so easily around the apartment. She plucked an apple from the plastic produce bag, wiped it on her shirt, and took a bite. 'Do you really think we'll get that blizzard?' she asked, apple juice dribbling down her chin.

'Well, *yeah*,' I said. I tried to soften the remark with a little laugh at the end, but I wasn't sure if it worked. We both heard my father fumbling at the door. He burst in, wearing a long, black wool coat and a bright red scarf. *He looks good*, I thought. *Really good.* His eyes were bright, his hands steady.

'It's freezing out there,' he said.

'So what are you guys doing here, anyway?' I asked.

'We need to go through the boxes. Goodwill is picking up the donations today. But maybe there are some other things in the "For Vermont" boxes that can go there as well. And we should move

426

them to the sides of the room, just to give us more space. It's like a maze in here.'

'Why do you need more space?' I asked. 'Is someone coming?'

My father ignored this, bustling to the first open box. 'Well, the realtor is coming,' Rosemary answered for him. 'She said she'd be by Monday.'

'Yes,' my father said absentmindedly. He glanced at me. 'Have you and Philip rented a van to move your things out of here?'

'Philip went back to Annapolis,' I said flatly.

My father widened his eyes. 'Did he take your things with him, or . . . ?'

'No.'

'So . . . then . . . how are you going to get your things out of here?'

'I haven't thought that far ahead,' I said.

'Well, maybe you should.'

'Richard . . .' Rosemary said quietly. 'I can help, if you want. We can find some movers.'

I couldn't move. I wasn't even sure where I'd send my things to – Philip's? Had that been merely a fight last night, or something much bigger?

'There aren't going to be any movers available. It's a weekend.' My father slapped his thighs and stared up at the ceiling.

'Movers work on weekends,' I reminded him. 'They work all the time.'

'And there's going to be a blizzard,' my father said dourly.

'Then why are we even having this open house?'

427

Rosemary said. 'If it's going to snow three feet, why bother?'

My father lowered his arms. '*Now* you're saying this? *Now* you believe in the blizzard? You've been telling me this whole time it's not going to snow!'

'What? I can't control the weather!'

'Why couldn't you have mentioned this, I don't know, when there was still time to back out?'

'Dad!' I said, startled by his tone. My father stepped back, surprised. Rosemary glanced at me, equally surprised at my defense.

Today, Rosemary's dark blonde hair was in a braid down her back, with various strands of hair straggling out from each braided lump. She wore a large piece of turquoise on her right pointer finger; my father had found it when they were on a vacation to New Mexico. They had gone there not long after the attacks, as a way to separate themselves from New York City, my father over-medicating himself to get through the plane ride.

She took an annoyed bite out of the apple, crunching loudly. 'I'm going down to Duane Reade for some Tylenol. I have a headache.'

'Can you get some packing tape?' my father called. 'I think we're running out.'

'It's on the list,' Rosemary responded, gruffly. She shrugged into her wool duffel coat and slammed the door.

For a while, my father just continued to shuffle around the boxes. Then he turned and examined the living-room wall. He reached into a blue duffel bag, pulled out a yellow and black measuring tape, and began to pull it from one side of the room to the other.

'I can't believe you can do that,' I said.

He stopped. The tape remained taut. 'Do what?'

'You used to be afraid of measuring tapes. You used to hate using them.'

He thought for a moment. As he moved his head to the side, I saw a smattering of gray at his temples. It was arresting; I'd never seen gray there before. 'I think that was kitchen knives,' he concluded, glancing again at the blank wall. 'I really don't know if we should knock this down or not.'

'I don't think you should sell this place, Dad.'

He looked at me blankly. I pointed to my sternum. 'I offered to take it over, remember?'

'You don't want to live here.'

'Why?'

'I don't think it's a good idea.'

I leaned back on the counter. 'Why? Is someone else moving in here, instead?' *My mother perhaps? My mother and you?* But did that make any sense? Why would he be putting it on the market? Why would he bother moving his things out?

My father pressed a button, and the measuring tape retracted back into its holder. I felt a big wave welling up inside of me, building, ready to break. 'I know what's going on,' I said.

He whipped his head up. 'Sorry?'

'I . . . I know you're talking to her.'

His mouth dropped open. No sound came out. I couldn't believe I was actually right. I thought about Rosemary, strolling down the street, her nose into the wind, her purse swinging by her side. She knew a lot, but she probably didn't know this. Perhaps they'd been communicating for a long time, and my father hadn't had the heart to tell her. Of course he'd still find it hard to tell people difficult things. Of course he'd still avoid conflict whenever he could.

'I wondered if you knew,' he said.

'It's okay,' I said quickly. 'I mean, I don't blame you. I understand.'

'You do?'

'I do.'

His face crumpled into a smile. He perched on the edge of one of the boxes, his hands in his lap. 'Wow.' He let out a sigh. 'Did you tell Steven?'

'Well, no. I haven't said anything.'

He sighed, staring at his palms. 'So.'

'So.'

'Well . . . perhaps this is a strange question, but would you like to see her?'

I fluttered my hands to my throat. Right now, Rosemary was weaving through the narrow Duane Reade aisles, pausing to buy Tylenol, tape, cough drops. Philip had asked me plenty of times what my mother was like. Each time, I stopped in my tracks. I knew *what* she liked – cashmere sweaters, imported olive oil, Himalayan cats, cooking utensils she didn't need, exercise crazes, her oversized

430

cell phone – but not exactly what she *was* like. 'She was very particular,' I always ended up saying. 'She had very specific tastes.'

All I knew was this: she'd still be beautiful, but cold and dismissive. She'd be effusive but mercurial and impatient. I'd still find her mysterious, another species. She'd be the same person as when she left us, her feelings out of arm's reach, always unspoken. And, as usual, I'd try tirelessly to snatch something from her, to coax her to tell me that I was, indeed, loved.

'Yes,' I whispered. 'I'd like to see her.'

'Okay.' My father smiled shyly at me. It felt like the first sincere smile he'd given me since before he'd admitted himself into the Center. Once there, his smiles became hazy, bogged down by medication or resentment. 'I'll call her, then.'

'Okay.' My heart beat fast. It was happening, whether I wanted it or not. I pointed to the door. 'I'm going to . . . I have stuff to do.' I didn't, but I felt like I needed to feel some air on my face. I wanted to walk to the river and stare at the buildings.

'That's fine,' my father said. 'And . . . Summer?'

'Yeah?'

He looked at me but said nothing. All at once, we were us again. He was grateful, and I was tall and competent. I blew him a kiss and walked out the door. The hallway was blue carpeted, the same as it had always been. And as I walked down one flight for the front door, I remembered another time when I was walking down these same steps, back when I was little. I was following my brother and mother; we were in bathing suits, headed to the community pool. It was one of those blisteringly hot days where you couldn't think straight, where everyone walked around on the streets squinty and cross. When we hit the street, we saw that one of the fire hydrants was spraying water everywhere. The neighborhood kids were playing in it – it was too hot and too stifling to resist. I looked at my mother, and she shrugged and put her hand on the small of my back. I pulled off my shorts and ran into the hose. Steven ran too. We screamed and pressed our faces into the water. And when we were finished, we walked the rest of the way to the pool.

I paused on the landing, smiling, remembering that. Sometimes, returning to places brought back good memories, too.

CHAPTER 29

Before Stella died, she pressed a piece of paper into my hands. She had written an obituary, she said. *The* obituary. But she didn't want me to read it until it was time to send it to the newspaper to be printed. She didn't want me to diverge from the text, either, but to dictate it exactly as it was written. 'I'll know it if you do,' she warned me. 'I'll see you. I'm going to follow you around when I'm dead.'

I had horrible thoughts about what the piece of paper would say:

Stella Rogers, mistakenly killed when an eagle dropped a large tortoise on her head, mistaking it for a stone.

or:

Stella Rogers, oldest woman in space, died on her mission because the parachute on her capsule failed to deploy.

Whatever it was, it had to be more extreme than those we'd crafted when the doctors had first diagnosed her – otherwise she wouldn't have made me wait until after she'd died for me to open it. I kept the obituary in the pocket of my suitcase, which I'd folded up and stuffed in the back of the Cobalt house's closet. I nearly forgot about it after she died.

It was late afternoon, and I sat at the old ice cream parlor near the Promenade, the one my father and I had gone to when he told me my mother had left us. I hadn't been back here since he'd made that announcement, staying away because the place had felt cursed. Despite the frigid temperature, the line for ice cream grew longer and longer. My father said he would meet me here, but he was late. I considered calling Philip. I wanted to tell him that he was right, that I had been distracted. That I was scared. That maybe I was running from something.

I dialed his cell phone, but it went to voicemail, the very same voicemail message I heard over a year ago, in the hospital with Stella. *I can't come to the phone. Thanks.* His voice sounded far away, aloof. Beep. I hung up.

I couldn't make sense of our argument last night – it was the equivalent of seeing the beginning and end of a movie but missing the middle. I called his phone again. 'It's me,' I said after the beep. I thought of everything I should say. Really, there was so much. Finally, I blurted out, 'Please call me. Please. Okay? I'm sorry. I need you.'

The voicemail beeped again. There was a lump in my throat; had I really just said that?

Rosemary plopped down across from me. 'So this is where you're hiding.'

'I'm not hiding.' I cupped the still-warm cell phone between my hands.

'No?' Rosemary was wearing an oversized burnt orange sweater with a small moth hole in the shoulder. She wrapped her hands around a small paper cup from the coffee cart on the corner. There was a smudge of pink lipstick around the sip top. 'You've been awfully quiet, Summer. Is everything all right?'

I shrugged.

'Did you and Philip have a fight?'

'I don't know.'

A few seconds passed. A woman at the counter was yelling, appalled that this ice cream store didn't offer anything for vegans. 'Have you talked to your father much?' Rosemary pressed.

I stared at the scuffed checkerboard floor. I didn't want her to get this out of me. My father should be the one to tell her about my mother. 'Not really.'

She cleared her throat. 'Are you two still upset at each other?'

I looked at her suspiciously. 'What do you mean?'

She smiled sadly. 'I know I'm not the right person to talk to you about this. I know that, I really do. But I know how things used to be between you two. I know how special your relationship is. If you ever need a friend to listen, I'm here.'

I folded my paper napkin into smaller and

smaller pieces. To be honest, I'd found it surprisingly pleasant to talk to Rosemary about a lot of things – gardening, New York, books, music – but when it came to my father, I just couldn't. It felt cheesy, like an invisible eye was somewhere above us, looking, chuckling. 'I'm okay,' I mumbled.

'I found something in the apartment that you might want.' She reached into her bag and pulled out a tattered white envelope. The Brooklyn apartment's address was written on it in what looked like my handwriting when I was younger, letters that weren't quite so slanted and rushed. There was a twenty-nine-cent stamp in the corner, but no postage marks to show it had been mailed.

I slid my finger under the paper and pulled out the envelope's contents. It was a single sheet of lined stationery, addressed to me.

> *Thursday, December 16, 1992*
>
> *Dear Summer,*
> *Thank you for your letter and your concern. It's nice to know that someone takes an interest in science these days; so few people do. I'm glad you like my theories, and I can only encourage you to read more and more so you can form your own. The only way we'll know the whole truth to everything scientific is to keep questioning and testing.*
>
> *As for further evidence supporting DNA and your family, I'm sure things will work out as they are supposed to work out. Your mother is*

436

a good person. So is your father. Try not to be hard on him if he forgets to buy popsicles at the store or throws his red shirt in with your white laundry. He loves you very, very much, and he is very sorry for any and all mistakes he makes in advance.

And last, you are a good person. You are the best person in the world. Please don't forget this.

Sincerely,
Your teacher, Mr Rice

I set the letter back down and raised my eyes to Rosemary. We watched each other for a long time. 'He has been keeping something from me,' I finally said. 'And not even the secret about you, I mean. Other secrets. He keeps secrets from everyone.'

Rosemary shifted in her seat. 'Maybe he keeps secrets for your own good. To protect you. Not all secrets have to be told right away . . . or at all. But you should talk to him. You two should sit down and air everything out. I know you both want to.'

'He keeps secrets from you, too,' I snapped sharply. *A big secret, maybe. One that might unravel everything.*

Rosemary tilted her head. Some of her hair fell over her face. Outside, a gust of wind kicked up, blowing trash around. We remained there for a few moments, saying nothing, letting this sink in. Then, I felt a hand on my arm.

'Summer?'

My father was standing above me. Next to him was a woman in her mid-thirties with shoulder-length brown hair, pink, glossy lips, stark freckles. She wore a down coat, a black dress, opaque tights over her slender thighs. Something about her looked familiar, but I wasn't sure why.

'Summer, this is Josephine,' my father said. 'Josephine, this is Summer. Josephine was good enough to take some time away from her conference to come out to Brooklyn.'

Josephine stuck out a small, pale hand. 'It's really, really nice to meet you. I've heard so much about you.' Her hands were cold and chapped. She had an open, friendly face, with one incisor crossing over the tooth next to it. There was a thin wedding band on her finger. A map of the New York City Subway system peeked out of her coat pocket.

Josephine. The name sliced through me. 'Hi,' I said back, more a question than a statement.

'Richard.' Rosemary stood up abruptly, her voice quavering. 'What are you doing?'

'It's okay. Summer and I talked about this.'

'You . . . did?' Rosemary looked startled.

'Wait, what?' I tossed my eyes from Rosemary to my father.

The woman, Josephine, looked down at the table and pointed at the letter from Mr Rice. 'Oh, that's Richard's handwriting, isn't it?'

'Can I talk to you for a second, Richard?'

Rosemary took my father's arm, nudging her chin at Josephine.

'It's all *right*,' my father repeated. 'Summer and I were talking about it this morning. Stella told her.'

Josephine's eyes darted back and forth. She drew her bottom lip in her mouth. 'Maybe this is a bad time?' she asked slowly.

'Stella told me *what?*' I couldn't remember my father and I having a conversation this morning about Stella. What had Stella told me? I examined Josephine again, my thoughts half-formed, like I'd just woken up from a dream.

My father's mouth hung open. He laid his palm flat on the table. 'Well, wait a minute. I mean, when we talked this morning, I just *assumed* Stella told you, Summer. I mean, I didn't know how else you *could* know.' When he registered my lost look, he tried again. 'Our discussion in the apartment today. After Rosemary left. This is . . . you said you knew we were talking. Stella told you, right? She told you about Josephine?'

Rosemary covered her face with her hands, took a few steps away, and circled back around. 'Richard, I think we should . . .'

It was as if time had stalled. They were in on the joke, while I was still floundering to get it. Josephine scratched her upturned nose and let out an uncomfortable laugh.

It was the upturned nose that did it. I saw a photograph, the one I found in my father's old

439

desk drawer in his bedroom and then moved to Stella's hutch, next to the important papers, after she came home to die. A girl smiling, her body tilted toward a guy. I remembered looking at her nose and thinking what it must be like to have a nose like that. On the back of the photograph was an inscription about two people who were secretly engaged in 1970.

And I saw the same face, older now, as the dark-haired, freckled girl in the picture that had appeared and disappeared in Stella's house, first under a *National Geographic,* then wedged into an encyclopedia. Once I even found it propped in the medicine cabinet in the downstairs bathroom – practically in plain sight. Stella knew I would see it.

The baby is healthy, Stella had screeched, steeped in dementia. *She's being taken care of. You think the world knows, but who cares if they do, Ruth? The only one who really cares is you.*

He's got something in hiding. Like the Nazis.

My mind was a sheet of paper. Someone had just pricked a pin through it, and a slice of light shone through. I stared at Josephine. Maybe Stella had given me the punch line before the joke. Maybe a lot of people had.

'Oh.' It popped out of me like a hard, lead BB, falling out of my mouth and plunking to the ground.

My father took a big step back. 'Oh, fuck.'

He turned around, stumbling over an empty

chair behind me. A few patrons looked up, startled. He passed the chrome trash can near the front, which was overflowing with crimped-edged paper plates, and practically fell through the door. I watched him disappear behind a bus kiosk, then found him again across the street.

'Oh dear.' Rosemary touched the edge of her cheek. 'I'd better . . .' And she darted after him, pressing out into the cold street.

It all happened so fast. I was still sitting at the table, the old letter in front of me. Josephine shifted her weight, still standing. 'Okay.' She let out a self-conscious laugh.

I glanced at her. The cold, icy shock had begun to thaw, not entirely, but enough for me to react. I hid my hands in my lap and curled them up, cursing my childish, incompetent father for leaving me here, alone, to grapple with what I didn't quite yet understand. My mouth puckered, about to say something dismissive, perhaps an excuse that I needed to use the bathroom. I could find a back door and escape. Or I could just get up and leave, like the rest of them had. I didn't owe this woman anything, not exactly. She probably knew much more about me than I did about her.

I had asked my father about this, of course. I had asked if the baby had died. He hadn't answered me. I hadn't lingered on it, though – I hadn't thought about it, because there was so much else to think about. And maybe because I hadn't wanted to consider it.

441

'Jesus,' I whispered.

They'd probably been corresponding for years, my father telling Josephine much more than he told me, using his sober, unglamorous words. Rosemary seemed to know Josephine, too.

I peeked at her. Josephine fidgeted with the strap on her purse and scanned the laminated menu, just for something to look at, because she wasn't sure of her place, or where she was supposed to go. She had a funny way of nervously smiling with only one side of her mouth. I felt a warm, bitter-sweet ache – Stella used to smile just like that when the irritatingly chipper nurse prepped her for her blood draws.

Something inside me reversed directions. I released my hands from the crimps in my lap and forced my shoulders down from their locked pos-ition. It was possible Josephine was more confused than I was. If she was who I suspected – it was beginning to make more and more sense – then what had her life been like? What sorts of prob-lems did she have? What kinds of questions and fears were inside of her?

I counted three long breaths.

'They make really good espresso milkshakes here.'

Josephine jumped. My voice even startled me a little. I swallowed, then continued. 'I used to get them as a little kid, probably when I was too young to really have coffee. They still have them on the menu. I know it's cold out, but do you want one?'

Josephine's entire face lifted. With just that, with those few words. 'Oh.' She fumbled with her purse. 'Well, sure. Let me give you some money.'

'I'll get it.'

Her eyebrows rose. She looked so grateful.

'No, it's fine. I'm happy to.'

I reached into my own purse and found my wallet. My hands were shaking so hard it was difficult for me to get the money out. While I fumbled, Josephine asked, 'So you lived in Brooklyn your whole life, huh?'

'That's right.'

'This is one of my first times here,' she said. 'I've mostly lived in Colorado, in the mountains. But I was born where your Dad's from. Cobalt. We moved when I was about eight.'

I know, I wanted to tell her. Of course I knew. I pushed my hands deep into my sweater's front pouch, begging them to stop shaking, and walked to the ice cream line. Outside, my father and Rosemary stood at the curb. It didn't look like they were saying anything, but just standing, staring. Josephine sat down at my table and looked at the letter my father had written to me, pretending he was Mr Rice. Reading every line. And I let her. Everything was there. *Things will work out as they are supposed to. You are the best person of all.*

There was the button nose. Not trapped in a faded photograph, but in front of me, real. She didn't notice me watching her, and I didn't let her know that I was. I tried not to think, tried not to react. Parts of me screamed in surreal confusion, while other parts felt crazily, carelessly fine. I put my hand over my mouth, stifling a laugh of self-awareness, like I was looking down at this from somewhere else.

The line crept forward, a mother leaned down and asked her kids what they wanted, the register person put a limp twenty into the till. And then it was my turn at the counter. I ordered two espresso milkshakes. The worker nodded, opened the big back ice cream freezer, scooped out enough ice cream for two, and turned on the blender.

CHAPTER 30

By the time I returned with our milkshakes, Rosemary was back at our table, explaining to Josephine that my father had to leave unexpectedly. There were prospective buyers at the apartment, she said, and he had to show it to them. My father apologized, and he would contact her tomorrow.

Josephine stood up, saying she understood, and that it was nice to meet both of us. She seemed a little relieved. After she left, Rosemary helped me gather the things from the table. 'Thank you, Summer,' she said, pushing our empty dishes and cups into the slot in the chrome trash can.

I found my father sitting on one of his favorite benches on the Promenade, staring out at the water. There was a bunch of newspapers on the seat next to him that I had to move aside before sitting down.

For a while, we watched the water in silence. It was so cold, I couldn't feel my toes. My nose ran and my legs were spasmed with shivers.

'Jesus, Summer,' my father finally said. He put his hands through his hair. 'Jesus, I'm sorry. I don't

445

even know what to say. I just couldn't be in there any longer, once I realized . . . Did she leave, or . . . ? Rosemary told her I'd call her later, right?'

I said yes.

'Okay.' He drummed on his knees nervously. 'Jesus. When you said you knew . . . I thought you meant you knew about her.' He still hadn't looked at me. 'I thought Stella had told you we were talking. I *figured* Stella had told you about the whole thing. She *said* she did.'

'She told me the first part,' I mumbled. 'About you and . . .' I swallowed hard. '. . . Kay. And about the accident. She mentioned Kay's baby, too, and it's my own stupid fault for not pushing her if the baby survived the delivery or not.' I looked at him. 'That *is* who Josephine is, right?'

My father nodded.

'I asked you, but you didn't answer. And I suppose Stella tried to tell me,' I went on. 'But she was so sick, so I didn't know whether to believe her.'

'I understand.' My father stared at his palms, then out at the boats on the water. The Sea Streak ferry chugged to Wall Street, its outdoor decks empty, all the passengers crammed inside where there was heat. 'Stella and I talked on the phone when I was in college,' he said. 'Nothing about what happened. Mostly just chitchat. But it helped. She even came to New York to visit me, once. We went to see a bunch of musicals. I took her to see the Rockettes at Radio City.'

I smiled. 'Stella was always talking about how,

once she beat cancer, she was going to try out to be a Rockette. She bought a video and everything. It was called *The Rockette Workout*.'

'I'm glad you got to know her,' my father said. He cleared his throat. 'We talked on the phone a few times while you were there. She was always telling me about you, Summer, how good you were to her. She called after the attacks, when the cancer was in her brain. Out of nowhere, she asked if I was in touch with Josephine. I'd never talked about it with her, so I was surprised that she knew. Although I shouldn't have been. That's why I thought she told you everything.'

I let out a stalled breath of air. 'So . . . Josephine . . . they delivered her while Kay was in the coma?'

My father nodded. 'Kay was kept on a ventilator until the baby was strong enough. They delivered Josephine prematurely. I never saw her. She lived in Cobalt for a while, but then Mark got a job out West. I never went back to see her, not once.'

'Why?'

He stared out at the water, wringing his hands. 'It's not that I didn't want to. My mother found out that Kay and I had been seeing each other. She wanted me not to meddle any further – she had to live here, she was the one who had to face everyone. She asked that I remove myself from the situation, as completely as I could. I'm not sure she realized it would be *that* complete.'

He stifled something, maybe a cough, maybe a sob. 'But I did remove myself for a long time, until

447

after my mother died. I thought it would be the best thing. Then I looked for Josephine when I was at the Center. It took me ages to find her – Rosemary helped me. I wrote her some letters. Then, I lost her again. After the attacks, all sorts of people did crazy things. I found her again by tracking her down on-line. Steven gave me some great people-finding sites, although I never told him what I was using them for. I asked Josephine if we could meet. I didn't tell her much . . . just that I had been good friends with her mother, but some things had come between Mark and me, and we didn't speak. I've only seen Josephine once before this. It's just a coincidence she's in New York this weekend – she's here for a conference. She asked to see me, but I told her it might not be the right time with all of you here. I said I'd have to see how things went. So when you said you knew that I was talking to her and wanted to see her, I called her.' He put his head in his hands again.

'I wrote her such crazy letters,' he went on, after a moment. 'At the hospital. It's a wonder she even wanted to speak to me. I wrote a lot of people crazy letters.'

My eyes stung. The inside of my mouth tasted tart, as if I'd just eaten lemons. 'Why didn't you write me any?'

He blinked, taking me in, genuinely surprised. 'Because you already know everything.'

Do I? I wanted to ask. It didn't feel that way. I ran my fingers over the edges of the Fair Isle scarf

Rosemary had loaned me when she understood I was going to the water to talk to him.

'I kept this a secret for so long,' he whispered. 'I told your mother parts of it, but not everything. Not about Josephine. I felt bad not telling you, but I wasn't sure if it was right *to* tell you. How do you even get in to something like this? And do I have the right to inflict this on other people – especially you? How much should I burden you to know? I feel like I'd put you through enough already. And I have a hard enough time grappling with it myself.'

I stared at him. 'I know,' I said. And suddenly, I did. 'It must be hard.'

My father and Rosemary had arrived in Cobalt the day after Stella died. Midway into the day, I remembered Stella's obituary. I apologized to my father in advance, saying that Stella's obituary might be crazy, but it was really, *really* the one she wanted to run in the newspaper.

She'd sealed the obituary in an envelope with a foil-lined sticker. When I opened it, the piece of paper still smelled a little like Stella, her peanut-butter cookies, her Charlie perfume. There was her cramped, loopy script. She never printed, always wrote in perfect cursive, even the hard letters, like Z and Q.

Stella Rogers, age 76, died due to complications of colorectal cancer. She was married to William 'Skip' Rogers for twenty-five wonderful years. She is a long-time resident of Cobalt,

449

Pennsylvania, and is survived by her nephews Richard and Peter, her grand-nephew, Steven, and her grand-nieces, Summer, Samantha and Josephine. Services will be held at Grinsky family funeral home in downtown Cobalt. Reception to follow.

I had turned the paper over not once but twice, certain she'd written something on the other side. But she hadn't. There was no shipwreck or mountain-climbing accident or case of the bubonic plague. The only error was that she had written she had an extra niece, someone named Josephine. Why hadn't she said she had sixteen extra nieces? Why hadn't she said she had twenty children and six husbands? Why hadn't she added that she knew every contestant on *Road Rules* and housemate on *The Real World*, that she had aspirations to compete in a triathlon, or how wonderful she was, how utterly, crazily wonderful? I scratched out Josephine's name, insulted by its paltriness.

My mouth wobbled now. It was upside-down, but then it contorted, turning right-side-up. My shoulders shook in laughter. The tears on my face were confused, not sure what side they were on.

My father pressed his shoulder against mine. 'I understand this is a shock, honey. It's weird, I know.'

'Actually . . .' I took a breath. 'It's . . . it's *not* that much of a shock. I mean, it is, but honestly? I'm kind of relieved.'

'Relieved?' He blinked.

'Yeah.' I sniffed through tears. *This* was the big secret he'd been keeping from me, the one I'd built and built and built up. This was the thing I'd worried about, the big evidence that glowed red and made everything in the experiment fall into place. I would look through a microscope, and there it would be, showing me everything. And this was it. It just didn't seem that scary.

'Huh.' My father sounded pleasantly surprised, but also confused, uncertain, as if he wasn't sure what emotion would erupt out of me next.

'So, does she know she's your . . . ?' I sounded out a *d*, but couldn't finish the word.

He paused. 'I don't know. And I don't want to know. It doesn't matter. She had a good childhood, a good life. Mark raised her. He remarried. She grew up in Colorado. Most of her childhood she was climbing mountains, breathing clean air.'

'I thought you'd been talking to Mom. I thought that's what this was about.'

He raised his eyebrows. 'Oh. *Oh.*'

A few things floated down the river. A Coke can. Driftwood. Gum wrappers. We could hear the cars on the BQE rumbling beneath us, swishing to far-flung parts of Brooklyn. My father must have been thinking of the BQE, too, because he said, 'Our first apartment here was right by a BQE overpass, out near the Tennis Bubble in Prospect Park. Your mother hated it.'

'She did?'

451

He nodded. 'She wanted to be in New York City proper, not Brooklyn. And especially that neighborhood. It was full of old Italian women wearing headscarves. And car thieves. Every morning, we would have coffee and look out the window, and we'd see these guys drive a car up to a spot in front of our building, get out, and start ravaging through the trunk. Sometimes they'd leave the car there. And then the car would sit there until someone finally towed it away. It would take days, but then the tow truck would come, and if we were home we'd both watch it. Once, the tow truck screwed up, and ripped a car's fender right off. Your mom thought it was just awful. She always threatened to call the police but she never did.'

My father had a faraway look on his face. 'She cried a lot, those first few years. She was so scared.'

'She was scared?'

'Everything about New York scared her. The subways, the people, the noise, the muggers, Times Square . . . everything. It was overwhelming to her.'

The idea of anything scaring my mother was unfathomable.

'It was a big change,' my father said. 'Everyone's afraid of big changes.' He looked up at the sky. 'We had fun, though. Once we moved here, to this apartment, and had Steven. He had the buildings on the skyline memorized by the time he was two. He knew exactly which companies occupied which building. He also knew the distance from the

Promenade to the East River, down to the last inch.'

'That sounds like Steven.'

'Yeah,' my father said. He swung his feet in front of him, almost kicking the Promenade's wrought-iron fence. 'There used to be times where I thought everything was perfect. Where I convinced myself nothing was wrong.'

I looked at him. 'So you always knew something was wrong?'

'I don't know. No. Maybe. Maybe I was deluding myself. Maybe I do that a lot.'

I turned my hands over, considered my thoughts. 'Do you think you're deluding yourself with Rosemary?'

He thought for a moment. 'I don't think so. I guess I'm an optimist. I still believe things can work. It's scary to try, but you have to try, don't you think?'

I stared at him, my eyes frozen. 'Maybe,' I whispered.

A series of horns sounded out from the BQE. When they finished, I asked, 'When Mom called you back when the towers were hit, did she tell you where she was living?'

He shook his head. 'She just called to see if I was okay. She didn't say anything else. Actually, I said I'd call her back. But I was in such a state that day, I didn't get her number.'

'It'll probably be another ten years before she calls again.'

'Probably.' He stretched out, crossing his ankles. 'It's a strange way to live, surfacing only every once in a while to check in on this huge part of her life. It reminds me of dolphins, or maybe whales. One of those can remain under the water for huge amounts of time, holding and holding and holding their breath. It makes me claustrophobic just thinking about it.'

'Me too,' I said quietly.

'But that's her way of living. It's not ours, is it?' I brought my mittens to my face, his words washing over me. 'No,' I whispered. 'It's not.'

Last month, at the pool with Claire and Frannie, I followed them as they marched for the platform diving board. Frannie's little legs scrambled up the stairs – it was so high, there was an industrial-looking staircase to get to the top instead of a ladder. After a while, Frannie appeared at the top and walked to the very edge. We watched her fall, her little arms crossed over her chest to make her body more aerodynamic. When she hit the water, she plummeted under, then resurfaced. She waved to her mother, just a tiny red speck among the lapping blue. The lifeguards leaned forward, poised to jump in and rescue her, but she paddled easily to the ladder. Then Claire climbed up to the platform, waved at me, and jumped off herself.

When it was my turn, I teetered at the top, the platform rough under my bare feet. The edge was solid, without any spring to it. I could see the old men in the sauna in the corner, the lap swimmers

454

making flip-turns at the far end of the pool. I could even see the parking lot through the windows, and wished I were sitting in one of the parked cars instead of shivering here, practically on the ceiling. Even when I was younger, I shied away from jumping off diving boards or skiing down mountains. I didn't like the idea of dropping from great distances.

'Come on!' Claire called from the deck.

I turned around. There was a girl of about fifteen waiting behind me, leaning her elbows on the stair railing. *I am twenty-six years old,* I said to myself. *It's about time.*

I screamed the whole drop. When I hit the water, I was first relieved, then thrilled. Frannie applauded, messily slapping her little hands together, and Claire waited for me at the edge of the pool. 'Did you like it?' she asked.

I got out without saying anything, but I could feel I was smiling.

I only went off that once. But sitting with my dad by the Promenade, I suddenly wanted to do it again. I wanted to bring Philip, too. I wanted to jump off the diving board holding his hand, even if the lifeguard didn't allow it. And when we hit the water, I wanted to open my eyes underwater, look at him, and wave. And when we got to the surface, I knew I would tell him, maybe for the second or third time, how I truly felt, something that I already knew would make him happy. The words wouldn't come easily, stumbling out of me like clumsy, newborn animals – wormy little birds, maybe – but at least I'd give it an attempt, and that would be something.

I looked out at the debris floating down the river. More Coke cans, old, partly disintegrated shipping pallets, and then, all of a sudden, a beautiful, blue-green glass bottle. It was mostly obscured in the water, so I wasn't able to tell what was inside, but there could have been all sorts of things. A potion, maybe. A tiny ship, like the ones that were trapped inside the bottles on my father's shelves. Even a letter, explaining all the mysteries in the world we still hadn't uncovered. But I knew, suddenly, that there was probably nothing inside the bottle except icy water from the East River. Realizing that made me a little sad, but also gave me a wise, stripped-down feeling, as if I'd really – finally – figured something out.

As I was watching the bottle float to us, it started to snow. The snow stuck to the bottle's curved sides. The flakes were huge and dry, perfect sledding snow.

My father opened his palms to catch the falling snowflakes. 'We might have to postpone the open house.'

'Maybe not,' I said. 'People might come anyway. You know people will do anything for real estate.'

My father laughed. I tried to imagine where we'd all be, a day or so from now, when this blizzard really took hold. I saw Steven and Angie sitting in the airport, gazing wearily at the departures

456

board, their flight indefinitely delayed. I saw Josephine at the airport, too, headed back to Colorado, calling her father, Mark, and telling him who she'd seen this weekend. I saw Mark sitting in a chair in a large, ski-chalet style of room, gazing at a photo of him and my father – the only one, perhaps, he'd saved. I saw Samantha soldiering on to another real-estate conference, her Mercedes windshield wipers churning. I saw Philip crunching through the snow to the corner market, stocking up on milk and bread and pancake syrup, pausing at the sporting goods store in town to buy a red plastic sled, the kind two people could fit on.

And I saw something else, too, farther in the future: I saw myself, sitting in a warm, quiet lab, flipping the switch of a microscope, turning the knobs on the side to focus. The image had a clean, sure feel to it, like a stone worked over by the ocean.

The bottle bobbed. The current shifted so that it floated close enough so that we could almost reach down and grab it. My dad pointed at it. 'If only it were summertime and hot out. I'd see if I could reach into the water and get that bottle for you.'

'I know,' I said, in a voice barely over a whisper.

And I did know. And maybe that was everything I needed to know about him – that he was the type of person and would always be the type of person who would save a bottle out of the East

River if I wanted it. And I would save it for him, too.

I placed my hand over his. It was cold, and my hand was probably cold, too. It felt like his hand always had, large and rough, each finger strong and sure. I grabbed on to his thumb and squeezed, and I saw him smile, just a little.

Neither of us had any way of rescuing the bottle, so we simply watched it bob gently down the river. It floated under the Brooklyn Bridge and passed the Sea Streak ferry and a garbage barge. The cars on the FDR streaked past toward the Bronx, the cars on the BQE lumbered into Brooklyn. We watched the bottle until it was a tiny green dot, and then until it was nothing.